The Meiji Guillotine murders

FŪTARŌ YAMADA is the pen name of Seiya Yamada. He was born in 1922 in Hyogo Prefecture, Japan, and graduated from the faculty of medicine at Tokyo University. He made his authorial debut in 1947 with the short story 'The Incident at the Dharma Pass' and went on to write over a hundred novels and short stories. Known for his versatility, he is best loved in Japan for his series of ninja novels and historical crime novels. Many of his works have been adapted for film, television, manga and anime. He died in 2001.

BRYAN KARETNYK is a translator of Japanese and Russian literature. His recent translations for Pushkin Press include Seishi Yokomizo's *The Village of Eight Graves* and Ryūnosuke Akutagawa's *Murder in the Age of Enlightenment*.

The Meiji Guillotine Murders

FŪTARŌ YAMADA

TRANSLATED FROM THE JAPANESE
BY BRYAN KARETNYK

PUSHKIN VERTIGO

Pushkin Press
Somerset House, Strand
London WC2R 1LA

First published in Japan in 2012 by KADOKAWA CORPORATION, Tokyo.

English translation rights arranged with KADOKAWA CORPORATION,
Tokyo through JAPAN UNI AGENCY, INC., Tokyo.

First published by Pushkin Press in 2023

1 3 5 7 9 8 6 4 2

ISBN 13: 978-1-78227-888-7

Map hand-drawn by Neil Gower
Designed and typeset by Tetragon, London

Printed and bound in the United Kingdom by Clays Ltd, Elcograf S.p.A.

www.pushkinpress.com

The Meiji Guillotine murders

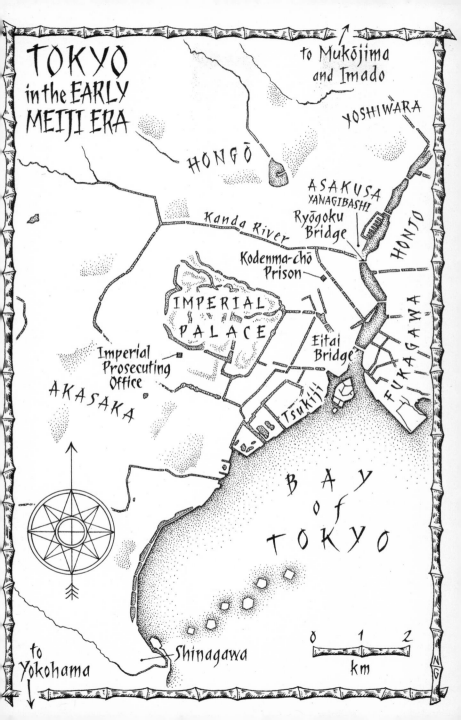

A Brief Historical Note

When Commodore Matthew Perry's notorious 'Black Ships' arrived at Uraga in 1853, Japan had been governed by the military dictatorship known as the Tokugawa shogunate for two and a half centuries. Throughout this time, the shogunate had enforced a strict policy of isolationism and seclusion, yet Perry's ships had come to end all that, forcing upon Japan a treaty that would see, among other things, the country opened up to international trade and diplomacy.

Anxiety over the influence that contact with the outside world would bring led the puppet Emperor Kōmei to issue an edict in 1863, breaking with centuries of tradition and calling for the foreign 'barbarians' to be expelled from Japan. When the shogunate failed to enforce the edict, however, a schism ensued, and samurai loyal to the emperor coalesced around the rallying cry *sonnō jōi*: Revere the Emperor, Expel the Barbarians! Following a spate of high-profile political assassinations, widespread unrest and rebellion eventually turned into a full-scale civil war, known as the Boshin War, with the southern provinces of Satsuma and Chōshū forming a military alliance against the shogunate.

While the victory of this alliance did bring about the restoration of imperial rule, the new Emperor Meiji's youth meant that power rested in the hands of an oligarchy of former samurai from Satsuma and Chōshū, the most influential of whom were Toshimichi Ōkubo, Takamori Saigō and

Takayoshi Kido. This new government soon realized, however, that without reform and modernization, Japan would lag behind the Western world and leave itself open to the threat of colonization. Consequently, it not only continued to trade with the West, but also pursued a policy of rapid Westernization—all of which consolidated a sense of betrayal among many of those who had fought for the emperor.

The ensuing years of social change and acute political turmoil are where this story begins. Readers should be aware that the old capital Edo has just been renamed Tokyo, and that dates are given according to the traditional Japanese calendar—that is, with years reckoned according to periods of imperial rule, and months according to the lunar calendar.

THE CHIEF
INSPECTORATE
OF THE IMPERIAL
PROSECUTING OFFICE

1

As great wars and great revolutions reach their end, most nations seem to enter a fallow period lasting several years.

After such tremendous bloodshed, troubles arising from the victors' arrogance and lust for retribution, as well as from the losers' sense of disgrace and resentment, will inevitably flare up and prevail over the hour of peace, yet still the vantage of history will somehow lend the impression that these years were in some way empty. The period after the Second World War is a case in point. And the early years of the Meiji era, too, were much the same.

Never had there been so nationwide a sense of collapse as there was when the Boshin War ended, but then nor had there ever been so profound a sense of heartfelt relief at the dawning of peace. It seems, however, that both sides then fell hopelessly into a state of total confusion, with neither one having any idea where to begin or what to do. For the people living then, those years must have seemed anything but fallow; rather, it must have been a time of great turmoil, of life-or-death struggle. It was a time when new government offices sprouted up like bamboo shoots, when new administrative orders came down from on high like rain, and when new customs and ideas came flooding in like a deluge from a harbour. By the same stroke, however, it was also a time when even stranger offices, laws and notions from the old days were revived like the souls of the departed and combined, as though mixing together the seven colours of the rainbow—who could say then whether for better or worse—with the end result a chaos of ash-grey.

This period of chaos-cum-fallowness seems to have lasted until around 1873, the sixth year of Emperor Meiji's reign, when the famed Iwakura Mission returned from its embassy travelling in the United States and Europe. From the observations made by this group of high-ranking officials, a blueprint was drawn up, one that sought to refashion Japan in Europe's likeness, one that would set her on course not only to catch up with, but to overtake the West, and one whose consequences would be felt not only in the Meiji era, but right up to the Second World War and even afterwards.

In his autobiography, the writer Yukichi Fukuzawa observes: 'The years on either side of the Meiji Restoration, from the second or third year of Bunkyū to the sixth or seventh of Meiji, were the most dangerous. During those twelve or thirteen years, I never ventured out of my house in Tokyo at night.' Lines such as these make clear the extent to which these supposedly fallow years were fallow also in terms of public order.

This does not mean, however, that the capital was entirely without law enforcement. In the first year of Meiji, 1868, while the loyalist army was stationed in old Edo, the magistrate's office was reformed as a municipal court. Later, the soldiers loyal to the various ruling clans took control of the city and, in the sixth lunar month of the second year, a hired militia was appointed to the role. Finally, by the eleventh lunar month of the fourth year, the *rasotsu* system was implemented, although the term itself was already in use beforehand. But whatever the name or the system, law enforcement itself was, at any rate, to borrow a phrase from the *Kojiki*, a tale of 'when the world was yet young and like unto floating oil, drifting medusa-like'.

And so, let us now go back to the autumn of the second year of Meiji.

There were once five *rasotsu* in Tokyo...

2

The district of Akashi-chō, where the Tsukiji Foreign Settlement was located, is bound to the east by the mouth of the Great Sumida River but surrounded on all other sides by canals and waterways. Each of the many bridges there had a guardhouse, and that was where the *rasotsu* were stationed.

The settlement had been built for the protection of foreign residents, but though guardhouses had been erected, very few foreigners actually availed themselves of them. And so, while in the early days there had been multiple guards stationed in them, now they had just one lone sentry.

At his post one afternoon, Sergeant Jirōmasa Saruki was having some sport with a drunken man.

Actually, it would be more apt to say that the man was sobering up. The foreign settlement, you see, also contained a pleasure quarter: Shin-Shimabara. It was open to foreigners, with the women having been brought in from the more famous Yoshiwara, but, as with the guardhouses, it was rarely frequented by its intended patrons, and on the whole its clientele was Japanese. The man seemed to be a regular of these establishments. For some reason, though, he had got so drunk that morning that he had been staggering about like a somnambulist. Saruki had brought him in 'for his own good'.

It had been about eleven o'clock in the morning when the man collapsed onto the floor of the guardhouse and fell asleep, snoring dreadfully. He had awoken only moments ago, a little before four o'clock that afternoon.

As he looked around in confusion, the drunk, who wore the clothes of a merchant, noticed the *rasotsu*'s monkey-like face with its upward-pointing moustache glaring at him from the desk, and sat up in astonishment.

'You're in the Karuko Bridge guardhouse, in the foreign settlement. You were so drunk that, as you were coming over the bridge, you looked as though you might fall over the railing at any moment, so I brought you here.'

'Oh… Thank you…'

'What were you doing drinking at such an ungodly hour?'

'Well, you see, I quarrelled with one of the working girls and she ran off in the middle of the night. I was so angry that I had one of the young serving lads fetch me some sake, and before I knew it, it was dawn. That's about as much as I can remember. Was I really that drunk?'

As he bowed and scraped in embarrassment, the man searched furiously inside the breast of his kimono and in the pockets of his sleeves.

'Look at me!' the sergeant barked. 'Who are you? I need your name, age, address, occupation…'

Wearing another look of astonishment, the man lifted his head.

'My name is Shimbei. Shimbei Takaya,' he replied, still groping all over his body. 'I'm thirty-eight, and I run a lamp shop in Kotobuki-chō, in Asakusa.'

'Looking for something?'

'It's just, my money… No matter how much I drank, there should still be a fair amount left.'

'It's here.' Sergeant Saruki tossed the man's coin purse onto the desk. 'I've been keeping it safe for you.'

'Ah, that's awfully kind of you. Thank you, Sergeant.'

With a show of gratitude, the man picked up his coin purse and set about inspecting its contents.

'One *ryō*, two *ryō*… two *bu*… and one *shu*,' he said, counting it all out. Then, having satisfied himself, he nodded and prostrated himself in gratitude on the floor. 'All present and correct. You've been a real help to me, Sergeant. Well, if that's all…' he said, getting to his feet.

'Just one minute,' said Saruki, stopping him in his tracks. 'If you'd collapsed like that in the middle of the street, any passer-by could have come along and robbed you, taking the whole lot. Thanks to me, you were spared from that injustice. Don't you think you ought to show a bit more gratitude?'

'Oh, but I already… What I mean to say is… Thank you. I really am most awfully grateful to you.'

'Come on, do you really think this is the sort of thing that can be repaid with words alone? Hmm?'

The lamp-seller blinked as he beheld the sergeant's face, his jaw thrust out over the desk. Suddenly, the man's face creased into an awkward smile.

'I hadn't realized… Of course, I must thank you properly,' he said, fumbling around in his coin purse. He extracted a two-*bu* gold coin and offered it to the *rasotsu*.

'Kindly accept this token of my gratitude, sir. Now, if that's all?…'

'It is not!' Saruki snarled, thrusting his chin out further still. 'Think about it. Why, if I hadn't rescued you, you'd have fallen off the bridge before you knew it. Is saving your life really worth only two *bu*?'

The lamp-seller panicked.

'Ah, well, when you put it like that... You can't really put a price on—'

'Don't you think that three, even four coin purses like this would still be nothing compared to a man's life? Hmm?'

The lamp-seller took a deep breath and looked at the man across from him. But the *rasotsu*'s face was deadly serious, and suddenly a look of irritation flashed in his eyes. A few seconds later, the lamp-seller bowed again, so low this time that his forehead practically hit the floor.

'I really do apologize. It's just as you say, sir. Here, please, take the purse and its contents,' he said, holding it out in desperation.

Saruki snatched it from his hands. Then, as the lamp-seller made his way out of the guardhouse, stumbling as he went, as though his drunkenness had suddenly returned to him, the *rasotsu* called after him in an ingratiating tone:

'It's a relief, in any case, to know that everything was "all present and correct".'

The sergeant then tipped out the coins and spread them across the desk.

There were gold coins worth two *bu* and silver coins worth one *bu* or one *shu*, all mixed together. Just as he had said: two *ryō*, two *bu* and one *shu* in total.

While there was all manner of chaos in those first years of Meiji, this was never truer than where money was concerned. In the previous year, the new government had immediately set about issuing banknotes, but these were hardly in common use. On the other hand, the coins from the old days of the shogunate were still in circulation, but both the values and the denominations of those coins were really quite negligible, and, to make matters worse, there were a prodigious number of counterfeits mixed in. Looking back, it seems miraculous that society didn't just fall apart in those days.

One by one, Saruki picked up the coins and dropped them onto the desk, checking whether or not they were counterfeit.

Despite the chaos, this was over two and half *ryō* in an era when you could buy a whole sack of rice for five *ryō* and still have change left over. He was thankful not to find a single worthless government bill. And better yet, each of the coins appeared to be the genuine article. As he listened carefully to the sound of each coin landing on the desk, Sergeant Jirōmasa Saruki was in a world of his own, his face ecstatic. But suddenly he noticed a figure standing in front of the guardhouse, and so he began to gather up the scattered coins in a fluster.

3

'Case closed!'

The man who had just stepped into the guardhouse was not stationed in the foreign concession, but he was a *rasotsu*. His name was Heikurō Imokawa, and he was an old friend of Saruki's.

Imokawa broke into a broad grin, revealing his rodent-like features.

'I just ran into a man staggering about outside... So, how much did you manage to get out of him?' he asked, rubbing his palms and his stubby fingers together.

'Ugh, you're just like a magpie,' said Saruki, clicking his tongue and tossing a one-*shu* silver coin onto the desk.

With tremendous dexterity, surprising in one so fat, Sergeant Imokawa took the coin in hand.

'Pure coincidence! Anyway, I came to tell you that, since Ichinohata seems to be so mysteriously in clover lately, I've been on at him to come to Yoshiwara or Shin-Shimabara one of these nights. Do you want to come along? You look as though you could do with it.'

'What, is that all?' Saruki spat out with contempt as he covered the money on the desk with his hand, tipped it back into the coin purse and placed it into his pocket. 'All right, fine. Shall we go and see Ichinohata, then?'

'Are you sure you can leave? The duty officer hasn't come to relieve you yet.'

'Don't worry. Half the time, nobody shows up anyway.'

With that, Saruki picked up his sword in its red-lacquered scabbard and, pressing Imokawa ahead of him, left the guardhouse.

Heikurō Imokawa gazed out at the many steamers plying the waterways and floating in the blue mouth of the river. As he looked back towards the foreign settlement, his eyes came to rest on a brick building, and he stared up at the exotic-looking tower atop the roof of the Tsukiji Hotel.

'Is this how everything's going to be in Japan now?' he muttered.

Saruki chuckled, his monkey-like face creasing into a sneer.

'What's it to us what happens to the country?'

'True enough,' Imokawa replied with a chuckle.

They walked off. Jirōmasa Saruki was of slight build, whereas Heikurō Imokawa was thick-set. The two were still wearing their uniforms.

The jacket looked like a cross between a modern-day suit and a frock coat, but, since it had no buttons, it fastened at the front like a kimono. The trousers—the so-called *danbukuro*, which looked like swollen elephant's legs—were completely black, but for the waistband of bleached cotton holding them up. This bizarre ensemble was worn together with a sword in a red-lacquered scabbard, and, crowning the head, an old-fashioned *nirayama*-style hat. Not one of the items they wore was in decent condition.

While it was still common for policemen to wear straw sandals, Saruki, surprisingly, had on a pair of shoes. They were monstrously large—almost one and a half times too big for him—and he had purloined them from an imported-goods shop in the foreign settlement. To secure them, he tied the laces around his ankles, and would go striding off with a triumphant clatter. If nothing else, they at least spared him the cost of straw sandals.

So, as the reader has seen, Saruki was the sort of sergeant who enjoyed menacing the general public and extorting money out of them, whereas Imokawa had the habit of sponging off of Saruki and others of his disreputable ilk. Whenever his friend came by some easy money, he would always somehow manage to appear out of nowhere. Hence Saruki's earlier complaint that he was like a magpie. It was never his style to threaten; he would just crease his rodent-like face into a broad grin, clap his hands together and flatter a person so brazenly that nobody could ever be angry with him. What's more, this man had an uncanny nose and could always sniff out petty crimes that promised to be lucrative. Only, he would never sully his own hands, having developed instead the habit of entrusting the matters to his colleagues and, no matter the money, taking only a small commission from them. And so, it was impossible to escape him.

As the pair walked in the direction of Nihonbashi, three or four strange-looking vehicles crossed their path. I say 'strange' because, although these were in fact rickshaws, they had only begun to spring up that summer, and, still curious to the eye, they looked like an odd combination of the old two-wheeled cart with a sort of palanquin set on top. Passing by with cries of joy and laughter, a group of what appeared to be students was speeding towards the Nishi Hongan-ji temple.

'What's all this?' Imokawa asked.

'It's all those spongers who live with that government bigwig Shigenobu Ōkuma in his mansion by Nishi Hongan-ji,' said Saruki, frowning. 'In the days before the Restoration, it belonged to one of the shogun's bannermen, a man by the name of Togawa. But these days, some upstarts in the government are loafing around the place, talking up some rubbish about how they're going to change the world, all argued over cups of sake. They say they're causing such a racket that the neighbours can't sleep, even though the grounds of the mansion are five thousand *tsubo*.'

On the streets running along the canals, there were many mansions lying empty that had once belonged to various daimyo, or high-ranking samurai. After their inhabitants left for their hometowns or else fled to who knows where, any residence of note had been seized and turned over to the new government or else sold to government officials. Under the shogun, however, some sixty per cent of the land in Edo had belonged to the old samurai clans, so there were mansions that had been left untouched all over the place.

'Hey, isn't that...' said Saruki.

In front of the entrance to one mansion in Hatchōbori, they spotted a large man shouting, and the two of them stopped in their tracks. The mansion had previously belonged to a bannerman, but the gate was in ruins and you could see from the street that the garden inside was overgrown with weeds.

'I'm a representative of the Grand Council of State and I have come about the garden! This place has failed its inspection! If you don't open up, this site will be seized immediately!'

Though he was facing away from them, the man cut an imposing figure, and he was brandishing a wooden noticeboard in his hand.

'He's up to something,' replied Imokawa.

'It's Tamonta Onimaru,' Saruki muttered.

Unsteady on his feet, an old man came hurrying out of the dilapidated entrance and started bowing and scraping before the imposing *rasotsu*. Sergeant Onimaru was tapping on the noticeboard as he carried on reprimanding him.

That summer, the new government had issued a proclamation ordering all owners of mansions with gardens to plant mulberry trees or tea plants immediately. (In those days, raw silk and tea were Japan's leading exports, so this was but one example of the heroic efforts the new government was making in the belief that it had to act, even if its ideas were in short supply.) What's more, it had also threatened to seize any vacant land and gardens that were not being put to good use and had been allowed to go to seed.

The noticeboard bore the words 'Crown Property'. However, Saruki and Imokawa were well aware that Sergeant Onimaru had written those words himself.

Before long, having extracted from the old man a certain sum to 'overlook' the incident, Sergeant Onimaru came out of the front entrance, noticeboard in hand, and scowled when he spotted the two other gentlemen. His bearded face was fearsome to behold.

They both held out their hands. Eventually, still scowling, Sergeant Onimaru opened the envelope and handed them one *ryō* each.

'How many places have you been to?' asked Imokawa.

'And just where are the pair of you going?' he fired back without answering the question.

'Where indeed!'

'We're on our way to Denma-chō, to see Sohachi Ichinohata,' Saruki replied.

When Saruki informed Onimaru that Ichinohata had, it seemed, lately found himself a nice little source of income, he said:

'Why don't I join you? I haven't seen Sohachi's face in a long while.'

With a nod, he snapped the homemade noticeboard in half with his foot and tossed it into the gutter at the bottom of the mansion wall. And so, the three of them set off together.

As they were about to cross the Edobashi Bridge, Imokawa suddenly looked around.

'Hmm, I wonder…' he said, twisting his neck.

'What is it?' Onimaru asked.

'You see that samurai walking over there, the one in the *fuka-amigasa* hat? Look! He's stopped dead in his tracks.'

A few paces behind them, just as he said, there was a man wearing a black-crested *haori* jacket and a pair of *hakama*, with a large straw hat covering his face, trying to light his pipe with a match.

'He's not been following us, has he?'

24

'Why would you think that?'

'He's been following me ever since the end of summer. I don't know about before that, but I've a feeling that I've seen him four, maybe five times since then. I don't involve myself in nefarious dealings like you two, though, so I can't think why anyone would want to follow me. There's nobody with a grudge against me,' said Imokawa.

'What on earth are you on about?'

'Do either of you recognize him?'

'I don't, no. That being said, it's an outrage that anybody should be following an officer of the law! Right, I'll arrest him and find out,' said Onimaru, ready to turn on his heels, when Imokawa quickly stopped him.

'Wait! Wait! He looks strong. I have a feeling that you're about to kick a hornet's nest. Besides, I could be wrong about this.'

'He's gone!'

After wasting three or four matches in the wind, the man in the straw hat, trailing behind him at last a cloud of blue smoke, had leisurely strolled off, disappearing into an alley-way. He did not seem to be aware of them, so unhurried were his steps.

The three men proceeded to cross the Edobashi Bridge.

The area was full of merchants' homes and shops, so the crowds of people were no different from what they had been in the years before the Restoration. In fact, there were no fallow days for those people who had to work in order to survive.

There was one sight that did differ from before, however. By the sides of the main thoroughfare, there were people spreading out rugs and woven mats, laying out furniture, swords, dolls, clothes, all manner of things. Mostly, their heads were covered with braided straw hats or the headscarves known as *okoso-zukin*, and they didn't call out to passers-by but instead just sat motionlessly, their heads bowed, or else with both hands pressed to the ground in supplication. Even though the bright autumn sun was streaming down, they looked like a host of shadows. Having lost their stipends in the collapse of the previous government, these samurai families had no idea how to survive in the new world in which they found themselves.

'Ugh... here we go!' said Imokawa in a strange voice.

'Is that Heisuke Yokomakura?' said Saruki, glancing over at the street corner.

The front of the little place was only ten feet wide, and on the half-open sliding door was written: Greater Denma-chō Police Station. (In days past, it would have been called a lock-up.) Behind it, they could just about see the head of a lone sergeant. It was none other than the long face of their friend, Heisuke Yokomakura, but in front of him, with his back to them, there was a man wearing a samurai's topknot, his head bowed, and beside him what appeared to be girl of sixteen or seventeen—perhaps his daughter, who was cupping her face in both hands and appeared to be crying.

When Sergeant Yokomakura noticed the three of them approaching, he said in a loud voice:

'Very well, I'll overlook it this time. Now be off with you!'

When the man turned towards them, the three spotted that he was holding a half-folded fan. They surmised that he must have just given some money to Yokomakura, observing the old custom of offering it on the object. The greying, refined but somewhat frail-looking man and the girl who appeared to be his daughter went tottering out of the police station.

'What was all that about?' enquired Sergeant Saruki.

'Oh,' said Yokomakura, rubbing his long face in irritation, as though regretting having just raised his voice. 'It's a father and daughter who run a shop over there on the main thoroughfare. I just happened to be passing by and heard her disparaging the new government, so I dragged her off. Since her father came to make amends, though, I let her off the hook.'

'How much did it cost him?' asked Imokawa.

'Two *bu*,' said Yokomakura, extracting the coins from his pocket and showing them. 'Apparently, that was all he had. It hardly seems worth the trouble.'

'But you do this several times a day, surely?'

'That was my first of the day! Anyway, who would want to be a *rasotsu* if it weren't for little bonuses like that?!' said Yokomakura, smirking unashamedly.

'Oh, I would! I'm a servant of the people.'

By nature, Imokawa was, of course, a tremendously lazy man.

Feeling little inclined to demand a cut of only two *bu*, the three of them, each wearing a wry smile, turned to leave the police station, but Yokomakura called after them, stopping them in their tracks. When he asked after Sohachi Ichinohata, it was decided that he, too, should accompany them. Although this would leave nobody manning the police station, he did not seem to mind in the slightest. And so it was that the group of three became a group of four.

Together, they set out for Kodenma-chō, joking and talking loudly, oblivious to the world around them.

4

At Kodenma-chō there was a single block, right in the middle of the neighbourhood. It was enclosed by a long, blackened mud-brick wall some eight feet high and topped with bamboo spikes. Nailed to the wall beside the entrance was a still-new sign bearing the words 'Tokyo Prison'. Which is to say, this was the notorious Kodenma-chō jail.

'Hello!' said Heikurō Imokawa, addressing the two sentries stationed at the entrance. 'I don't suppose Sergeant Ichinohata's around, is he?'

Though the world might have changed drastically, the new government seemed, for the time being, loath to touch the prison's facilities or its set-up, and the old jailers had been allowed to remain in their posts. Naturally, however, quite a few of them had panicked and run off, and so the situation was that a number of *rasotsu* had been hired to fill their jobs.

The sentries were also friends of theirs.

'He is!'

'Come in!'

With these words from the sentries, the group piled in.

The prison was not a nice place to visit. Just setting foot inside was enough to send shivers down your spine. Sohachi Ichinohata, who worked there, had once offered to give them a tour, but all of them had politely declined, and usually, after a brief chat in a place called 'jailers' row', which was used these days for meetings between visitors and prison officials, they would beat a hasty retreat.

It was this room that they were now heading for.

As they got closer, they could hear a loud voice coming from further inside the building.

'Give it back! Give me back the money!'

With suspicion written across their faces, the four entered.

In a corner, Ichinohata was standing there crestfallen, his head slumped on his chest. In front of him, a man was reprimanding him, his arm outstretched and almost prodding Ichinohata on the nose.

'To say nothing of the fact that you're a just a guard here—'

He turned to look at the four *rasotsu* who had just entered, but showed no sign of fear.

'In any case, how is it that an official of His Imperial Majesty's government could defraud the people?!'

The four of them all turned to one another with looks of embarrassment. Just who could this man be? He must be an outsider, of course, but he was an imposing, fine figure of a man, somewhere in his mid-thirties. He wore a commoner's topknot and had on a striped kimono that he had tucked up into his waistband, revealing a pair of purple undertrousers. He had a large mouth and a strong jaw, as well as a very lean, sinewy physique, but he didn't look at all like a samurai. For one thing, he didn't even carry a sword. And yet, despite this, Ichinohata, who was by nature a timid sort, though still a *rasotsu*, was visibly trembling in the corner.

It was Onimaru who spoke first.

'And just who the hell are you to be raising your voice in a place like this?'

'I, sir? My name is Yukichi Fukuzawa.'

The four of them turned pale. This was no ordinary commoner. Even they knew that this was the name of the renowned Western scholar, who had opened a great place of learning called the Keiō in Shiba Shinsenza.

'And ju-just what do you mean by "Give me back the money"?'

'Well, I have some business, you see, with a certain prisoner here. Ever since the summer, I've been coming to this jail, bringing him books, clothes, money and what have you. Or at least, that was my intention. I simply assumed that the prisoner was here. When I first came to make a few enquiries, it was this man who told me that he was, and ever since, he's acted as the intermediary for these provisions,' said Fukuzawa, his face still puce with rage. 'But, as it so happens, it was all a sham. Yesterday, I learnt that the man in question is not being held at Kodenma-chō at all. This man has cheated me. How dare he tell such a barefaced lie?! So, I've come for an explanation, and to demand the return of all the goods and money I've handed over. Are my anger and my demand unjustified?'

He was no longer shouting, but his voice, let alone the meaning of his words, had a force that is difficult to convey.

It was little wonder that Ichinohata was so afraid.

'They are unjustified!' Saruki piped up in a high-pitched voice.

'In what way are they unjustified?'

'It is, by and large, considered improper to bring inmates goods and money. It's only natural that they should be confiscated!'

'If it's improper, then why were they not returned to me in the first place? Ah-ha! Got you there, haven't I? Well, in that case, I'm not the only one guilty of wrongdoing, am I?'

'I won't stand for this!' said Onimaru, slapping his red scabbard. 'You need cutting down to size, you do!'

'Cut me down? Don't make me laugh.'

Unbeknownst to the *rasotsu*, in May of the previous year, at Keiō University, when the rumble of cannon at the Battle of Ueno reverberated like distant thunder, this man had simply carried on with his lecture on Francis Wayland's treatise on economics. Now, as then, he did not so much as flinch, and instead merely spat out:

'I was relieved when the overbearing and corrupt officials of the shogunate disappeared, but it appears that, no matter how much the world may change, officials will still be officials. But then, I don't quite know whether these newfangled *rasotsu* even count as officials. Apropos of which, let me tell you something. The *rasotsu* may be policemen in name, but if you ask me, they're nothing more than roving gangsters. I really shouldn't say this, but just the other day I went to brief Lord Iwakura on the West's system of law enforcement, but I didn't manage to convince him. If a *rasotsu* were to cut me down with his idiot-meter, then we might see reform a damn sight sooner.'

'What's that? Lord Iwakura?'

'Idiot-meter?'

The *rasotsu* were dumbfounded.

'He means your sword! He thinks its length is a measure of your idiocy...'

With a hearty laugh, Fukuzawa suddenly turned towards the open door. There, just outside it, with the setting sun behind his back, stood somebody new. There was a note of madness in his voice, and he cut a very odd figure. The *rasotsu*, with the exception of Ichinohata, all stared in astonishment.

Not one of them, Fukuzawa included, could put a name to the attire worn by the man, but he had on a pale-blue *suikan* robe, a pair of *hakama* with legs that were tied at the ankles and traditional *kegutsu* furred boots.

'Can we help you?' came a suspicious voice from the crowd of *rasotsu*.

'And who might you be?' Fukuzawa finally asked.

'Chief Inspector Keishirō Kazuki of the Imperial Prosecuting Office, at your service.'

Looking the man over again as he entered, they now saw that he had jet-black hair, worn knotted at the back, and he even had eyebrows drawn on his forehead, as noblemen did in bygone times. Hanging at his waist was a sword that looked like an old-fashioned samurai's *tachi* rather than a *katana*, and in his hand he carried a folded fan made of cypress-wood. Though still a young man in his mid-twenties, this most elegant and handsome figure looked like a courtier who had stepped out of the Heian period.

'The Imperial Prosecuting Office? I see,' said Fukuzawa, flabbergasted, mumbling as he thought for a moment. 'The name of the body is familiar to me. Although I'm astonished that our new government has seen fit to bring out of retirement such an ancient and venerable institution from the annals of our country's history... even if I do agree with the spirit of it. Simply put, it's an office to catch malfeasance carried out by government officials, isn't that it? Well, if so, then I have something important to tell you. I am Yukichi Fukuzawa, rector of Keiō University.'

He introduced himself and once again launched into his tale.

'There's a soldier of the old shogunate by the name of Takeaki Enomoto, who, after surrendering in the Battle of Hakodate in the fifth month of this year, was sent to Tokyo. Now, I'm a native of Nakatsu, in Kyushu, and have no connection whatsoever to this Enomoto, but in the summer, quite by chance, I heard that his family, having no inkling what happened to him afterwards, was extremely worried about him.

As I say, I myself don't even have a passing acquaintance with Enomoto, but I was impressed by the fact that he had fought for the shogun right to the bitter end. They lost, I believe, only because they lacked numbers. So, I decided to go out of my way to help. Well, I said to myself, since the man would be deemed a criminal, why not go to the jail in Kodenma-chō and find out? So, when I came here, whom did I happen to meet but that scrawny weed over there. He was the one who had the audacity to tell me that Enomoto was here and that he was looking after him, so, ever since, I've been duly coming to drop off books and money and so forth for him. But would you believe, Enomoto has never in fact been here! Yesterday I learnt that he's being held in the military prison in Tatsu-no-kuchi. That's why I'm so irate and have come to protest. I don't regret the money or the goods in the slightest; however, I cannot forgive such a wicked and humiliating lie—*rasotsu* or not. In fact, it's precisely because he's a *rasotsu* that this *cannot* be overlooked. Tell me, kind sir, is my objection unreasonable?'

'It's perfectly reasonable,' the young chief inspector replied.

His voice sounded clear, sweet even. He then turned his narrowed eyes towards Ichinohata.

'Return it.'

'But... but I can't,' said Ichinohata, flustered.

'You mean to say it's all been disposed of?' asked Kazuki. A wry smile creased one of his cheeks. 'At any rate, this matter will be duly investigated, and it is the government's responsibility to compensate you for any goods or money that have been misappropriated. Sergeant, if you commit a crime like this ever again, you can be sure that you'll be punished.' Kazuki looked not just at Ichinohata, but at all four of the others. 'Is that understood? You will be punished by the

33

authority of the Imperial Prosecuting Office,' he repeated. 'Dismissed.'

The five *rasotsu* left the meeting room in a daze—in fact, each of them looked as though he had had a narrow escape.

'Please forgive me,' said Kazuki, bowing to the rector, who wore a look of considerable dissatisfaction. 'It's still early days for the new government, and there are all kinds of disreputable sorts swarming around. It's hard to catch all of them. The Imperial Prosecuting Office has begun conducting citywide patrols only recently.'

'Do all the officials of the Imperial Prosecuting Office dress like you?' Fukuzawa enquired, voicing a question that had been nagging at him.

'No, I'm afraid it's just me,' Kazuki replied with a laugh. 'If I may, sir, you look as though you have something on your mind.'

'I'd heard about the establishment of the Imperial Prosecuting Office,' said Fukuzawa, 'but, to be honest, I hadn't much of an idea what it did. Later, I found out that it was a revival of a Heian-period administration set up to investigate and root out official corruption. Rumour has it that there are some very old-fashioned people in its ranks… At any rate, as far as I can see, it isn't just the likes of the *rasotsu* that are up to no good. Higher up, there seem to be plenty more disgraceful types trying to line their pockets amid the chaos of the changing times. With all due respect, how much does the Imperial Prosecuting Office know about this, and what measures is it taking to deal with it?'

Looking straight into the eyes of Fukuzawa, who had put the question so bluntly, Kazuki replied:

'What measures, indeed? As you're doubtless aware, sir, right now in Tokyo the former residences of various daimyo are lying unoccupied. There are several gangs who, amid all the confusion, would very much like to get their grubby hands on them. We're conducting secret investigations into such cases. Ah yes, of course! You mentioned your recent visit to Lord Iwakura, to teach him about the Western system of policing. I'm also aware that a mansion in Mita, which belonged to the daimyo of the Shimabara Domain—with a building of some 769 *tsubo* and grounds of more than 14,000 *tsubo*—came under discussion. You apparently asked whether it could be sold to you for the low price of one *ryō* per *tsubo*, as compensation for your advice.'

Startled, Yukichi Fukuzawa drew a sharp breath, while Keishirō Kazuki merely grinned, revealing a beautiful set of teeth.

'Sir, how do *you* think the Imperial Prosecuting Office should go about treating such cases?'

5

That evening, at an *izakaya* in a backstreet of Nihonbashi Bakuro-chō, four of the *rasotsu* were drinking.

Having been detained by work at the prison, Ichinohata was running late. By the time he eventually arrived, the others were getting ready to leave.

When asked whether he had been questioned any more about the events earlier, he told them that he hadn't. Hearing this, Jirōmasa Saruki immediately asked:

'Hey, Sohachi, so what's the score with that devil from the Imperial what's-its-name?'

'I don't know,' replied Ichinohata, cocking his head. 'He started coming to the prison about ten days ago.'

'Could he be investigating one of the inmates?'

'No, but he's up to something strange.'

'Strange?'

'Yes… at the back of the prison, there's a spot for beheading criminals. He's had a new hut built there and a large dais erected in the yard. Then, two or three days ago, a wooden box twice as tall as a man was brought in from Yokohama. Well, strictly speaking, it came from France, but it seems to have been ordered by the chief inspector.'

'What? From France? What could it be, I wonder…'

'I've no idea what's inside it,' said Ichinohata, shaking his head feebly. 'But never mind that. I'm still in trouble after they found out about those packages.'

'But didn't you just say that there wasn't going to be any investigation?'

'True, but I can't make any money through that wheeze any more, and I've still got plenty of mouths that need feeding and palms that need greasing.'

Leaning over his cup of sake, Ichinohata held his head in his hands.

'Besides, that chief inspector may look like a soft touch, but still, there's something uncanny about him.'

'He did say that you could "be sure of punishment" if you ever did it again…' said Onimaru, sticking out a generous lower lip from beneath his beard. 'The little upstart had the cheek to take that high-and-mighty tone… Hey, innkeeper! More sake!'

'Do you think the Imperial Prosecuting Office will really be keeping an eye on us?' asked Heikurō Imokawa, beset by anxiety once again.

'Even if they wanted to, they'd never catch up with us—not

if they had thousands of men working for them,' said Heisuke Yokomakura with a chuckle.

They were truly an incorrigible lot. They wore their authority as a mantle and made it their daily task to cheat people out of their money with all manner of empty threats, extorting and swindling wherever they went. Their hapless victims just assumed that everyone in a position of authority did likewise. That was far from the case, however.

'That upstart must be from Satsuma or Chōshū, or one of the domains that overthrew the shogunate. Don't you think? And just what kind of chief inspector goes around in that get-up? Whatever he may say, there's something crooked about him.'

'After all, only two or three years ago all these so-called government officials were wanted by the police. Half of them were arsonists, bandits and murderers.'

'And now they preach to us about "society" and "the nation" and what have you.'

'Whereas in actual fact, day after day, night after night, they're buying up every last place in Yanagibashi and having a grand old time of it!'

'They're the same people who drummed up unrest and went marching through the streets, chanting, "Expel the barbarians!" They're the same people who overthrew the shogun and then, when all was said and done, played dumb, as if to say, "Who were all those people chanting? They've simply vanished!"'

They began to gabble excitedly over one another, and it was not just the alcohol talking. They were filled with genuine indignation over the state of the country.

'They aren't just playing dumb! They've been allowed to give full vent to their greed and lust with absolute impunity.

Ichinohata, next time you meet that devil, tell him that if he means to go after anyone, it's the top officials he should be looking at! The government ministers and councillors of state. Why, they aren't much older than we are! In fact, some of them are even younger!'

'And they're all raking it in, while we have to go to these unspeakable lengths just to scrape together enough money to buy some cheap whore from the pleasure quarter.'

'It's a world gone mad, damn it… Innkeeper! We're out of sake! And hey, give us all that octopus you've got there!'

The innkeeper wore a pained expression. He had no other customers, for they had all skulked off the moment they saw the *rasotsu* traipsing in.

The five of them were all former members of a security unit that was set up at the end of the Edo period: the so-called Shinchō-gumi. In the early 1860s, the shogunate had scraped together the masterless samurai known as *rōnin* to keep order in the city of Edo, but in their final days, far from keeping order, they had turned into a plague, blackmailing and extorting money from the citizens. Thinking back on it now, though, while their conduct used to be more brazen, they had nevertheless had high hopes for the future.

Nowadays, they all lived in the tenement houses near the slums. The heroic-looking Tamonta Onimaru, still unmarried, lived with his sixty-three-year-old mother and eighty-eight-year-old grandmother; Jirōmasa Saruki, who fell into a trance whenever he was counting money, had a wife who ate so prodigiously that she looked like a sumo wrestler; Heisuke Yokomakura, whose philosophy was that the best way is always to do nothing at all, had, unaccountably, seven children; Heikurō Imokawa, who used flattery to cadge money from his colleagues, might have had no wife, but he did have five younger siblings to look after; and the sickly-looking weed Sohachi Ichinohata had a hot-tempered spouse, who at least once a day would strike her husband's sunken cheeks and send his head spinning.

As chance would have it, only the previous day, they had all got it in the neck from their mothers, come to blows with their wives or been reduced to tears by their siblings and children. And so, to distract themselves, they had all thought of buying a woman—oddly enough, a love of prostitutes was the only thing they shared. For some reason they had ended up placing their faith in Ichinohata, who seemed to be in the money, to make this happen. But when they visited him at the prison, they had been frightened by that odd-looking devil from the Heian-period court, which dampened their ardour—and that was how they had wound up drinking in a backstreet *izakaya* instead.

'If things get any worse, we can kiss goodbye to surrounding ourselves with beautiful *maiko* from Yanagibashi and discussing the great affairs of state,' drawled Onimaru. 'Maybe I'll never hold a beautiful woman in my arms again. My hopes, my dreams—all gone!'

With that, he hung his bearded head over his plate of octopus and began to weep. He was awfully prone to weeping after a drink or two.

'Can we really be done for?! Unlike you lot, I still have so many things that I want to do. No, not just the women! There are things that I ought to have done as a man.'

'"Unlike you lot"?! That's a bit harsh, isn't it?' said the lazy Yokomakura, pouting. 'I have things that I want to do, too!'

'You?! Such as?'

'Well, I don't really know, but still... I just have this feeling that there are things I want to do.'

'I wish that I could be a man!' cried Onimaru, tears welling in his eyes. 'I don't know how, but I'd like to die having done something that would make people think I'd lived a meaningful life.'

'Hear, hear!' shouted Imokawa. Then, after a pause, he got to his feet. 'This bar isn't exactly lifting my spirits. Why don't we all pile down to Yoshiwara anyway?'

Seeing the group clatter towards the exit in a flurry of excitement, the innkeeper quickly called after them.

'Gentlemen! Your bill!'

'I'll settle up with you next time I'm on patrol in the area,' said Saruki. 'You can wait until then.'

'I'm sorry, but that just won't do. We run a hand-to-mouth sort of establishment.'

Having been bawling his eyes out only a moment before, Onimaru now looked over his shoulder and yelled at the owner: 'Don't be absurd! Just who do you think it is who makes it possible for you to run "a hand-to-mouth sort of establishment" in such a treacherous world? Aren't we the ones who go without sleep, just to keep the likes of you in business?'

6

Having left the *izakaya* behind, the five *rasotsu* set off in the direction of Asakusa.

Their arms around each others' shoulders, the group marched in a line down the lawless, moonlit, already deserted streets, singing a popular ditty of the day at the top of their voices.

Up ahead of them, the shadow of the palace gate at Asakusa drew into view. But just then, somebody came running out of a side alley.

'Who's there?' the figure called out, having heard the singing and stopping it dead. He peered at the group through the moonlight. 'Oh, sergeants! There's robbers, I'm being robbed! Help me, please!'

He practically ran into them, falling to the ground and clutching at their ankles.

'There's three of them,' he said in a shrill voice. 'They had their swords drawn and were threatening me. One false move and they would have killed me. Oh, how glad I am! How happy I am to see you, sergeants! Quickly, now, it's the Sumiya pawnshop just over there.'

Imokawa shook off his hands.

'Terribly sorry, but right now we're on urgent official business. There's a police station just up there, by the palace gate at Asakusa. Go there, if you want.'

The five of them spun around. They had all sobered up the moment they stopped singing, and so now they marched off with a true sense of urgency.

At the crossroads directly in front of them, however, were two silhouettes, coming towards them and barring their way. Who could they be?

Before they could ask the question, the *rasotsu* were startled. In the moonlight, they recognized the silhouette of a *suikan* and also the outline of a *fuka-amigasa*.

'Go back!' said the figure in the *suikan*.

'Is there a law that permits *rasotsu* to run away,' the man in the *fuka-amigasa* added, 'even after being informed that there are bandits around?'

The second man spoke with a Satsuma accent.

'Turn back!' he commanded.

The five *rasotsu* were stunned. They spun around and retraced their steps in confusion.

'Which one of you was it who told him to go away?' the man in the *fuka-amigasa* asked.

'It… it was me,' replied Imokawa, trembling.

The man who had approached them earlier was nowhere to be seen. He must have run off to the police station in Asakusa. Leaving the figure in the *suikan* and the *rasotsu* where they were, the man in the *fuka-amigasa* marched off into the alleyway by himself.

Moments later, he returned and said, 'All right. It's the pawnshop five or six doors down. The only way out is through this alley.'

'Kazuki, would you flush them out? I'll wait here and shoot them when they come running.'

From the breast of his kimono he extracted something that astonished the *rasotsu*: a pistol.

'No, wait! We don't want to kill them,' said the man in the *suikan* with a shake of his head. 'I need them alive. Better you shoot the pistol here. The bandits will come flying out and down the alley. That's where I'll catch them.'

'Are you sure that's best?'

'I think so.'

When they saw the object that he drew from his waist, the *rasotsu* were wide-eyed in amazement. It was not a sword, but the folded cypress-wood fan that they had seen earlier that afternoon.

Then, his furred boots muffling his footsteps, he entered the alley.

Rather than ask how on earth he was going to arrest the bandits with only a fan, the *rasotsu*—and especially Imokawa—could not resist asking a question that had been plaguing them from the outset.

'Sir,' they called out to the samurai wearing the *fuka-amigasa*. 'Who on earth are you?'

'I'm Chief Inspector Toshiyoshi Kawaji,' the man replied, 'of the Imperial Prosecuting Office.'

He raised the arm in which he was holding the pistol.

Down in the alley, the cypress-wood fan opened with a flourish.

'Excellent!'

The blast of the gun rent the moonlit sky.

A few moments later, a tangle of figures appeared in the alleyway. They peered out of the darkness into the street, then gave a cry of alarm, and hastily beat a retreat, before stopping dead in their tracks.

The *rasotsu* saw the flash of several swords being drawn, a flurry of movement, then all was still.

'Over here!' called the figure in the *suikan*, stepping out of the shadows.

Seeing him stand there on his own, the *rasotsu* were taken aback.

Drawn by the sound of gunfire, locals began appearing from all over, curious to find out what the commotion was. When they saw the fantastic vision of a Heian courtier, seemingly floating before them in a moonlight-drenched Tokyo alleyway, they stopped, spellbound.

'There's no cause for alarm,' said the figure in the *suikan*, slowly undulating his cypress-wood fan. 'The robbers have been dealt with.'

When the five *rasotsu* came running, he pointed with his fan to the three silhouettes lying at his feet.

'Take them into custody.'

7

It was to be a night of surprises.

The first surprise was that the young man from the Imperial Prosecuting Office, using only his fan, had seemingly made the three robbers faint with fear. The fan was made entirely of thin strips of cypress, and since it was almost a foot and a half long, it could be used as a baton when folded, but the *rasotsu* were unaware of this, and, even if they had known, it would still have stunned them to learn that he could defeat three sword-wielding robbers with it.

The second surprise was that among the robbers there was a woman in her thirties, which they did not immediately realize on account of her wearing a mask and a man's kimono. Lifting up the three figures who had been knocked unconscious, the *rasotsu* either slung them over their shoulders or dragged them by their hands and feet to the jail in Kodenma-chō, where the third surprise awaited them.

After arriving at the prison, they were all herded into a cell of their own.

'Hey! What's all this?' they protested, panic-stricken.

'No idea,' replied the guard on the other side of the bars. 'Chief Inspector's orders.'

Naturally, it had come as a quite surprise to them to learn that the samurai in the *fuka-amigasa* was also a chief inspector, and that he was a colleague of that devil in Heian garb.

'But in that case,' Imokawa muttered, looking worried, 'maybe the chief inspector has been following me all this time! Maybe they've been following all of us!'

The other four turned pale.

'Do you think that's why we've been thrown in here?' asked Saruki, cradling his head in his hands.

'But wasn't Ichinohata let off the hook after he was taken to task by that Western scholar this afternoon?' asked Yokomakura. 'Besides, all *rasotsu* do this sort of thing. Why are we the only ones being locked up?'

Whatever the reason, the fact remained: they had been thrown behind bars, which did nothing to relieve their anxiety.

'So, might the two chief inspectors be around?' Onimaru asked the guard.

'They might,' the guard replied, before adding: 'They appear to be doing something at the execution ground.'

The five *rasotsu* looked at one another.

'In the dead of the night?' asked Ichinohata, his voice hoarse.

'Mmm-hmm… Oh, and just a little while ago, somebody arrived by palanquin. Apparently, the chief inspectors summoned him.'

'What?!'

Their anxiety levels shot up.

'Who is it?'

'I've no idea, but he was shown, still in his palanquin, straight to the execution ground. Ah yes, about those three robbers you brought in earlier,' said the guard, changing the subject. 'They were some pretty big fish, you know. One is Wild Dog Kinbei, another is Scarface Taji, and the third is Ballbreaker O-Aya.'

45

'Never heard of them.'

'You're all pretty new around here, so it's only to be expected,' the guard said. He had served there as a guard since the old days.

'I don't know how many people they must have killed. They were the most feared gang we had here, but they were let out under the new regime. Don't ask me why. But, hey, you did good catching them again.'

'Hey! Maybe they're going to be executed,' Imokawa suggested.

'Hmm, I doubt they'd do it at this time of night.'

'So do I,' added Ichinohata, who knew the place well. 'I've never heard of them carrying out an execution in the dead of night. In fact, I may as well tell you: one of my jobs here is to deal with the bodies after the beheadings.'

The four others stared at Ichinohata in horror.

Nobody dared joke whether he would be 'dealing with' his own corpse that night.

It was about half an hour later that several prison officials arrived and the *rasotsu* were conducted from their cell to the execution ground. Needless to say, this sent the five into a terrible panic.

Terrified by the sound of jeering voices, they all began to tremble. Saruki, for one, failed to spot that one of his enormous shoes had slipped off, while the heroic-looking Onimaru seemed to suffer a fit of cerebral anaemia and went crashing to the ground. In the end, the prison guards had to prop him up on both sides.

After passing through several wooden doors, they saw that the night sky ahead of them was aglow. Something was burning down below.

'What's that fire?'

'I've no idea. But that's the execution ground over there,' answered Ichinohata, his teeth chattering.

Eventually, they arrived in front of a small gate cut into a mud wall. A palanquin had been set down beside it, but the *rasotsu* didn't even have the time to realize that this must be the one the guard had told them about.

'You're ordered to go through,' the guard said. 'Quickly, now.'

The door opened and through they went.

Then the door closed behind them.

8

What awaited the already half-dead *rasotsu* on the other side was a scene that could have been dreamt up only in the hereafter.

The execution ground was enclosed by a mud wall that was cracked and crumbling all over, and, right in the centre of the square, four bonfires were burning. These were what was turning the night sky red. Staked in the ground beside them were canes of green bamboo with their leaves still on them, bound together by the kind of rope ordinarily reserved for Shinto ceremonies, with the zigzag paper streamers attached to the rope fluttering in the wind.

In the middle of the square, a three-tier scaffold had been erected, upon which stood two solid-looking pillars side by side, twice the height of any man, with just enough space between them for somebody to pass through. They were connected at the top by a thick board—but what was that thing attached to the board?

The object was glittering a bright red in the light cast by the bonfires. Plainly, it was an iron blade, and it was slanting downwards. There was another board at the bottom of the two pillars, with a square basket fixed to the nearest side of it. There was also a rope dangling from the top of the structure.

Though the spectators did not know what this device was intended for, the very sight of the grim spectre sent a shudder straight to the depths of their souls.

On the far side of it stood three silhouettes. Two of them belonged to Keishirō Kazuki and Toshiyoshi Kawaji. Kazuki was in his usual attire, but Kawaji had removed his hat. He must have been around thirty-six or thirty-seven, wore a sharp, upward-pointing moustache and had a look of considerable resolve about him.

Without even glancing at the *rasotsu* who had just entered, Kazuki turned and said:

'Well, are we ready?'

'*Oui,*' the figure next to him replied with a nod.

It was a woman's voice, and there was something odd about it.

Who on earth was this? Once again, the *rasotsu* could scarcely believe their eyes. She was wearing something fluttery and pink—almost like a mosquito net. They didn't know the name for this either, but the woman had on a broad-brimmed *ichimegasa* hat, which had a long cylindrical veil trailing down from it.

'Right, you men!' said Kazuki, turning to the *rasotsu* for the first time. 'You see those three bandits over there? Bring the one with the scar on his face up to the scaffold first.'

The five men finally noticed the figures of the two men and one woman sitting directly beside the entrance. There was no doubt about it: these were the robbers from earlier. By now, of course, they had all regained their senses, but their hands had been tied behind their backs, and, as they beheld the strange sight before them, they seemed to look on with eyes devoid of consciousness.

'The rest of you, keep a close eye on the other two!'

The penny finally dropped: the bandits were the ones for the chop.

'Ah, yes, sir!'

As though propelled by springs, Ichinohata and Yokomakura stepped forward. For Ichinohata, the reflex was almost automatic, since he had been assisting with the beheadings for some time already. Yet for the lazy Yokomakura, his uncharacteristically enthusiastic response was more the result of a burst of elation and delight.

'Get to your feet!'

The one they were dragging off had a grisly scar—the vestige of a terrible burn—covering the right half of his face: it was Taji.

They approached the scaffold from the one side on which there was no rope cordoning it off and climbed the steps leading to the platform. They followed the commands issued by Kazuki's voice and fan, but they were stunned when he gave the order to lay the prisoner face down on the bench.

Ichinohata and Yokomakura knew that this man was to be beheaded—but the exact means of this eluded them. Just as they were wondering how on earth they were going to do it, they looked up and suddenly saw the enormous blade hanging overhead. Then a chill ran down their spines. Finally, they realized what this instrument was for.

'The board at the foot of the pillars is in two parts. Lifting the top one of them will make a hole. That's where you are to place the criminal's neck. Then, using the leather straps, tie his body to the bench.'

Kazuki walked around the ropes as he spoke and then climbed up onto the scaffold himself.

As though under his spell, the two of them did exactly as he said. When they lifted the upper board, they found that it had been hollowed out into the shape of a crescent moon, and together with the other board it made a neat, round hole.

Taji, who had been strangely unperturbed until that point, was finally struck by a fear that this was no ordinary execution and began to resist furiously; however, because his hands were tied behind his back, they had no trouble pinning him down and placing his neck against the bottom of the hollowed-out crescent Moon. When the other board was lowered from above, only his head stuck out on one side, while the rear was just a writhing trunk of human flesh. Then the two *rasotsu* strapped him to the bench.

'Scarface Taji, you will know that in the past your conduct would have warranted the hell of a crucifixion. You are to be put to death, but in this enlightened age you will be beheaded in the French fashion,' Kazuki boomed, as he clutched the hanging rope. 'At least you will have the honour of being the first in Japan to be subject to an experiment of this kind. You may be grateful, moreover, to know that you are being given the most painless kind of death known to man.'

He pulled on the rope.

There came a noise that defies description: the hiss of iron, and then a cry that mixed wonder with horror. The cry was not that of the condemned man, but rather a mingling of the gasps of the two *rasotsu* standing on the scaffold with those of the spectators and the sound of the prisoner's neck being cut.

The triangular axe had fallen along the grooves cut into the two pillars and, with the force of its own weight, severed the head that was poking out of the hole, which then tumbled down into the basket below. A tremendous amount of blood surged up, bright crimson, into one of the bonfires.

After a few moments of terrible silence, Kazuki spoke:

'Gentlemen! Bring down the body and take it over there. Then fetch the next one: Wild Dog Kinbei.'

As though having finally awoken from his stupor, Kinbei started howling and raging. Though he was still tied up, he tried to escape. Saruki tackled him to the ground, but he managed to roll over and send Saruki flying. Had it not been for Onimaru's Herculean strength, who knows what might have happened. And if Onimaru was keen to use the situation to show off, the fact remained that both he and Saruki were desperate to present themselves in a good light before the fearsome chief inspectors.

The corpse on the scaffold was taken down by Ichinohata and Yokomakura. The headless body continued to spew up blood, leaving a slippery streak of red across the scaffold.

In his place, Wild Dog Kinbei was dragged up and, true to his name, even after his head had been placed in the hole, he continued to struggle and rage.

'And now for the second one,' announced Kazuki, as the iron axe dropped.

As if by magic, Kinbei fell silent.

Now, in Kaishū Katsu's memoirs, the statesman tells of three villains whom he supposedly 'admired'. The first of them, he wrote, would commit a robbery in Edo and, not spending the stolen money straight away, would instead bury it, and flee to Kamigata. Once there, he would commit another robbery, bury that money too, and, when the dust of his previous crime had settled, return to Edo to dig up the money and spend it. This man went on, alternating like this, and nobody clocked that he was a robber for the longest time. And his name was Taji.

The second villain had been arrested and interrogated by a police sergeant. Where most men would give any excuse to wriggle out of the situation, this one gave a full confession, saying that it couldn't be helped, that his arrest was the will of Heaven. Then, when he was to be put to death the very next day, he was suddenly released amid the chaos of the shogunate's downfall. However, while his fellow inmates were in a frenzy of excitement, he never even so much as blinked, and instead merely said, 'Oh, I see. Well, I'll be off, then.' And with that, he waltzed out of the prison. This one was Kinbei.

That incident happened just after the government forces took Edo Castle, when Katsu was, for a time, entrusted with public security in the capital. 'What did it matter?' he later wrote. 'Even if we beheaded fifty or sixty prisoners, the world wasn't going to be short of murderers and thieves, so I let them all go.'

The woman's story ran as follows. 'There was also a female prisoner in her thirties,' he wrote. 'I wanted to learn the nature of her crime, so I paid somebody to go and question her in person. She claimed never to have spoken about it to anyone and said that she would tell it only to me. "Because of my alleged beauty," she said, "I've been approached by many lascivious men. So, whenever a rich-looking one would come along, I would open my heart to him, and when we would [redacted], I would twist his [redacted], killing him in the process. Then I would just grab the money and play innocent. Even when the doctor would come to examine the body, since there was no wound, he would say it couldn't be helped. I must have killed no fewer than five men in this way." Truly, is this not the height of boldness?' May it please the attentive reader to fill in the redacted words for themselves. So much for the third figure: O-Aya.

When Heikurō Imokawa dragged the temptress up onto the scaffold, even she half-fainted before the prospect of the iron axe. And when the blood spurted from her self-avowed 'beautiful' head as it fell into the basket, not one of the men, for all their love of women, would regret her loss. Instead, they merely averted their vacant eyes.

But, no… Truth be told, the five *rasotsu* did not witness this spectacle at all, for their eyes were elsewhere. That the third condemned prisoner was a woman might well have aroused an irresistible curiosity, yet the figure in the *ichimegasa*, who until that point had been standing at the back, now floated forward and looked up at the scaffold from beside one of the bonfires. This is what had drawn their attention.

Peeping out from the veil, which opened at the front, was a pair of blue eyes. Her complexion was as white as snow. And, billowing beneath the veil, they could see hair of what appeared to be spun gold! Was this figure who looked like a Heian noblewoman in fact a lady from another land?

'My word,' said Kazuki, as he examined the fallen blade. 'That's some fine craftsmanship. Not even a scratch on it.' He smiled at the woman. 'But since we have the opportunity, I think we ought to test it out a little more.'

He then turned to face the five *rasotsu*.

'Now then… Your misdeeds have already been investigated thoroughly. As *rasotsu* charged with maintaining public order in the capital, this is inexcusable. As if that were not enough, you are guilty furthermore of gross professional misconduct. When a citizen informed you of a robbery, not only did you ignore him, but you even tried to run off. What kind of men are you!? What kind of policemen are you!? It is utterly unforgivable!'

The five men gulped as they stood there, petrified.

'This afternoon, I told you that you would be sentenced to death without fail if you committed another crime. And you have done just that.'

Once again, the triangular blade swished up.

Silhouetted in his *suikan*, the chief inspector from the Imperial Prosecuting Office took the rope and said in a clear voice, which echoed delectably:

'You are to be put to the guillotine one by one. Now, which of you will be next?'

ESMERALDA THE *MIKO*

1

At around three o'clock in the afternoon on the eighth day of the eleventh lunar month, a young man of twenty-three or so came galloping towards the Imperial Prosecuting Office, which was located just opposite the Sakurada Gate at the southern end of the imperial palace.

As the cloud of dust settled behind him, the rider, who was dressed like a student, jumped off his horse by the gatehouse and, after a few brief words to the sentry, handed him the reins and hurried in through the vermilion-lacquered gate. As he entered, he was spotted by Toshiyoshi Kawaji, who was walking through the grounds in the company of Keishirō Kazuki.

'Well, if it isn't Heihachirō!' exclaimed Kawaji.

The youth looked puzzled when he saw Kazuki in his *suikan*, but he bowed right away.

'Is Kaieda here?' he asked, betraying an accent very similar to Kawaji's. 'I have news that won't wait.'

'What is it?'

'Masujirō Ōmura died in Osaka on the night of the fifth.'

The chief inspectors looked at one another.

Some two months previously, Vice Minister of War Masujirō Ōmura had been injured in an assassination attempt made by eight assailants in Kyoto. At first, the wounds appeared to be healing, but the one on his right knee had become sceptic, and so the following month he had been transferred to Osaka, where, under the knife of a Dutch military surgeon, his right leg was amputated. He was reported to have been making good progress since then.

'It's my first time at the Imperial Prosecuting Office,' said the young man. 'Can you tell me where I might find him?'

'I'll take you there,' said Kawaji, leading the way.

As they walked, Kawaji turned and asked the youth where he had come by the news. Those were, of course, the days before the telegraph, so it was only natural to wonder how news could travel all the way from Osaka in only three days.

'When I went down to the wharf earlier today to meet somebody off the steamer, I happened to run into a government messenger—an acquaintance of mine—who was on his way to the Grand Council of State.'

'I see. But why is the news so important to Kaieda?'

'I believe that last month, at a meeting at his house, Kaieda expressed a deep concern for Ōmura's well-being.'

'He'll be delighted, I'm sure.'

The young man turned towards Kawaji. He couldn't quite understand what he had meant by this.

Without saying another word, however, Kawaji walked on, a smile appearing on his cheeks. They didn't go in through the main entrance, but passed through a side gate with a wooden door and then skirted along a garden. Kazuki walked behind them.

It was a warm, sunny day, and all the *shōji* paper screens facing onto the garden had been opened wide. In each of the tatami rooms, they could see groups of people sitting at their desks, writing or researching. The desks were all piled high with papers. Though they could only catch glimpses as they passed, what they saw was the now-rare spectacle of frenzied activity in government offices.

After a lengthy walk, they arrived at the furthest tatami room, where they found half a dozen people sitting.

When the youth, who had been so taken aback by Kazuki's *suikan*, saw the place, his eyes widened. The figures seated there were all wearing *eboshi* hats and ancient ceremonial robes.

'Gentlemen,' said Kawaji, announcing himself. He approached and bowed. 'Heihachirō Tōgō has come from Yokohama with urgent news.'

The youth approached the threshold and repeated the news of Ōmura's death. Unsurprisingly, there was an outcry of shock in the room.

Tōgō further elaborated on what he had heard from the messenger. At the very end, Ōmura had left a farewell poem written in pencil in a Western-style notebook:

> *I do not regret laying my life down for the emperor,*
> *My only thought is for the fate of the country.*

He added, however, that the writing was apparently so thin and shaky, like an earthworm crawling over the paper, that it had been exceedingly difficult to decipher.

'And he had the nerve to look down on Saigō!'

The one who now spoke was First Secretary Tomozane Yoshii.

Hearing Yoshii's words, the man beside him, Second Secretary Yajirō Shinagawa, turned his head.

'Now, let me see,' said Shinagawa. 'Where have I heard those words before?'

'Last words are like sutras: they all sound the same,' said Second Secretary Yukimasa Ozaki.

Shinagawa clapped his hands together.

'I've got it!' he cried. 'They were Uta Nagai's last words—you know, the one from back home, who advocated opening the country up to foreigners, and who was forced to commit *seppuku* in the third year of Bunkyū. Hmm… It's just like Ōmura to borrow somebody else's words for his own death—he who showed such contempt for others!'

'It wasn't so much his contempt for others,' said Togama Kōno, 'it was his total lack of spirit!'

'For a vice minister of war, it's not exactly an impressive death,' chided Ryōsuke Yasuoka, spitting out his words.

'That's just the kind of man he was!' came a hoarse cry.

The voice belonged to the man whom Tōgō had come to see: Nobuyoshi Kaieda.

'I wonder, though. Did he show contempt for others right to the bitter end, or had he lost what little spirit he had left by the time death finally came for him? Either way, that's what happens when you're so strongly influenced by Western military ideas and lose the spirit of the Empire.' A broad set of white teeth flashed between his heavy lips. 'I'm sorry, Shinagawa, but Ōmura was a disgrace to the Chōshū Domain.' Kaieda then turned his attention to Tōgō, who was still standing in the garden. 'Thank you for bringing the good news, Heihachirō. You may go.'

He bowed and began to walk off, but after only a couple of steps, he turned around with a troubled look on his face.

'But what about the navy, sir? Is it not to be westernized, too?'

Kaieda seemed to be at a loss for an answer.

'I've fought aboard Western-built warships,' Heihachirō continued, his face solemn. 'I'm not quite convinced when you say we'll be slaughtered if we adopt a Western-style military system.'

Only a short while ago, this youth had told Kawaji that he had come as quickly as possible because Kaieda had voiced

60

concern for Ōmura's well-being. What he had not known, however, was under what circumstances and with what intonation Kaieda had made those remarks, and it now seemed likely that he had laboured under a misapprehension.

'The navy has no choice,' replied Kaieda with a wry smile. 'But if we only imitate the West, then we're bound to lose the war with them when it comes. Even if the guns on our battleships are borrowed from the West, don't forget the Japanese spirit. Ōmura seemed to think that unless we westernized the Japanese spirit as well, Japan wouldn't have a leg to stand on. In his testimony, the assassin said many things—that Vice Minister Ōmura was using his influential position to advocate for westernization; that, if he continued to do so, he would jeopardize the Empire. I must say, his sentiments on the matter accord with my own.'

Having finished his monologue, he suddenly turned towards another figure in the garden.

'Kazuki, you've been to France. What do you make of it all?'

The sleeve of Kazuki's *suikan* fluttered in the wind. Placing his arms by his sides, he bowed deeply.

'I hesitate to say the words aloud, but as His Majesty the emperor has seen fit to observe, availing ourselves of the foreigners' weapons and tools is scarcely apt to harm the Japanese spirit.'

'Ah, so that's what you think!'

'It is, sir. From where I stand, you esteemed gentlemen seem to regard the fortress that is the Yamato spirit as though it were the great assembly of deities that repose in the high heavens... or at least that's what I, with all due deference, would venture to say.'

'Enough, enough, Kazuki!' cried Yukimasa Ozaki, frantically waving his hands about. 'Somehow, you always manage to make everything sound like a mystical incantation.'

2

The Imperial Prosecuting Office was originally established in the eighth century, during the Nara period, to find and root out corruption among government officials and courtiers. It had been dusted off and brought out of retirement along with the restoration of imperial rule in the second year of Meiji, and Michitaka Kujō had been appointed to the post of director.

Below Kujō were the deputy and assistant directors. For generations, their titles had been retained ceremonially by the families that had first held them, but since the Restoration these positions had been revived. In reality, however, they were handed out to the old feudal lords one by one, and, as with the director, their presence did nothing more than add a sense of grandeur to the office.

Below the directors were secretaries of the first and second rank. There were three of each, and these men, in effect, made up the nervous system of the Imperial Prosecuting Office. Among the former were Nobuyoshi Kaieda and Tomozane Yoshii, both of whom hailed from Satsuma, and also Ryōsuke Yasuoka, a native of Tosa.

Yajirō Shinagawa, Togama Kōno and Yukimasa Ozaki made up the secretaries of the second rank, and beneath them were more than a dozen other ranks, including commissioners, inspectors, investigators and so forth, making up some one hundred and fifty or sixty men all told.

Its powers combined what would later be separated into the Prosecutor's Office, the Metropolitan Police, the Military Police, as well as the Board of Audit.

Nobody would have ever thought the first and second secretaries, who were responsible for the running of the place, to be the sorts likely to distinguish themselves in office. Stubborn and inflexible, they all hailed from an elite and had, moreover, been appointed to the roles on account of being the right sex and having been in the right place at the right time. Yet it would be fair to say that, during those years of chaos, among the many government agencies that simply let themselves be swept along by the wind, it was the Imperial Prosecuting Office that first began to operate at full speed and with a certain sense of purpose.

And just what was that sense of purpose? In a word, it was conservatism.

Back in the Nara period, not only had the Imperial Prosecuting Office been willing to denounce a minister or a prince of royal blood, but if ever the government of the day tried to move off in a new direction, even by the smallest degree, they would inevitably slam the brakes on.

And the current Imperial Prosecuting Office was no different. Now they criticized any proposed reform, asking:

'Hadn't the ministers called for the restoration of the monarchy? And hadn't the lords advocated for the foreigners to be expelled?'

In the face of such outright defiance, there was not a single lord or minister who had a word to offer in his own defence. The government was bewildered, embarrassed and had already begun to regard the Imperial Prosecuting Office as a den of conservative reactionism.

All the same, the officials of the Imperial Prosecuting Office were deadly serious about their work. As we have just witnessed, when they held their meetings, they wore *eboshi* and ceremonial robes—and this was not a joke, nor was it eccentricity: they did this because they placed such great faith in the restoration of the monarchy and order.

And yet, the news of Ōmura's death just now had brought a smile to Kaieda's lips.

The fact was that on the fifth day of the first lunar month, the influential politician Shōnan Yokoi had been assassinated in the streets of Kyoto's temple district, and now, even though most of the six assassins had been taken into custody, Kaieda still stubbornly refused to consent to their execution.

According to a letter explaining the assassins' motives, Yokoi supposedly had the evil intention of spreading 'the Jesus faith', and in so doing planned to inflict terrible damage on the Empire, et cetera, et cetera. When the government attempted to impose the death penalty immediately, Kaieda had opposed them, saying that the assassins' aim had been a just one. So sympathetic to them was his argument that there were even outraged voices from within the government, wondering whether it had not been Kaieda who instigated the assassination in the first place. What was more, the death penalty could not be imposed without the approval of the Imperial Prosecuting Office, and so the government now found itself between a rock and a hard place.

The Imperial Prosecuting Office had, moreover, begun to demand that its officials be allowed to attend and observe cabinet and privy council meetings. They were also quick to raid government offices and examine their ledgers, and, if the ledgers recorded a pair of scissors bought for ten *sen*, then these scissors would have to be produced, and if they could not be found, the department would be accused of falsifying accounts; and if an office recorded ten sacks of charcoal weighing four *kanme* each, they would order the sacks to be brought out and weighed, and if they were found to weigh only three *kanme* and 150 *monme*, the accountant would be investigated for accepting bribes from merchants.

In addition to this, they sent out all manner of patrols about the city and dispatched secret envoys to spy on the various clans.

There is one story that sounds like a funny tale on the face of it but is really far from it.

Decades later, Toyomi Yamamoto, who served as deputy director of the Treasury's accounting directorate, was asked why—year in, year out—he looked as though he were chewing a wasp. 'When I was young,' came his reply, 'I served in the Imperial Prosecuting Office and was ordered always to scowl whenever I found myself in a government office, and so every day I'd practise in front of the mirror, training myself to look stern and grim. The habit stuck, and now this is the only face I can make.'

The story goes that he said all this still looking as though he were chewing a wasp.

In short, the Imperial Prosecuting Office was a source of the most terrible dread for government officials back then.

3

Still looking dazed, Heihachirō Tōgō left the Imperial Prosecuting Office through the vermilion gate, together with Kawaji and Kazuki.

Tōgō took the reins of his mount from the sentry but had little choice but to walk alongside the two chief inspectors, as Kawaji had begun talking to him.

'That's a Western horse. Whose is it?'

'I belongs to Mr Wagman, from the English-language school I attend in Yokohama.'

'Oh, you're studying English these days?'

'Yes, indeed. Now, I'm very sorry, but I really must be on my way. I have to return the horse.'

With that, Tōgō bowed, leapt onto the horse and galloped off.

'A fine young man, don't you think?' muttered Kazuki as he watched him go. Kazuki had not been so very different from him in his youth. 'Daring to disagree with old Kaieda like that!'

'He seems a little slow on the uptake,' Kawaji replied, 'and just as headstrong. I think he'll go far.'

Then they began to discuss what they had just heard.

Tōgō had served as a third officer in the Satsuma navy and had combat experience, fighting off Enomoto's fleet last year, in the Battle of Awa, and more recently, in the Battle of Hakodate. However, because of his reserved, ponderous, somewhat awkward character, he had been promoted later than the comrades of his age.

'He's not unlike you in fact,' said Kazuki, laughing.

'Isn't he?'

'Well, he's sincere, plodding… hasn't made much of himself.'

Kawaji laughed.

Toshiyoshi Kawaji hailed from Satsuma, and had fought at Hamaguri Gomon and Toba-Fushimi, at Ueno and Aizu, distinguishing himself in each of the battles. And yet, while Kaieda and Yoshii and others of their clan had risen to the upper echelons, Kawaji, though he was now in his mid-thirties, for some reason still held only the rank of chief inspector.

'Besides,' said Kazuki, 'from where I'm standing, you both look as though you could go far.'

'You flatter me!'

'Oh, it isn't flattery. In any case, there are a lot of things I don't quite understand about you.'

'For instance?'

'What can I say? I just can't get to the bottom of you, Kawaji. Or rather, each time I think I do, there always seems to be something else hidden beneath it.'

'Now that you mention it, I'm not sure I can, either. I always try to be frank with you, though.'

A vague smile appeared on Kawaji's face. For all the outward calmness and composure of his strong features, they belied profound emotional depths.

'Speaking of hiding things,' said Kawaji, casting a sidelong glance at his colleague's *suikan*, 'I have a hunch that you're hiding something up that sleeve of yours.'

'Me?'

'Well, near enough everything you say to them in that office comes out sounding like an incantation. You're not pulling their legs, are you?'

'I most certainly am not,' replied Kazuki, casually rolling up his sleeves. 'Nobody goes around in this get-up for a joke.'

The few passers-by all stared at him in amazement, before walking on with an air of comprehension. Perhaps the robes seemed to reconfirm for them that old Edo Castle had once again come into the possession of the emperor and his court. There was no doubt about it, though: this was indeed a strange-looking outfit.

'You've been to France—' Kawaji began to say, but Kazuki looked up and cut him off.

'We're already at Hibiya Gomon,' he muttered. 'I'm going home. Which way are you heading?'

Kawaji considered for a few moments and said, 'Actually, I'd like to talk to you a little more. I'll walk with you. May I?'

'Of course.'

Although the two men would visit the headquarters of the Imperial Prosecuting Office whenever the need arose, their main role was to investigate cases and patrol the city. And so, there was no such thing as being 'off duty'.

4

Although the young Keishirō Kazuki had a kind, attractive face, there was something uncanny about him. His subordinates feared him, and even his peers were known to feel uneasy in his presence. And this was not just because of his bizarre attire. Toshiyoshi Kawaji, meanwhile, despite being the man of the moment, did not much care for going out with his bosses, nor did he appear to have any close friends from back home.

The two of them seemed to get on well only with each other. Though Kawaji was some ten years Kazuki's senior, he never took exception when the younger man addressed him on equal terms.

'Just because somebody's been to France, it doesn't mean they're crazy about it,' Kazuki replied a little while later. 'There are so many who've already been to France, England and the United States, and they can be broadly divided into two categories: those who are completely taken in by it and become followers of the barbarian religion, and those who react by becoming more Japanese than the average Japanese. From where I'm standing, the ratio seems to be about fifty-fifty so far.'

'And you rank among the latter?'

'Well, I suppose you could say that.'

'Then why did you procure that French beheading block?'

'Ever since the Restoration, people have been saying that the old Japanese way of beheading is no good and that it should be replaced by the Western method of hanging, so a specimen gallows was brought to the prison from England. Having learnt of this, Lord Kansō heard that the French had an instrument of execution called a *guillotine* and wondered what it could be. I merely saw to it that he found out.'

A faint smile passed his lips.

'The manner in which somebody is put to death often looks more painful than it really is for the person undergoing the ordeal. And what they call "a peaceful death" is, on the contrary, often closer to a living hell. They adopted the *guillotine* in France because they believed it to be the most painless form of execution. My test the other day confirmed this. You were of the same opinion, I trust?'

'So why did you summon the woman from France?'

'How many times have I told you? She wasn't summoned. She followed me of her own accord. I'm at a loss to explain it myself.'

He appeared truly perplexed.

'If it were just everybody gawping, that would be one thing, but in this brave new world of ours, there are people clamouring for her to be put to death.'

'Have you tried sending her back?'

'She won't go. Besides, ever since there was talk of killing her and what not, I've begun to dig my heels in.'

Kawaji still looked unconvinced. But then, Kazuki was a man who hardly radiated good cheer even when he smiled.

'There was a time, though, after you came back, when you flaunted those foreign ways. I heard some people even got so tired of it that an attempt was made on your life.'

'Where did you hear that, I wonder?'

'Now, who was it who told me...?'

'You wouldn't happen to be investigating me as well, now, would you?'

'Perish the thought!'

As he stared at Kawaji, a wry smile played on Kazuki's lips.

'Ha!' he said after a brief pause. 'In any case, I seem to have been freed of the evil spirit that possessed me and mended my ways. Those people I mentioned earlier were never simply divided into two neat groups—pro-foreign and pro-Japanese—and if some wavered between the two, then others also switched sides. I certainly did. Because the grass is always greener. In fact, it's the difference between heaven and earth. That's why I lamented the state of affairs in Japan and grew depressed and angry. But when I think about it now, I realize that, no matter how much we imitate them, imitation is an eternity away from the real thing. Both sides have different histories stretching back millennia. For better or worse, east is east and west is west. Or, to put it another way, I had the painful realization that Japan will forever be Japan. But when I look around these days, I see that there is much unrest in the government, and that they all seem to be falling over themselves to imitate the West blindly. That's why I snapped and decided to assist the Imperial Prosecuting Office. They've taken a shine to me because I wear the same old ceremonial robes and hats as they do. But I'm also half serious about this outfit.'

'Was that all?'

'What do you mean, "was that all"?'

'Your reason for joining the Imperial Prosecuting Office,' said Kawaji, tilting his head. 'Just because you sympathize with their brand of nationalism? I should have thought that someone who'd been abroad would be a valuable asset in Japan these days. Are you satisfied being a chief inspector?'

'Are you?'

'I like catching the bad guys.'

'So do I.'

Kazuki reached out his hand and shook Kawaji's.

'Neither of us chose the job just for the sake of it, Kawaji. I joined the Imperial Prosecuting Office because it's what I wanted to do. That's why you and I get along.'

And it was true. The reason they had first come to accept one another, and since then had grown closer than other colleagues, was the extraordinary passion they shared for the work.

'I don't like using their words, but in France they have a word for it: *rivalité*. That is, rivalry. In the best sense of the term, let's be rivals.'

'That's more like it,' said Kawaji, nodding vigorously.

'You asked me if I was happy being a chief inspector,' Kazuki continued enthusiastically. 'The fact is, I believe that the Imperial Prosecuting Office should become the central organ of government—the supreme organ, even. The government must be a just government. And we must make that happen.'

'Now, hold on a minute, Kazuki. Don't you think that's going a bit too far? Government is a means of protecting the people, and the judiciary should be one of its organs.'

'You're wrong there. Listen, I've no idea how many people died in the rebellions and wars that led to the Restoration, but across the whole of Japan it must have been over ten thousand. What was the point of it all, if we paid so dearly for it, yet the government stays the same?'

'But we won't have the same government.'

'Oh, but we will, Kawaji. The signs are already there. What caused the fall of the shogunate? On the face of it, it was the strain of the upheavals that started with the arrival of the Black Ships bringing foreigners. But really the fall had nothing to do with a desire to kick the foreigners out or close the country again. Put simply, it was because the shogunate was rotten and corrupt at its very core. That was the real root of it.'

As he looked up at the early winter sky with its wispy, rippling clouds, Keishirō Kazuki's eyes lit up with a dreamy light, while he argued passionately.

'Corruption is, after all, the muddying of the distinction between the public and the private, between right and wrong. That's why the public lost faith in the shogunate. Truly, it's a good thing that it fell. And yet, the newly formed government is already showing signs of corruption. You ought to know this better than anyone. Otherwise, what was the point of our revolution? Or will there be another, and then another? Would it not be absurd to go on repeating it for all eternity? The government doesn't exist merely to protect the people. Its aim must be the embodiment of justice. That's why I want to place the Imperial Prosecuting Office at the very heart of government.'

'But that's just it, Kazuki,' said Kawaji, his words heavy. 'Isn't that dangerous?'

'What are you talking about?'

'I had more or less guessed your views on the matter. Your logic may well be right, but governments are not like that. In this world of men, a government cannot embody justice. It makes me nervous to hear you say it, Kazuki. Aspiring to such things can be dangerous.'

'Dangerous?' said Kazuki, raising an eyebrow. 'I'm ready for danger! My dear Kawaji, I used to have a high opinion of you, but if I understand you correctly, you're not so very different from the rest of the chief inspectorate, and what's more—'

But before he could finish, he spotted a large gate up ahead. Once again, he turned to Kawaji.

'Hey, we're already at the Saga mansion…'

5

Earlier, when Kazuki had said that he was heading home, the place he had in mind was the former Edo residence of the Saga Domain. Of course, it is unimaginable that he should be the owner of such an abode. Kazuki was merely a resident in the row of tenement houses that were built in place of walls around the daimyo's mansion.

While most of the mansions that once belonged to the supporters of the shogun had been seized or lay empty, this one was in fine fettle. The four provinces that had largely been responsible for the Restoration—Satsuma, Chōshū, Tosa and Hizen—now enjoyed power and prestige. Among the lords of Hizen on Kyushu, none enjoyed this more than Naomasa

Nabeshima, the former daimyo of Saga. Although the Saga Domain did not distinguish itself especially during the Boshin War, it did, for that very reason, manage to preserve its men, and since these men were capable and intelligent, having been trained from an early age by the clan leader Nabeshima himself, who was in some respects exceedingly enlightened, the new government had little choice but to appoint them.

That was why this mansion was still in good shape. Lord Nabeshima had been appointed governor of Hokkaido but had dispatched his retainer Yoshitake Shima in his stead, while ensconcing himself in his residence in the imperial capital.

'Well, I'm going to take a stroll before I head home,' said Kawaji, bowing his head.

As he was about to turn around, however, he saw two men coming his way from the direction of Saiwaibashi Gomon. Though they were still too far away for him to make out their faces, he heard one of them call out:

'Hullo, brother!'

'Well, if it isn't Keigorō,' Kazuki replied, turning to look at the other men.

'I've brought Etō-san!' Keigorō shouted.

The two groups advanced towards each other. When they met in front of the gate of the Saga mansion, Kazuki introduced his colleague:

'This is my associate, Chief Inspector Toshiyoshi Kawaji.' Then, turning to Kawaji, he explained: 'This is the Saga clan's gifted chief treasurer, Judge Shinpei Etō. And this one here is my younger brother, Keigorō.'

With his bushy eyebrows and high cheekbones, Etō's face suggested that he was a man of strong character.

'Oh-ho,' said Etō. 'And you must be Kawaji, from Satsuma?'

Perplexed, Kawaji fixed Etō with narrowed eyes.

'How do you know who I am?'

'Saigō-sensei once told me that if he ever wanted somebody from Satsuma to lead the police when the day finally comes to reform it properly, Kawaji would be the first in line. I've always remembered that name.'

'What? Saigō-sensei said that?' Kawaji was flabbergasted. 'I'm flattered, but… I very much doubt I'm the man for such an important job.'

'Ha! There's time yet. Besides, we can't have Satsuma and Chōshū taking over everything now, can we?' said Etō, laughing defiantly. He then turned to Kazuki and added: 'Now, Kazuki… It is in fact you that I've come to see.'

'Me?'

'Well, if not you, your wife would have done.'

'My wife?' Kazuki laughed and shook his head. 'She isn't my wife. In any case, how can I help you?'

'I wanted to have this translated.'

Etō extracted a thick book from his pocket. It was evidently foreign.

'It's French, you see. A treatise on criminal law.'

Kazuki took it and read the cover.

'I'm afraid my French is a bit rusty.'

'But you speak French with that woman of yours, don't you?'

'My French isn't to be trusted, I'm afraid. And lately she's begun to understand Japanese, so we muddle through. But a legal treatise? A single mistake and you'll be in trouble.'

'Oh, come, I don't mind a little mistake here and there,' said Etō, raising his eyebrows. 'In Japan today, it's essential that we know even the gist of laws made in the West at the earliest opportunity.'

Kazuki pondered this for a moment, before finally nodding.

'I suppose something may come of it if we work together. I'll give it a go; only, please, Etō-san, would you mind letting the rest of the clan know about this?'

'Whatever for?'

'As you're doubtless aware, there are those among the clan who would gladly draw their swords just because she's a foreign woman. The job could offer her some protection.'

'I see. Well then, so be it.'

Etō cast his eyes towards the gate.

'In any case,' said Kazuki, 'let's go inside. Kawaji, if you'd care to join us?'

And with that invitation, Etō hurried inside.

Discussing something with his brother Keigorō, Kazuki followed Etō's lead, and behind them trailed Kawaji, wearing a look of astonishment.

According to the traditional way of reckoning age, Shinpei Etō was in his thirty-sixth year. He had been born to a minor branch of the family, and, although his name had not been lined up for inclusion in the family shrine, he had already established an outstanding reputation for himself within the clan.

In those days, many young men were in awe of him. Even Kazuki's twenty-one-year-old brother Keigorō was a disciple of his. Five years later, though, there would come a twist of fate and, after having been the ringleader of the failed Saga Rebellion, Etō would be put to death along with Keigorō. Even Toshimichi Ōkubo, who gave the order for their execution, was so impressed by his last moments that he noted in his diary that Keigorō had 'looked like a man among pirates'—but of course, at this point in time, only the celestial deities knew what the future held.

Unaware of this tragic fate, Keigorō walked and talked with his brother fondly, as though they had not seen one another in some time. Like Kazuki, he had a handsome and energetic appearance, as well as the naturalness of youth.

Eventually, Kazuki called out to the briskly walking figure in front of him.

'Etō-san!'

'Yes?'

'Kawaji and I were debating on the way here. The question was: can there be a just government?'

'Oh-ho!'

'To sum it up, it is my contention that the government must be, in the first instance, the seat of justice. Whereas Kawaji here argues that a government cannot make justice its primary concern, and that it's dangerous to be too attached to such ideas. I think Kawaji might even be tempted to call my ideas naïve. That may be so, but I still cannot bring myself to agree with him. What do you think, Etō-san?'

'I think you're right,' Etō replied. 'The government must be the seat of justice.'

The answer was as unequivocal as it was abrupt. And yet, a faint smile crossed Shinpei Etō's lips.

Later, after he became lord justice, he would use this very argument to denounce the Chōshū oligarchy; yet from an ethical standpoint, his justice was but a weapon to defeat his political opponents. The faint smile that had appeared on his lips as he gave his unequivocal answer to Kazuki's question must have seeped out from the cracks in his multi-layered personality. Heedless of this, however, Kazuki looked back at Kawaji, elated.

'My dear Kawaji, would you care to repeat your argument?'

But Kawaji just smiled his usual vague, hazy smile, and carried on walking in silence.

As they passed through the mansion grounds, which were lit by the setting sun, every passer-by would bow when they spotted Etō, and he would cheerfully acknowledge them with a 'hello, hello'.

'Setting all that aside, Kazuki,' began Etō, 'I hear you executed some criminals the other day, using a beheading device you acquired in France.'

'Yes, indeed, sir.'

'And how did that go?'

'It really is a well-made instrument.'

'I haven't had the chance to see it yet. How does it work, exactly?'

Kazuki provided an explanation. To Etō's questions of who had created such a device, and when, and why, Kazuki replied that, even though a precursor had apparently been devised long, long ago, a doctor by the name of Guillotin had, during the French Revolution, and in consultation with a man called Sanson, who himself came from a long line of executioners, improved on the original design in order to dispatch a great many of those criminals condemned to death in a way that was not only quick and reliable but also painless and humane. He then told him how the instrument had been named after this Guillotin, how the criminal would be laid out on the scaffold, and how afterwards the iron axe would drop down from above, severing the criminal's head. But, he added, simply letting the blade fall squarely would ruin it, and so, to reduce the shock, they had devised the idea of making it triangular. The irony was that soon afterwards, the sovereign, Louis XVI, and later his queen, Marie Antoinette, had themselves been put to the guillotine. Moreover, even after the tempest of the Revolution had blown over, the device had become so esteemed that, some eighty years later, it was still being used to carry out executions in France.

'Did you ever see one in action while you were in France?'

'Alas, no,' Kazuki replied. 'I heard that during the Revolution they used to do it in public squares, but these days they carry out the executions in prisons. I tried it out for the first time just the other day.'

Some years earlier, the shogunate had sent an embassy to Europe to negotiate the scrapping of a treaty that had opened up the port of Yokohama to foreign trade. At just twenty years old, Keishirō Kazuki, said to be one of the most skilled swordsmen in the Nabeshima clan, was appointed the chief delegate's guard.

Ultimately, not only did the mission's six-month embassy in Europe fail to achieve its aim, but, having gone out for wool, they came back shorn. When the group returned, they were all enthusiastic supporters of opening up the country—and that is why they were all immediately placed under house arrest.

Fortunately or unfortunately, Kazuki had fallen ill during his time in Paris and had been unable to return with the rest of the mission. Even after his recovery, it had been exceptionally difficult to find a decent ship to Japan. By the time he managed to eventually return, secretly, aboard a French ship, he had been in Paris a total of three years.

'Of course, it was His Lordship who procured the guillotine, but it must have been you who informed him about it. Still, I'm surprised the French government allowed such a thing to be exported.'

'Actually, I had it specially made,' Kazuki replied in a whisper. 'You recall that man called Sanson whom I just mentioned, the one who came from a long line of Parisian executioners? Well, it was the fourth generation of that family who put the king and queen to death during the French Revolution. Apparently, it was the custom, whenever a man was guillotined, to take him by his bloodied hair and hold the head aloft for all and sundry to see. However, the profession was still abhorred by the public, and the Sansons seemingly became repulsed by it, too, and gradually left the work to others, until by the seventh generation the family trade was finally abandoned. Only, I happened to make the acquaintance of a member of the eight generation, to whom I sent for the guillotine.'

'And how exactly did you come to meet this man?'

'I happened to lodge with his family when I was left behind in Paris on my own.'

'I see…'

Shinpei Etō fixed Kazuki with a strange look, but just then there came an unusual cry from up ahead.

#

'Ah!' shouted Kazuki, immediately dashing off without so much as bowing to Etō and the others. It was as if he had been suddenly struck by an idea.

Nabeshima's mansion, as the reader will remember, was surrounded by rows of houses on all four sides. The row at the front was reserved for those with the rank of samurai, while those at the sides catered to the lower ranks. At the rear was another row where former retainers, clan elders and even their servants lived. This was where Kazuki rented his little house.

As it transpired, the ruckus was taking place just outside his house.

A dozen or so samurai had gathered there, all ranting and raving, gripping the hilts of their swords. Two or three of them had even drawn their weapons.

Facing them down were two men standing in front of the doorway, their swords drawn, shouting back at the samurai. Alarmed by this sight, Kawaji had instinctively broken into a run, racing after Kazuki.

'You can't come in here!'

'You'll have to kill us if you want to get past us!'

The men in the doorway were in fact two *rasotsu*: Tamonta Onimaru and Jirōmasa Saruki.

The group of men recognized Kazuki and the others as they approached.

'Oh, Etō-sensei!' one of them gasped, quailing at the sight of him.

Two or three of the men began to cry out:

'Before you say anything, sensei, you should know: there's a golden-haired fox with nine tails nesting in your house!'

'It's a stain upon the Nabeshima house to allow such a thing to live here! The fate of the whole clan is at stake!'

'That's why we've come to drive it out. Surely you wouldn't prevent us, sensei?'

Though Etō had only just set foot in the mansion for the first time in a long while, he understood in an instant how this scene must have come about.

Judging by their slovenly appearance, these men had undoubtedly arrived in the capital from Saga only recently.

And though this was a new age of government, it did not necessarily follow that everybody supported the opening up of the country. The simple and naïve believed that the policy to expel the barbarians would be continued, because the group which previously advocated it now held the reins of power. Many in the Saga clan were relatively open-minded, but there were also those who had been brainwashed by the bushido code espoused in Tsunetomo Yamamoto's influential *Hagakure*, and adhered more stubbornly to the old ways than other clans did. And so, having heard that something strange was living in the mansion, the rabble must have marched there, unable to ignore it.

It looked as though the men had already come to blows. Of the samurai from Saga, some had their kimonos torn, while others had bloodied noses; meanwhile, the *rasotsu* Onimaru's hat had been knocked off, while Saruki's face was purple and swollen.

As Kazuki pressed ahead, Etō stopped him. 'Wait, wait!' he shouted. 'Give me that book.'

He took the volume he had just given Kazuki and marched ahead himself.

'It's not that I don't understand your feelings, but all the same, this won't do.'

'But why not, sir?'

'I have important business with the very person you're trying to oust.'

'What business might that be, sir?'

'This is a book on French law, and I need it translated urgently,' he said, brandishing the volume. 'You may well want to cause a ruckus, but I have orders from the Grand Council of State. This is absolutely vital to the national interest!' Etō's voice boomed as he glared at each of them in turn. 'If you prevent me, then this old man will suffer the consequences. If that's what you want, then be my guest!'

Shaken by this, the samurai turned their backs and walked off, grumbling and foaming at their mouths.

The two *rasotsu* collapsed to their knees.

'That was a close shave,' said Kazuki as he approached.

Hearing his voice, the two men quickly got unsteadily to their feet.

'Are you both all right?' he asked.

'So long as we're on guard, nobody gets past us!' they boasted.

'My sincere thanks,' he said, with tears in his voice.

Kawaji noticed that this young colleague of his, who could be so curiously hard-nosed, also had another side to him: one that was easily moved to tears. He was, moreover, stunned to see those two *rasotsu* there on duty.

Only ten days ago, he and Kazuki had caught five corrupt *rasotsu* and threatened to use the newly imported guillotine on them. They had been so afraid that they couldn't even stand up. Kazuki had been half-joking, of course, and later pardoned them. But to see them now, on guard here, came as quite a shock to Kawaji.

'I decided to have them come here in shifts on their days off,' Kazuki explained. 'It just so happened that two were here today. Those men from Saga are dangerous. My instinct was right.'

Kazuki opened the door and stepped inside. Kawaji, Etō and his brother followed him, but immediately stopped in their tracks, standing there on the earthen floor.

In one of the back rooms, a woman wearing a white short-sleeved *kosode* kimono over a pair of scarlet *hakama* was sitting cross-legged. Seeing them, she shot up and cried out:

'Oh, Keishirō!'

Rushing over and throwing her arms around Kazuki's neck, she hugged him and kissed him on the lips. Then she began prattling away in a foreign tongue, whose words recalled the warbling of birds. One could easily imagine, however, that she was describing the terrifying ordeal.

Of course, Kawaji had met the foreigner at the recent testing of the guillotine, and naturally both Etō and Keigorō had known of her existence since her arrival in Japan the previous summer. But it was the first time the latter two had set eyes on this blue-eyed woman who wore the traditional garb of a *miko*, a Japanese shrine maiden. They could see, moreover, laid out in the room opposite, all manner of strange objects used in Shinto rituals, including a *kaen-daiko* drum decorated with flames, a plain wood offering-stand with rice piled on top of it, a round mirror, a bow, prayer beads and even bamboo leaves.

'It's all right, it's all right,' said Kazuki, turning and addressing the others. 'Gentlemen!'

For the first time, the golden-haired *miko* seemed to notice the presence of other people.

To Kawaji, her wide blue eyes seemed like a pair of mysterious jewels. Though he had seen them before, he could not help feeling mystified that such a beautiful creature could exist upon this earth.

Then, suddenly, she launched into Japanese.

'I… was praying… to the gods. I was praying… to Amaterasu… The gods of Japan… are helping me… I am sure of it…'

'It's all right. We'll discuss a better way to deal with this situation later. In the meantime, you just wait over there for a little while,' said Kazuki, pointing to a room in the back.

As she walked off, the woman's golden hair flowed all the way down her back to her red *hakama*. Suddenly, Kawaji recalled that one of the samurai from Saga had called her a golden-haired fox with nine tails. But even Tamamo-no-Mae, the great courtesan of legend, could not have been as bewitchingly beautiful as this woman.

When the *shōji* closed, Etō, who had until then been standing bolt upright, watching this scene unfold, muttered, still keeping a firm grip on his emotions:

'Was that what they call "a kiss"?'

'In France, it's called *un baiser*. It's a custom of theirs, I'm afraid to say,' said Kazuki, now blushing slightly.

It pleased Kawaji no end to think that this man was not impervious to embarrassment.

'Still, it's mightily impressive that a woman of such otherworldly beauty would go running after you. How on earth did you get to know her?'

'Well, as I was telling you, she's the daughter of the family I lodged with in Paris,' replied Kazuki, pausing and smiling mischievously. 'You see, she's the ninth generation of the Sanson family of Parisian executioners I mentioned. Her name is Esmeralda Sanson…'

7

The group proceeded to the formal tatami room, but they had all been stunned into silence by what Kazuki had just said. Not only Etō, but Keigorō and even Kawaji, who had witnessed at first-hand the guillotine in action, had vaguely assumed that the Frenchwoman had been summoned to read the instructions for the device. This was the first time they had learnt of her background.

Once again it was Kazuki who broke the silence.

The fact of the matter was that he had brought her to live in the Saga mansion because he thought that it would be less dangerous than having her live somewhere else in Tokyo. The result, however, was the scene they had just witnessed. While the old residents seemed to have gradually come to tolerate her, the new arrivals from Saga were trouble. They had been sent packing for now with that excuse about the translation of the French legal treatise, but her future seemed far from secure. 'Does Etō-san happen to know of any place she might be given refuge?'

'I'm not sure that I do,' said Etō, looking doubtful, for he himself knew perfectly well just how pig-headed the people of Saga could be.

'Kazuki, you really are going to a lot of trouble over this,' Kawaji put in. He recalled how, just the other night, Esmeralda had come to the prison disguised in a long veil. Since she could never have gone there wearing French clothes, he had assumed that Kazuki had dressed her as a *miko* as a last resort, but now, much to his surprise, he found that he dressed her as one at home as well.

The disguise was no doubt for the benefit of the men from Saga, and was likely worn for very same reasons that Kazuki wore the *suikan* at the Imperial Prosecuting Office. Still, Kawaji could see the clouds already gathering on the horizon, and he, too, had no idea where they might take the foreign lady.

'Brother,' Keigorō whispered anxiously, with a look of concern, 'couldn't we just send her back?'

Just then, raised voices could be heard outside.

'You can't come in here!'

'No, no, you can't! You must leave!'

It was the two *rasotsu* again.

In response, a hoarse voice reprimanded them.

As Kazuki strained his ears, a look of consternation and bewilderment came over his face, but he immediately called out:

'Oh, this one's all right! Please, let him in!'

The old man who entered was not alone. He must have been around sixty, and he was accompanied by a beautiful young girl wearing a high *shimada* chignon.

'Oh! You've brought O-Nui?'

There was a swelling note of panic in Kazuki's voice, but the old man suddenly cut in, looking somewhat surprised:

'Ah, Etō!'

After the two of them had exchanged pleasantries, Kazuki made the introductions. Kawaji, he explained, was a colleague of his from the Imperial Prosecuting Office, while the old man was Naotsugu Manabe, a former official in the Saga Domain who now occupied high office in the Ministry of War. The young lady was his daughter, O-Nui.

Manabe turned to Kazuki.

'I was on my way to call on His Lordship, when I heard about the disturbance.'

The man with the half-grey *chonmage* looked every bit the sweet old gent, but at the same time, he was clearly displeased.

'If we let it carry on like this, then sooner or later something bad is going to happen,' he said, suddenly casting a glance towards the neighbouring room. 'Is she in there?'

'She is,' Kazuki replied, before calling out in a foreign language. The only word that the others could make out was the name Esmeralda.

'*Oui*,' came the reply from the next room. It was soon followed by a quiet and curious kind of singing. Or rather, it was not so much singing as it was chanting or incantation.

'*Achime... ohhh... ametsuchi ni... kyurakasuwa... sayurakasu... kamiwagamo... kamikosowa... kinenikikō... kyuranaraba...*'

Manabe's face clouded over with fear. 'What's that sound?'

'It's an ancient Japanese *kagura* song.'

'What? You mean to say that's Japanese?'

'I learnt it from an old priestess who served at one of the Shinto shrines, but even she couldn't tell me what it meant,' said Kazuki, laughing for the first time since they had arrived. 'Still, if she's singing, then she won't be able to hear what we're saying.'

'Keishirō,' said Manabe, appearing to come to his senses. 'I've told you I don't know how many times: send the girl back.'

'I myself have told her I don't know how many times. But she just won't listen.'

'Whether she listens or not, so long as the girl is here, we can't do anything about O-Nui. Why, she's twenty-two already! How long do you intend to make her wait?'

'Father, please,' said O-Nui, hurrying to stop him. Her cheeks were blushing a deep red. 'I don't mind. Is that why you came here?'

'Well, no... it isn't. But I'm saying this for Keishirō's sake. After all, I'm like a father to him. Who was it, if not old Manabe, who raised him and his brothers?!'

'Father!'

'No, I'm not looking for gratitude.' Although he may have looked like a sweet old man, Manabe seemed determined to have his say. 'I doted on those brothers and raised them with my own hands. Each of them, and, especially you, Keishirō, has a bright future ahead of him. I'm sure of it. But of all things, to lumber yourself with some Western savage. What in heaven's name has got into you? Who would be fooled by this cheap imitation of a *miko*?' His voice was trembling. 'You've entered the Imperial Prosecuting Office. Whatever your position there is now, you're certain to go on to great things. I truly believe that. But with something like that shackled to you, you'll lose everything. You'll ruin your chances of getting on in life, and I can no longer turn a blind eye and indulge this. Keishirō, you must send the girl back to France tomorrow!'

'I'm afraid I'm going to have to disappoint you,' said Kazuki, casting a sidelong glance at Etō. 'Etō-san has entrusted me with having this book on French law translated as a matter of urgency, and so the girl's presence is vital.'

'What's this?' said old Manabe, glancing at Etō. 'That sort of work shouldn't take long—no more than six months or a year. Very well, then. Do it if you must. But wait, didn't you just say that it was needed urgently? In that case, a month should do the trick. And then, once you've finished the job, send her back immediately!'

Kazuki gulped.

'And besides,' the old man continued, slapping his knee, 'when His Lordship heard about the commotion earlier, he said he was concerned for the girl.'

'He did?'

'I do not think it right to cause His Lordship such concern. And you're wrong if you think I'll permit the source of all this trouble to live under our roof!'

Having received this final blow, Kazuki was unable to utter a single word and was left looking at the old man like a fool. He merely nodded in agreement.

'We'll do as you say,' he said eventually.

'You will? You'll send her home? When? When will you do it?'

'When the work is finished—in around a month's time. Or rather, before the month is out,' he said flatly.

Meanwhile, the girl's singing continued unabated.

'*Achime... ohhh... satsuoraga... motakinomayuki... okuyamani... mikarisurashimo... yuminohazumiyu...*'

Kawaji tilted his head, wondering whether Kazuki could really make such a promise, but just then Kazuki spoke:

'Uncle, I fear your expectations of me are simply too great... Do you really think I have a career ahead of me in the Imperial Prosecuting Office?'

Although Kazuki was not related to Manabe by blood, he always called him 'uncle'.

'So long as you steer clear of that vixen, you do.'

'Of course. By the way, Uncle, have you met young Kawaji here? He's a fellow countryman of Saigō-sensei. He's been touted as one of the future leaders in law and order.'

'What on earth did you say something like that for?!' said Kawaji, flustered.

'Ah, you're from Satsuma?' said Manabe, raising his eyebrows. 'I don't much relish the idea of letting men from other clans feel so comfortable in our house.' He had little goodwill towards men from Satsuma, on account of the habit the higher-ups at the Ministry of War—namely, those who came from Satsuma and Chōshū—had of throwing their weight around.

'So, this man is my competition, as it were,' said Kazuki calmly, paying no mind to the old man's complaints. 'How about I put your mind at rest by showing you just how determined I am to get on at the Imperial Prosecuting Office?'

'Determined? How?' asked the old man, his eyes wide with astonishment. 'You mean to prove it to me?'

'Well, all kinds of cases are brought before the Imperial Prosecuting Office. Then there are those that we find, too. Of the next two or three difficult ones, say, or even the next four or five, I'd like to show you which of us, Kawaji or I, can solve them the quicker.'

As he said this, Kazuki turned to face Kawaji and, using the eye that old Manabe couldn't see, winked at him. He had intended it as a sign for Kawaji to play along, but his friend was so taken aback by this strange and unexpected proposal that he was at a loss for words. He recalled that, on the way there, Kazuki had said something about being rivals, but that had been strictly between the two of them. And besides, the old man seemed to have something against people from Satsuma.

'I'd very much like to see that myself,' said Etō, grinning. He, too, had little affinity with people from Satsuma.

'I don't know about all that, Kazuki,' said Kawaji, getting to his feet. 'But I'm afraid I really must be going now.'

'Oh?' said Kazuki breezily. 'Keigorō, see him out.'

When Kawaji stepped outside, the odd-looking pair of *rasotsu* stood to attention and bowed to him. They seemed to have learnt their lesson the other night. Kawaji had no time to laugh about it now, and with arms folded, he made his way to the gate.

Young Keigorō saw him to the door. Quite unexpectedly, however, they were followed by the girl. She had such a pure and delicate beauty, like a ray of light amid the twilight, that it was hard to believe she was the old man's daughter.

'He may be my brother, but he is a bit of an odd one. He's smart, capable, and most of the time he's kind and acts normal, but he does have his eccentricities, and there are times when even I don't understand him,' said Keigorō, walking four or five steps behind Kawaji. 'I feel sorry for you, too,' he said, turning to the girl. 'Truly I do. But I'm relieved that he at least gave his word to send that girl back to France.'

'Do you think really he'll send her back?' she said.

'What makes you ask that?'

'I'm not quite sure myself.'

'I understand your concern, but I think you know as well as I do that even my brother could never take that woman as his wife. You're betrothed to my brother. Have a little faith. Why he hasn't held the wedding yet, I'll never know.'

'The foreign lady arrived in Japan last summer. Even before that, Keishirō was…'

Like a sigh, her voice trailed off. What she meant was that even then Kazuki had seemed reluctant.

'Surely, you don't mean to say that he—'

'No,' she replied with a resolve that was surprising for one so tiny. 'I believe that Keishirō loves me.'

A STRANGE INCIDENT AT THE TSUKIJI HOTEL

The following relates the particulars of an exceptionally difficult case, in which a body was discovered almost cut in half in the great hall below the bell tower of the Tsukiji Hotel. There was evidence to suggest that the individual who discovered the body had sworn an oath never to kill again; there was also evidence, however, that he was in the tower at the time of the crime.

— From a report made by Chief
Inspector Toshiyoshi Kawaji of
the Imperial Prosecuting Office

1

Shirōzaemon Tsuge was my father. But his name probably means nothing to anybody today. That is only to be expected. Were anyone to say that my father died without contributing anything to the world, that he merely withered away like a weed, I would have to concur. Still, a few additional words are all it would take for people to exclaim, 'Ah, yes, of course!' Those few words are as follows: 'Shirōzaemon Tsuge was the man who beheaded Shōnan Yokoi.'

These are the opening lines of Mori Ōgai's historical tale *Shirōzaemon Tsuge*. Narrated by the son of the eponymous figure, the story describes what kind of a man his father, one of Yokoi's assassins, was, what his background and ideology were, and attempts to speak on his behalf.

'My father was born in the first year of Kaei, 1848. His childhood name was Shikata,' it says. Hence, when the assassination took place in the second year of Meiji, he would have been a young man of only twenty-one.

Ōgai goes on to tell how Tsuge, who was born to the village headsman in Ukita-mura, in Bizen Province's Jōdō County, had been strongly influenced in the days of his youth by the calls to 'expel the barbarians' and had come to believe that it was an act of treason to bow down before the menace of the Black Ships; how, having learnt the art of swordsmanship, he became what was known as a *shishi*—a self-styled 'man of high purpose', whose only aim was to serve the emperor—and found like-minded comrades including Rippu Ueda,

Tokuzō Yanagida, Matanojō Kashima, Rikio Maeoka and Toneo Nakai; and finally, how he had come to plot the assassination of Shōnan Yokoi, who had long been seen as a believer in the Christian faith. He has the following to say about that fateful day:

It happened on the afternoon of the fifth day of the first lunar month in the second year of Meiji, 1869. Shōnan Yokoi was on his way from the Grand Council of State, and his palanquin had just come down the Teramachi to the section south of Goryōsha. Flanking both sides of the palanquin were his followers, Sukenojō Yokoyama and Shikanosuke Shimozu. In addition to two attendants, Yūjirō Ueno and Kinzaburō Matsumura, a sandal-bearer also accompanied the party. Suddenly a pistol shot shattered the leaden air of that rather cloudy day; from between two merchants' houses half a dozen warriors stepped out, drawing their swords in unison.

Ōgai goes on to describe how the group of assassins crossed swords with Yokoi's followers, who were ready for this eventuality and stood their ground, and how Yokoi himself even stepped out of his palanquin, drew his weapon and engaged Tsuge in a sword fight. 'Met by Yokoi's unexpected resistance, Shirōzaemon flared,' Ōgai writes. 'Finally, under the vicious onslaught of Shirōzaemon's blade, the dagger was knocked from Yokoi's hand, and Shirōzaemon quickly seized the opportunity. He shoved Yokoi to the ground, took hold of his topknot and beheaded him.'

Tsuge then ran off with his head.

Meanwhile, Yokoi's disciple Shimozu, undaunted by the gash on his forehead administered by Yanagida earlier on, ended a hard-fought struggle by making a deep gash in one of Yanagida's shoulders, whereupon, unable to bear the pain, Yanagida slumped to the ground. It was just then that Shimozu saw Shirōzaemon take his master's head and flee the scene, so he abandoned Yanagida and set off in pursuit of Shirōzaemon.

Pursued in this fashion, Tsuge then threw away Yokoi's head and at last managed to escape.

Now, the first case in which Chief Inspectors Kazuki and Kawaji would compete was tied up in events that resulted from the sorry fate of Shōnan Yokoi. His assassination, of course, was a tragedy for all those concerned, but it also gave rise to another incident that was an extraordinary and absurd tragicomedy. All this will be revealed in due course, but for now, let us say only that this is where the figures that appear in the following tale have their origins.

2

A little after noon on the twenty-third day of the eleventh lunar month, Kazuki and Kawaji, having just arrived at the Imperial Prosecuting Office, were taking tea in the room that served as their office. Just then, their superior, Deputy Commissioner Kunai Nagasaka, came in, accompanied by Deputy Inspector Tetsuma Sugi, enquiring whether they might see the infamous guillotine for themselves.

The French contraption was stored away in a hut that had

been erected on the execution ground at the Kodenma-chō jail. When Kazuki cheerfully asked whether they would care to see it right away, their answer was an eager yes.

After a brief pause, Kazuki looked his superior in the eye and said, 'Actually, sir, maybe it would be better if you waited a little while.'

Nagasaka was in his mid-forties, with a balding pate and a face as full and round as that of Ebisu, the god of fishing and good fortune. He was good-natured and popular, but he could be rash, which caused much laughter in the office, and he made a lot of mistakes, which could not be laughed off so easily. Though he held the rank of deputy commissioner, his reports were forever filled with the most preposterous errors. Nevertheless, his suaveness always saw him through such mishaps, and he was truly a ray of light in the ordinarily gloomy office.

'No, no,' said Nagasaka, turning to Sugi. 'We'd really like to see it.'

Sugi was a man of thirty, tall and sinewy, and, with a steel-blue tinge to his complexion, made a rather grim impression. Though he was only a deputy inspector, he was said to be exceptionally capable.

Being of the Hosokawa clan, both men hailed from Higo Domain, and that summer they had been transferred from the Imperial Prosecuting Office's branch in Kyoto.

'We'd like to see just how good this guillotine really is,' said Sugi.

Kazuki looked doubtful.

'If it's a demonstration you're after, I don't think we have any criminals whose execution has been authorized.'

'A bundle of straw will suffice,' said Sugi. 'I've taken the liberty of bringing some with us.'

It seemed rather presumptuous of the man to have arranged this without even asking Kazuki's permission, but he broke into a smile and said, 'In that case, let's go. Kawaji, will you join us?'

Kawaji nodded.

The four left the office via the back door and, as they passed through the gardens, Sugi picked up a large bundle of straw, neatly and securely bound.

Then, just outside the Red Gate, they caught sight of two figures, one large and one small, both remonstrating with the guard. Looking their way, one of the figures said in a loud voice:

'Hey, isn't that Nagasaka-san?'

Startled by this, Nagasaka and Sugi stopped in their tracks.

'And there's Sugi,' the other one growled.

With a look of resignation, the two men then approached the group.

'What are you doing here, Kawakami?' asked Nagasaka.

'Petitioning for clemency for Shōnan Yokoi's assassins,' the man replied. He was small, slight, and must have been in his mid-thirties. With his pale complexion and quiet manner, he had the air of a scholar. 'So, this is where you've been hiding? While I've been dealing with these fine people. Couldn't you put in a word for me? I simply must see the director.'

'Surely you don't mean…? What, you? Meet Lord Kujō?' Nagasaka's eyes widened. He spread his hands as if to say that it was a ludicrous idea. 'For one thing, His Lordship doesn't ordinarily come to the office.'

'Well, in that case, I'll see his deputy.'

'That won't be easy. Besides, the Imperial Prosecuting Office can't be expected to take up each and every petition made by an outsider without an introduction. Isn't that so, Kawaji?'

He turned to his colleague, looking for help.

Kawaji and Kazuki stepped forward and were introduced by Nagasaka.

'And this is Gensai Kawakami, a fellow native of Higo,' he said, introducing the young man, before adding with a note of deference: 'He is the one who killed Shōzan Sakuma.'

In saying so, Nagasaka likely intended to convey that this was the reason he could not act as Kawakami's intermediary.

Kawaji and Kazuki both looked at the man in astonishment. Although Kazuki had not been in Japan when Shōzan Sakuma was killed in Kyoto, he still had the impression that this assassination had been different from other such incidents.

Unperturbed, Kawakami stared back at Kazuki in his *suikan*, with a look that seemed to say, what a strange fellow! 'So,' he said, returning his gaze to Nagasaka, 'perhaps you would be so kind as to give me an introduction? No?'

A look of fear came over Nagasaka's face, and now he turned to Sugi, looking for help.

Kazuki and Kawaji saw Sugi exchange an uncomfortable look with Kawakami's companion. The man in question stood about a foot taller than Kawakami: in addition to his naturally imposing stature, he wore a tall pair of magnolia-wood *geta* on his feet. He also sported a tremendous beard and radiated a spirit of fearlessness.

'You must be Tetsuma Sugi,' said the man in a deep voice. 'Was it you who killed my brother?'

'Kill him? I didn't kill your brother,' said Sugi, with a look of defiance. 'But then again... Your brother committed *seppuku*. I merely helped him.'

'Helped him?'

The young man wearing *geta* had a terrible gleam in his eye. 'There are rumours going around Kumamoto that you had a personal grudge against my brother, and that you had him laid across a mound of earth and used him to test the sharpness of your blade. You did once work as a sword-tester in Kumamoto, after all. It stands to reason!'

'Just because I used to do that doesn't make the rumour true. Besides, seeing as your brother, Shikanosuke Shimozu, and I were regarded as worthy opponents when it came to swordsmanship, his supporters were bound to try and blacken my name. And anyway, people will talk. Then again, Ushinosuke, your brother *was* appointed as Yokoi's bodyguard, wasn't he? He didn't do a very good job of it, now, did he? Those assassins managed to make off with Yokoi's head. Don't you think it would be better to let people think that he committed *seppuku* out of a sense of responsibility, lest the Shimozu family be disgraced for generations to come?'

Momentarily lost for words, his opponent gripped the hilt of his sword and exclaimed: 'Just tell me whether you did it or not!'

'I'll leave that to your imagination,' said Sugi, a faint yet fearless smile playing on his lips. 'I take responsibility for everything I do—be it as the Hosokawa clan's sword-tester or as a deputy inspector,' he bragged. 'Come now, are you really going to attack an official of the Imperial Prosecuting Office? Please! You don't hold a candle to your brother. Do you really think you can cut me down? I, who am every bit as renowned a swordsman as your brother?'

Sugi threw down the bundle of straw that he was carrying and clutched his own sword.

'Wait! Wait!' cried out Nagasaka, who had until then been looking on helplessly. 'Shimozu, you've come here to file a petition, not to get into an altercation with an official. Doing that will only scupper your chances. Surely you agree, Kawakami? End this.'

'Quite so,' said Kawakami, smiling quietly as he watched this extraordinary scenario play out. 'Ushinosuke, you didn't come all the way from Kyushu to seek revenge. You're here as my bodyguard. Tomorrow is another day: for now, leave it.'

'Your bodyguard? You need a bodyguard, Kawakami?'

'I've vowed never to cut down another man. Ever since taking Shōzan's life.' He looked at the ground. 'Sugi, what is that you've just thrown down? It's not for testing another blade, is it?'

Sugi shrugged his stiff shoulders.

'It is, as it so happens,' he said. 'We were just about to go and try one out. Only...'

Sugi hesitated, realizing that he was under no obligation to explain himself to this man.

Kawakami, for his part, seemed little inclined to press the matter further. 'We'll take this and be on our way,' he said, approaching Sugi and picking up his bundle of straw.

Oddly enough, Sugi, who remained standing there bolt upright, didn't try to stop him. As he had just had occasion to witness, his opponent was full of fighting spirit—and besides, for all that he may have looked like an unimposing scholar, he exuded an air of exceptional menace.

'Take this and let's go,' said Kawakami, handing the bundle to the young man in *geta*. 'We came to file a petition. Getting into a fight with an official from the Imperial Prosecuting Office would only make matters worse. Ushinosuke, let's take our leave, shall we?'

Nagasaka nearly fainted with relief.

'Kawakami,' said Sugi, 'I should add that, where the assassination of Yokoi is concerned, the powers that be in the Imperial Prosecuting Office have long been sympathetic to his killers, and the fact is that they have not yet given their approval for their execution. As such, I doubt there is any need for your petition.'

'But that's precisely why we've come here,' replied Kawakami, glaring at him. 'You see, Sugi, once the Yokoi affair has been put to bed, Shikanosuke's death can be re-examined.'

With that, urging his bodyguard on, Kawakami turned abruptly and walked off. In the white winter sunlight, they looked like two inauspicious white crows.

3

'Shall we go?' asked Kazuki.

Nagasaka turned with a quizzical look on his face.

'Go where?' he asked.

'To the jail, of course.'

'Let's go!' said Sugi, regaining his composure quicker than Nagasaka.

The group walked off in the opposite direction from Kawakami and his friend.

'Ugh,' said Nagasaka at last, after looking over his shoulder a few times. 'There's no way I can allow somebody as dangerous as that to meet His Lordship.'

Five years previously, on the eleventh day of the seventh month in the first year of Genji, 1864, Shōzan Sakuma, who had dubbed himself the greatest of his generation, and who, owing to this estimation, had been fearless enough to advocate vociferously for opening up the country, was passing through the Sanjō Kiyamachi district of Kyoto on a horse with a Western saddle, when suddenly he was set upon by two assailants. When he tried to escape, lashing the scoundrels with his whip, he came across a third assassin lying in wait. When this man blocked his path, the horse reared and threw Shōzan to the ground. The very next instant, the assassin's blade glinted and was plunged into Shōzan's chest. This was followed by a second blow that severed the man's famously elongated head, before the killer vanished like a gust of wind.

Keishirō Kazuki had been well aware that the assassin was a man from Higo by the name of Gensai Kawakami.

'But if he killed Shōzan, an advocate of opening up the country,' said Kazuki, 'isn't it only natural that Kaieda and his supporters will consider him to have been even more justified than Shōnan's assassins?'

'Indeed. It isn't so much that, though,' said Nagasaka, shaking his head. 'He's a fearsome man, that Kawakami. After all, it's not for nothing that in Kyoto they used to call him "Cutthroat Gensai". It was said that, once, when a group of loyalist samurai were drinking at a restaurant, one of them expressed their indignation over a certain somebody who worked for the Military Commissioner of Kyoto. Moments later, Gensai, who had slipped out without anybody noticing, suddenly reappeared, saying, "Gentlemen! Let's drink some more, with this to whet our appetites!" And with that, he apparently threw down the freshly severed head of the official who had just been mentioned.'

'You'd never know it, just by looking at him.'

'That's what makes him all the more impressive.'

'Quite.'

'You understand why I wouldn't allow his petition to reach the level of His Lordship, don't you? Introducing a man like that would do no good for the people of Higo further down the line.'

Such was the conversation as they made their way to Kodenma-chō.

'The warriors of the Hosokawa clan were always tremendously loyal to the emperor, so by rights they should get on well in today's world, but it seems our man is rather contrary and is displeased with the way the new government is doing things. Last I heard, he was in a place called Tsurusaki, in Bungo Province, a Hosokawa enclave, where he was sent to keep him out of trouble. However, I also heard a rumour that he was up to something, gathering disaffected elements, but I doubt he'd come all the way to Tokyo to stir up trouble.'

'Yokoi must have been quite a big name in Higo. Doesn't it strike you as odd that Kawakami would come all the way from Kyushu to plead for the lives of his killers? He's from Higo as well, after all.'

'He's an old-style fanatic, with a touch of madness about him too.'

Come to think of it, for all that Kawakami seemed so quiet at first glance, when you looked at his face, you could not fail to mark an eerie shadow cast over it, as though he had been possessed.

'By the way,' said Kawaji, speaking for the first time in a long while, 'who exactly was that man accompanying him?'

'Him?' muttered Nagasaka, casting a sidelong glance at Sugi. 'He's an underling from the same province who appears to have become one of Kawakami's followers.'

'Sugi, what was all that about his brother?' asked Kawaji.

'Ah, yes, that…' replied Sugi. 'The man you met is Ushinosuke Shimozu, and, as you just heard, his older brother, Shikanosuke, was a follower of Yokoi-sensei. He was so proud of his strength and skills in swordsmanship that he even volunteered to be one Yokoi-sensei's bodyguards. Only, there wasn't much of a struggle when Yokoi-sensei was killed. It was a truly unforgivable blunder, and so Shikanosuke and the other bodyguards were interrogated by the Imperial Prosecuting Office in Kyoto. While they were in custody, however, Shikanosuke, so ashamed of his earlier boasting, and probably thinking there was no way out, committed *seppuku* when the opportunity presented itself.'

'Didn't he say that you'd used him for sword-testing or something?'

'He did, but what happened was that I found Shikanosuke moments after he'd plunged the blade into his abdomen, and so I performed the duty of a *kaishakunin* and beheaded him. But because I'd been the clan's chief executioner during my days in Kumamoto and had carried on in the role even after I was appointed to the Imperial Prosecuting Office in Kyoto, and because back in Kumamoto, Shikanosuke and I had been considered worthy rivals when it came to swordsmanship, that baseless rumour spread throughout our province. Evidently, Ushinosuke has decided to believe it. Truth to tell, it's a real nuisance.' Sugi then turned to Nagasaka. 'I may be a senior officer, but I can't just go around trying out my sword on just anybody, let alone on someone from my own clan. Isn't that right, Deputy Commissioner?'

'Oh, yes, quite right,' Nagasaka replied with a nod. 'But why did he make off with that bundle of straw? Given his pedigree, it makes me nervous.'

'What have you to fear when you've done him no wrong?' said Sugi with a shrug. 'Besides, you and I are no ordinary men from Kumamoto. We are representatives of the illustrious Imperial Prosecuting Office.'

As they walked along, the *rasotsu* they encountered stood to attention and bowed. At first, Kazuki thought they were bowing to him, but soon he realized that their deference was directed towards Deputy Inspector Sugi.

'Yes, yes,' said Sugi, nodding haughtily to each of them in turn. The deputy inspector seemed to have quite a hold over the *rasotsu*.

At last, they reached the prison at Kodenma-chō, where, upon enquiring, they learnt that there were two prisoners whose executions had been authorized five days ago. There was little scope for sympathy in either case. One was a man who had broken into a merchant's house to 'commandeer funds' for an anti-government movement, killing three people in the process, while the other was a woman who envied her neighbours' good fortune so much that she had killed their little girl by throwing her down a well.

Ordinarily, the chief headsman, Asaemon Yamada VII, who had held the post since the old days of the shogunate, would have beheaded them by now, but he had been laid low with ill health recently, and so the prisoners were still awaiting execution.

'Since the bundle of straw is no longer necessary, you may see the guillotine at work, sir, if it so pleases you,' said Kazuki.

'Oh, my,' said Nagasaka, wincing. 'You mean for us to see the real thing? Thank you.'

'Even better,' said Sugi.

The two heinous criminals were fetched.

This was in fact only the second time that the guillotine had been used. Once again, the triangular blade fell, singing a song of bone and flesh and blood.

'It must be terrifically sharp,' said Nagasaka.

When Kazuki turned around, he saw the deputy commissioner slumped down on the ground and looking deathly pale.

'Yes, indeed,' said Sugi with a look of wonder in his eyes. Presently, however, he cocked his head in puzzlement. 'So, is this how capital punishment is to be meted out from now on?'

'Not necessarily. The gallows has also been proposed, but the decision rests with those in higher places. What is certain, however, is that the old method of beheading by sword is on the way out.'

'I must say, I hope not,' said Sugi. 'In fact, when I heard about this instrument, I was worried, along with my fellow samurai, but the truth of the matter is that it is far crueller and more heartless an instrument of punishment than I was led to believe, and I doubt it would bring peace of mind to any criminal. However wicked a person may be, they are still a human being. Does our beautiful and ancient Japanese tradition not at least send them into the hereafter with a blade that carries the spirit of the headsman?'

Kazuki stared at the man intently without uttering a word.

'Having seen it now with my own eyes, I am ever more convinced that this cannot go unchallenged. Chief Inspector Kazuki, it may be presumptuous of me, but I should like to lay my career on the line and form an anti-guillotine movement with like-minded colleagues. With your permission, that is.' Sugi glared at Kazuki and, turning to Nagasaka, continued: 'Don't you agree, Deputy Commissioner? If so, I should like you to take the lead.'

Still slumped on the ground, Nagasaka opened his mouth to speak, but words failed him as he spluttered and stammered unintelligibly.

After Nagasaka and Sugi left the prison, the two chief inspectors talked things over.

'I hope I'm not speaking out of turn,' said Kawaji, 'but are you aware that Sugi has been doing his best to get rid of old Yamada and install himself as the new government's chief headsman?'

'I am indeed aware,' said Kazuki with a laugh. 'In fact, that's why I brought him here—to see what he would say. Fancy wanting to become an executioner!'

'Well, you mightn't think it, but it's apparently quite well paid. Besides, he used to serve as headsman for the Hosokawa clan. If the shoe fits… Perhaps he thinks that to become the new government's executioner is the surest and quickest way up the career ladder.' Chief Inspector Kawaji's eyes seemed to light up. 'At any rate, he's extremely competent and popular among his colleagues and the *rasotsu*. He'll fine someone on the least pretext, but won't report it, and then, rather than put the money in his own pocket, he'll treat his colleagues and subordinates.'

'He throws his weight around with his superiors as well,' grumbled Kazuki.

'You mean Nagasaka? The man's incompetent.'

'It isn't just that. I get the distinct impression that Sugi might have something on the deputy commissioner.'

'Now that you mention it, I wondered the same myself. Only, Nagasaka's character hasn't damaged his reputation. I've heard it said that the reason he was able to go from caretaker at the Hosokawa mansion to a position in the Imperial Prosecuting

Office in Kyoto was because he'd curried favour with Lord Kujō. If he leads the call to get rid of the guillotine, then I dare say he's not one to be messed with.'

'Mind you, I'm not such a fan of it myself.'

This conversation took place as they watched one of the prison officers and the *rasotsu* Ichinohata clean up the mess left behind by the guillotine. The corpses were placed in coffins and stored temporarily in the mortuary, after which they would go to Kozukappara for burial.

The sight of the guillotine seemed to provoke a thought.

'How's the translation of that French penal code coming along, Kazuki?'

'Oh, that? It's getting there.'

'You promised to send Esmeralda back to France after a month or so, didn't you? Well, it's been two weeks already.'

'Yes, indeed it has,' said Kazuki, with a strange look on his face.

4

'I have to go with Esmeralda to the Tsukiji Foreign Settlement tomorrow,' Kazuki announced all of a sudden, three days later. 'Would you like to come along with us, Kawaji?'

Kawaji blinked in astonishment.

'What on earth are you going there for?'

'It's been more than a year since the girl arrived here in Japan, but she's never yet left the Saga mansion in broad daylight. She's been begging me to let her see Tokyo, if only once. But if I were to let her go parading through the city as she is, she wouldn't be sightseeing so much as making a spectacle of herself. So, I hit upon the idea of the foreign settlement. It isn't the *real* Tokyo, I grant you, but as it's a district for foreigners, I needn't worry so much.'

'I see.'

'I thought she should at least be given an outing before her time here is up.'

'Kazuki…'

'Yes?'

'You do still intend to send her back, don't you?'

'There's nothing else for it.'

Kawaji felt somewhat disappointed.

At around three o'clock the next day, as promised, Kawaji met Kazuki and Esmeralda at the Shinpuku-ji Bridge, one of more than a dozen leading into the Tsukiji Foreign Settlement.

Esmeralda had come by palanquin. She was not wearing the costume of a *miko*, nor did she have on her long veil.

'*Bonjour*,' she began, but immediately corrected herself. 'Hello, Monsieur Kawaji.'

Under a long, billowing light-purple skirt, she curtseyed.

Although her broad bonnet blocked out the winter sunlight, her face, framed by a black-lace ribbon tied beneath her chin, seemed to shine a bright white. Though she was a foreigner, she was so captivating that even Kawaji thought her the very picture of beauty.

If you were to catch so much as a glimpse of her in passing, you would have guessed that she was in some ways quite childlike and mischievous—never would it have occurred to you that she could be the daughter of a long line of Parisian executioners.

The eastern side of the Tsukiji Foreign Settlement faced the mouth of the Sumida River, but the other three sides were bounded by a series of broad canals, and each of the bridges slung across them had a small sentry hut, where, according to the rules, anybody acting suspiciously could be stopped and questioned.

As they entered the foreign settlement, there was, to the right, a narrow canal that enclosed a block of a dozen or so buildings. This was the red-light district.

As they passed it, Kazuki and Esmeralda began to speak in a foreign tongue.

'She's determined to see Shin-Shimabara,' said Kazuki with a chuckle.

They walked along the canal and turned right, coming onto a broad street that was more than a hundred feet wide. On the left was a large gate, just like the one in Yoshiwara, and through this gate lay the so-called Shin-Shimabara pleasure quarter.

The shopfronts were grand and impressive, and the vermilion of the latticework was as vivid as the day it was painted, but the pillars and window bars were all covered in dust. Perhaps because it was midday, there were few potential customers to be seen, but there were scarcely any young boys cleaning up, either. (These were the young servants of the pleasure quarter who had yet to come of age.)

Plans for the settlement had been drawn up in the closing years of the shogunate and carried out by the new government. It had finally opened in the eleventh month of the previous year, and even a pleasure quarter for foreigners had been set up there. As has just been intimated, however, surprisingly few foreigners availed themselves of it. Foreign legations and diplomatic missions were situated more centrally, while trading companies, having already set themselves up in the more convenient Yokohama, declined to relocate. Consequently, the settlement itself was something of a white elephant.

They walked along the deserted red-light district's main thoroughfare: the Nakanochō-dōri. As they went, pale faces would materialize behind the red lattices, and eyes would suddenly appear and follow them—so surprised were they to see a man in Heian-period dress and a foreign lady in a splendid foreign costume pass by.

'It's hard to tell who's gawping at whom,' Kazuki muttered.

'They say that among these women are many daughters of the samurai who supported the shogun,' said Kawaji.

The fact was that the pleasure quarter had started catering to a Japanese clientele, but since it had been originally intended for foreigners, the women who had come here were sure to be the those who had fallen on hard times.

All the while, Esmeralda kept warbling away to Kazuki, to which he would merely respond a brief yes or no in Japanese. Kawaji thought that he seemed to be preoccupied by something.

Exiting the pleasure quarter, they found themselves in an ordinary-seeming neighbourhood. Only, it wasn't quite ordinary. The narrow streets were laid out neatly in a regular grid pattern, and here and there Western-style brick buildings were visible, while the wooden shops had been painted to give them a Western look.

Among the shops were bakeries, cobblers, purveyors of foreign goods, even a glassblower's workshop, and places selling Japanese trinkets including folding fans, picture books and dolls. As it was all geared towards foreigners, the place had a vaguely exotic feel to it. Peeping over the rooftops, a group of warehouses could be seen lining the waterfront.

Here, there were far more sightseers wandering about than there would be in the environs of a Japanese-style pleasure quarter. And, just as one would expect in a foreign concession, there were a few non-Japanese thrown into the mix.

The passers-by would turn to gawk at Kazuki's *suikan*, after which their eyes would move naturally to Esmeralda—and only then would they widen in surprise.

At the far end of the neighbourhood, a magnificent building came into view. Its outer walls were topped with black tiles, while the walls were ornamented with white plaster in a diamond pattern. It had only two floors, but it was twice as high as any ordinary building, and rising up from it was a tower that, with its two-tier copper-plated roof, looked just like a festival float for some religious procession. The Tsukiji Hotel had been completed only a year previously.

Let us borrow a description of the building from Samuel Mossman's *New Japan*, which was published around that time:

It was built on a picturesque site by the margin of the bay, surrounded by grounds very tastefully laid out with paths among flower beds, shrubberies and grassy knolls. The... campanile tower sixty feet high, which commanded from its enclosed top an extensive prospect of the capital—now called Tokyo, but which will always be named Edo by foreigners—the magnificent Bay of Edo, and the native-adored mountain of Fuji-yama rising grandly in the distance... Here a foreigner could obtain excellent meals and lodging at the reasonable charge of three dollars, or nine *itsibus*, equal to thirteen shillings and sixpence per diem.

Perhaps owing to sightseers, the square in front of the main entrance was strangely crowded, so they went around the side and, after Kawaji had shown his card at the gate there, entered through the garden.

There was a total of one hundred and two rooms, sixty-three on the ground floor, and thirty-nine upstairs. Each room came with a fireplace and a veranda, and they were all of them quite splendid.

The three daytrippers were shown around by a porter in a navy-blue uniform. Both Kazuki and Kawaji had seen the building from the outside before, but this was the first time that they had set foot inside it. All the while, Esmeralda kept warbling away, apparently critiquing various aspects of it.

Hardly anybody was staying there, however. There were conspicuously few foreigners, and all the Japanese guests seemed to have come from the provinces. It made the hotel look rather deserted and gave Kawaji the impression of some kind of Western temple—even though he had never seen one.

This impression was deepened further by the vast hall in the middle of the hotel. Right in the centre of it stood an enormous wooden pillar, more than three feet in diameter, which rose up all the way to the vaulted ceiling. Around the pillar a spiral staircase wound its way up to the tower.

Esmeralda marvelled at it.

When she enquired who had built this hotel, she appeared very impressed to hear that it was a Japanese man by the name of Kisuke Shimizu. The hotel, she learnt, was made entirely of wood, and no iron had been used to support the structure. The idea of wrapping a spiral staircase around this thick central pillar as a means of climbing directly up to the high tower was certainly an ingenious one.

Led by the porter, the three ventured up.

The stairs were steep and rather narrow—only three feet wide, so two people could not walk abreast. On both sides were thin, elegant handrails made of smooth teak.

Round and round they went, all the way up to the top. Mossman set the height of the tower at sixty feet, but in truth it was much higher than that: almost one hundred feet to the very top of the roof.

5

As he reached the top, Kazuki cried out in surprise. Ahead of him were several others. In addition to Deputy Commissioner Nagasaka and Deputy Inspector Sugi, there was a group of half a dozen women and children, and even Jirōmasa Saruki.

The others seemed equally surprised to see Kazuki.

'Enjoying a spot of sightseeing?' he asked.

'Yes,' replied Sugi. 'Just got off duty. I found Saruki here at the guardhouse on the Karuko Bridge and asked him to show me around.'

Still looking bewildered, Saruki bowed. It seemed that Sugi's authority extended to this *rasotsu* as well.

'My children have been begging me, you see,' said Nagasaka amiably. 'May I present my family.'

His family consisted of an elegant middle-aged woman, a beautiful daughter of eighteen or nineteen, and what appeared to be her younger siblings, among whom was a sweet-looking young boy of around five.

'And w-w-who is…'

Their eyes were fixed on Esmeralda. Nagasaka and Sugi also seemed to have heard about the French girl with whom Kazuki had become involved, but their curiosity soon turned to admiration.

After the introductions and pleasantries, Kazuki and his group went immediately over to the east-facing window.

On all four sides of the tower, there were large glass windows making the shape of a great temple bell, and from the weathervane that crowned the copper roof, chains stretched out to the four corners of the eaves, each hoisting several bronze wind chimes, just like on the ancient five-storey pagodas.

As they looked out of the window, they could see the wide estuary and on it a multitude of ships, some stationary, others plying the waters. Most of them were simple barges, but they could also see four or five paddle steamers and Western sailing ships. Further afield lay the island of Tsukuda and the vast blue sea.

Kazuki and the others began to move around the windows one by one. Never had they seen a panorama of Tokyo from so high up. They had such an all-encompassing vantage over the foreign settlement, surrounded as it was by water on all sides, that it was as if they could reach out and pick it up in the palms of their hands. Although it had been renamed Tokyo, it was still, to be sure, the old capital of Edo, but the new foreign settlement looked like a lone painting in black ink amid a copperplate engraving. To the west, the immense winter sky stretched as far as snow-capped Mount Fuji. When she saw it, Esmeralda cried out for joy.

It was, by all accounts, a bell tower, and indeed a great Western-style bell did hang from the ceiling, but it had never yet been rung, and the tower was in fact used as a viewing platform.

'We should be going,' said Nagasaka's wife, ushering the children off.

The family presented a charming and happy sight, but Sugi, with his rather glum expression—probably because he had accompanied them only by reason of his being a fellow native of Higo—seemed out of place.

Suddenly stepping away from Sugi, the girl who appeared to be the eldest daughter, went over to the west window and looked down.

'What's going on down there, I wonder?'

She was a beautiful girl, but she was nothing like her plump, jolly father. Her long, oval face even had a somewhat frigid look about it. Evidently, she was her mother's daughter.

'What is it, Miss O-Kumi?' asked Sugi, sidling up to her again, while everybody gathered around.

In the square in front of the hotel, a group of people had formed a circle. A strange object had been placed in the middle of it, and beside it stood two men who looked like *rōnin*. One of them had drawn his sword, which seemed to have attracted quite a crowd. These must have been the people whom Kazuki and the two others had noticed as they entered the hotel, but they were no ordinary sightseers.

The strange object in the middle was a bundle of straw that had been placed on a dais.

'Isn't that Gensai Kawakami?'

'And that's Ushinosuke Shimozu.'

Nagasaka and Sugi groaned.

And sure enough, the one wearing a headband and a sash and brandishing his sword was indeed the renowned assassin, while the other one, standing a little further away, his arms folded and *geta* on his feet, was the other Higo youth.

'What on earth are they doing?' asked Sugi.

'For two or three days now, every day at this hour, they've been gathering a crowd and showing them what they call "a Japanese sword-trial",' the porter informed the group. 'We're having trouble stopping it because they're guests of the hotel.'

'What?!' exclaimed Nagasaka. 'You mean to say he's staying here? That civilization-hating Kawakami? In the Tsukiji Hotel?'

'It looks as though he's saying something,' said Sugi, rushing to open the window.

As he pulled the glass towards him, the wind, which had been inaudible until now, rushed in, carrying with it snatches of what they were saying.

'Yes, you red-headed barbarians! Listen to me if you have ears! Or, if you don't understand the language of this sacred land, then watch closely with those bead-like eyes of yours and witness the sharpness of the Japanese sword!'

Shimozu was the one doing all this shouting.

'This bundle of straw is harder than a man's torso! If you dare to look down on Japan, your bodies will taste the sharpness of this blade!'

Kawakami's sword flashed like lightning as he swung it down, slicing the large bundle in two with a single stroke.

Piled up nearby were another four or five bundles of straw. They looked very similar to the one snatched from Sugi.

'What idiotic behaviour! He must have stayed here deliberately to do a stunt like this,' said Nagasaka, tutting. 'Frankly, I'm surprised we didn't come across him on the way in.'

'What does it matter even if we do run into him?' said Sugi, feigning a lack of concern.

Yet Nagasaka suddenly grew nervous.

'Still, it would be better not to involve ourselves with them,' he said. 'Let's get out of here quickly. Sergeant, is there any way to leave without their seeing us?'

Then, having barely taken their leave of Kazuki and the others, Nagasaka bundled his family off, down the spiral staircase.

6

'Oh, they've forgotten something!' the porter cried out, shortly after Nagasaka and his party had disappeared from the tower.

On the window ledge lay a smoking pipe.

'It must belong to Nagasaka,' said Kawaji, picking it up. 'He's always forgetting things. Here, you'd better take this and run after him.'

After the porter had gone tearing down the staircase, Kazuki turned to Kawaji.

'Nagasaka is certainly devoted to his family, don't you think? That's rare for an official these days.'

'He's very fortunate. It's just a pity they let him work in the Imperial Prosecuting Office.'

'By the way,' said Kazuki, 'that Saruki... I doubt he was there simply as their guide. Sugi's caught him by the tail, it would seem. I suppose it's only to be expected, given he's got Nagasaka by the tail as well. It was only a hunch the other day, but now I'm more and more convinced of it.'

'Did you notice something?'

'Well, you saw Nagasaka's daughter? Sugi seems to be awfully interested in her, although she was giving him a wide berth. Nagasaka can't be unaware of this. And yet, still he won't tell his subordinate to back off. I'm beginning to think Sugi must have something on him. Or am I being overly suspicious?'

'I suppose it takes a ladykiller like yourself to pick up on such subtleties between men and women.'

This strange compliment made Kazuki laugh.

'Well, you're not wrong that Sugi has one over on Nagasaka,' said Kawaji, nodding. 'I know somebody else who used to be in the Kyoto branch of the Imperial Prosecuting Office around the time of the Yokoi case, and I found out a thing or two from him.'

'Oh?'

'Apparently, Nagasaka bungled the investigation—twice over.'

'Bungled it how?'

'It's a long story, but hear me out. On the fifth day of the first month, Yokoi-sensei was attacked by six men, but one of them, Tokuzō Yanagida, was struck down by Yokoi-sensei's attendant, Shikanosuke Shimozu, and, though severely wounded, he was taken into custody. Yanagida died before he could be interrogated, although his name was enough to establish who his accomplices were...

'Of the accomplices, Shirōzaemon Tsuge, who had been hiding out in Kyoto, was caught on the fourteenth, and, two days later, despite having made it all the way to Mount Kōya, so were Rippu Ueda and Matanojō Kashima. Yet in the confusion, the remaining two, Rikio Maeoka and Toneo Nakai, had managed to slip past the cordon that was set up at the city limits, and their whereabouts are still unknown...

'Nagasaka's first mistake was to do with Nakai's escape. As head of the Imperial Prosecuting Office in Kyoto, he was in charge of the checkpoint at Awataguchi, and reports came in, saying that Nakai was heading in that direction. They didn't know what he looked like, but they were told that he was a ferocious and cunning man with a large beard, and that he would be carrying a three-foot sword in a red-lacquered sheath. So, all the men who approached Awataguchi carrying long swords were stopped and questioned, but it was later discovered that Nakai had sailed straight through, having shaved his beard and carrying only a short sword in his belt...

'It was an appalling blunder to make. It wasn't the only checkpoint he slipped past, so Nagasaka alone wasn't to blame. But then he went on to make a second mistake...

'On the fourteenth, as I've just said, one of the assassins, Shirōzaemon Tsuge, was arrested. Since the name Shirōzaemon is so pompous and old-fashioned, more often than not he was called by his childhood name—Shikata—and so at first, that was the name under which the authorities tried to find him. But then there was Shikanosuke Shimozu, Yokoi-sensei's attendant from Higo—which is to say, Ushinosuke's elder brother. Such a formidable man, he managed not only to kill Yanagida, but also to pursue Tsuge part of the way after he'd run off with Yokoi-sensei's head. In the end, though, he'd failed to protect Yokoi-sensei, and he was detained by the Imperial Prosecuting Office...

'This is where it gets interesting. Yokoi's attacker was Shikata, and his bodyguard was Shikanosuke. What are the chances of the men on either side having such similar names? You couldn't make it up...

'Anyway, the execution of the culprits—who are still in custody—was delayed by objections from Kaieda's office, but immediately after the incident, the Kyoto authorities had, of course, been in a state of such excitement that orders were given to behead them all immediately, including Shikata Tsuge. In fact, it was none other than Nagasaka who signed the execution orders. Only, he'd inadvertently written down the culprit's name as Shikanosuke…'

'What?' It was only at this point that, for the first time, Kazuki could not contain his astonishment.

'Actually, I don't know the ins and outs of it. The man who told me wouldn't go into details. The other half is my imagination. I'm sure I'm right though. Shikata and Shikanosuke. Of course, nobody would mix them up saying the names aloud, but it's easily done when you write them down. Only that careless Nagasaka could have done it. But still, Shikanosuke was also from Higo, so that name must have been familiar to him. Maybe he wrote the name down in a moment of madness.'

'Hmm…'

'It was Sugi who received the order and executed Shikanosuke Shimozu accordingly. He apparently thought that Shikanosuke was being put to death for having failed to protect Yokoi-sensei. After all, when Naosuke Ii was killed, his bodyguards were all held responsible for his death and duly executed. So, there was a precedent. Still, this was different. There are reasons to believe that Sugi was aware of Nagasaka's mistake and, without questioning it, deliberately killed the wrong man. What's more, that business about the sword-testing seems to be true. It was revenge for some disagreement they'd had back in Kumamoto.'

Kazuki was silent.

Kawaji continued, 'I doubt that Nagasaka would have deliberately written the wrong name with some ulterior motive. It was a careless mistake, but not one without consequences. When he found out about it later, he was horrified, and that's when Sugi tore into him. As he said, people began to talk, and, back in Kumamoto, there were rumours that, because of a grudge, he'd used Shikanosuke to try out a new sword. Sugi took the brunt of the notoriety, and that's why Nagasaka is in his debt...

'If all this is true, it's astonishing that they've been able to keep it under wraps. But then, it's so absurd that it would have been difficult to make public without calling the new government's competence into question. The man who told me also warned me not to make it public. On the other hand, Nagasaka's winning character must have played a part in this as well. After all, he's a favourite of Lord Kujō's. As for Sugi, he doesn't want to have anything to do with his native Higo, which has become a backwater since the Restoration, so he seems to have calculated that the only way he'll advance his career is by sinking his teeth into Nagasaka. Well, what do you say to all that?'

'I'm in shock,' said Kazuki, staring intently at Kawaji. 'Shocked at the findings of your investigation, but more shocked by the fact of the investigation itself. Your colleagues had better watch out!'

What was perhaps most surprising of all, however, was the calmness with which Kawaji had just relayed all this.

Esmeralda, thankfully, had been enthralled by the scene outside throughout this conversation, but at this point she finally turned around and said something.

'Is the show already over?' asked Kawaji, to which Kazuki nodded and smiled vaguely.

'Yes, but apparently something's about to happen.'

Far-sighted though Chief Inspector Kawaji was, what happened next well exceeded any premonition he might have had.

7

On the night of the twenty-eighth of the eleventh lunar month, an incident occurred in which an Englishman by the name of Long was attacked.

The man was an overseas teacher at a government school—it later came to light that he had been a barber in his native country—and he had taken a Japanese woman as his mistress. On the evening in question, while accompanying her on a walk in Kanda-Sudachō, where the night stalls were open, he was suddenly set upon by an imposing figure brandishing a sword and sustained a serious wound to his shoulder. When a crowd gathered, attracted by the mistress's screams, the assailant fled. Though Long narrowly escaped with his life, the British envoy, Sir Harry Parkes, lodged a formal protest with the Japanese government.

The assailant was said to have sported a beard and looked like a samurai, and what's more, he apparently wielded an exceptionally large sword. Although his name and whereabouts were unknown, within a matter of days, Kawaji learnt that there was a suspicion in the Imperial Prosecuting Office that the man was none other than the fugitive from justice Toneo Nakai.

On the third of the following month, Kawaji heard about another curious incident from Kazuki.

A report had come in from Jirōmasa Saruki, the *rasotsu* attached to the Tsukiji Foreign Settlement, that, on the morning of the second, a bundle of straw used for sword-testing had been found lying at the bottom of the stairs in the great hall of the hotel, cut in two.

'What could it mean?'

'I've no idea. Apparently, the porter found it.'

Truly, it was a mystery.

'Incidentally,' said Kawaji after a pause, 'did you know that there's a rumour going around that the assailant in the Long case might have been Toneo Nakai?'

'I'd heard that, yes.'

'What are they basing it on?'

'The fact alone that the assailant used a long sword?'

'I don't really know. From what I gather, Nagasaka and Sugi seem to think so and are operating on that basis. Perhaps they know something we don't.'

'Hmm…'

'It wouldn't surprise me to learn that Nakai's ideas had led him to attack a foreigner.'

'Couldn't you say the same for Gensai Kawakami and Ushinosuke Shimozu, though? Apparently the man was well built and had a beard. That sounds rather like Ushinosuke.'

'That one's capable of anything, but they have *alibis*. On the twenty-eighth, they were both at the Tsukiji Hotel from morning till night.'

Kazuki had taught Kawaji the word 'alibi', and hearing it now made him laugh.

'You've done your research.'

'Indeed I have,' said Kawaji, looking slightly embarrassed.

'Nagasaka may not be the most reliable officer when it comes to a manhunt,' said Kazuki, 'but if Nakai really is the culprit, then Nagasaka will have some answering to do. It's only natural that he's eager to catch him by any means necessary. Only, it seems that Sugi is even more determined to score a victory with this. Incidentally, their alibis for the night in question aside, Kawakami and Shimozu are both claiming they had nothing to do with the bundle of straw. I expect you already knew this. Still, there's something that doesn't quite add up about their stay at the Tsukiji Hotel…'

The incident that well exceeded any premonition that Kawaji might have had, however, was not the attack on the foreigner. Instead, it was the tragedy that was discovered in the afore-mentioned hall beneath the bell tower of the Tsukiji Hotel on the morning of the seventh, some four days later.

That morning, at around half-past eight, in the small house that he rented in Kyōbashi, Kawaji received an urgent message from Sergeant Imokawa.

'Sir, please come to the Tsukiji Hotel immediately. Chief Inspector Kazuki has requested your presence.'

'The Tsukiji Hotel? Kazuki? What's happened?'

'There's been a murder, sir.'

'A murder? Who's the victim?'

'I received the order from Sergeant Saruki, so I'm afraid I don't know, sir. But he said to come as quickly as possible.'

Kawaji and Imokawa raced to Tsukiji as fast as their legs would carry them. It was so cold that they could see their breath.

Following Sergeant Imokawa, Kawaji entered, as he had done before, by the side gate, then passing through the garden to arrive at the bottom of the tower. A door opened onto the vast hall, where he found a group of people standing like frozen silhouettes at the foot of the great column.

The late winter's morning had already long dawned, but the hall was still in darkness. A dozen or so men stood there in a semicircle, mostly with their backs to him, and the first faces he managed to make out were those of Gensai Kawakami and Ushinosuke Shimozu. The others were mostly *rasotsu*, but one figure then turned to look over his shoulder: it was Kazuki.

'Thank you for coming,' he said.

Kawaji drew nearer until he stood next to Kazuki. Among the figures, he noticed Nagasaka and his daughter—O-Kumi, he thought, wasn't that her name?—and a porter too. Then, right in the middle of them, he saw a body stretched out on the floor. There, lying in a pool of blood, his abdomen clearly cut open and his innards spilling out, was Tetsuma Sugi.

8

'I came as fast as I could when Saruki told me the news, and this is the scene I was faced with,' said Kazuki. 'I've heard various views from the people involved, but my head's in a spin. I'd like to hear your opinion, Kawaji. If you wouldn't mind, Deputy Commissioner? From the top.'

Deputy Commissioner Nagasaka was quivering like a jellyfish. Though, in effect, he was being questioned by his subordinates, he did not object, and, with trembling lips, he began his tale.

'Well, you know about the case of the attack on Mr Long? It was Deputy Inspector Sugi who suggested that the assailant might have been Toneo Nakai, the fugitive involved in the assassination of Yokoi-sensei. There are certain circumstances regarding this individual's escape for which I bear responsibility. That being so, Sugi and I wanted to apprehend him ourselves at any cost and were desperate to learn his whereabouts. Anyway, the day before yesterday, Sugi reported that Nakai's mistress was apparently somewhere in the Shin-Shimabara pleasure quarter of the foreign settlement, and that the wounded Nakai was hiding there.'

This startling fact, which he was hearing for the very first time, made Kawaji's eyes widen in astonishment.

'Sugi didn't tell me to which establishment the girl belonged. He had great faith in his own abilities, so he only made me aware of the fact itself. Then, yesterday morning, we learnt that two of Nakai's associates were also hiding out in the establishment, posing as customers, so, if we were to arrest them, we would have to prepare for a considerable number of casualties. He expressed his reservations about causing a bloodbath in the foreign settlement of all places.

'Then, yesterday evening, Sugi somehow managed to arrange things with the woman, and the next morning again— that is to say, this morning—Nakai left the pleasure quarter alone and went on his way. Sugi had said that he intended to apprehend him at the guardhouse, and that Nakai would of course be unaware of our movements.

'However, although it was easy enough to get Nakai to leave the establishment, nobody knew which direction he would go or which bridge he would attempt to cross. As everybody knows, there are more than a dozen bridges leading out of the settlement. There are even ones without guardhouses. Naturally, Sugi said he would take the precaution of having *rasotsu* stationed at every one of them, but, so that Nakai wouldn't notice him following, he wanted to go on ahead and wait for him at whichever bridge he was headed for.

'So, Sugi suggested that I go to the Tsukiji Hotel this morning under cover of darkness and keep watch from the top of the tower.

'As Kazuki and Kawaji saw only the other day, there are large windows on all four sides there, giving a panoramic view of the foreign settlement. By the same stroke, the tower, with me going around and around inside it, can be seen from anywhere in the settlement—including the guardhouses. From my vantage point, I could communicate Nakai's whereabouts and the direction he was headed, using gestures. The idea was that Sugi would follow my instructions, while the *rasotsu* would be on alert at their posts.

'What's more, Sugi didn't just ask me to keep watch, but he wanted my daughter O-Kumi to accompany me as well. When I asked why, he replied to the effect that I couldn't be trusted. I am known to be a little careless at times, so I could see his logic. He added that it would made me look good. "You'll be commander-in-chief of the operation to capture Nakai," he told me. To tell the truth, I agreed with him, and I was grateful to him for this bizarre-seeming method of surveillance and direction.

'So, this morning I did just as he said. I came here while it was still dark and had the porter show me to the top of the tower.'

The porter nodded. Given Nagasaka's rank, he would not have been able to refuse him.

'O-Kumi and I went around and around, keeping watch. Night turned to day. But no matter how we looked, there was no sign of Sugi or the man with the long sword in its red-lacquered sheath. At that early hour, it wouldn't have been hard to spot anybody in the streets of the foreign settlement, but, even with our eyes peeled, we couldn't see a thing. Isn't that right, O-Kumi?'

His daughter nodded, her complexion like pear blossom.

'Meanwhile, six-thirty went by, then seven o'clock. I know this because I heard the clock tower of the American Trading Post opposite the Akashi Bridge strike the hour with its loud bell. I believe it tolls at seven o'clock in the morning, at noon and then again at seven o'clock in the evening. Just as the chimes were fading away, I heard a strange sound come from the bottom of the stairs. I don't quite know how to describe it.

'We both looked at one another, and so, bracing myself, I left my daughter to keep watch, while I made my way down the spiral staircase. And that's when I found Deputy Inspector Sugi lying like this, with Gensai Kawakami and Ushinosuke Shimozu standing by his side.'

Kawaji crouched down and looked at Sugi's corpse.

His abdomen had practically been cut in half. It seemed to have been slashed in a single clean blow from one side to the other. It must have taken some skill. Horrifying was the only word for it. Death would have come instantly, but still, the corpse's eyes seemed to glitter with rage.

Kawaji then noticed the fresh blood splattered around, not just on the floor, but up the first half a dozen or so steps of the spiral staircase. He also spotted, next to Kawakami and Shimozu, a sword some three feet long, drenched in blood, and, beside it, a pair of magnolia-wood *geta*.

Kawaji shot a look at Ushinosuke's feet. He was not wearing his usual *geta*, but instead had on a pair of sandals like those provided by the hotel.

'It looks like somebody has been testing their blade,' said Kawakami, as he looked at the body and forced a smile. 'If he did use Shikanosuke to test his sword, as they say he did, that's exactly how he would have done it. But I regret to say that it was neither Ushinosuke nor I who did this—the reason being that we do not yet have conclusive evidence regarding Shikanosuke's case.

'A short while ago, we heard a knocking at our door. When the door opened, we saw the porter and this *rasotsu* standing there.'

He nodded towards Sergeant Saruki.

'He said there was something to do with Shikanosuke's case that needed to be discussed, and that Deputy Inspector Sugi was waiting in the garden behind the hotel, so would we come with him immediately? By all means! we thought. We checked with the porter, who told us that it was the garden between the bell tower and the water. Without having to ask, we knew that you could get there through this hall.

'After the *rasotsu* and the porter left, we dressed and headed out. It must have been… Ah, yes, just before we entered the hall, the big clock in the hallway chimed. Thinking about it, it must have been seven o'clock. That was when I heard this strange noise. So, I rushed to open the hall door, and when I entered, I found the poor bastard lying here like this.

'I looked around but saw nobody. When I opened the door on the other side, the long corridor was deserted. Ushinosuke went to the door leading into the rear garden, but again, there was no one there, except that *rasotsu* who was standing on the opposite side.'

Kawaji looked in the direction where Kawakami was nodding and saw Sergeant Yokomakura.

'The deputy inspector told me to wait there,' explained Yokomakura.

'Did you arrive with Deputy Inspector Sugi?' asked Kawaji.

'I did, sir. Then the deputy inspector entered the premises via the back door by himself.'

'At any rate,' said Kawakami, 'we returned to Sugi's body, and were wondering what on earth had happened, when who should come down the stairs but Nagasaka.'

'Sergeant Yokomakura,' said Kawaji. 'At what time did Deputy Inspector Sugi arrive here?'

'The American clock opposite the Akashi Bridge began tolling just after the deputy inspector went inside... Then, not long afterwards, the samurai with the beard opened the door and peered out. He had a terrible look on his face. Next, I saw Saruki come round the outside from the main entrance, and, after a brief discussion with him, he went to investigate. Shocked and horrified by what he saw, he told me to go and send for Chief Inspector Kazuki.'

After Kazuki had arrived, he must have had Sergeant Imokawa run and fetch Kawaji.

'But just what was Sugi doing here?' Kawaji asked the *rasotsu*.

'I believe he said something about having urgent business with one of the guests, sir,' said Saruki, after which he and Yokomakura said in chorus:

'That's all we know, sir!'

Kawaji's eyes now looked elsewhere. 'What are those doing there?'

He walked over to the pair of *geta* lying in the pool of blood and picked them up. They were large and made of magnolia wood, and had thick straps.

'They look just like the ones I've been wearing,' grumbled Ushinosuke. 'Mine are in my room. I don't know whose these are.'

Although the building mixed both Japanese and Western styles, nobody was likely to go around in *geta* indoors. Then again, nobody but this man seemed to wear *geta* like this.

133

'On the face of it, it looks like we did it,' said Kawakami after a pause. The trace of a bitter smile still played on his lips. 'But I didn't kill him. As I said the other day, I've taken a vow never to kill again.' This excuse was unlikely to pass muster, at least not with this individual. 'Now you'll be wondering whether it was Ushinosuke who did it. But, no. Show them your sword, Ushi.'

At his request, Ushinosuke slowly unsheathed the sword at his waist and showed it to them.

They all stared in amazement. Though the red-lacquered scabbard was three feet long, the sword that emerged from it was useless, the blade having been broken in half.

'Because of my actions, there's many a man who would want to try to kill me. But I've vowed never to kill again—that's why I take strapping Ushinosuke with me everywhere as my bodyguard, even making him wear *geta* so that he'll seem all the more imposing, but it's all for show.'

'Nobody has suggested that you used that sword to kill him. It's the one lying there that did it,' said Kazuki, pointing to the long sword covered in blood on the floor. It was clear that this was the murder weapon.

'It would appear that we've been caught in a trap,' Kawakami said in an imperious tone. The faint smile on his lips was fast disappearing. 'And just what was Nagasaka-san doing up in that tower anyway? Doesn't that strike you as most suspicious?'

'I've already told you my reasons for being there,' Nagasaka cut in. 'In any case, you claim that you've fallen into a trap and that somebody else is to blame. But where else would we find somebody who could cut Sugi—a man who was famed throughout Higo as a master swordsman—so magnificently in half. I could never do it. I'm no swordsman. And besides, just the other day a bundle of straw was found in this very

134

room. Cut in two, they say. I've no idea what it means, but I'm certain that was your handiwork as well.'

'This is outrageous! We had nothing to do with that!'

'Well, leaving that aside, you must have seen me come down from the very top of the tower when you discovered the body,' said Nagasaka. 'According to everybody's testimony, Sugi must have been killed at around seven o'clock. For now, let's say that it was at seven. I was in the tower at that time—my daughter can confirm this. And if her testimony isn't good enough, there are others who witnessed it.'

Most of the *rasotsu* nodded. They must have been the ones keeping an eye on the tower from their posts.

'At any rate, I couldn't just run up and down this steep spiral staircase in an instant. Why, it's absurd even to suggest that it was me. For one thing, I had no reason to kill Sugi.'

'Objectively speaking,' said Kawaji, turning to Kawakami, 'it would appear that I must ask you to accompany me to the Imperial Prosecuting Office.'

'No! I won't go!' he said, shaking his head, his voice growing more and more irate. 'I won't! You government dogs, you're all in on it. Going to these lengths to trap me, are you? Is that how much I scare you? Well, if you mean to take me down, I'm ready for you.'

Kawakami sounded as though he were about to kill someone, whether or not he himself realized it, but Kawaji shook his head with composure:

'No, there are some things that still need to be cleared up.'

'Such as?' asked Kazuki.

'For one thing, why Deputy Inspector Sugi came here in the first place,' said Kawaji. 'And what about Toneo Nakai? Where has he gone?'

'But, as far as the murder of Sugi is concerned, there's nobody except those two who could have done it,' said Nagasaka in a shrill voice, as he backed away and hid behind Kawaji. 'Chief Inspector, take him to the Imperial Prosecuting Office at once! That's an order!'

'Do you understand it, Kawaji?' asked Kazuki.

'I don't. At least, I don't understand Sugi's behaviour... Do you?'

'No, I can't work it out either. That's why I called you here.' Kazuki tilted his head slightly and stared off into the distance. 'For starters, I think we should send for Esmeralda.'

'Esmeralda? You mean that French...' began Kawaji, wearing a look of bewilderment. 'Whatever for?'

'It's a long story and we don't have the time to go into it right now. But suffice it to say, I've had her trained as a *miko*. Curiously enough, the old priestess who taught her has made surprising progress. Lately, she's even been able to summon the dead.'

Everybody was dumbfounded.

'If we send for her, we can have her summon the spirit of Deputy Inspector Sugi.'

'But that's absurd!'

'I'm sorry, but a corpse can't tell us why Sugi came to this hotel. I want to hear it from the mouth of the man himself. Just let me do this one thing. Oh, and while we're at it, there are a few others I'd like you to send for as well.'

Without divulging the details, Kazuki called over Saruki, Yokomakura and Imokawa, and gave them their orders.

The three *rasotsu* then bowed and went racing out the door and into garden.

9

Before even an hour had gone by, a convoy of palanquins arrived in quick succession, bringing the people Kazuki had sent for.

To the surprise of Kawakami and the others, it included none other than Nobuyoshi Kaieda and five other grandees from the Imperial Prosecuting Office, who must have come straight from the department itself. Even Naotsugu Manabe and his daughter O-Nui were there, both looking perplexed and wondering why they had been summoned. Yet what drew the eye more than this pageant of dignitaries was of course the beautiful foreign lady in their midst.

Kaieda and his colleagues were dressed in their usual *eboshi* and ceremonial robes, but Esmeralda entered the hall wearing an *ichimegasa* with a long veil. These were removed to reveal underneath a blue-eyed woman with long golden hair trailing down her back, dressed in a pair of scarlet *hakama* and a white silk *haori* with long sleeves. It was little wonder that Kawakami's jaw dropped, and for a moment he was quite speechless.

In the time it took them to arrive, Kazuki had ordered a porter and a *rasotsu* to place a table in front of the large column in the hall and to lay out Sugi's mutilated corpse on top of it. He also had six chairs brought in separately.

Having seated the officials in these chairs, Kawaji proceeded to give them an outline of the case and to explain who was involved in it. Meanwhile, Kazuki and Esmeralda arranged the mirrors, a bow and prayer beads that she had brought with her around the body and covered it with bamboo leaves, leaving only the face visible. All the while, they whispered together in a foreign language.

Esmeralda had had a large cart brought, which had carried, in addition to the above items, ancient musical instruments, including a large *kaen-daiko*, decorated with a pattern of flames, as well as several smaller *kakko* hourglass drums. Pushing and pulling the cart were Sergeants Onimaru and Ichinohata, who had until now been nowhere to be seen.

'Ye deities in heaven,' began Kazuki. 'I, Keishirō Kazuki, do respectfully summon the spirit of the deceased Deputy Inspector Sugi.'

As he spoke, the instruments were laid out on the floor, and the five *rasotsu*—the usual suspects—sat down cross-legged beside them.

'Though still inexperienced,' said Kazuki, now speaking plainly, 'these men have, at my bidding, undertaken to learn the art of *kagura*.'

Each of the *rasotsu* wore a dignified, solemn look.

Nobody dared laugh. The dead man's body was lying face up on the table. The scene was set, and the hall, with its enormous pillar in the middle, seemed to be transformed into a temple.

Onimaru struck the *kaen-daiko*, whereupon the flutes and drums began to play, and the strains of solemn music flowed.

Still standing, the golden-haired *miko* closed her eyes and began to chant slowly.

> *Awariya, asobihasutomo, mōsanu, asakurani,*
> *Amatsukami, kunitsukami, orimashimase...*

At first, the observers thought the words were foreign, possibly because some parts of the intonation did not sound very Japanese. The musical accompaniment was also in disarray, but that only added to the other-worldly effect.

> *Awariya, asobihasutomo, mōsanu, asakurani,*
> *Naruizuchimo, orimashimase…*

As she chanted, Esmeralda moved and twisted her body in an uncanny manner.

Kawaji stood there, dumbfounded. As all this was going on, he saw Kazuki say something to the porter, after which the porter went over and said something to Kawakami, who, as if he were not bamboozled enough already, nodded, looking more and more perplexed, after which the porter left the hall.

> *Awariya, asobihasutomo, mōsanu, asakurani,*
> *Sugi Tetsuma no mitama, mairitamae…*

The *kagura* bells that the *miko* was holding suddenly rang out.

'*Ima… mairu!…*'

The atmosphere in the still-gloomy hall seemed to grow even darker.

'*I am… the spirit… of Sugi Tetsuma…*'

Everybody in the room was startled. The *miko*'s voice had changed, and for the first time they could understand the words. Though the timbre was different, the voice was still unmistakably Esmeralda's, with its strange accent. Yet it looked as though the body on the table, its eyes still staring heavenward, had just moved its mouth.

'*For the first time… since arriving in the land of the dead… I can see… the land of the living… without hindrance… Before my death… I did not know why I died… But now, at last… I know… The man who killed me… was Deputy Commissioner Nagasaka…*'

'Wh-What is the meaning of this?' exclaimed Nagasaka in a strange voice. 'What is Sugi—or rather, that woman—saying?'

The *kagura* bells rang out once more, cutting him off.

At this point, Kawaji saw the porter come in carrying a length of rope and a bundle of straw under his arm. He then saw him place it, with the help of one of the *rasotsu*, on the fifth or sixth step of the staircase, then take the rope and set about tying it to the railing on both sides. Standing over him, Kazuki whispered his instructions, and then picked up the bloody sword and the *geta*.

Nobody apart from Kawaji, however, appeared to notice this.

'*Nagasaka said… that Toneo Nakai… was hiding in the foreign settlement… But all that… was a lie… Knowing that it was a lie… he ordered the rasotsu… to their posts… and climbed the tower…*'

'This is an outrage!'

'*I had no idea… that Nagasaka would do such a thing… Early this morning… I was summoned… by Sergeants Saruki and Yokomakura… They told me… that Nagasaka and his daughter, O-Kumi… had been kidnapped by Kawakami… and were locked up… in the tower… I immediately… rushed over…*'

'End this! This is preposterous! Dead men don't say things like this!' protested Nagasaka.

A shiver ran down Kawaji's spine. The substance of what the *miko* had to say was startling enough, but, despite what Nagasaka said, the voice was undoubtedly that of the late Sugi. There was no other explanation for it, for how else could the foreign lady who had only just arrived know how he spoke? Then again, was it possible that the deceased could know things in death that he hadn't known in life?

Even Kawaji had not noticed, however, that during all this, Kazuki, who had been standing at the top of the stairs, had suddenly vanished—who knew when or where?

'I entered the foreign settlement... and was told... by the rasotsu... to look at the top of the tower... There I saw Nagasaka... and his daughter, O-Kumi... I believed... that they had been kidnapped... by Kawakami... I ran into the hotel... in a daze... and raced up the stairs...'

Just then, the people in the hall heard a strange sound, like something sliding.

'Meanwhile... Saruki lured Kawakami and Ushinosuke... to this hall...'

Something came flying down the stairs at a terrific speed. The glinting object appeared and disappeared three or four times as it made its way around the great pillar.

'After I had taken... five or six steps...'

Five or six steps from the bottom, there was a sudden snapping sound. Everybody looked as the bundle of straw that had been standing there was sliced in two and the unbound top half tumbled down the stairs.

The cut had been made horizontally by a single long blade. The sword had something strange attached to it on either side, but as soon as it cut the bundle of straw, it went flying, while the attachments dislodged themselves: two magnolia-wood *geta*.

'I was... slain...'

They all stared at this terrifying mechanism, as if petrified, realizing that the teeth of the *geta* had hugged the handrail, allowing it to slide all the way down the staircase.

'The sword... had been slipped through the straps... so as not to slide... At the same time... the weight of the sword... held the two geta in place... preventing them from coming off... and speeding up their descent...'

All this time, the strange, other-worldly music was still

playing: the five *rasotsu* were all puffing out their cheeks and beating their drums with great intensity and zeal.

'*As I ran up the stairs... leaning forward... the speeding sword... cut right into my stomach... At this point... the straps of the geta... were touching the back of the blade... so they could not... cut them...*

'*Ordinarily... as soon as the sword touched me... I would have been knocked back... but because the staircase is spiral... it cut me at an angle... in a single blow... just as it would have done in a sword fight...*

'*Just before that... I heard a strange sound above my head... but the hall was still in darkness... and because of the spiral staircase... I couldn't see the weapon sliding down...*

'*This is how Nagasaka... was able to kill me... from all the way up in the tower.*'

There was a noise amid the crowd of people. Nagasaka's daughter had collapsed.

'*The only reason Nagasaka said... that Toneo Nakai was about to leave the foreign settlement... was so that he could have the* rasotsu *testify... that he was at the top of the tower when the murder took place...*'

Kazuki came down the stairs, having provided this 'demonstration' of the murder.

'*Nagasaka came up with this trick... after seeing the guillotine... Five days ago... he cut a bundle of straw here... to see whether the sword would slide well... and whether it would really cut it... The reason he left it where it lay... was so that he could throw suspicion on Kawakami and Ushinosuke later... Of course... this is also why they were lured to this hall today...*'

Before he knew it, Nagasaka was cowering beside the unconscious O-Kumi, his balding pate pressed to her body.

'The unscrupulous Nagasaka planned this elaborate murder...
It was an act of villainy... His resolve came from his desperation to
protect his own happiness... Not only did he want to murder me...
because of my love for O-Kumi... but at the same time... he wanted
to do away with Kawakami and Ushinosuke... who were trying to
expose his old failures...'

The *kagura* bells rang out once more.

'Is it right for a man who reports to the Imperial Prosecuting
Office... to murder for the sake of himself and his family?... Surely,
he must be put to the guillotine...'

With a dull thud, Onimaru struck the *kaen-daiko*.

Esmeralda, who had given voice to this fearsome 'lament
of the dead', seemed to fall into a trance and spoke no more.

'It looks like it's over,' said Kazuki, suddenly appearing at
Kawaji's side.

However, Kawaji, together with the other representatives
of the Imperial Prosecuting Office, and even Kawakami and
Ushinosuke, just sat there, motionless, like shadows in the
realm of the dead.

'All this would make Miss O-Kumi here an accomplice,' said
Kazuki, turning to the assembled dignitaries, 'but, in light of
the circumstances, I would ask that she be pardoned.'

Still, none of them uttered a word.

'Take Deputy Commissioner Nagasaka to the Imperial
Prosecuting Office,' Kazuki then ordered.

The five *rasotsu* approached Nagasaka, who was still
cowering.

'But, Kazuki,' said Kawaji, returning to his senses, 'doesn't
this mean that some of the *rasotsu* could be complicit too?'

'That may well be so. I'd even say it's highly likely,' said
Kazuki, almost in a whisper. 'But it's also likely that they had

their arms twisted by Nagasaka. Though I suspect they'll be glad to see the back of Deputy Inspector Sugi, they did ultimately help to solve the case. We'll reprimand them later. For the time being, at least, I think we should overlook this.'

However, before Kawaji could say anything else, Kazuki went over to Manabe and his daughter.

'As you've just heard, sir, it would appear that I've won this round with Kawaji. As for the translation, it's finished, and tomorrow will be one month to the day, just as promised, but I do think it would be a good idea to let the girl stay in Japan a little while longer.'

Manabe, however, seemed not hear Kazuki's words, for Esmeralda, once again wearing her long veil, was walking towards O-Nui. Her eyes widened in astonishment as the French woman bowed to her with all the elegance of a lady of the Heian court.

'*Bonjour,*' said Esmeralda, smiling through her veil. 'How do you do, Mademoiselle O-Nui?…'

FROM AMERICA WITH LOVE

The following relates the particulars of an exceptionally difficult case, in which, on a snowy night, a rickshaw carrying a man plunged into the Kanda River, whereupon the man in question drowned. No footprints were left in the snow by the individual pulling the rickshaw, however. It was almost enough to make one believe in the existence of ikiryō—*those living manifestations of the soul that are spawned from the intensity of individual's hatred.*

— From a report made by Chief Inspector Toshiyoshi Kawaji of the Imperial Prosecuting Office

1

It was a sunny afternoon towards the end first lunar month in the third year of Meiji, and Sergeant Onimaru was taking a leisurely stroll down Asakusa's Nakamise-dōri, heading towards the main temple.

The street was not, of course, the thriving, prosperous shopping district that it is today. The Kaminari Gate had burnt down at the very end of the first year of Keiō, 1865, and if you walked past its ruins, to your left you would see the blackened walls of the smaller Sensō-ji temple, and to your right rows of stalls made from simple reeds and, dotted among them, street vendors with their wares set out on little stands and straw mats.

The air was filled with the cries of merchants selling their goods, the noise of whistles attracting customers, women laughing and children crying. The bustling crowd was so dense that the customers jostled with one another.

As he walked down the street, Sergeant Onimaru was munching on a stack of sliced fried tofu, which he had just deftly pinched from a vendor along the way.

This was not his first meal of the day, however. Already he had taken a boiled egg from another stall, and some sweets from yet another. And his pilfering didn't stop there, either. He had also pocketed a faggot of kindling, flagrantly helping himself as though he were taking his very own property.

Seeing the arm reach for their wares, the vendors had naturally wanted to cry out and stop the thief, but when they saw that the arm was attached to a hulking great *rasotsu* with an impressive beard and moustache, they bit their tongue before it could speak. Needless to say, Tamonta Onimaru's face was now more menacing than ever.

'Ah!' he exclaimed, as he approached the Niō Gate and stopped in his tracks.

Bowls, dishes and lacquerware were laid out there on the straw mats. They were antiques, and one of the ceramic flasks caught his eye. It could hold only around three *gō* of sake, but it had a fine shape and the lustrous patina of age.

Onimaru reached out his hand, and his face met that of the vendor sitting on the other side of the mat. He had on a faded black-crested garment, his hair had grown out, and his beard was scraggly—in a word, he looked down on his luck, yet his features were surely those of a samurai who had at one time been fearless. He must have been around thirty, and he had a child of three or so sitting quietly beside him.

The two men glared at one another. Onimaru flinched, wondering whether this was such a good idea, but the next moment he bared his teeth.

'I'll just take this and be on my way,' he said, snatching the flask.

And with that, he walked off, leaving the samurai-looking man speechless.

With a haughty swagger, the sergeant strutted through the Niō Gate and found himself in front of the main temple, amid a flock of pigeons. Just then, a voice called out behind him:

'Hold it!'

The voice belonged to a woman, so he thought she must be calling for somebody else, but then she called out again:

'Wait! Sergeant!'

When he turned around, his eyes grew wide.

Running after him was a woman of twenty-five or so, wearing a patchwork kimono. Her face was lean and stiff, and she was gasping for breath.

'Sergeant! You just took something from my shop without paying! Yes, you! I must ask you to return that flask!'

Onimaru quelled his sense of panic.

'What are you talking about?! This was given to me!'

'My husband says he has no recollection of doing that. That flask is one of my most valuable pieces. And anyway, no matter what the value, I'm sorry, but you can't just go pinching things like that. A man of your standing, taking from poor people trying to earn money by selling their own possessions!'

'Shut up, you!' shouted Onimaru, towering over her.

Clearly, she was the man's wife and must have heard what had happened from her husband before chasing after Onimaru. She was a brave woman.

'How dare you cause a scene like this and falsely accuse a public official!'

'It isn't a false accusation. Isn't that my flask you're carrying? Is it right for a *rasotsu* to steal?'

'What's all this about stealing, eh? Why, I should kill you where you stand for that insult!'

'Go right ahead, you crook!'

Suddenly, the pigeons scattered. Onimaru was astonished to see the woman place her hand into her *obi* and extract a small dagger.

A circle of people had quickly formed around them. At this rate, he'd have no choice but to drag the woman off to the police station. He certainly couldn't back down now.

'Hey! Hey, you bitch!'

Having clocked the flask held in Onimaru's outstretched hand, the crowd burst out laughing, but what made the sergeant's face blush an even deeper shade of scarlet was the sight of a familiar face among the crowd. It was Chief Inspector Kawaji, looking at him blankly.

Onimaru stopped dead in his tracks.

At that moment, a strange and noticeable change came over the woman, too, as her gaze turned away from Onimaru, and she paused.

'You may have that flask, Sergeant,' she finally said. 'I apologize for any misunderstanding.'

He was in a state of shock. The crowd of spectators looked equally perplexed and began to disperse.

The woman just stood there staring. Onimaru noticed that her eyes were fixed on a single figure in the crowd: the back of a woman in an *okoso-zukin* headscarf. Apparently having already paid her respects at the temple, she was passing through the Niō Gate and making her way down the Nakamise-dōri.

A few moments later, the shopkeeper's wife, without so much as another word to Onimaru, headed off, clearly in pursuit of her.

2

'Onimaru…'

The voice came from beside him. It was Kawaji.

Onimaru blushed again.

'What was the matter with her?' asked Kawaji. He seemed preoccupied, however, and before Onimaru could answer, he said: 'I think we should see what all this is about.'

With that, he walked off, leaving Onimaru with little choice but to follow him.

As she passed by her shop—or rather, the mat where her husband was sitting—the woman glanced over but said nothing. Perhaps she worried that he might leave the child unattended if she called him. The husband, meanwhile, just sat there, hanging his head, appearing not to notice her.

The woman in the headscarf pressed on through the bustling crowds on the street. She was not what you would call fat, but she had a voluptuous figure and a most coquettish walk. Though the woman in pursuit could easily have caught up with her, strangely enough she maintained her distance, keeping a close eye on her.

Before long, the other woman turned onto the main road, just as a rickshaw was passing. She hailed it and got in, after which the rickshaw sped off.

In a fluster, the woman following her looked around, but it so happened that there were no other rickshaws to be seen.

Then, when she turned round and saw Sergeant Onimaru drawing nearer, she suddenly ran back and grabbed his hand. The momentum made him drop the flask, which was still in his hand, but when it hit the ground, smashing to pieces, the woman didn't seem to mind.

'Sergeant!' she cried. 'Sergeant, you're just in time. That woman in the rickshaw… You must follow her and find out where she lives!'

She was like a different person. Or rather, it was as though she had recovered that same assertiveness she had when she had first gone to remonstrate with Onimaru.

He didn't know what to say.

'Then,' she continued, 'once you've found out, tell me. You'll find me in the spot where you stole that flask.'

Onimaru glanced back. After a nod from Kawaji, he ran off in the direction of the rickshaw that had vanished.

Meanwhile, Kawaji approached the woman and introduced himself as a chief inspector from the Imperial Prosecuting Office.

The woman seemed surprised.

'You're quite a piece of work,' he said. 'Who was she, that woman in the headscarf? Clearly, she wasn't just any ordinary woman.'

The young woman struggled to find an answer.

'No matter,' said Kawaji. 'The *rasotsu* will find out at any rate.'

'Yes,' said the woman, composing herself. 'My name is Io, and I'm from Karatsu, on the island of Kyushu. That woman just now, the one who was hiding her face with the headscarf… I'm sure it was the mistress of Lord Ogasawara.'

'What, you mean the shogun's former chamberlain and the Intendant of Iki Province? But then why were you trying to follow her?'

'At first, I wasn't really thinking, sir. I was so surprised to see her and just wanted to find out how she was doing and where she was living these days. So, I went after her. But as I did, I noticed something odd. She appears to be with child.'

'She did?'

'Maybe five or six months…' (Only a woman could notice such a thing.) 'It's just a hunch, but I'm almost certain of it. No more than seven months, to be sure.'

There was a trace of tension on Kawaji's face.

'Ah, yes, of course!' he said. 'The rumour is that Ogasawara's fled to America.'

'That's right, sir. Last year, around the time of the Battle of Hakodate. I must have heard about it back in the fifth month,' she said, counting on her fingers. 'I was trying to work it out while I was following the lady. It's been eight months since His Lordship left Japan. He would never have taken her to Hakodate, so the last time he would have seen her must have been before that. But if she's five or six months pregnant...'

'You mean to suggest that Lord Ogasawara is in Japan?' Kawaji exclaimed.

The woman seemed curiously startled by this. Evidently, she had not considered this possibility.

'Well, if not that, then what exactly were you thinking?' he asked.

Though she must have been around twenty-five, her face, for all its almost masculine dignity, now blushed a pale shade of crimson.

3

That evening, as he was arriving at the Imperial Prosecuting Office, Kawaji bumped into Naotsugu Manabe by the Red Gate. Kawaji nodded to him, but the old man simply passed him by, wearing a sullen look on his face.

When Kawaji entered the office, he found Kazuki sitting alone at his desk, resting his chin on his hand. His attire only added to the impression of refinement and elegance.

'I just ran into your uncle outside.'

'Oh? I didn't see him. I believe he's been holding some serious talks with the directors.'

'He wants to have Esmeralda sent back to France?'

'Yes.'

'So, what did the directors say?'

'I haven't heard yet. But I doubt they'll have agreed to it. Before, they were of course sceptical about her, but now, after the incident at the Tsukiji Hotel, they seem to have taken a more positive view of her.'

Kazuki laughed.

'Kazuki?'

'Yes?'

'That business with Esmeralda as a *miko*. It surprised me too, but… when I thought about it later, there was something that struck me as odd.' Kawaji trained his eyes on Kazuki's face. 'Before Esmeralda solved the mystery and identified the culprit, you seemed to be making preparations to explain it yourself… Did you know in advance?'

'In fact, I did,' said Kazuki, scratching his head. 'You see, the night before, while we were having relations, she let it slip just as she climaxed. Not in so many words, of course, but a few feverish phrases here and there. Apparently, it's necessary for her to get into that state as a prelude to her *miko* act.'

Hearing this, Kawaji lost the nerve to ask any more questions, and his eyes darted around in bewilderment.

'Ahem… On another note, I stumbled across a curious incident in Asakusa earlier today.'

'Wait! Before we discuss that, have you ever heard of Lord Ogasawara, the Intendant of Iki Province?'

'I'll say! He was Lord of Karatsu, in the domain next to Saga. And he was on the shogun's council of elders, too, wasn't he? They say he fled to America after the collapse of the shogunate,' said Kawaji.

154

Even if this was not the case, the primary aim of the Imperial Prosecuting Office was to keep tabs on officials, as well as to expose traitors, and so it seemed only natural to have such knowledge of a formerly high-ranking official who was now missing.

Kawaji continued, 'I've seen the woman who apparently used to be his mistress.'

'Yes?'

'She must be five or six months pregnant…'

'Yes?'

'The thing is, Ogasawara fled to America in the fifth lunar month of last year—though we ought to check on this, just to be sure. In any case, it doesn't add up.'

'Perhaps she had an affair. Although, it can hardly be called that if Ogasawara abandoned her,' said Kazuki wearily. But then, all of a sudden, a thought struck him. 'Kawaji, how exactly do you know how far along she is?'

'I'm basing it on a woman's observation.'

'A woman?'

'Your presumption of an affair matches hers. But my first thought was that the rumour about Ogasawara's flight to America could be false.'

'Ah-ha!' Kazuki's eyes grew wider, whereupon Kawaji began to tell him all about the incident in Asakusa.

As strange a request as it was, Sergeant Onimaru had gone after Ogasawara's mistress at the behest of the street vendor's wife and found her to be living at an address next to the graveyard in Yanaka Hatsune-chō, along with a maid who was apparently both deaf and mute.

Kawaji, meanwhile, had waited behind with the couple selling antique teacups and sake flasks, and once again, he had enquired why the woman was so interested in Ogasawara's mistress, even though she was born in Karatsu and did not know the man.

'The woman was bolder than she appeared,' he told Kazuki. 'Her name is Io, and she was born in the temple at Karatsu, but even from a young age she was strongly influenced by the "Revere the Emperor, Expel the Barbarians!" slogan. Apparently, there was a time when she would disguise herself as a man, take a sword and associate with loyalists in the western regions—the likes of Ryūma Sakamoto and Shinsaku Takasugi.'

'You don't say!'

'She was extremely dissatisfied with Ogasawara's various deeds on the council of elders—in fact, that's putting it lightly. She was once married to a priest from Karatsu, but later, after leaving her husband, she took up with a *rōnin* from Mito by the name of Hikogorō Koibuchi. This new husband of hers apparently even convinced her to be taken on as a maid in the Karatsu Domain's Edo residence in the hope of killing Ogasawara.'

'Quite a woman, it seems.'

'I was shocked myself. Seemingly it was the mistress, O-Yumi, who spotted her.'

'I see. So, just how was it that this woman-loyalist was reduced to opening a street stall?'

'Well, not only did her native Karatsu Domain become something of an enemy state under the shogun, but her husband—the second one, that is—joined in the Mito Rebellion, which led to his downfall, and then, after the collapse of the shogunate, they were forced out onto the streets. The man seems to be utterly hopeless when it comes to earning a living. He just sits there on his mat, looking crestfallen. They really are an unfortunate pair.'

'So, what does this shadow of her former self intend to do now that she knows Ogasawara's mistress has conceived a child with some unknown man?'

'Well, that's just it. The woman, of course, isn't very well disposed towards Ogasawara even now. Nevertheless, she said she finds it unforgivable that his mistress would have a child by another man, and she seems to be in a rather distressed state of mind.'

'I see.'

'That in itself is one problem, but as I just said: what if Ogasawara is hiding out somewhere in Japan—maybe even here, in Tokyo? If he is, then...'

'It would be quite something if he were,' Kazuki agreed.

At that time, dozens of 'war criminals' were being sought by the new government, but the Intendant of Iki Province, Lord Ogasawara, must have ranked among the most wanted.

'When it comes down to it, my knowledge of Ogasawara is rather patchy. After all, I did spend the three years prior to the Restoration abroad. I'm sorry, but could you fill in the blanks for me, Kawaji?'

'Well, when you put it like that, there are things that I'm not too sure about either.'

What Kawaji meant by this was that he knew more about the man's career than he did about the man himself.

Kawaji began: Nagamichi Ogasawara was born to a wealthy and powerful clan in Hizen Province's Karatsu Domain and rose to become a member of the shogun's council of elders. His father had died when he was two years old, and so another member of the family—although in truth, he was no blood relative—had been invited to become the new head of the Ogasawara clan. This was because, holding the role of Nagasaki

Guard, the Ogasawara clan was not permitted to have a child daimyo. And so, although he was the first-born of the previous daimyo, he was treated as a man of lesser status. It was not until he reached the age of thirty-seven that he was proclaimed the rightful heir—and even then, only because Tosa's Lord Yōdō interceded on his behalf. This, however, took some considerable effort, because by then the Ogasawara clan had already sprouted various branches that had become entangled with one another.

In the event Ogasawara did not become the daimyo of Karatsu Domain, but, owing to his status as heir, in the second year of Bunkyū, he became a member of the shogun's council of elders. This unprecedented appointment showed just how widely recognized his brilliance was, and how his skill could be relied upon during that period of terrible strife, when the campaign to kick the foreigners out reached its peak just as the country was opening up to the rest of the world.

That is why, on the face of it, Karatsu gave the impression of having two lords.

Ogasawara had backed the opening of the country unequivocally, and there was even evidence to suggest that he had conspired in a hair-raising *coup d'état* against the imperial court. In the end, however, all his efforts came to naught, and the shogunate fell. He advocated continued resistance and made it to Hakodate, where Takeaki Enomoto and his soldiers were holed up. That much was clear. Yet by the time Enomoto and his men had at last surrendered, Ogasawara was nowhere to be found. Upon further investigation, it was discovered that on a certain day in the fourth lunar month, Ogasawara, along with two retainers, had boarded an American ship anchored in Hakodate Bay and fled to the United States.

Afterwards, the Karatsu clan explained to the new government that Ogasawara's actions had been completely out of the clan's control. The new head of the Karatsu Domain, Nagakuni, explained that two factions now existed within the clan—the one loyal to him, Nagakuni, and another still loyal to Nagamichi Ogasawara. Nagakuni swore that he would report on Ogasawara the moment his whereabouts became known, and that if he was found to have returned to Japan, the clan would arrest him immediately and hand him over to the authorities. Thus, by the skin of his teeth, did he manage to ensure the domain's continued existence.

As so often happens in the world, the Karatsu clan had taken great pride in—and advantage of—Nagamichi's influence with the shogun, yet now, in these life-or-death circumstances, they well and truly scapegoated him.

'Well, there you have it... more or less,' said Kawaji.

'Indeed. Back then, his actions would have seemed quite reasonable. Compared to the other opportunists that were around, he even seems to have shown some backbone.'

'And yet, I don't have much sense of the man himself.'

'Meaning?'

'Well, you know I was saying about his having been commander-in-chief during the Summer War? He apparently looked quite splendid in his fiery-red *jinbaori* and his helmet with its enormous two-pronged crest, each prong said to be more than two feet long, which he wore over a black-lacquered *hachigane*. Only, one day, a certain daimyo came to inspect the troops and was so impressed by his battle attire that he took the helmet in his hands. He was surprised to find it was so light that it practically floated on air and realized immediately that the shiny black helmet was made from finest paulownia wood. The daimyo laughed and said, "I see you're only playing at generals. When you flee through woodland and forest, there's a risk that a crest as big as yours could get caught and cause you to fall from your horse, but this will snap right off." Ogasawara also told the daimyo that if he turned his *jinbaori* inside out, he'd find that it was black—the proper colour for a military overcoat. This, he said, might also have been of help when Ogasawara inevitably fled.'

Chief Inspector Kazuki was astonished.

'Then there are reports that, when he was a member of the council of elders, he would happily take bribes from anybody who came to see him. If anybody kicked up a fuss and he had to return it, you could be sure that the other party would be back again ere long. And anyway, there simply wasn't the time to deal with each and every one of them. It was easier to let him take the bribes. Besides, he would always roar with laughter and claim that the bribes had no effect—and apparently this was true enough.'

'He seems like quite a man.'

'That's one way of putting it, Kazuki. You almost seem impressed. But wasn't it you who was once so indignant at the shogunate's corruption? Isn't this just another proof of that?'

'Well, when you put it like that... How old is he?'

'He must have been going on fifty when he fled.'

'I see,' said Kazuki, looking straight at Kawaji. 'In the unlikely event that Ogasawara is the man who impregnated that woman, it would be the biggest capture in recent times. Well, Kawaji, shall we see which of us can find our adversary first?'

'It shouldn't be so difficult to find out. All we'd have to do is keep an eye on her, or else take her into custody and question her.'

'If only it were that easy,' said Kazuki.

'Meaning?'

'Well, I've only just heard the story from you, so who knows. But didn't you say it was Onimaru who'd been tasked with keeping an eye on her? He may have managed to establish that the woman lives alone, but he isn't skilled enough to shadow her and get that sort of information without her noticing. What would he do if our adversary stopped him? And what if he arrested her and under questioning she gave a false name to hide the real identity of the man?'

'We'll have to cross that bridge when we come to it.'

'Well, to each his own,' said Kazuki. 'By which, I mean that I'll investigate from the sidelines. You, though, must do as you see fit. But I suspect it may not go quite as planned if you have the woman investigated directly.'

'Oh, very well, I take your point…'

4

Searching for a man who had impregnated a woman was, ordinarily, not something that the Imperial Prosecuting Office would do. But when one of the parties was a major criminal—and one who at the same time had the unprecedented distinction of having fled the country—it was another matter entirely.

Despite Chief Inspector Kazuki's challenge, Kawaji was in high spirits. The curtain was rising on the second act of the detectives' rivalry.

The next morning, together with Sergeants Onimaru and Yokomakura, Kawaji made his way to the address in Yanaka Hatsune-chō that Onimaru had tracked down.

Onimaru had received the order to accompany Kawaji the previous day, but Yokomakura came along of his own accord. Having heard about the old man's mistress and so forth, even this idle young man could not resist sating his curiosity.

To the south of the Tennō-ji temple, whose five-storey pagoda was in later years famously depicted by Rohan Kōda, a vast grave-yard spread out, bound by a lattice fence. On the opposite side of the road leading along this fence were a dozen or so shops huddled together There was a tofu vendor, a charcoal dealer, a shop selling household goods, even a seller of joss sticks. It was a winter's morning, and so each of the shops had only one or two doors open, making the scene appear even more dismal. Other than that, there was only the low wall of the temple, for the ben-efit of which alone the shops seemed to be open.

'That's the woman's house over there,' said Onimaru, as they stood in front of one of the shops. Around five yards away, three enormous gingko trees towered up, while under their bare branches stood a small but elegant-looking house.

'Is that the shop where you made your enquiries?'

'The very one, sir.'

Through the door of the household-goods shop, Kawaji glimpsed the figure of a woman who appeared to be the owner. He poked his head in and enquired about the residents of the house in question and others who frequented it.

'Ah, you're the one from yesterday!' exclaimed the owner, seeing Sergeant Onimaru with his enormous beard. She sensed immediately that Kawaji must be his superior and, wearing a look of dread, started prattling on.

The facts, such as she related them, were largely the same as those reported by Onimaru the day before: that a beautiful woman was living there alone, with only a maid; that they had

162

been living there since the sixth lunar month of the previous year; that the woman rarely ventured out and that, whenever she did, she would always cover herself with a headscarf; and that it was the maid who ran errands and did shopping and the like.

Then she added something odd. Although she had never seen anybody come to visit the woman, apparently, once every month or two, a rickshaw would arrive, carrying a woman who looked like the mistress of a foreigner.

'A foreigner's mistress?' said Kawaji, tilting his head in puzzlement. 'You mean to say that she was dressed in Western clothing?'

'No,' the woman replied. 'That's not it. I just mean that she wears a choker about her neck, and her make-up has a whiff of something foreign about it. She says barely a few words on the doorstep, and then, before you know it, she's gone.'

'Hmm,' pondered Kawaji. The case was murkier than it originally seemed. 'And you've never seen a man arrive?'

'Correct.'

'So, what can she be living on?'

'Well, she seems to lead quite a lavish lifestyle. Everybody's saying that she might be a mistress who's been paid off hand-somely by her former lover.'

The presumption of her being a mistress was right enough.

'Is the main road the only way of getting to the house?'

'Yes, unless you count the graveyard. That said, there's something queer about that graveyard.'

'What do you mean?'

'It has to do with the ghosts.'

'Oh? Are they not coming out when they're supposed to come out?'

This was all the humour that Kawaji could muster.

'Well, I've lived here for decades and never heard anything like that. But last summer, late one night, O-Yone, the incense seller, happened to be looking in the direction of the graveyard. Shall I go and call her, sir? O-Yone, I mean.'

'Hmm? No, let's hear your story first.'

'Well, it was a moonlit night, and I saw something white moving towards the graves. It was an odd time to be paying a visit to a grave, and it didn't look like a priest either, so I called Yoshi, my husband, and we both ventured into the graveyard. As we got nearer, I saw it behind a grave—it was floating in mid-air, this high!' she said, gesturing with her hand. 'Then it just seemed to vanish into the distance. Later on, though, Zen, the tofu vendor, said that he saw something similar early one morning, in the faint light of daybreak. It was a black shadow that time, but sure enough, he said it was drifting in mid-air.'

Just then, the woman cried out. Kawaji turned around and saw a girl of around fifteen, with round, frostbitten cheeks, peering in at the door. As soon as their eyes met, the girl went tearing off in the direction of the house, her sandals clattering, carrying something wrapped in a *furoshiki* cloth under her arm. She must have been on her way home after doing some shopping, when suddenly she had seen Kawaji and the others in the shop. It was anybody's guess how long she had been standing there.

'She must have been listening,' the woman muttered, embarrassed.

'I thought the girl was deaf-mute?'

'Oh, no, she can hear all right. Deaf, my foot!'

Getting near the house would be difficult now. Then again, Kawaji had come here only to make a preliminary investigation; this was an unexpected bonus. But what exactly were those black and white shadows that had been spotted in the graveyard?

'The woman took up residence there in the middle of last year, did she not? Was it only afterwards that these strange occurrences in the graveyard began?'

'Would you care to go and take a look, Chief Inspector?'

'No, not yet. To go now might scupper our investigation.'

Kawaji left the shop and pondered for a moment. Suddenly, he turned around.

'Onimaru, go and buy yourself something to eat. I want you to keep an eye on the graveyard for the time being. Just make sure that nobody sees you.'

Sergeant Onimaru gulped.

'You mean… this graveyard… where there are ghosts?'

'If you do happen to see any, arrest them, won't you?'

'And… you w-want me to do this… myself?'

'You're big enough and strong enough not to need any help!'

'And… you w-want me to be here at night as well?'

'Of course! After all, she said it comes out at night. Do it until you receive new orders.'

'H-hey! Yokomakura!' said Onimaru. 'You can stay here with me!'

Already halfway out the door, Sergeant Yokomakura turned to look at Kawaji.

'There's no need for two men to do a job where one man would suffice,' the *rasotsu* responded in a shrill voice. 'It would be a waste of valuable resources!'

'Come, come,' replied Kawaji. 'It wouldn't be a waste. Indeed, this case demands the use of our valuable resources!

You can take it in turns.' He stared blankly at Yokomakura. 'Didn't you come along so that you could lend a hand? After all, a friend in need is a friend indeed.'

Without looking back at the two *rasotsu*, both of whom were standing bolt upright, both wearing a look of dejection, Chief Inspector Kawaji ventured out into the cold wind and set off at a brisk pace.

5

Before long, Kawaji found himself back in Asakusa.

When he came to the stall selling antique plates and sake flasks, the woman was gone. Only the husband and child were sitting there, in the shadows.

'I must apologize about yesterday,' Kawaji began. 'Is your wife not working today?'

'No, she's, um…' said Hikogorō Koibuchi, hesitating. 'After meeting you, sir, my wife and I talked. She's gone to see a former official from Karatsu, in connection with the mistress we found out about just yesterday.'

As it so happened, Kawaji had gone back to Asakusa because he had a premonition that the man's strong-willed wife would never have been content to sit idly by. He had even wondered whether he might run into her in Yanaka.

Since it could hinder the investigation if she were to kick up a fuss now, Kawaji had returned to warn her off. Could it be that she had already gone there?

Kawaji knew, of course, that he would have to investigate Ogasawara's contacts in Karatsu thoroughly, but as there was nobody for the moment who sprang to mind, he had been wondering where to begin. Koibuchi's words, however, made him smile to himself.

'My wife, you see, can't help herself. You could say she's the very embodiment of justice, a woman who won't let things be swept under the carpet. But you could also say she's just a meddlesome busybody—in that respect, she's not unlike other women. These days, however, all her efforts are doing our family no good at all,' Koibuchi lamented. 'As you can see, sir, she leaves our child unattended, which is a real nuisance.'

The man seemed a far cry from the one who had once stolen his principled wife away from her former husband, let alone from the samurai who had once sent his wife to dispatch Ogasawara. Indeed, he had changed since then: he seemed earnest and made a good impression.

'Now we have nothing to do with Ogasawara, let alone with his mistress. On the contrary, I think she's inviting unnecessary trouble, but my wife's like a wild horse, sir: she doesn't listen to a word I say. As someone from the authorities, couldn't you try to reason with her?'

'Hmm… So, just who is this former official from Karatsu whom you mentioned?'

'He's called Sagen Tagusari. He's one of Nagakuni's supporters—which is to say, he's leader of the faction that opposes Nagamichi Ogasawara.'

'Where does he live? And what does he do these days?'

'I heard he was living in the Kobiki-chō neighbourhood of Kyōbashi and that he'd been appointed an undersecretary in the Ministry of Popular Affairs. I think that may be where my wife was headed.'

'Ah, he's working for the government now?' Kawaji was

surprised to hear this. There were few such men from the Karatsu Domain. 'Very well, I'll go and ask him.'

From there, Kawaji made his way to the Ministry of Popular Affairs in Marunouchi, which was no easy task, as he had to make the entire journey on foot.

Having produced his card, he enquired about Tagusari's availability and was shown into a meeting room, where the undersecretary finally joined him.

He was a burly man with a stern-looking face and the dignity befitting a former retainer of the Karatsu clan, but his expression changed when he walked in. While his title may have suggested a certain grandiosity, he was, in fact, a rather low-ranking official. Nevertheless, as a member of the Karatsu clan, the would-be heir to which was a 'fugitive criminal', he was lucky to find himself with a position in the new government.

To Kawaji's first question, asking whether a woman by the name of Io, who hailed from the same province, had already paid him a visit, he replied that she had come a short while ago. As he said this, he wore a look of dejection. Kawaji then asked whether he knew the whereabouts of Ogasawara's former mistress and, having suggested that she was now pregnant, enquired whether he had any idea who the father might be.

'Of course I have no idea where a woman like that might be living!' he replied indignantly. 'Should you deign to look into the matter, you'll find that back in Karatsu I was a member of the loyalist faction—that is to say, I sided with Nagakuni's lot—and that I opposed Ogasawara's appointment to the shogun's council of elders. Lord Ogasawara was disastrous for the Karatsu Domain, and since then the clan has suffered a most lamentable fate. I've heard it said that Ogasawara fought with the shogun's army until the bitter end and that only afterwards did he flee to America, but in truth I find his recklessness outrageous. Still, I suppose none of that matters now. This mistress of his may well be with child, but the identity of the father is none of my concern.' He practically spat out these last words. 'Yes, that Io woman did come here. Lord Ogasawara's absence is one thing, but that his mistress should be with child is, I should say, scandalous. Of course, if the former loyalists of the Karatsu clan got wind of this, there'd be hell to pay. I believe that is why Io came to see me, to stir up trouble. But I sent her packing. I told her that such a deed would bring disgrace upon the Karatsu clan, and that they have no appetite for any more needless folly.'

'Has it ever occurred to you that the rumours of Ogasawara's defection could be false and that he might still be in Japan— perhaps hiding here in Tokyo?' asked Kawaji.

Tagusari was speechless.

'Of all the ridiculous things to say!'

'Nevertheless, you have no concrete evidence that he is in America, do you?'

'That's... well, that's true enough, but... our belief that he fled to America is not entirely baseless. After all, the fact that he boarded the American ship was witnessed by several of the shogun's vassals who were in Hakodate at the time. Besides, if Lord Ogasawara really were in Japan, the Nagakuni faction would not have turned a blind eye.'

'And you haven't heard anything about his whereabouts via the members of this Nagakuni faction?'

'Well, no...' Tagusari groaned, at a loss, but after few moments the flow of words came gushing forth again. 'When the Karatsu clan managed to receive official pardon, they pledged that, if by any chance Lord Ogasawara were found to be in Japan, they would apprehend him immediately and hand him over to the authorities. On behalf of the Karatsu clan, I, Sagen Tagusari, do hereby declare that we will not go back on our word.'

'Is that so?' said Kawaji, a slight trace of disappointment on his face.

If this former official from Karatsu had, despite his antipathy for the opposing faction, never doubted Lord Ogasawara's escape abroad, then it was hard not to wonder whether the suspicion that now gripped Kawaji might be delusional.

He bowed and turned to leave. 'By the way,' he added just as he strode out of the meeting room, 'I've ordered a *rasotsu* to be posted at the graveyard of the Tennō-ji temple, not far from where the mistress lives. If the father does decide to pay her a visit, I'll be sure to know about it. Until then, if that woman should come here again, try to reason with her and see that she doesn't cause any more trouble.'

6

'I've also come across somebody connected with the Karatsu clan,' said Kazuki four or five days later, after Kawaji had informed him of his recent sleuthing.

Although they were technically rivals, Kawaji didn't yet feel that way and had only the case in mind. However, he seemed to have hit a dead end and had just been relaying all this to his colleague with a wry smile.

Kazuki, for his part, was still investigating. Not only was the identity of the father still a mystery, but there was also something peculiar about the woman in question.

'I'm from the neighbouring domain, so I imagined I'd have a lot of people in common, but they're surprisingly thin on the ground. Few men from Karatsu have been given positions in the new government, so my investigation was proving pretty fruitless. But then I came across Magobei Akamatsu, this big shot among Nagamichi's supporters—he even once served as the daimyo's chief minister in Edo.'

'One of Nagamichi Ogasawara's supporters? But how can that be?!'

'He was a minor functionary in the Treasury, but, because he was seemingly very capable in economic matters, he was promoted. He's now in charge of exchanging the clan's scrip for national currency.'

'I see.'

'So, I thought I'd meet him and ask him myself. Only, we'll hit a brick wall if he decides to play dumb. After all, you can't rely on a man to talk.'

'Indeed you can't.'

'But it appears that this Akamatsu goes to Yokohama on the fifth day of every month. He even takes official leave in order to do so.'

'Oh? What business does he have there?'

'I've no idea. That's all I've been able to find out. Though I doubt they're sightseeing trips. There's something fishy about it, that's for sure. At any rate, tomorrow is the fifth. I'm going to try to follow him there. Will you join me?'

'With pleasure!'

'I'm told he lives in Takebe-zaka, in the Hongō district. He usually leaves early, so shall we say around seven o'clock? Wait for me on the north side of Suidō Bridge. I'll have Sergeant Imokawa put on guard there.'

The following day, Kawaji arrived just before seven o'clock. From the bridge, he walked down the street on the north side, skirting the Kanda River. Along the southern edge of the road was a steep embankment, while to the north several little hills rose gently up. Which of these was Takebe-zaka? he wondered as he walked. At the foot of one of the slopes stood a couple of rickshaws, waiting for fares, and on the footrest of one was sitting a *rasotsu*, engaged in conversation with the rickshaw driver. When he spotted Kawaji passing him by, however, his face crumpled, and he pretended not to see him. It was Sergeant Imokawa.

Kawaji walked on a little further, but then turned and headed back to the Suidō Bridge. Just then, Kazuki arrived, wearing his usual *suikan*.

Then, as he looked down at the deep ditch, he told Kawaji how, a few days previously, a rickshaw had gone tumbling over the edge not far from Ochanomizu, and how the driver had somehow managed to swim over to the embankment and grab hold of a branch while the fare drowned.

'I'm told that another rickshaw that was coming along the road tried to get out of the way but ended up falling in as well. With so many rickshaws and the like around, maybe they ought to erect a fence along the south side of the road.'

'It's criminal what these rickshaw drivers get away with. They ought to be licensed.'

As they stood there chatting in the bitter cold, they could not help stamping their feet, trying to keep warm. Suddenly, Sergeant Imokawa came running up to them.

'He's on the move!' he shouted.

A few moments later, a rickshaw passed, bearing inside it a man in his forties, with a long, oval face and a serious demeanour.

As it crossed the bridge, the two empty rickshaws appeared. Waving his hand, Imokawa flagged them down.

'I took the liberty of arranging some rickshaws, just in case,' said Imokawa. 'Quickly now, sir!'

Kawaji realized that the rickshaw driver with whom he had seen Imokawa talking earlier had not just been waiting for a fare.

'Follow that rickshaw,' said Kazuki, having already hopped on. 'I believe it's headed for Yokohama.'

The rickshaw had in fact developed like magic. When it first appeared in the summer of the previous year, looking as though somebody had placed a box on top of a two-wheeled cart, everybody laughed at it, but since then it had been improved, and new types were popping up practically every day. Now the wheels were made of iron, and the passenger's seat appeared to have been borrowed from the Western perambulator. Some also had collapsible hoods, and some could carry two passengers, too. However, it still seemed like a ridiculous mode of transport. The rickshaw-pullers did not, as they did in later years, wear smart uniforms and hats; and many simply hitched up their robes and wore a twisted hand-towel about their heads—or worse still, some, even in winter, wore little more than a *fundoshi* about their waist and looked every bit like the ruffian palanquin bearers of yesteryear.

There had already been talk of building a railroad between Tokyo and Yokohama, but nothing had yet been done about it. There was opposition to the project, and, as usual, the most vociferous opponents were to be found among the higher-ups in the Imperial Prosecuting Office.

The journey from Tokyo to Yokohama took more than five hours by rickshaw, so by the time they arrived in the port town it was already past midday. Even so, Kawaji could not help but admit that the journey by rickshaw had been far preferable to walking.

'Well, well,' Kawaji murmured as he saw where the rickshaw in front of him was headed.

Tokyo was still much as it had been during the Edo years, but Yokohama had an air of exoticism about it that blew in with the sea breeze. The streets were wide, and several rickshaws could run abreast of one another.

'He's heading for the foreign settlement!' exclaimed Kawaji.

They kept a safe distance from the rickshaw, lest its fare notice that he was being followed, but from the very outset the possibility had not seemed to cross his mind, and so he entered the foreign settlement without hesitation.

His rickshaw stopped in front of a Western-style house that stood at the foot of the Yato Bridge and faced the road running along the waterfront. There were dozens of people queuing out its front door, all the way to the main street. All of them were Japanese, and all appeared sickly. Akamatsu alighted from the rickshaw and disappeared somewhere around the side of the house.

'Isn't that Doctor Hepburn's house?' asked Kawaji.

The building was elegant and made of wood painted a pale blue; its frontage must have been more than forty feet wide, and while you couldn't really tell how far it went back, it must have covered a good hundred *tsubo*.

7

The name Hepburn was known to Kazuki. Ten years ago, this American physician and missionary had come to Yokohama to preach 'the Jesus faith' and to help the sick and the poor.

'Have you been here before?' asked Kazuki.

'Yes, I have. Last year, towards the end of the eleventh month, there was an incident in which a foreign teacher by the name of Long was attacked by some thugs. He sustained a serious cut to his shoulder and was later carried here on a makeshift stretcher. I was the one ordered to supervise his transportation.'

Just then, a man dressed in white appeared in the front door and was about to begin sorting through the patients in the queue, when suddenly he looked in their direction.

'Hullo!' he called out, making his way towards them. 'It's Chief Inspector Kawaji, isn't it?'

Beneath his white coat, he appeared to be wearing clothes from another world. He was a tall and bearded man in his late thirties, and although he was wearing what looked like a white headscarf, you could see that his hair was cropped in the Western style. Yet there was no doubt about it: this man was Japanese.

Kawaji recognized him as Ginkō Kishida, Doctor Hepburn's assistant. Kishida shook Kawaji's hand in the Western style and, as he asked how he could be of assistance, he looked up and down at Kazuki's odd garb.

Having introduced the two men, Kawaji began to explain: 'We saw a man entering the building just a moment ago. His name is Magobei Akamatsu, and he was once the lord of

Karatsu's chief minister in Edo. We'd like to have a word with him, if possible.'

'Ah, Akamatsu-san! Of course, it's the fifth today, isn't it?'

'I believe he comes here on the fifth of every month. What are these visits for?'

'That's correct. They're… err…' he began, but stopped himself. 'I'm not sure it's my place to tell you. At any rate, please, do come in. If you'll follow me?'

He set off towards the entrance.

The two chief inspectors passed through the entrance and were shown into a large reception room immediately on the left. On the wall hung a picture of the Virgin and Child, and the shelves were adorned with a statuette of Christ, a globe and other curiosities.

'Kishida's involved of all manner of business in Yokohama,' Kawaji explained. 'He started a newspaper, founded a shipping company and even ran an oil company. But since meeting the venerable Doctor Hepburn, he's been utterly devoted to him. Not only is he helping the good doctor to compile Japan's first Japanese–English dictionary, but he also assists him in performing surgery.'

'And you said he was called Ginkō? That's a funny-sounding name, no?'

'Ah, yes. I believe his real name is Ginjirō, but one way or another he seems to have adopted the less-than-flattering nickname. He's a decent sort.'

Presently, they were joined by Kishida and Akamatsu. Kishida was holding what appeared to be a bundle of documents in his hands.

'Are you the gentlemen from the Imperial Prosecuting Office?' asked Akamatsu, forgoing the usual pleasantries.

'And you're interested in the reason for my coming here each month?'

'The fact of the matter is,' said Kazuki with equal candour, 'that your name has come up in our efforts to establish the whereabouts of the Intendant of Iki Province, Lord Ogasawara.'

Akamatsu shot a grave and pensive look at him.

'I see. Well, since you ask, it would appear I can conceal it no longer. As Kishida-san here can confirm, I come here in order to receive letters and remittances from His Lordship in America.'

'Remittances, you say? And what exactly is Lord Ogasawara doing over there?'

'His Lordship has become an advisor to a whaling company somewhere on the west coast of America. I believe the town is called San Francisco. He sends his correspondence by ship every month. I have no way of receiving letters from America at home, and, moreover, since His Lordship is, as you know, in exile, I have had to exercise caution, so I asked the good doctor if he would receive these letters for me. That, gentlemen, is why I come here once a month.'

'I assumed that you had come in connection with this,' said Kishida, setting down the bundle of letters on the table. 'Unfortunately, no post arrived today, but here are the letters that Doctor Hepburn has previously received from Lord Ogasawara.'

Kawaji picked up a few of the letters automatically, but the envelopes were inscribed with only English characters, and he was unable to make out any of it.

Kazuki also picked up an envelope and peered inside it.

'I'm afraid they're all in English,' Kishida laughed. 'His Lordship must have had somebody else write them.'

As he looked at the figure dressed in the *suikan*, his smile almost seemed to mock him.

'You said something about remittances?' said Kazuki, as he extracted the letter. 'Remitted to whom exactly?'

'That's right, err...' Akamatsu hesitated.

'To you?'

'Absolutely not! Nor should I have any reason to receive something like that from His Lordship. It is, in fact, for somebody else.'

'And would that "somebody else" happen to be his mistress, O-Yumi?'

'You're very well informed,' said Akamatsu in astonishment. 'You are correct. Doctor Hepburn then exchanges it for Japanese money and has it delivered to Miss O-Yumi.'

Just then, Kawaji interrupted him.

'Is it possible that the person who delivers it is a woman?'

'Ah, I wonder,' said Kishida, nodding, before briskly striding out of the room.

A little taken aback by this, Kazuki regained his composure only after watching him go.

'Incidentally,' he said, 'are you aware that this mistress of Ogasawara's, this O-Yumi who resides in the Yanaka district of Tokyo, is with child at present?'

Kazuki had cut straight to the chase. Akamatsu's face visibly stiffened.

'What's more, no matter how you look at it, all the evidence points to the conception having occurred after Ogasawara's escape. What do you make of this?'

Akamatsu heaved a deep sigh.

'So, you know about that, as well?' he said. Then, staring off into space, he added: 'Believe it or not, it was the doing of Ogasawara's *ikiryō*.'

'His what?! His *ikiryō*?'

Just then the door opened, and Kishida peered in. Behind him stood a young woman dressed in white, just like him.

Kishida said, 'This is O-Den... She helps us at the hospital, but she's also the one who's been delivering the money.'

Her hair was tied up in the style traditionally worn by married women, and she had on a kimono, but she also wore a choker about her neck, which lent her a beautiful, exotic air.

Kawaji had only heard the tale from the owner of the household-goods shop in Yanaka, but now, seeing this woman, he was left in no doubt that this had to be she.

'Thank you,' he said with a nod.

The nurse then vanished as suddenly as she had appeared.

In the summer of the previous year, she had come knocking on the door of Doctor Hepburn's house together with her leper husband. Now her husband was undergoing treatment, and, alongside nursing him, this virtuous wife lent a youthful and efficient hand in the hospital. (Around ten years later, Chief Superintendent Kawaji would have the 'temptress' O-Den beheaded, but back then only the Devil himself knew this.)

'About that money,' said Kazuki. 'Why didn't you deliver it to Yanaka yourself?'

'It's as the saying goes: despise a monk, and you will despise his robes,' replied Akamatsu. 'Just as there are many who have despise Lord Ogasawara, so too are there those who do not care much for Miss O-Yumi. That's why I've tried to keep her whereabouts as secret as possible. Still, it isn't beyond the realms of possibility that some powerful men in the capital have got wind of it. But, as I am a known supporter of Nagamichi Ogasawara's, there could be no question of my delivering the money. I knew that it would be better for our safety if the courier had nothing to do with us. If O-Yumi and I were seen together, tongues would wag, and that would be dangerous. So, I decided that under no circumstances would I meet O-Yumi in person. I'm ashamed to have had to go to such lengths, but that's why I had to trouble Doctor Hepburn to have the money delivered.'

'I see. So, do you mean to say that men are prohibited from visiting her?'

'Not at all. Only that I myself don't go there.'

Kazuki returned to the strange words that he had heard earlier.

'You were saying something about Ogasawara's *ikiryō*?'

'Yes, I was sceptical about it myself, but not so long ago there was a letter from His Lordship to Miss O-Yumi, in which he apparently said that he would return to Japan from America as an *ikiryō*, so that he might enfold her in his arms once more. Since then, His Lordship has appeared at the house in Yanaka several times, and Miss O-Yumi claims that the pregnancy is a result of this.'

'Of all the absurd things!' cried Kazuki, sneering. 'I don't suppose the letter also said that the *ikiryō* travels by telegraph, did it? Anyway, if you were having nothing to do with O-Yumi, then how could you possibly know all this?'

'Well, it's just that, after she fell pregnant, Miss O-Yumi wrote to me once or twice, you see. As I said, I didn't believe it at first, and I worried that, if she truly was pregnant, and if the other clansmen in Tokyo came to find out about it, there'd be no telling what kind of trouble it would cause.'

'Forgive my asking, but couldn't O-Yumi simply have taken a lover, as some are saying?'

'And just what do you mean by that?' asked Akamatsu, his eyes flashing. 'The only reason I haven't drawn my sword on you is that I know that this investigation is being conducted by the Imperial Prosecuting Office! Why, what you're saying is preposterous! Only those who don't know how much His Lordship loved his O-Yumi, nor how much Miss O-Yumi pined for His Lordship, could think such a thing!'

It must have annoyed Kazuki to hear his words dismissed like this, when only a moment ago the man had spoken of living ghosts.

'So, you're saying that the black and white shadows spotted in the Yanaka graveyard are Ogasawara's *ikiryō*?' muttered Kawaji, as forbiddingly pragmatic as ever.

'You'd think a country like America *could* at least send a man's *ikiryō* by telegraph!' said Ginkō, roaring with laughter under his impressive beard. Immediately, however, he resumed a more solemn demeanour. 'The Virgin Mary conceived by the power of the Holy Spirit. In fact, our own Doctor Hepburn converses with the Holy Spirit daily. Even in this modern age, miracles of faith are possible,' he added, crossing himself.

Doctor Hepburn was seemingly too busy administering treatments, so in the end the chief inspectors were unable to see him. What was apparent, however, was that the letters and money sent by Ogasawara were handled by the saintly doctor himself, proving that Ogasawara had to be in America.

'I'd call that a perfect alibi, wouldn't you?' said Kazuki, a faint, cryptic smile crossing his lips.

It was a curious choice of words, for they seemed to suggest that Ogasawara was across the Pacific Ocean congratulating himself on getting away with something—yet that was exactly how Kawaji felt about it, too.

8

It should be noted at this point that Kazuki and Kawaji were not the only representatives of the Imperial Prosecuting Office to have dealings with Doctor Hepburn. These other men had, moreover, an altogether different purpose in contacting him—one that was only to be expected of the 'Jesus faith'-loathing Imperial Prosecuting Office.

In a letter from Hepburn dated 2 March 1871, he writes:

> *There is nothing we can expect from the Jap. govt. It seems to be directly opposed to Christianity, with the intention of driving it out of Japan entirely. You may be aware of the Christian pamphlet I translated and published a few years ago. The govt. is trying to ascertain the identity of the Japanese who helped me with its publication. To do this, the Imperial Prosecuting Office has dispatched an agent to investigate both me and the individual involved.*

For several days after their suspicions were dispelled and the mystery only deepened, Kazuki seemed troubled.

'For all his show of solemnity,' he told Kawaji, 'that Akamatsu is corrupt. He's fiddling the scrip-exchange.'

'Oh? What makes you say that?'

'It's all very complicated. I've spoken to Kaoru Inoue over at the Treasury, but the long and short of it is this. He says that even if an official in charge of scrip is up to no good, it's nigh impossible to find proof of it these days, so he's advised amateurs like us not to get involved. If you ask me, there's something fishy about that Inoue, too, but I can't exactly do anything on a hunch alone. My instinct tells me Akamatsu's definitely up to something, though.'

'Hmm…'

'And yet, my investigation turned up that his house in Takebe-zaka is small, that he has no family, and that he lives frugally, with only an old maid. On the other hand, that opponent of Nagamichi Ogasawara's, Sagen Tagusari is a real drinker and womanizer; he leads a life of luxury, spending all his time in Yanagibashi and the other pleasure quarters. He may well have had a fortune back in Karatsu, but it just doesn't add up for a low-paid functionary in the Ministry of Popular Affairs.'

'But… what does all this have to do with the woman in Yanaka?'

'I'm not sure. But these are the facts,' said Kawaji.

'I've been thinking about it since the other day, as well. I just can't bring myself to believe what he said about the *ikiryō*. You don't think the child's father could be Akamatsu, do you?'

'It's possible, but if that were so, he could have taken the money to her directly. And if he were trying not to invite suspicion, then why would he go to such lengths as to involve Doctor Hepburn as an intermediary? It's truly baffling. And besides, it's too far-fetched that a man who once served as a daimyo's chief minister in Edo would try to attribute a woman's pregnancy to an *ikiryō*.'

'In that case, isn't it time we asked the woman herself?'

'*Ikiryō* or not, the law has no cause to punish whoever fathered that child, so long as it wasn't Ogasawara, having sneaked back into Japan.'

'That's true enough,' said Kazuki.

'Still, just to be on the safe side, I'm having Tagusari watched by Sergeant Saruki, Akamatsu by Sergeant Imokawa,

183

and Sergeant Ichinohata's keeping an eye on that Koibuchi couple. Who knows whether anything will come of it. They're not a very trustworthy lot, but they'll have to do for now…'

A few days later, on the thirteenth day of the second lunar month, Sergeants Onimaru and Yokomakura rolled up at the headquarters of the Imperial Prosecuting Office, where Kawaji and Kazuki had just arrived.

'We saw it! We saw it!' they both cried out.

'What did you see?' asked Kawaji.

'Ogasawara's *ikiryō*!'

'What on earth are you on about?' Even the ordinarily composed Kawaji raised an eyebrow at this. 'Where?'

'In the graveyard at Yanaka.'

Lost for words, Kawaji fixed the two *rasotsu* in his gaze.

'Oh, you two were still there, were you?'

'Still there?! But you ordered us to keep an eye on it!' they both cried, bowled over by Kawaji's forgetfulness.

Both faces looked drawn with hunger and the colour had vanished from their cheeks. And little wonder: for nearly half a month now, right in the middle of winter, they had been staking out the graveyard in Yanaka.

It was not that Kawaji had forgotten about them entirely; every now and then, they would suddenly pop up in his mind, but he knew that O-Yumi had been receiving visitors and, what was more, after hearing the strange tale from the Koibuchi woman, he had expected word from them any day now—and let half a month slip by in the process.

'Oh, I do apologize. What were you saying about an *ikiryō*, though?' he asked, surprised that these two had even heard of such a thing.

184

'Actually, sir, before we do that,' said Yokomakura, 'there's something else you should know.'

'That's right,' added Onimaru. 'If we don't tell you, you might never believe it.'

The pair were mumbling, their jaws trembling.

'I'm sorry to say so, sir, but, you see, for the last three days, there've been others helping us with the surveillance,' said Yokomakura.

'Others? Who?'

'Well, three nights ago, there was a man by the name of Sagen Tagusari, and another called Hikogorō Koibuchi.'

'What?!'

'Tagusari apparently used to be the chief minister for the Karatsu Domain, but now he's working in the Ministry of Popular Affairs. He said he wanted to catch the guy who got Miss O-Yumi pregnant and asked whether we'd let him join us. He said you'd told him, sir, that we were staking out the area.'

Hearing this reminded Kawaji that he had indeed told Tagusari about the surveillance.

'Then, Tagusari got in touch with this Koibuchi guy, who came along too. Ah, that's right: apparently his wife was more interested in the investigation, but, since a woman with children can't very well stake out a graveyard at night, she sent him instead. He didn't seem too happy about it, truth be told.'

Having mentioned the *rasotsu*'s surveillance in order to rein in their wayward behaviour had, it seemed, backfired.

'Then,' Yokomakura continued, 'the night before last, a guy called Magobei Akamatsu came along. He greeted Tagusari as though he hadn't seen him in a long time—he'd apparently even been the domain's man-in-Edo at one point. He said he'd heard from a lady that two *rasotsu* were keeping watch at the graveyard, so he'd come to see how it was going. I think he had some suspicions about us, though.'

Yokomakura scratched his head.

'Of course, sir, you told us to make sure we weren't spotted, but that was impossible! You can't just sit out there, being buffeted by the wind on a winter's night, without some sake to drink and a fire to keep you warm. Never mind at night: even during the day, we had to keep moving about to keep warm—otherwise, we'd have caught our death!'

'Why didn't you report these other men at once?'

'Tagusari told us not to! He was ever so menacing. And, well, it was only a couple of days.'

'Besides, we thought some company would help distract us from the cold and the boredom.'

'Oh, very well. Proceed with your story.'

'Well, sir, Akamatsu told us about Ogasawara's *ikiryō*. Apparently, he heard it from His Lordship's mistress. Naturally, we all told him there's no such thing. Akamatsu said he was sceptical himself, but that if an *ikiryō* really was visiting the place, he wanted to see it for himself, but he couldn't have the lady knowing about this, so he joined us, crouching behind the gravestones.'

Truly, it was an unexpected gathering of those factions for and against Lord Ogasawara.

'And it appeared at last this morning! Yes, in the early hours, around the tolling of the sixth hour. We were all there. We had a fire going and were talking about all the changes since the Restoration, and—'

'Enough about your idle chatter! What exactly did you see?'

'Well, all of a sudden, in the distance, I thought I could hear a strange, faint sound—it was going *ki-i-kuru, ki-i-kuru*…

We all jumped up to take a look, and there, coming from the vicinity of the house, we saw a shadow floating in mid-air— well, not mid-air exactly, but it seemed to be gliding over the gravestones. It was just as dawn was beginning to break, and the world seemed to be shrouded in a thin layer of ice.'

Perhaps it was all the talk of ghosts and spirits, but Onimaru's narrative had taken an uncharacteristically literary turn.

'He looked like a warrior. He had on a helmet and a *jinbaori*.'

Even Kawaji thought he could feel a drop of perspiration trickling down his back.

'We were all terrified, but we began to creep towards it, with Akamatsu leading the way.'

'He went ahead and stood right in its path,' Yokomakura piped up. 'He was riding in a rickshaw! The sound we'd heard was the noise of the wheels. Only, there was no runner pulling it!'

'What do you mean?' shouted Kazuki.

'Even though there was no runner, the shafts of the rickshaw were parallel to the ground, and just like that it came our way, bearing the warrior along. He was wearing a black-lacquered *hachigane*, a helmet with an enormous two-pronged crest, each prong more than two feet long, and a pitch-black *jinbaori*. Akamatsu cried out, "But... but... isn't that His Lordship?"'

'I saw him, too, sir,' interjected Onimaru. 'Or rather, I didn't see him. You see, there was no face looking out from under the helmet. What there was, I couldn't say. It was as though the air itself had donned the helmet.'

'With a voice like a strangled chicken, Tagusari challenged the ghost before drawing his sword and rushing towards it. And as he did, the faceless warrior spoke. His voice was terrifying beyond words, sir,' said Yokomakura. '"You dare to draw

187

your sword against your lord, Sagen Tagusari," he said. "I have shown myself for the benefit of those who do not believe. Let it be known: that anybody who dares to hinder the nightly visits of Lord Ogasawara's *ikiryō* will be possessed and slaughtered."'

'His words knocked us clean off our feet, sir! Then the rickshaw set off again, making its way between the graves—or rather, no, it went off as though the graves weren't even there, just making that same sound: *ki-i-kuru, ki-i-kuru.*'

Both Kawaji and Kazuki just stared at the two *rasotsu*, unsure what to make of this.

'Th-this must be some kind of a joke,' said Kawaji at last, but his words were perfunctory and meaningless.

'A joke?' said Onimaru. 'If you think this is a joke, sir, then have those three other men brought here and ask them yourself.'

Yokomakura began to stroke his long beard.

'There's one thing I don't understand, though,' he said. 'According to what Akamatsu told Tagusari, it was Ogasawara's *ikiryō* that fathered the woman's child. But if the *ikiryō* doesn't have a body, then how did it manage to get her pregnant?'

Speechless, Chief Inspector Kawaji paused and, only after quite some time, let out a protracted roar:

'*Damn it!*'

9

It was not until a week later that the actual murder took place.

Moreover, it was not by chance that Kazuki and Kawaji found each other at the scene of the crime immediately after the curious incident occurred.

Here is how it happened.

It was the twentieth day of the second lunar month, and the rain had been falling since morning. In those days, of course, the lunar calendar lagged somewhat behind the Western one, so this would have been sometime in late March. Although it was still bitterly cold, the rain already carried the distinctive scent of spring. As usual, Tokyo had become a city of mud. But later in the afternoon, the temperature plummeted, and the showers of rain turned into flurries of spring snow.

That evening, after their offices had closed for the day, Sagen Tagusari and Magobei Akamatsu met at Yanagibashi to have few drinks in the company of some geisha. Later, at around nine o'clock, they hailed rickshaws and headed for Akamatsu's house. By then, Tagusari, who liked a drink and was already a little worse for wear, was in the mood to have some sport with his companion.

There, in Takebe-zaka, they had the old maid prepare some snacks and recommenced their drinking. They asked that the rickshaws wait outside the house and, since it was snowing, invited the two pullers into the kitchen and plied them with sake.

Meanwhile, two *rasotsu* were following these events closely.

In fact, for some while Saruki had been keeping watch over Tagusari, Imokawa over Akamatsu, and Ichinohata over the Koibuchi couple, but, in spite of this, the three *rasotsu* were unaware that these three men had gathered at the graveyard in Yanaka the night on which the aforementioned *ikiryō* had made its appearance. Unable to bear keeping watch in such bitterly cold weather, all three had decided to skip work.

It later transpired that Akamatsu had spotted Imokawa, invited him round, won him over and given him money to go out drinking. The whole thing was a shambles.

Perhaps they knew Kazuki had only asked them to keep an eye on the men as a precaution, and perhaps that was what led to their negligence.

But now that night, the twentieth of the month, acting under strict instructions, Imokawa and Saruki followed the two officials from Yanagibashi to Hongō, winding up in Takebe-zaka. They were already aware that Akamatsu and Tagusari, despite having held positions of influence within the Karatsu Domain, were on opposing sides of the Ogasawara debacle and did not enjoy an especially close relationship, to say the least. Yet after their evening drinking in Yanagibashi, one of them had invited the other to his house.

Something like this had to be reported to the chief inspector. In fact, the two men knew that if they didn't, they would be hauled over the coals for it. As they discussed their observations, they saw the rickshaw-pullers enter the house and begin drinking, and so, surmising that the situation was unlikely to change for some while, Imokawa raced off to the Saga mansion to tell Kazuki, while Saruki rushed to find Kawaji in Kyōbashi.

It was the strangest thing: by chance, the two *rasotsu* were both given the same order to flag down two rickshaws, and, together, the four all made their way to back to Hongō.

The snow was letting up, but there was already a good two inches of it on the ground. At this time of night in this kind of weather, the streets were practically empty, and the few rickshaws carrying people with some business to attend to stood out. There was no moon, but the nocturnal city was bathed in an uncanny light reflected from the snow.

It was a little after eleven o'clock when, not far from Takebe-zaka, Kazuki alighted, leaving Imokawa and the rickshaw behind. There were no footprints or rickshaw tracks on the road running along the canal.

'Kawaji isn't here yet,' Kazuki muttered to himself as he looked around by the light of the snow.

Just then, he spotted two rickshaws crossing the Suidō Bridge one after another. It was Kawaji and Saruki.

Joining together, the four of them then turned left off the main road and began to climb Takebe-zaka. It was a narrow, gently inclining slope, with snow-laden branches of bamboo drooping over the walls on both sides. As he climbed the hill, Kawaji was struck by a most peculiar sensation, but at the time he had no idea what the cause of it was.

Akamatsu's house stood about fifty yards up.

'The rickshaws are gone!' Imokawa whispered to Saruki.

'Tagusari must have gone home,' he replied.

The light was still on in Akamatsu's house, however, and voices could be heard shouting. Just then, the lattice door at the front opened, and five yards from where Kazuki stood frozen to the spot, three figures came clattering out.

'Hey, where are the rickshaws?' a familiar voice shouted, having realized their absence, too. 'Has Tagusari left already?'

The voice belonged to a somewhat drunken Akamatsu.

'Left? But who would he have to pull him?'

'Hey! Mine's gone as well,' shouted one of the rickshaw-pullers. 'Where could they both have gone?'

They followed the rickshaw tracks with their eyes and looked startled when they first noticed the group standing in the shadow of the wall.

'So, we meet again. Chief Inspector Kazuki of the Imperial Prosecuting Office. We were just doing our rounds. How have you been keeping?'

Patently untrue though this was, Akamatsu asked without thinking:

'Have you just arrived?'

'This very minute!'

With no time to doubt them further, and seeming to have forgotten the conversation at Doctor Hepburn's residence the other day, Akamatsu said:

'That's very good of you. Only, I was entertaining a guest here at my house, and he seems to have vanished all of a sudden. We were just looking for him.'

'I'm sure he wouldn't have been so impolite as to leave without saying goodbye,' said Kazuki, cocking his head and looking at the snow.

'But the rickshaws are gone! And you can see their tracks leading off,' Akamatsu suddenly shouted, raising his hand as Kazuki and the others tried to draw nearer. 'Please, don't move.' He turned and called into the house: 'Bring the lanterns, old woman!'

Then, turning back to them with a somewhat more sober look on his face, he began to explain:

'Well, gentlemen, I'm not sure exactly how much the Imperial Prosecuting Office knows already, but, judging from what you said the other day, I'd imagine it might be a fair bit. You see, Tagusari was the leader of the group that made His Lordship anathema within the Karatsu clan. Well, he and I do not see eye to eye, and, ever since the Restoration, even though we both work for the new government, we haven't exactly been on the friendliest of terms. So, the other day, when he and I happened to bump into one another for the first time in a long while, there was much to discuss, and I ended up having a drink with him this evening in Yanagibashi. There had been misunderstandings on both sides—there were some points we were able to clear up, and others that we weren't, so I invited him here, where we could talk to our heart's— Just a moment! Don't move,' he said, raising his arm again. 'Now, be that as it may, just a short while ago, while I was reciting some poetry to him, Tagusari lay down, using his arm as a pillow, and began to drift off. Suddenly, however, he must have felt an urge and got up to go and relieve himself. When he didn't come back, I went to find him, but he was nowhere to be seen. He seemed pretty inebriated, so I wanted to see whether he was sleeping it off somewhere, but, try as I might, I just couldn't find him. It was then that I called these rickshaw-pullers, who'd been drinking in the next room, and when we came out here to check, we found the two rickshaws missing.'

The old woman brought the lanterns.

'It's odd enough that the pullers are here while the rick-shaws themselves have disappeared, but I've just noticed something even more bizarre,' he said, bringing the lantern in his hand lower, so that it lit up the ground. 'Would you look at that! The rickshaw tracks are there, but there are no footprints from the person pulling it.'

Sure enough, there were signs that the rickshaws had been turned around in the snow, and there were even some footprints, too—but when the chief inspectors followed the tracks in the direction in which they had moved off, there were wheel tracks with no footprints between them.

'It was still snowing when we got back, so these must have been made more recently. Let's follow these tracks,' Akamatsu said, setting off, lantern in hand.

Wearing a look of bewilderment, the two rickshaw-pullers followed behind him. As they made their way down the gently sloping hill, Kazuki and others set off after them. They could see all the way down the hill the footsteps they had left as they came up, but they couldn't really tell whether there were any footsteps from before that.

'He's right, you know,' Kawaji groaned. 'That must've been what gave me that odd feeling earlier on—the wheel tracks without any footprints!'

The wheel tracks overlapped an awful lot, but if you looked carefully enough, you could tell that there was more than one set. They went down the fifty or so yards of Takebe-zaka, now overlapping, now parting, before cutting across the main road and vanishing over the embankment of the river.

It was only after half an hour of frantic searching in the dark that there, below the embankment of the Kanda River, two rickshaws were found half-submerged. And it was a good hour after that, and after having sent for more lanterns and several ropes, that the two rickshaws were hauled out of the river, along with the drowned corpse of Sagen Tagusari.

'There was nothing I could have done to prevent this,' Akamatsu sighed. 'Though it does rather unavoidably cast suspicion on me.'

As he looked down at the terrible sopping-wet corpse lying on the snow-covered embankment, he shuddered.

'Not only were our relations as I described previously,' he continued, 'but after he came to my house, he had the temerity to disparage His Lordship and contradict me. I'm sure these rickshaw-pullers must have heard us arguing. Of course, they were drinking in the kitchen, but you've seen how small my house is, and the walls are made of mere paper.'

Their teeth chattering in the cold, the two rickshaw-pullers nodded.

'Still, my recitation seemed to lull him to sleep. Say, did you two happen to hear me reciting the verses?'

'We did!'

'It was after that that all this commotion began. But surely you don't think that I bundled Tagusari into a rickshaw, pulled him all the way down the hill and pushed him over the edge, before making my way back up?'

'And what about the second rickshaw?' said Kazuki, casting a quizzical look at Akamatsu.

'That's just it!' he replied. 'I don't know what it means either. But there's no way that one man could pull two rickshaws. He'd have to go up and down the hill twice over, and if I'd done that, there's no way that these gentlemen wouldn't have noticed.'

'Yes, that's quite right,' the rickshaw men agreed. 'We could hear him reciting the poetry the whole time.'

Despite this agreement, however, they exchanged bewildered looks with one another.

'What puzzles me is that there are no footprints,' Kawaji grumbled again. 'No matter how you look at it, a rickshaw needs somebody to pull it. You don't have any ideas, do you, Kazuki?'

'I'm afraid not,' he replied. 'I can't fathom why there were two rickshaws. Was one empty, or was it carrying someone other than Tagusari-san?'

'It must have been His Lordship!' Akamatsu suddenly exclaimed, his serene features trembling. 'Lord Ogasawara must have been riding in the other rickshaw! Yes, that night in Yanaka, His Lordship appeared riding in a rickshaw with nobody pulling it. His *ikiryō* must have lured away the disloyal Tagusari and meted out the ultimate punishment!'

As Akamatsu lifted his icy eyes up to the dark sky above, Kawaji thought he could see, drifting down the snow-lit slope, the ghostly apparition of two driverless rickshaws, one carrying Tagusari, the other carrying a warrior in a pitch-black *jinbaori* and a jet-black helmet with a long crest.

10

The following night, a strange ceremony took place on Takebezaka. Two empty rickshaws were positioned in front of Magobei Akamatsu's house, and opposite them three braziers were lit. The body of Sagen Tagusari, having been conveyed to the Imperial Prosecuting Office already, was brought back and laid there. Except for his face, his whole body was covered in green bamboo leaves.

A series of stools had been set up along one side of the hill, and on these sat the assorted grandees of the Imperial Prosecuting Office in all their finery, their faces grave and austere. They were joined by old Manabe and his daughter, as well as Kawaji. The gradient was so exceedingly gentle that it was not at all uncomfortable sitting there, but the snow had of course melted and was now replaced by mud.

On the opposite side, five *rasotsu* sat cross-legged on a straw mat, holding their instruments in their laps.

Beside Kazuki in his *suikan* stood Akamatsu, dumbfounded by the spectacle before him—and most of all by the sight of a golden-haired, blue-eyed *miko* bathed in the light of the fires.

Since the Imperial Prosecuting Office was at a loss to explain the curious events of the previous night, the *miko* had been called in to summon the spirit of the deceased and solve the mystery.

The large *kaen-daiko* rang out, struck by Sergeant Onimaru. The other four then joined in, calling forth the strange, eerie strains of the *kagura* music.

> *Awariya, asobihasutomo, mōsanu, asakurani,*
> *Amatsukami, kunitsukami, orimashimase…*

Holding the *kagura* bells in one hand, the *miko* began to sing and dance.

> *Awariya, asobihasutomo, mōsanu, asakurani,*
> *Naruizuchimo, orimashimase…*

Her beautiful yet extremely slow chanting carried on.

> *Awariya, asobihasutomo, mōsanu, asakurani,*
> *Sagen Tagusari no mitama, mairitamae!*

As her chanting swelled to its climax, the *kagura* bells rang out.

'*Ima… mairu!… I am… the spirit… of Sagen Tagusari…*'

In that instant, the uncanny voice of Tagusari's spirit raised goosebumps on Akamatsu's back.

'*For the first time since arriving in the land of the dead… I can see the land of the living without hindrance… I now know… that Lord Ogasawara never did go to America… At Hakodate, he boarded the American ship… but when it called in at Yokohama… he stole ashore and hid himself in Tokyo…*'

'What?!' came a cry from the audience. However, this was not Akamatsu but Kawaji.

'*As he hid in Tokyo, Lord Ogasawara ventured out to visit O-Yumi in Yanaka regularly… They did not live together, lest he be discovered and O-Yumi implicated in the crime... And yet, he could not stop seeing her... This was very typical of His Lordship...'*

'That is an outrageous thing to say!' exclaimed Akamatsu.

'Once or twice, Lord Ogasawara was spotted at the graveyard in Yanaka... Each time, he escaped by putting on a paulownia helmet and a jinbaori that he always carried to disguise himself... This, too, was typical of His Lordship...

'Of course, Akamatsu knew all this... In fact, he even embezzled his superiors' money in order to help His Lordship... What's more, Akamatsu had no direct contact with Lord Ogasawara at all... and just delivered the money straight to O-Yumi... who, in case she should ever be questioned... went to the trouble of asking a certain American in Yokohama to make it look as though His Lordship was sending the money from the United States...

'As they had feared, the Imperial Prosecuting Office eventually came to question this American... They were shown Lord Ogasawara's letters from America... One of the officers was fooled, but the other, who knew a little English, saw through it immediately...'

Hearing this, Kawaji winced.

'But there was one person who had known all this all along... And that was I, Sagen Tagusari...'

In that instant, to the astonishment of all, the mouth of Tagusari's corpse even appeared to move.

'To catch Lord Ogasawara and turn him over to the authorities... I thought I would first have to flush him out... So, I kept a close watch on Akamatsu's movements... and saw that he was up to something strange... Akamatsu realized this and offered me money to keep quiet...'

'My only dishonour was in giving you money... Your greed knew no bounds!' cried Akamatsu, as though forgetting himself. He looked around in alarm, but nobody said a word.

'To my shame, I said nothing... I, the leader of the Nagakuni faction in the capital, was no better than the Nagamichi faction's Akamatsu...

'We thought that nobody else knew... But the source of our failure lay elsewhere... O-Yumi fell pregnant... and this was spotted by a certain meddlesome woman...

'Akamatsu had been worried about this for some time... If it were to become known... If the Nagakuni faction were to discover that Ogasawara himself was the father of the child... he would find himself in danger... But if the Nagamichi faction were to believe that the child was the result of adultery... then O-Yumi would be in danger...

'The very notion that it could have been His Lordship's ikiryō was patently absurd, but it was our only way out of a desperate situation...'

As he watched Akamatsu's face turn ashen, Kawaji could feel the blood rush from his own cheeks, which had been burning only a moment ago.

'When our attention turned to that meddlesome woman, I panicked... If she caused a fuss and the members of the Nagakuni faction took notice, there would be trouble... Meanwhile, the Imperial Prosecuting Office had ordered some rasotsu to keep watch on the graveyard in Yanaka... If the truth were exposed, both Akamatsu and I could be sure that we would suffer the consequences...

'So, unless the meddlesome woman and Imperial Prosecuting Office saw His Lordship's ikiryō, we would find ourselves boxed into a corner...

'After hastily discussing it with Akamatsu, we realized there was no need to physically show them... Buying off the rasotsu and that meddlesome woman's husband would have the same effect... So, we decided to give them a lot of money and have them tell tall tales about a ghostly warrior...'

Kawaji turned and glared at Onimaru and Yokomakura, his eyes as incandescent as the flames in the braziers.

Perhaps they were deaf to the lament of the deceased that was coming from the *miko*'s mouth, but Onimaru, who besides his drum had a gong as well, and Yokomakura, who had his flute, just kept striking and blowing on their instruments like madmen.

'*The foolish* rasotsu *were easy enough to pay off... but we weren't so sure about the woman's husband... In the end, however, he too agreed...*

'*Though he was once a proud samurai from Mito, he had fallen on hard times long ago and wanted to get one over on his henpecking wife...*'

Hikogorō Koibuchi was not present at this scene, but in later years his wife would leave him and go on to greater things.

'Tell them what happened next,' said Akamatsu through gritted teeth, half in defiance and half in resignation.

'*Soon, however, I began to worry... I wondered how long a deception like this could hold up... Then, I received word from Akamatsu... He was even more worried than I was... We met in Yanagibashi to talk things over...*

'*Now I realize that his biggest concern was me... He thought that I might betray him at any moment and he had to deal with me while he still could...*

'*Akamatsu got me drunk and brought me back to his house in Takebe-zaka, where he plied me with even more alcohol... Between that and waking up in the land of the dead, I recall nothing... But I fear he must have laced my drink with sleeping pills procured somewhere in Yokohama...*

'*While plying me with this sake, he stepped out for a moment and started to position the two rickshaws...*'

In a flash, Kazuki shot up and set about standing the two rickshaws facing one another.

'He stacked the shafts on top of each other...'

Kazuki did as the *miko* said, and then bound the four poles together with a length of thin twine.

'They were tied so that they would hold the shafts firmly but snap under the right pressure...'

Kawaji's eyes were bulging. Before him was no longer a rickshaw, but a rather bizarre-looking four-wheeled chariot!

'Later, as the recital continued, I fell asleep... He carried me outside, sat me in one of the rickshaws and tied me to it, using the same thin twine...'

By now everybody was sitting there frozen, their eyes wide with astonishment, for, following the *miko*'s words, Kazuki had picked up Tagusari's body and was placing it in the rickshaw.

'It was all over in the blink of an eye... Akamatsu gave the rickshaw a push, and off it went all by itself...'

The *kagura* bells rang out.

And sure enough, all by themselves, the two rickshaws set off slowly down the gently sloping hill.

'Akamatsu then returned to the tatami room and began to make a commotion... The two drivers who had been drinking in the next room, oblivious to all this, then joined him...'

The two rickshaws appeared to move as one, gradually gaining speed as they progressed down the slope, until at last they vanished over the edge of the embankment. From where they were sitting, not even a splash could be heard. The grandees of the Imperial Prosecuting Office were speechless.

'As it had been snowing that day, Akamatsu believed he could have the drivers testify to the mysterious absence of footprints left in the show... But even if it hadn't snowed, he reasoned that it would have been the same with the mud...

'*Immediately after that, two members of the Imperial Prosecuting Office turned up, lending credence to his story... But even had it just been the two rickshaw-pullers, he was sure that things would go smoothly...*

'*Now I realize that it was Akamatsu who concocted the story about the warrior being carried through the graveyard by the driverless rickshaw... so he must have already been thinking of ways in which to murder me even then...*'

The *miko*'s voice was becoming fainter and fainter.

'*Because the two rickshaws fell over the embankment one after the other, the twine holding them together snapped, as did the twine holding me in place... That is how I came to find myself in the land of the dead...*'

The *miko*'s golden-haired head slumped forward.

Suddenly, Kawaji jumped to his feet. 'Tell us where Lord Ogasawara is hiding!' he shouted.

'*His Lordship is en route to America...*' came the faint, otherworldly reply.

With that, the *miko* fell silent, as though having lapsed into deep slumber.

A picture of composure, Sergeant Onimaru struck the *kaen-daiko* twice in quick succession, bringing the ceremony to an end. As he did so, Akamatsu collapsed onto the muddy ground.

'I'll deal with him,' said Kazuki. 'You lot, go and fetch the body and the rickshaws out of the water again.' He then turned to Kawaji. 'The show seems to be over.'

Fixing Onimaru and Yokomakura in his baleful gaze, Kawaji was about to go running after them, but Kazuki barred his way.

'Wait,' he said. 'They're like cleaning rags. You can't use them without sullying your own hands, though they do have their uses. I'd appreciate it if you'd go easy on them in this case, if only for my sake.'

Kazuki smiled sweetly as the five *rasotsu* went racing down the hill.

Across the way, Esmeralda, dressed in her *miko*'s attire, approached old Manabe and his daughter. Standing there in her long, specially made scarlet *hakama*, she curtseyed to them.

'*Bonjour!* I'm very pleased to see you again, Mademoiselle O-Nui…'

*

A brief digression on Nagamichi Ogasawara:

It was not until the middle of the fifth year of Meiji, 1872, that the Class-A war criminal Nagamichi Ogasawara, who had been hiding all along in the Hongō's Tsumakoi-zaka, reappeared, having kept a close eye on the release of Takeaki Enomoto. At the time, however, he sent a report of his homecoming to the new government, claiming that in the second year of Meiji, while voyaging from Hakodate to Tokyo, his ship had run adrift because of the winds and waves, and that only now was he able to return to Japan. At any rate, just as he had calculated, he was not subjected to any punishment.

Ogasawara lived until the twenty-fourth year of Meiji, 1891. Having sired more children in his twilight years, he died peacefully and was buried in the graveyard at Yanaka.

THE HANGED MAN AT THE EITAI BRIDGE

The following relates the particulars of an exceptionally difficult case, in which a man was found hanging from the railing of the Eitai Bridge over the Sumida River. Though it was clearly a case of murder, it was also apparent that the suspect could not have been at the scene of the crime when the murder took place.

> — From a report made by Chief Inspector Toshiyoshi Kawaji of the Imperial Prosecuting Office

1

One fine spring evening, Keishirō Kazuki was walking with his colleague Toshiyoshi Kawaji through the Saga mansion in the Gomon neighbourhood of Yamashita, when suddenly he heard a voice calling him. As he turned around, he saw that it was Naotsugu Manabe.

'So, you've brought him with you again, have you?' said the old man, grimacing. His daughter, O-Nui, was standing close behind him as usual. 'I thought I told you not to go bringing people from other domains here without permission?'

'Greetings, Uncle,' said Kazuki, bowing. 'You know, although Kawaji here is from Satsuma, he really doesn't pay much attention to all that. Why, you wouldn't even know he's from that place!'

'He has a Satsuma accent, doesn't he?'

'Yes, but that sort of thing's inevitable. It's a question of attitude.'

'Disregarding your roots is also a question of attitude. And not exactly an admirable one, either! A man like that cannot be a decent sort. There'll be no chance of his getting on in life!'

'But, Uncle, Kawaji is the same as me: a humble chief inspector in the Imperial Prosecuting Office.'

'It's your *future* prospects that I'm interested in!'

Old Manabe clearly had a strong sense of loyalty to his roots, but, after letting slip this glimmer of his private views, he then seemed to recall another source of indignation that was closer to home.

'More importantly,' he said, 'you still haven't sent that French woman back, have you?'

'I haven't, but that's nothing to do with me. The powers that be at the Imperial Prosecuting Office won't permit her return on account of her skills as a *miko*—skills that you yourself have witnessed.'

For a moment, the old man fixed his gimlet eyes on Kazuki, but in the end he shrugged.

'Have it your way, Kazuki. But O-Nui has received two further proposals lately.'

'How lovely for her…' As Kazuki watched O-Nui blush and tug at her father's sleeve, he asked, 'And who are the suitors?'

'Father, please!' she cried.

'Kazuki, you're a grown man of twenty-three. I won't be kept waiting for someone if it's a pointless exercise. One of them came from Heima Tsunakawa, if you must know. He serves at the Ministry of the Imperial Household. He's tried his luck any number of times before, but O-Nui has always refused him. Only three days ago, his parents demanded an explanation, wanting to know what our objections were. Tsunakawa is a man of pedigree, intelligence and good looks. He could have his pick of suitable women.'

'He'd never do,' said Kazuki, shaking his head.

'Whatever do you mean?'

'He's the sort of man who'd sell his own mother to get on in life. If that egotist ever fell in love with a woman, he'd be crazy about her for a while, but soon enough he'd lose interest and throw her out without giving it a second thought.'

Manabe stared at Kazuki in astonishment.

'You're a fine one to talk!'

'I won't say another word against him. Only, please, don't choose him. Where did the other one come from?'

'That is an altogether curious tale,' the old man began. 'But it's not for you to know just yet. For now, suffice it to say that there *is* another one. Let's go, O-Nui.'

And with that, he turned and walked off.

For a few moments afterwards, Kazuki watched them go. Then, as the two chief inspectors made their way towards Kazuki's house, Kawaji turned and said:

'Say, did you see his daughter's face?'

'Of course I did. What of it?'

'I meant the look on her face when you advised them to turn down that whatever-his-name-was.'

'Oh? And what kind of face did she make?'

'Well, I wouldn't quite say her eyes were sparkling, but something along those lines anyway.'

'How very uncharacteristically observant of you,' said Kazuki, laughing. 'Tsunakawa's a very unimpressive man. She was probably relieved to hear somebody say it wouldn't work.'

'Is that all, I wonder?'

'Meaning?'

'Could she have been relieved because it was *you* saying it?'

'And why would that be the case, Kawaji?'

'The very fact that you would speak ill of somebody else's proposal of marriage is a sure sign that you have feelings for the girl. Or rather, I'm not putting it very well, but isn't that at least the impression that Miss O-Nui must have got?'

'Nonsense! There are plenty of instances where people raise objections to a proposal out of sheer kindness. I'm sorry, but if I had any wicked intentions, I would never have said anything!'

'Wicked intentions?'

Kazuki looked a little shaken by this.

'Miss O-Nui once said she believed that you loved her. Would you refute these words?'

Kazuki walked on in silence.

'Why don't you put the old man out of his misery?'

'I don't have time for marriage and the like just yet.'

'And the same applies to that French girl, does it?'

'Of course.'

'But why? Why can't you get married?'

'Because of my work,' said Kazuki, quickening his pace. 'Let's just leave it.'

When they reached the house that Kazuki rented, Esmeralda came out, as she always did, and gave him something called *un grand baiser*.

It was a familiar sight, but each time Kawaji saw it, he couldn't help but see in his mind's eye the question mark that appeared in Western books. It pertained not so much to Kazuki's actions as it did to his state of mind.

As it happened, there was no particular reason for Kawaji's visit to the Saga mansion; it was, as usual, just an excuse to continue the discussion they had been having en route home from the office, about whether or not there could be such a thing as a just government.

Kazuki ushered Esmeralda into the next room and fetched some sake. The discussion continued, but, for one reason or another, their talk soon turned to the great samurai Saigō, Ōkubo and Kido, and which of them was the greatest man.

'I believe that Saigō once said there's nothing more formidable than a man who has no want of name, money, fame or rank,' said Kazuki. 'Yet Saigō himself is one such man. They say he had a hand in appointing the directorate of the Imperial Prosecuting Office. Why he wasn't made the director is beyond me.'

'He's too grand,' said Kawaji with a wry smile.

'Yes, that's true enough. After all, he did once serve as supreme commander. Ever since the Restoration, though, his mind seems to be elsewhere. He leaves just about everything in the hands of Kido and Ōkubo. His surfeit of money and rank, formidable though it is, is turning out to be no good thing. Then again, a man with his brand of charisma is a rarity in this country.'

'Saigō is without question a top-notch man. Everybody who meets him is always very taken with his charm, but just think how many people a man can meet over the course of a life—it can only be in the thousands,' said Kawaji coolly. 'But Ōkubo... Now there's a man who knows how to organize things. A man with that kind of power can change the lives of tens of thousands, whether they know him personally or not. Speaking for myself, it's Ōkubo I'd be afraid of.'

Just then, Esmeralda called Kazuki from the neighbouring room.

Kazuki stood up and began to say something in French. Kawaji couldn't understand a word of it, of course, but the girl's voice sounded like the chirping of some Western bird, although with a hint of complaint about it. In response, Kazuki's voice also took on a note of irritability, and in the end it became clear that they were quarrelling.

Suddenly, Kawaji got to his feet and stepped outside.

Around twenty minutes later, Kazuki sat down again, and, just as he turned quizzically to look at the door, Kawaji strolled back in.

'I'm sorry about that,' said Kazuki, scratching his head. 'Our little tiff is over now.'

Kawaji smiled wryly, without asking what it had been about.

'I really ought to be going,' he said. 'Only, before I do, I ran into O-Nui out there. She seemed worried about you and had come to check on you without telling old Manabe.'

Kawaji's face suddenly took on a serious expression.

'I availed myself of the opportunity to ask her about that other proposal… It isn't of marriage, per se. Apparently, Lord Iwakura has asked her to be his adopted daughter.'

'What?!'

Even Kazuki's head was turned by this most unexpected news. He hurriedly donned his straw sandals and stepped outside.

'She may not have been forthcoming with all this, but she wasn't exactly hiding it either,' Kawaji added. 'Apparently Manabe received word from Lord Iwakura's people the other day, but that was all she knew. In any case, the old man doesn't seem to have taken it particularly seriously. And on that note, I really must be getting home. No, thank you, I can see myself out.'

After a couple of steps, Kawaji turned around.

'You know, thinking of the great men of state today, I'd have to say that Lord Tomomi Iwakura is the most terrifying.'

2

'Kazuki, I've received a rather odd request to guard somebody.'

Kawaji's announcement came around ten days later—it was the third year of Meiji, and, while the troubles of the world around continued, the cherry blossoms were beginning to fall, unnoticed.

'To guard somebody? Who?'

'A man called Kokuten Kodama.'

'Kodama!' exclaimed Kazuki, while Kawaji put on a puzzled expression.

'Have you heard of him?'

'Err, yes... lately, Kawaji.'

'What do you mean, "lately"?'

'Well, I'd prefer to hear what you have to say first.'

'I'm surprised you've heard of him. He's such a reclusive figure. In fact, I found out about him only recently as well, but he's supposed to be Lord Iwakura's right-hand man—or even, so they say, his brain. You see, in the years before the Restoration, Lord Iwakura, for all his grand designs, had become a recluse in the old capital. But during that period, he seemingly devised various secret plans to revolutionize society. Those helping him were known as the Willow Lane Group. Have you heard of them?'

'No, never.'

'Well, in Kyoto, at a place called Willow Lane, in the Muromachikashira district just north of Imadegawa, Lord Iwakura had a number of secret agents working for him at his hideaway. The head of these was none other than Kodama. Since the Restoration, however, Iwakura has effectively become one of the most powerful figures in the new government, whereas Kodama has vanished from public view. Few people know what's become of him. I myself found out only after making some enquiries. At any rate, he seems still to work for Lord Iwakura's secret organization. He's listed as private secretary to the Iwakura household.'

'A man of many talents,' Kazuki laughed. 'Does he have bodyguards?'

'About a week ago, Kodama was set upon by an assassin here in Tokyo, in Kanda's Renjaku-chō district. While he was riding in a palanquin, a young man suddenly appeared from an alleyway and stabbed him in his right thigh before fleeing the scene. There goes another one who's slipped the net!'

'But I didn't see a report on that.'

'Kodama's lot didn't want word getting out. Lord Iwakura is, I think, widely misunderstood, but as for his right-hand man, who did things around the time of the Restoration that earned him a reputation as one of the most cunning men in all Japan, I doubt there's any dearth of reasons that people might want to see him dead even now. So, when His Lordship grew concerned, he took the matter up with Saigō, who mentioned my name and told him to leave it with me. At least, that's what Kaieda told me when he gave me my orders.'

'I see,' responded Kazuki.

'So, I went to see Kodama yesterday.'

'Oh?'

'Lord Iwakura's mansion stands just outside the Hibiya Gate. Kodama doesn't live there, but his house backs directly onto the mansion. The door doesn't even have a nameplate, so it isn't the sort of place that people would notice.'

'Clever fellow...'

'It's difficult to describe him in a few words. He must be around fifty. His hair is bizarre: closely cropped all round, like a chestnut in its burr. Anyway, boil him or roast him, he's a hard nut to crack, and every bit as indigestible. I suppose it's little wonder that Iwakura keeps him close. He was lying on his side, still recovering from his thigh injury, but there's a real strength in his voice. "Ah, you must be that bodyguard Saigō sent," he said. "Pleased to meet you." But I had the distinct impression I was just in the way. Oh, yes, there was one other

214

thing he did say, though. "I appreciate your guarding me," he said, "but I don't want people from the Imperial Prosecuting Office traipsing in and out of my house, and I certainly don't want anybody knowing that I'm being guarded." Saying that only made me more determined. Which means that, for the time being, this is what I'll be doing... Only, how is it that you've come to hear of him lately?'

'That's just it,' replied Kazuki. 'I came across him in connection with what you told me about Lord Iwakura's designs on O-Nui.'

'Oh?'

'Well, the story just seemed so far-fetched. But when I looked into it, it turned out to be right enough. While it's true that old Manabe didn't take it seriously, and that some of the details are still unclear, I understand that the proposal was made through a third party and that the person who came with the proposal was none other than Iwakura's private secretary, Kokuten Kodama.'

'What!?'

'The only thing was, old Manabe says he has no recollection of having ever set eyes on the man. Then, when I looked into Ōkuma's part in this, I found that somebody else—another girl from Saga, would you believe?—had received the very same proposal. That being said, this girl, too, is a renowned beauty, just like O-Nui.'

'Hmm...'

'After that, I ordered our five usual suspects to go and find out whether there were any other such stories going about town. Naturally, I didn't expect them actually to find anybody who'd received such an offer, but there are always rumours. I didn't put much faith in them, but they do have a reasonable nose for this sort of investigation. Believe it or not, I've received three reports so far!'

'Really?' exclaimed Kawaji.

'They're all renowned beauties from families that used to be retainers of the shogun, or at least from clans loyal to him. Now the families are all eking out pitiful lives with no prospects at all. I've only received the three reports, but at this rate, there's bound to be more of the same going on.'

Kawaji stared at Kazuki in astonishment.

'In other words, Lord Iwakura's building himself a pretty little collection,' said Kazuki.

'But to adopt them?! Doesn't he have four or five daughters already? Why would he want to adopt more?'

'And why is he targeting only beautiful women?' said Kazuki, looking puzzled. 'There are any number of men in the new government who've attained high office, only to keep mistresses and to indulge their pleasures. But Iwakura? He didn't strike me as the type. But then, common sense would suggest that any man, having worked his way to the top of government, would be tempted by the luxuries afforded by extreme wealth. What do you think?'

Kawaji was at a loss for words.

'Kodama is a man who worked busily behind the scenes during the Restoration, yet now he seems to be working as Lord Iwakura's private pimp. You'd think the recent attack would be the result of the former, but we surely can't rule out the latter,' said Kazuki.

He looked straight into Kawaji's eyes.

'Are you still willing to act as Kodama's bodyguard?'

Kawaji thought for a moment, and then replied with a serious expression:

'I am.'

Then, a few moments later, he added: 'That being said, I really couldn't manage it all by myself. Maybe I should take one of those *rasotsu* as an assistant. What do you think?'

3

In the blink of an eye, the garden of the Hepburn residence in the Yokohama Foreign Settlement had burst into a lush, vivid green. The rear of the house backed onto a street running alongside the canal, and, for more than two hours now, Kawaji had been gazing at the beautiful blossom on the dozen or so tall trees lining it, behind an iron railing.

Kawaji had no idea what kind of trees they were. They were as large as cherry trees, although their branches didn't spread out as much, and their red-and-white petals looked even smarter and more elegant than cherry blossom. They did not look Japanese and Kawaji could not take his eyes off them.

He was standing at the foot of the Yato bridge, which constituted one corner of the more or less triangular plot of land on which the Hepburn residence stood. From there, you could see both the road running along the waterfront and the alley passing behind the house. Ships of all sizes were afloat in the springtime harbour, but the sight of them no longer held any novelty for Kawaji.

Today there were dozens of people lined up along the main street outside Doctor Hepburn's house, and, until a few moments ago, Kodama's palanquin had also been in that queue. Now, at last, it seemed to have entered the clinic.

The wound on Kodama's thigh, which had appeared to be healing, had become infected. He was worried, having heard that Masujirō Ōmura had died of something similar, and had requested that the renowned doctor make a house call. Doctor Hepburn had informed him that he had too many patients to countenance that, but that Kodama could come and see him at the clinic in Yokohama if he so wished. And so, Kodama had little choice but to go there by palanquin. The doctor may not have appreciated that he was dealing with Lord Iwakura's right-hand man, but it is unlikely that his reply would have been different, even had his patient been a great minister of state.

And so, Kodama had travelled to Yokohama, but when he arrived there, he was astonished to find that he would be made to wait in the line like any ordinary man. When Doctor Hepburn's assistant, Ginkō Kishida, told this to Kodama's attendants, they flew into a rage, but Kodama showed his true character when, from inside the palanquin, he ordered them to wait as they were bidden.

That was some three days ago, and this was now his second visit to Doctor Hepburn's clinic. It was also ten days since Kawaji and Kodama had first met and, of course, Kawaji had accompanied him. The palanquin was carried by two bearers plus four attendants, but Kawaji and his dogsbody, Sergeant Imokawa, kept watch from a distance so that nobody would notice them.

'Sir!' cried Imokawa, as he came running through the gate. He was not wearing his *rasotsu*'s uniform, of course, and had hitched up his kimono, tucking the hem into his waistband. 'He's just come out. But a man in the queue of patients suddenly spotted him getting into the palanquin, and now he's ranting and raving at him!'

Kawaji made a dash towards the house.

By the gate, the line of people had broken up and formed a large, irregular circle, in the middle of which there was a man remonstrating.

'Now see here, Kodama!' He was around twenty-six—an artisan, by all appearances. 'In the old days, I was paid handsomely, and even after the Restoration I served as chief of the Yokohama Port Raw Silk Inspection Office, but now I've been reduced to cutting hair for the likes of foreign sailors, and it's all because of you!'

From his palanquin, Kodama stared out at the man berating him. His eyes were narrowed, but there was a strange glint in them.

Besides the four attendants, there were the two palanquin bearers, all of them ashen-faced, all of them standing there stock-still.

'Oh, don't worry,' the man ranted on. 'I don't have a razor blade on me. In fact, I cut my finger on a razor blade and it's given me a whitlow. It's so painful that I've had to come here. Even if I had a dagger, I wouldn't be able to hold it. So, you needn't worry yourself. For now, just listen to what I have to say.'

Kodama said nothing. Not because of he was reassured by the man's words, of course, but because he was overwhelmed by the look of menace being directed at him.

Though the man may have looked like a mere artisan, he had a tremendous intensity, even greater than that of a samurai. Truly, he was a man filled with anger and curses, and for a moment even Kawaji felt intimidated.

'You may be Lord Iwakura's private secretary, but you're also, so it would seem, the general manager of his woman-hunt.'

'Chief Inspector, arrest this man,' said Kodama, speaking for the first time. 'And don't let him go until I tell you to do so.'

Kawaji approached them. The man greeted him with baleful eyes.

'So, you're from the authorities, are you?' said the man. 'So be it. If you throw me in jail, there'll be nothing more you can do to add to my misfortune.'

He grinned and placed both his hands behind his back. There was a bandage on his right middle finger—this must have been the injury he had just described.

'Wait!' a voice shouted.

It was Kishida, standing behind the palanquin in his white coat. Kawaji had already spotted him and assumed that he had come out to see Kodama off.

'This patient may have to undergo an operation. Are you really going to arrest him, knowing that?'

Just as he was about to take a rope from Imokawa, Kawaji turned to Kodama, rather flustered. Seeing that Kodama did not deign to speak, however, Kawaji turned to the man and said in a low voice:

'I will not tolerate this abuse of a gentleman of rank any more. If you leave now, quietly, this matter will go no further.'

'Is that so? Very well. There seems little point venting grievances like this here anyway. I've said all I had to say. And you may well tell me to leave, but if I don't get treatment for this finger, the pain will be intolerable. It's Kodama who should be leaving.'

Having said this, he grinned provocatively and made his way back into the disorganized queue.

'Chief Inspector, Kishida-san, would you mind stepping this way with me for a moment? I'd like to have a word with you both,' said Kodama.

Kodama gave his orders, and the palanquin set off through the crowd of patients. He told them to stop somewhere quieter, and, having passed through the gate, the palanquin bearers set him down at the rear of the building, on the spot where Kawaji had been standing only a short while ago.

'My leg aches, so you'll have to forgive me for not getting out,' he said, lifting the curtain. 'I am indebted to you both for your assistance just now, and feel I owe you some explanation.'

He poked his close-cropped head out of the palanquin.

'Say, Kishida, what exactly are these trees?' he asked.

'Those, sir? They're called dogwood. Doctor Hepburn brought them over from America and planted them almost ten years ago now.'

'I see. They're even lovelier than our cherry trees,' Kodama said with perfect composure.

He was a little on the heavy side, but he was not portly, and, with his closely cropped hair, he had an unusual kind of elegance. His eyes were narrow and his lips heavy, and though you could not say he was good-looking, he nevertheless had a dignified air about him that inspired confidence and loyalty.

Kodama ordered his four attendants and the two palanquin bearers to stand aside and keep watch a short distance away. He then looked at Imokawa, but, recognizing that he answered to Kawaji, refrained from saying anything to him.

'Now, where was I?' he said, returning to the matter in hand. 'Chief Inspector, since you came so highly recommended by Saigō-sensei, I suspect you must already know a certain amount about me. As for you, Kishida, I wouldn't want Doctor

221

Hepburn to think he's dealing with dangerous patients, be it me or that man just now, so I'd like you to set the record straight for me.'

'Just a moment,' said Kawaji. 'That man—he wasn't the one who inflicted that wound on you, was he?'

'No,' replied Kodama. 'I saw the face of the man who attacked me in Kanda from the palanquin, and it was not the man you saw just now.'

'Do you know who he was?'

'I vaguely remember his face, but not his name. In any case, it would be pointless to try and remember it now.'

'But there's a risk something similar could happen again.'

'If I worried about such things, there would be no end to it. Besides, I have a man like you by my side now. That kind of unpleasantness no longer surprises me. Compared to what I had to deal with during the Restoration, that was child's play. I have already given my life to my lord—or should I say, to the nation,' he said solemnly and with resolution. 'In fact, this last year or so I've been finding beautiful women from all over and adopting them for the Iwakura house. I appreciate it may sound as though I'm seeking out women on whom His Lordship might lavish favours, but that is not the case. His Lordship would never stoop to that. The truth of the matter is that these women are being sought for a higher purpose.'

'Come again?' said Kishida, confused.

'Well, I'm not sure I should say this in front of a man from Satsuma like Kawaji here, but... The most important offices in the new government are held almost exclusively by men from Satsuma, Chōshū, Tosa and Hizen. And it isn't only the top spots—it's a real stroke of luck if anybody from outside those four domains holds any position in government, right down to the lowest ranks. This is really not good at all. And not only is it not good for those not from those provinces, but it's not good for the future of Japan. That is my considered opinion—and it's not a new one. I predicted the current state of affairs right after the Restoration, and it has come to pass. Moreover, even at a practical level, it's very difficult to appoint people from outside those four provinces, no matter how talented they may be. So, after giving it much thought, I proposed a plan to Lord Iwakura. It involved finding and selecting beautiful girls from all over—and not just beauties, but those who were intelligent too—having His Lordship adopt them, marry them off to some brilliant young man from outside the four provinces, and then have these men appointed. After all, would any girl object to being adopted by His Lordship?'

The listeners were stunned into silence.

'This may be a rather underhand means of promoting those whose talent has yet to be seen by the world, but, for the time being, this seems to be the only option. When I tried it out, however, I found that those who passed this modest test were few and far between. Over the last two years, I've picked out twenty-three women and seventeen men. They were given private interviews with one another, with a view to marriage, but only thirteen couples liked each other enough to marry. The conditions were such that the man had to have decent enough prospects to enter government and rise up, while the woman should be beautiful enough to entice the man and clever enough to produce an outstanding child. However, I've been rather disappointed that things haven't been going as well as expected.'

Still, nobody dared to interrupt him.

'Of course, I would approach the parents discreetly and ascertain that no other offers of marriage were on the table. But even when the parents were interested, I found instances where the children had promised themselves without their parents' knowledge. And, more often than not, the other party didn't fit the bill. There were also those who had fallen in love with the girls and, after finding out that they were to be adopted by His Lordship, would fly into a frenzy and come to my house unannounced and in a terrible rage. That's what happened with the man you saw just now. As he said himself, he used to be a retainer and receive payment of three hundred *koku* of rice. He was also at one time an officer in the shogun's navy. Well, after the Restoration, he was appointed chief of the Raw Silk Inspection Office here in Yokohama. I heard a rumour that he was too good for that sort of work, and so I summoned him for a meeting and found him to be a man of exceptional talents. When I asked him, he told me that he had no marriage plans and readily agreed to meet the girl I had selected. So, when the time was right, I arranged their meeting, and would you believe it...'

A faint smile appeared on his lips.

'The man was already engaged, but before he had even met my proposed match, he decided in a flash to accept my offer, gave the other girl's parents some excuse and called off their engagement. Unbeknownst to me, however, his betrothed was in fact none other than the very girl I'd chosen. It was a real bind. From where I was standing, it was a complete coincidence, but in the end it may well have been an act of divine providence. The girl was shocked and livid. I happened to be there, and, from the get-go, I saw what a strong-willed girl she was, but, dear me, what a face the man had! He could barely bring himself to look at her. In truth, I myself had begun to take a very dim view of him—ah, that's it! his name is Nijūrō Teranishi—on account of the fact that he'd made a fool out of me. So, I informed the Treasury and had him dismissed. All that was about a year ago, however. He said he was cutting the hair of foreign sailors or some such for a living these days, but can he really have sunk so low? Such, in any case, are the details of the story. I think it's perverse and unreasonable of him to hold a grudge against me. He brought all this on himself, after all. What do you say, Kishida? You seemed to be defending him before.'

'No, that wasn't my intention at all. Did I really do that?' said Kishida, laughing nervously and scratching his head. 'At any rate, I dare say he can't do anything dangerous with his hands for the time being. Right now, he comes here for regular treatment, so I'll make sure he doesn't make a nuisance of himself again.'

'You know, I'm serious about this adoption business. You could even say that the rest of my life depends on it. That's why I get so angry when reckless individuals like that get involved. So far, I've had success with only thirteen couples, but when I think of the children that will be born from them, I truly believe that this will go no small way to protecting against the harm caused by clan discrimination. What do you think, Kawaji of Satsuma?'

'Truly, I'm at a loss for words, sir,' Kawaji replied, bowing.

4

Those words were not meant as flattery. It was hard to tell how serious Kazuki had been when he described Kawaji as a man who cared little about his roots, but that was not the case at all. Kawaji was a Satsuma man through and through, but even he had to admit that this hare-brained scheme of Lord Iwakura's right-hand man had its merits.

All this, moreover, was no fiction dreamt up by some author. As is recorded in Shidankai Dōkō's *Accounts of Early Meiji*:

> There are a couple of stories from around the fifth year of Meiji that I recall hearing but cannot find recorded in any book. There was a rumour that Iwakura was having beautiful girls brought to him, and that he would adopt them, look after them and marry them off to eligible men. In brief, he seems to have been trying to gather up all the young people of quality and promise under his own roof.

It was in fact Kodama who had come up with the idea and begun to implement it, but of course he was acting with Lord Iwakura's consent. Kawaji's fear of Lord Iwakura had always stemmed from the vague belief that this shrewd and wily man excelled in the grandiose scope and meticulous planning of his stratagems, and now, quite by chance, he had seen the proof of it.

Kodama had foreseen the harm that would be done by the alliance of Satsuma and Chōshū before any other man and had set about trying to prevent it. Moreover, he had hatched a plan to adopt outstanding youths from outside the alliance and, though them, to rear a future elite—a plan that was already underway. Truly, one could not help being deeply impressed by this.

All this clarified why Lord Iwakura was gathering together beautiful women, and, since clan affiliation was not of particular importance where the women were concerned, it also solved the question of why O-Nui had been put forward as a candidate.

'I just thought you should know,' said Kodama, before summoning his attendants. 'By the way, Kishida, the wound on my leg was disinfected earlier, and it's feeling better than ever. Doctor Hepburn said that I should be back on my feet in another week or so. I paid for the medicine, of course, but I feel I ought to thank you all somehow.'

'That really isn't necessary, sir!'

'I understand that, but still, I'd like to offer you a token of my thanks at least. I hear you're not averse to a drink now and then. Perhaps I could tempt you up to Tokyo one of these days?'

'There's really no need…'

'Think about it, in any case!'

And, with a laugh, Kodama let the curtain fall. The carriers came and picked up the palanquin and set out into the main street. They passed the front entrance to the Hepburn residence and then headed north along the embankment, returning to the city.

Watching them go, Kishida, Kawaji and Imokawa walked back.

'What did you make of that story, Chief Inspector?' asked Kishida.

The two of them were acquainted well enough to be frank with one another.

'As I said before, I'm rather at a loss for words. That man is a strategist, and he's also a patriot.'

'I wonder whether all that was intended for me, though,' said Kishida.

'What makes you say that?'

'So that I should know what kind of a man he is.'

'But why? Why would he want you to know that?'

'I think…' Kishida began, but suddenly he glanced towards the sea. 'Ah! My steamboat has returned!'

There were all kinds of foreign ships out in the azure waters of the bay. At the time, of course, there was no pier large enough for the bigger ships to moor, so they all had to anchor a short distance offshore, while little barges would ferry back and forth. But here was a boat that was not a barge: in fact, it was a comically small steamer drawing up alongside the embankment.

Kishida waved and ran off towards it, leaving Kawaji in a state of confusion.

The chief inspector should escort Kodama on his way back to Tokyo, but Kishida's words were weighing on his mind. The words 'my steamboat' only pushed his curiosity further still.

There was nothing else for it: he would have to go catch up with the palanquin later. Besides, Kodama had his four attendants with him, so there was nothing to worry about.

'Imokawa!'

'Sir?'

'Go back to the Hepburn residence and keep an eye on this Teranishi fellow. I'm going with Kishida. But if that man does anything odd—unlikely though that may be—come and find me at once. You won't have any trouble spotting us in the crowd: just look out for Kishida's white coat.'

With that, Sergeant Imokawa went running off to the gate of the house.

The front of the Hepburn residence looked over the waterfront. There were few pedestrians around, but if you crossed to the southern end of the Yato bridge, which took you towards the bluff, you would have to weave your way through waves of people. Naturally, there were a lot of foreigners in the area, but there were also many Japanese who would come to look at them. From the foreigners' perspective, there were a great deal more locals strutting around there in *hakama* and wearing *chonmage* topknots with traditional headgear than in Tokyo, and so this too was a sight worth seeing. One could also spot there the flitting outlines of palanquins and rickshaws, and even horse-drawn carts.

When Kawaji came up to Kishida, he asked, 'What exactly did you mean when you said that Kodama was letting you know what sort of a man he was?'

'On his previous visit here,' replied Kishida in his deep voice, 'he learnt that some four or five years ago, I travelled to Shanghai. Not alone, mind you—I went there with Doctor Hepburn. At the time, Doctor Hepburn was producing his Japanese–English dictionary, but in Japan there was no type-face with which to print it. There was in Shanghai, though. So, we went there to print the dictionary. Two years it took! That's what I told the gentleman. He seemed to have done his homework, though, for he even managed to wheedle out of me that we'd returned with a small quantity of opium for medicinal purposes.'

As the two of them walked, Kishida continued his narrative:

'Well, while he was being treated, he asked all kinds of questions about opium. Where in Shanghai you had to go in order to procure it, how you smoked it, what effect it had… Later on, Doctor Hepburn lamented that it wasn't good for anyone but doctors to take an interest in opium. I've really no idea what that man wanted with it.'

'Hmm…'

'I wonder whether he didn't tell me that story to make me believe that he's a respectable sort. Telling me alone would have been a bit obvious, though, so I suspect he brought you in as a decoy.'

Kawaji wasn't sure how to respond to this.

'A man like that could make you believe that opium would do Japan the world of good,' said Kishida with a laugh, his large white teeth showing through his beard. 'That being said, I didn't think much of what we heard just now. I appreciate that he thinks he's doing something great for the nation, but, while the abolition of clan factionalism may be a good idea, the means he's proposing to achieve it is absurd. It's not exactly in good taste, either.'

Kawaji wasn't so sure, and he was surprised to hear Kishida express that opinion. He looked askance at this imposing figure, at this outré man with the beard of the legendary warrior Guan Yu; a man who had a hand in all these bewilderingly new enterprises, from newspapers and shipping to petroleum and much besides, and who had assisted the great American doctor in the manufacture of his dictionary. This was the sort of grievance that only a freeman who had disregarded such factionalism from the very start could express. Even though he hadn't yet got to the bottom of Kishida, Kawaji felt, despite his innate love of subterfuge, that to continue his line of questioning would be risky.

'By the way, what did you mean, "your steamboat"?' he asked, changing the subject.

'Just that. I own a steamboat. It's called the *Ginkō*-maru.'

Kishida looked out over the water. The vessel could have had only around fifteen horsepower at most, but still, they could see clouds of smoke billowing out of the chimney stack in the middle of the roof and, below it, the captain standing in the wheelhouse, holding the ship's wheel.

'You see that man there?' said Kishida. 'He used to captain the shogun's warships.'

It was then that Kawaji recalled that Kishida had once run a shipping company. He had heard that that was all behind him now, but evidently he kept this ship for his own pleasure.

'We're testing it out all over the place.'

Kawaji could see the words *Ginkō*-maru written on the prow of the ship (although, strictly speaking, it used different characters from those in Kishida's name). As the ship drew nearer, Kawaji could make out that the captain was middle-aged, with fine features and a handsome moustache, and that he was wearing a so-called *rekushon* uniform that resembled the admiral's uniform that existed the old days of the shogun.

'Say, isn't that Kazuki-san?' asked Kishida, after suddenly turning away from the sea.

And sure enough, making his way through the crowds lining the waterfront was none other than Kazuki. Even there, in a place not lacking in strangely attired people, the chief inspector cut an odd figure. He was accompanied by Sergeants Onimaru, Yokomakura and Saruki. They all appeared to be looking for someone intently.

'I say, Kazuki!' Kawaji called out, surprised to see them.

The group came running towards him.

'What's the matter?' he asked.

'We're chasing Gitetsu Hikita,' Kazuki replied.

'Who?'

'Ah, I haven't had the chance to tell you. He's the man who attacked Kodama back in Kanda.'

'Well, I never!'

'We combed through the crime scene in Renjaku-chō again and, thanks to some good investigating by this lot, we finally found somebody who saw the criminal's face and even knew his name. That was last night. His name is Gitetsu Hikita, and he used to be one of the shogun's retainers. We've managed to establish that he lives in the Aikawa-chō neighbourhood of Fukagawa.'

Kawaji was impressed.

'This morning, when we returned to the scene of the crime to look for solid evidence that it was him, there he was, stepping out of a sake shop in one of the backstreets. He practically barged right into us, although I don't think he suspected what it was all about. He told us he was going to see an acquaintance down in Yokohama. In fact, when we followed him down to the Eitai Bridge, Sergeant Yokomakura pointed him out, having just seen him cross it. Only, that's where he seemed to notice us and took to his heels.'

Kazuki and the three *rasotsu* were still trying to catch their breath.

'We gave chase and very nearly caught up with him, but we lost him around Shinagawa. But, having seen that he'd made it all the way there, I was pretty sure that he was on his way to Yokohama.'

Kazuki turned to look at the *rasotsu*.

'At Shinagawa, I jumped in a rickshaw, and the two pullers carried me as far as the entrance to the foreign settlement. You don't think I could've overtaken him, do you?'

He turned back to Kawaji.

'What on earth are you doing here, anyway?'

'I was here guarding Kodama.'

'Oh, of course. You said he was being treated by Doctor Hepburn. Ah, Kishida-san! Right on time,' said Kazuki, beaming.

Kishida returned Kazuki's smile with more affection than he had shown Kawaji, but he said nothing. With seemingly little interest in Kodama and his affairs, Kishida turned back towards the waterfront, where the little steamboat was drawing nearer, its bow parallel to the embankment.

'Damn it!' cried Kawaji, coming to his senses.

He had just remembered that Kodama's palanquin had already set off for Tokyo. If a villain like that was on his way from the capital, they could easily run into each other, and then there was no telling what would happen.

'Quick, you lot, come with me!' he shouted. 'You know what he looks like!'

Unusually flustered, Kawaji set off running along the waterfront.

5

It was about a week later, one evening towards the end of the third lunar month, when Kishida and Kodama got together for a drink in Yanagibashi.

By today's calendar, this would have been sometime in late April. It was a dismal, gloomy day, however, and, rather than spring showers, there was a torrential deluge more like a monsoon. Despite this, Kawaji and Sergeant Imokawa were pacing about in the rain, dressed in capes and hats, not far from Kodama's residence by the Hibiya Gate. Nothing out of the ordinary had happened the day that Kodama made the journey back from Yokohama, but since Hikita's whereabouts were still unknown, they were keeping a close eye out.

Kawaji had shared various pieces of information with Kazuki, but their exchange was a most odd affair. Of all his colleagues, Kawaji was of course closest to Kazuki, but there were certain things that Kawaji did not tell even him. He wasn't sure whether Kazuki was mindful of their rivalry, but he could sense that there were things being hidden from him, and there were times when he even laughed at the thought that each was trying to outfox the other. What Kawaji concealed depended on complex considerations that he himself intuited only vaguely.

Despite all this, Kawaji had learnt from Kazuki that this Hikita had once been a retainer with an income of 250 *koku* but had supposedly gone to Hakodate to fight in the civil war. After his surrender, he was imprisoned in Edo, and, upon his release, he had found his house confiscated and the where-abouts of his family unknown. These days, he was living in a hovel in Fukagawa's Aikawa-chō district, and it was unclear what he now did for a living. He had at one time apparently had a fiancée, but she had been ensnared somehow in Lord Iwakura's search. Because she loved Hikita, she had refused at first, but due to the family's circumstances, they had had no choice but to accept. Apparently, she had ended up hanging herself. Hikita had learnt the truth of the matter only recently and was outraged.

This was, more or less, what Kazuki had managed to glean from the old woman who owned the glue shop next door to Hikita and who looked out for him.

One way or another, however, Hikita realized that he was being watched, and ever since Kazuki's chat with the woman, he had vanished, never again returning to the house in Aikawa-chō. There was a rumour going around that he had once been an exceptional student of the renowned Kenkichi Sakakibara, who belonged to the Jikishinkage-ryū school of swordsmanship. What's more, he was impulsive and only twenty-five, so there was no telling what he might do in a state of desperation.

So, as he was patrolling the area around Kodama's house that day, Kawaji was on his guard.

At around half-past two that afternoon, a servant appeared— the one who always accompanied Kodama whenever he went out. He found Kawaji and announced that Kodama would shortly be going to a restaurant in Yanagibashi.

'I believe he's meeting the gentleman with the beard from Doctor Hepburn's house,' the servant said.

'What, you mean Ginkō Kishida?' asked Kawaji, somewhat taken aback.

'Yes, sir. The gentleman is an odd sort, is he not? He feels awkward drinking with a man of such rank and in the presence of four attendants, so the master has asked whether he might go alone, and, if there are concerns for his safety, that the chief inspector be stationed outside.'

'Did the invitation come from Kishida?'

'That, sir, I don't know. I've only just heard about it myself, but it's possible they arranged it in advance. Since the gentleman has to return to Yokohama, he's asked that they meet early. I'll leave this in your capable hands.'

And so it was that on that rainy day Kawaji had to accompany Kodama alone to Yanagibashi.

Having flagged down a rickshaw with a canopy, Kodama left the premises at around three o'clock. Kawaji knew this because he looked at his treasured pocket watch, which he had bought from a dealer of Western antiques.

Though he was still limping, Kodama could actually walk now, and so he climbed into the rickshaw himself. As he got in, he gave Kawaji a look as if to say 'thank you'—and there was even a glimmer of a smile in his eyes, which was a world away from the irritable looks he had once given him. Even Kodama, it seemed, had finally come to appreciate the labours of the faithful chief inspector, although Kawaji had already seen hints of this in their private conversations.

At Yanagibashi there was a great stylish restaurant called the Azuma-ya, which was a frequent haunt of government officials. Kawaji stopped at the bottom of the little street leading up to the building, but Kodama's rickshaw set him down right in front of the entrance. Several rickshaws were already parked there, so it was unclear whether Kishida had already arrived. Kawaji did not spot him going in, though, and it occurred to him later that, no matter who had invited whom, Kishida would have arrived first and waited for Kodama because of their difference in rank.

It later transpired that Kishida was indeed the first to arrive, although this did not appear to have been out of any especial courtesy. As proof of this, Kishida was the first to leave.

The reason was very characteristic of Kishida.

The light that day was odd—neither dark nor bright. The afternoon felt curiously gloomy, and though it was only around four o'clock when they arrived at the Azuma-ya, the lights of what appeared to be several oil lamps were burning brightly, and the shadows of geisha going in and out of the place floated like phantom butterflies. Kawaji was astonished that this kind of world still existed in Tokyo, and he surveyed the scene not as a mere precaution, but captivated by its charm.

After an hour, however, he grew weary of the spectacle, so he took a short stroll with Sergeant Imokawa, whom he had brought along. When they returned, they very nearly collided with Kishida.

'Oh!' Kawaji exclaimed, surprised to see him. 'You're leaving already?'

'I am,' replied Kishida.

It was still raining, so Kishida, in his Western apparel, was carrying an appropriately Western-style umbrella. The expression on the face under it, however, seemed ill-tempered.

'It was all a bit of a bore, so I've made my excuses.'

'What about Kodama?'

'He's having a gay old time of it with some geisha. Quite the dark horse, isn't he? Don't get me wrong, I myself used to enjoy that sort of thing a lot. When I was younger, I even worked as a geisha's *shamisen* carrier. But now that I help Doctor Hepburn, it doesn't sit well with me.' He laughed. 'Still, I don't mind a drink now and then. Would you care to join me?'

Kawaji was astonished.

'Thank you, but I'm on duty.'

'Nonsense! He'll be there for at least another hour or two. Besides, it seems absurd for you to be standing out here, keeping guard while he's in there, drinking in the company of beautiful women and getting up to all sorts. Never mind the fact that you're soaked through! And as for you, Sergeant, well, you make quite a sorry sight—you look like a drowned rat.'

Kishida pointed to the other side the street.

'You see that little door over there? I, for one, would much rather be in a place like that. Why don't you join me? Just for a little while?'

Kawaji was sorely tempted. It wasn't that he wanted to drink, but rather that he thought this would be a good chance to talk to Kishida, whom he had been forced to leave right in the middle of their conversation the other day. He looked at his watch. It was five o'clock precisely.

'Well, maybe just a quick one.'

Kawaji gave Imokawa a nudge, and together they walked down the street to the door, where they parted the rope curtain and stepped inside. The place was bigger than the façade suggested, and, as it was the dinner hour, it was full of merchants and workmen, all making a terrible din. Little did the policemen know that an ill wind was about to blow past outside that rope curtain.

As soon as their drinks arrived, Kawaji asked the reason for Kishida's meeting with Kodama.

'I only came because he was so insistent about it! And just as I suspected, it was about the opium again,' said Kishida, gulping down a cup of sake. 'When I told him I didn't want to talk about it, he soured, grew indignant—and that was that. So, I left immediately. I've no idea why he was after it, but the fact that he was so insistent makes me think that it can't have been anything good.'

As he claimed that their conversation had ended there, there was nothing more that Kawaji could ask. The look on Kishida's face made clear that he no longer wished to discuss the matter, so the topic was changed.

As Kishida carried on talking, he imbibed an awful lot of sake. This was not just because he wanted to blow off some steam. He was, by his own admission, a heavy drinker. It was hard to believe that this was the same meek-faced man in white whom they had met at the Hepburn residence.

His talk grew increasingly incoherent, but it was, for the most part, a history of how he had grown up as an orphan in Mimasaka Province, studied and become tutor to the lord of a certain domain, only then to make his way to Edo and fall upon hard times, working in all manner of jobs, from an attendant in a bathhouse to a pimp in the pleasure quarters, from a geisha's *shamisen* carrier to a dishwasher in a back-alley snack bar. Back then, of course, he hadn't the least inkling of the dramatic life events that his later years would bring.

The story was certainly an interesting one, but it was not the time for long and rambling tales. From time to time, Kawaji would try to interrupt him by asking questions: about whether Teranishi's whitlow had to be operated on in the end; about the steamboat and whether Kishida thought that Japan would ever control the maritime transport in Tokyo, Yokohama and their surrounding areas; and finally about a man called Naochika Asakura, who had been reduced to poverty and whom they were looking for.

'Well, it's getting on,' said Kawaji. 'Shouldn't you be getting back to Yokohama?'

Kishida seemed unconcerned.

'I intend to open a shop here in Tokyo one of these days, so I rent a house in the Tsukiji Foreign Settlement. It's lying empty at the moment, so I can stay there tonight.'

Just then, Imokawa suddenly turned towards the entrance. What he saw made him drop the slice of devil's tongue that was hanging from his mouth.

6

Kawaji looked up and was similarly startled to see Sergeant Yokomakura at the door, parting the ropes and entering the establishment.

Spotting them there, Yokomakura quickly put his finger to his lips.

It seemed unlikely that he had just happened to be passing and dropped in on the off chance. Had something happened? As Kawaji tried to control the pounding in his chest, he knew he couldn't leave Kishida. Eventually, Yokomakura found a seat on a bench and beckoned Imokawa over.

The *rasotsu* bowed and went over to him but returned three minutes later, his face looking extraordinarily pale.

'Sir, it looks as though Hikita is here.'

'What? Where is he?'

'In the corner over there.'

Kawaji turned his head, and sure enough, sitting there in the corner, gulping down sake, was a young man who, with his impressive moustache and shaved head, looked every bit the masterless samurai. Not so much a dauntless figure as a man with nothing left to lose.

'Hmm... So that's Hikita? I wonder how long he's been there.'

'I believe he came in just a few minutes ago. Yokomakura says he spotted him by chance near the Ryōgoku Bridge. He followed Hikita all the way to Yanagibashi, and he came straight here. Yokomakura didn't want to be noticed, so he waited outside a little before coming in. The guy doesn't seem to have noticed that he was followed, but Hikita seems unsure what to do next.'

'Does he know that Kodama's in Yanagibashi right now?'

'I'm not sure… Aah!'

The sound barely escaped Imokawa's mouth.

Having finished off a little flask of sake, Hikita left some change on the table and looked as though he was about to leave. Kawaji felt a sense of panic rising.

'What the matter?' asked the inebriated Kishida, finally realizing that something was amiss.

'Nothing, nothing,' said Kawaji, brushing the question aside, as he watched Hikita part the rope curtain and leave. He then followed him through the drunken crowd and poked his face out through the curtain.

The young Hikita was staggering off. He was headed not for the street on which the Azuma-ya could be found, however, but rather in the opposite direction, towards the Ryōgoku Bridge.

'Follow him!' Kawaji ordered the two *rasotsu* who had come running up behind him. 'And if he looks as though he's turning back, one of you run back and tell me.'

Kawaji returned to his table, from where, squinting through a mist of inebriation, Kishida had been watching these developments. But, whether from a lack of interest or the inability to see, he merely picked up the conversation from where they had left off.

'Now, my dear Kawaji, even if you made me run all the way, it would take me five hours to get from here to Yokohama. If there were a train, it would take only half an hour, but I hear the Imperial Prosecuting Office is against the idea. I mean, really, what a shower of old contrarians!'

Kishida was beginning to bluster now.

Although no report had arrived from the two *rasotsu*, Kawaji was growing increasingly concerned, and the thought of Kodama over in the Azuma-ya weighed on his mind.

After around thirty minutes, he finally couldn't take it any longer.

'If you'll excuse me for a moment, Kishida-san,' he said, getting to his feet, and heading across the way.

Arriving at the Azuma-ya, he heard something that startled him: Kokuten Kodama was not there. Worse still, he was told that Kodama had announced his intention to return home not ten minutes after Kishida's departure, and had left the restaurant.

Back then, there was no such thing as a private rickshaw, so the one in which Kodama had arrived would have been long gone. Consequently, the restaurant had called a palanquin for him. This must have been only a short while after Kawaji and Kishida entered the establishment down the road.

Kawaji was baffled. When he asked at the Azuma-ya where they thought he had gone, they gave him a quizzical look and said that, naturally, he must have gone home.

Wherever he had headed, the two *rasotsu* following Hikita had ended up who knew where and had not yet returned. And since Kawaji had ordered them to report to him there, he couldn't move.

As a precaution, he asked one of the boys at the Azuma-ya to go to the house by the Hibiya Gate and ascertain whether Kodama had in fact returned home. Meanwhile, he positioned himself at the street corner where he could both see the Azuma-ya and the bar and lament his blunder. As he stood there, he saw Kishida finally leave the place, stagger off with his Western umbrella, and clamber into a passing rickshaw, but he had little desire to run over and call out to him. The sun had long set on that spring day, but the rain was still coming down in sheets.

By the time Imokawa came running back, almost an hour had passed since he and Yokomakura set out in pursuit of Hikita. But still, he arrived back sooner than the boy from the Azuma-ya did.

'Sir!' shouted Imokawa, his face grim. 'Kodama has been found hanged!'

'What?! Where?'

'From the railing of the Eitai Bridge.'

7

In the early years of Meiji, there were only five bridges spanning the great Sumida River. As you moved upstream, they were, in order, the Eitai Bridge, the Shin-Ōhashi Bridge, the Ryōgoku Bridge, the Azuma Bridge and the Senju Great Bridge. They were all of them wooden, needless to say.

In those days, the roads were such that it was a journey of almost two miles from Yanagibashi, which lay immediately to the west of the Ryōgoku Bridge, down to the Eitai Bridge, so it is little wonder that it took almost an hour to get there and back.

Kawaji looked at his watch. It was half-past six. By the time he and Sergeant Imokawa reached the Eitai Bridge, having run there as fast as their legs would carry them, it had already gone ten to seven.

According to the report, Kodama, who had been escorted by Kawaji to the restaurant at Yanagibashi only three and a half hours previously, had been found with a noose around his neck, hanging from the railing, right in the middle of the Eitai Bridge.

The night rain was still torrential. Though it had been a gloomy day and night had now fallen, there was, perhaps because of the broad surface of the river, an uncanny brightness all around. To Kawaji, the entire scene seemed other-worldly.

On the bridge, standing in a daze beside Sergeant Yokomakura, was Gitetsu Hikita. He was not tied up, nor did he seem to be trying to escape.

'Are you from the Imperial Prosecuting Office?' he exclaimed when he saw Kawaji. 'So, the wrath of Heaven has befallen the bald old lecher who had his eye on every young virgin in the street, made us the victims of his sinister designs and was so deluded that he believed it was all an act of patriotism.'

He let out a scornful laugh, his eyes glittering.

'It wasn't I who carried out the will of Heaven, though. If I'd done it, I'd have used a sword!'

He provocatively slapped the hilt of his sword, and it was only then that Yokomakura rushed to grab his arm.

It would have been understandable if Yokomakura had refrained from restraining Hikita before then because he was waiting for support, but the real reason was as follows.

For one thing, it was Hikita himself who had discovered the incident. After leaving the establishment in Yanagibashi, he said, he had strolled aimlessly along the bank of the Sumida River. At some point—he couldn't say when—he had acquired a broken umbrella, and he was a little unsteady on his legs because, apparently, he had gone somewhere for a drink earlier. He passed the waterfront at Hamachō, where the Shin-Ōhashi Bridge stands, and arrived at the Eitai Bridge. Crossing it into Fukagawa would have immediately taken him back home to the Aikawa-chō neighbourhood. He had in fact been hiding out in Shinagawa, but that day he had finally decided, or so he said, to go home and show his face.

When he reached the middle of the bridge, however, he received a shock.

As he was walking along the railing on the southern side, he suddenly tripped over something. It was a broken bamboo hoop. He looked down and saw another one, securely fixed at the bottom of one of the posts of the railing. He also saw that there was a rope twisted around it. He didn't think much of it, but as he walked on, he happened to peer down towards the river. That was when he saw the man's head hanging in mid-air.

It was odd to have been able to see this on such a rainy night, but there was a ghostly light in the air, and even Kawaji, when he arrived later, had been able to make out that face, albeit through a haze. Perhaps it was because the head of the hanged man was bent backwards slightly, as though looking up. The average person, however, would have found it impossible to tell exactly what the face looked like.

Hikita told them that, when he saw the face, he had gasped and cried out the name of his reviled nemesis, whom he had even seen in his dreams. It was then that Yokomakura and Imokawa had finally caught up with him: the former had been carrying a lantern, while it was the latter who recognized Kodama.

'You were following me, weren't you?' Hikita laughed, seeing Sergeant Yokomakura and seeming to realize this for the first time. He had made no attempt to resist or escape, though. Quite the opposite. 'Well, if you've been following me, chaps, then you'll know that it wasn't me who did this. I, for one, should very much like to know how he came to meet his end like this. Go and call your superiors.'

He had said all this of his own volition and waited there patiently with Yokomakura until Kawaji arrived.

Two hours later, having received the urgent news, Chief Inspector Kazuki arrived by rickshaw, bringing with him Onimaru and Saruki. Only then was the body hoisted up and identified conclusively as Kokuten Kodama.

Splitting up, Imokawa and Saruki were dispatched to Kodama's house and the Imperial Prosecuting Office respectively, while Hikita was tied up and taken away by Onimaru, and Yokomakura was ordered to stand guard with his lantern. Meanwhile, Kawaji and Kazuki looked down at the pitiful sight lying at their feet—a corpse that belonged to a man who was once reputed to be Lord Iwakura's brain.

'I just don't get it,' grumbled Kawaji. 'Where did he go after leaving the Azuma-ya and why? And to strangle a man like that so easily… I can only think it was the work of a demon. And why hang him here? What does it mean? It's a total mystery.'

'But, my dear Kawaji, surely he wasn't strangled. It looks as though he hanged himself!'

'What do you mean?'

'I just noticed it myself. Look here. The rope marks on the neck aren't the horizontal ones you get when strangling a person: these ones run diagonally, from the throat up to the ears and behind them. Don't you think this is proof that he hanged himself?'

'You're saying, then, that this man put the rope around his own neck and jumped right off the bridge?!'

For several seconds, Kawaji was at a loss for words.

'But what about the rope?' he finally said. 'The rope wasn't tied to the railing. It was fixed to something resembling a hoop from a small bucket that had been cut in half and fixed to the railing, while the other end was dangling down, long enough, by the looks of it, to reach the river. I don't know why, but I can't help feeling that there's another hand involved.'

'I agree, of course, that this fellow wasn't the type to hang himself. And yet...'

'The only possible suspects I can think of, Kazuki, are Gitetsu Hikita and Nijūrō Teranishi.'

'They say that Hikita's fiancée hanged herself...'

Kawaji let out a plaintive sigh.

'Be that as it may, this tragedy is my fault. I was supposed to be guarding Kodama.'

Three days later, they caught up at the Imperial Prosecuting Office.

'What have you found, Kawaji?'

'Nothing. That's to say, I've found things, but I don't know what they mean.'

'Namely?'

'Well, first there's Kodama's movements that night. When I checked with the palanquin bearers that the Azuma-ya called, they said that he asked to be taken to Hamachō and was dropped off at the riverside. The bearers thought they were going there because of the *hanamachi* red-light district. I would be inclined to agree... but then, why, after having been dropped off in Hamachō, did Kodama make his way all the way down to the Eitai Bridge, when the distance there is even greater than what he'd already covered coming from Yanagibashi? Did he take another kind of transport? Or did he limp there on foot? There are no witnesses, and I can't work out why he did it.'

There was a brief silence between the men.

'Then there's Gitetsu Hikita. The man seems to think that because he was followed, the testimony of the *rasotsu* proves that he isn't the killer. He even made light of it, but really he's on shaky ground. Of course, the *rasotsu* followed him after he left Yanagibashi, but where's the evidence that he hadn't already committed the murder by the time he turned up at the bar? Only, I've ended up being Hikita's alibi for this. The timings are approximate, but Kishida left the Azuma-ya at around five o'clock. Then, ten minutes later, so did Kodama, supposedly. But it had been almost an hour since Hikita left the bar when Imokawa came running back to report the murder at half-past six, and Hikita must have already been drinking in the bar at half-past five. At that time, Kodama would have still been in the palanquin on his way to Hamachō. No matter how you look at it, there's no way that he could have gone with Kodama to the Eitai Bridge, then made it all the way back to Yanagibashi. It's almost two miles.'

Another brief silence ensued.

'Then there's Nijūrō Teranishi. On the night in question, he was in Yokohama—or so he says. Two days before, he underwent surgery for his whitlow, performed by Doctor Hepburn. He says he felt much better almost right away, so the very next day (the day of the hanging) he came to Tokyo to run an errand he had been putting off for some time. Only, when he got there, the pain began to get worse, and that night, after he returned to Yokohama, it was so intense that he went to see Doctor Hepburn again at around eight o'clock. If Kodama left the Azuma-ya at ten past five, then, given that the Eitai Bridge is almost two miles away, it would have been at least twenty to six by the time he got there. And if Teranishi was at the Eitai

248

Bridge, there's no way he could have got back to Yokohama by eight o'clock. Even by rickshaw, the journey takes five hours. Besides, with his finger in that state, he apparently wouldn't have been able to tie his own waistband, let alone strangle a big man like Kodama and hang him from a bridge. And that's coming from Doctor Hepburn.'

'Hmm,' was all Kazuki could muster.

Kawaji sighed.

'As it's Kodama we're dealing with, I dare say there are plenty of others who would have liked to see him dead. But if our killer wasn't Teranishi or Hikita, I wouldn't know where to begin...'

8

Awariya, asobihasutomo, mōsanu, asakurani,
Amatsukami, kunitsukami, orimashimase...

The following evening, at dusk, a beautiful, bewitching voice rang out over the Eitai Bridge.

The bridge had been closed, and right in the middle of it stood the two chief inspectors. Beside them, sitting on the ground, were Gitetsu Hikita and Nijūrō Teranishi, both bound with ropes. In front of them, holding her *kagura* bells and chanting, was Esmeralda.

The grandees of the Imperial Prosecuting Office, together with old Manabe and his daughter, were lined up along the southern railing of the bridge, while the *rasotsu* sat opposite them on the northern side, playing their ancient instruments. It was the usual set-up, but there were only three of them. Onimaru and Ichinohata were missing.

Awariya, asobihasutomo, mōsanu, asakurani,
Kokuten Kodama no mitama, mairitamae…

The *kagura* bells suddenly rang out.

'*Ima… mairu!… I am… the spirit… of Kokuten Kodama…*'

No matter how many times they had heard the incantation, this moment never failed to make the sweat run down everybody's backs.

'*For the first time since arriving in the land of the dead… I can see the land of the living without hindrance…*

'*That night, I went from Yanagibashi to Hamachō… This was because Ginkō Kishida, during our conversation at the Azuma-ya, mentioned that his steamboat was docked in Hamachō… Kishida said that he had recently been having his men investigate places along the Sumida River where steamboats could moor…*

'*At the restaurant, Kishida's mood soured all of a sudden… He left the table, and I thought he must have gone to meet the boat, so I decided to follow him there… When I got to Hamachō, I saw, in the dim evening light, a small steamboat floating like a ghost ship through the rain…*'

Just then, the assembled guests caught sight of a little steamboat upstream, heading downstream towards them from the Shin-Ōhashi Bridge where Hamachō was located.

'*As I approached the boat, I suddenly felt a blade being held to my neck… I turned around and saw a man with a razor… Still holding the blade to my neck, he made me board the boat and stand on deck…*'

The assembly of people saw two figures, one big and one small, standing on the little deck of the approaching steamboat. These could only be the missing *rasotsu*.

'*The man had been at Doctor Hepburn's house that day and had overheard Kishida agreeing to meet me in Tokyo… He hatched a*

250

plan and followed me out of the Azuma-ya... He had decided to wait for me to return home, intending then to take me to the boat in Hamachō by any means necessary... Did destiny take me in hand that night? I wonder... Whatever the reason, I ended up going on the boat of my own volition...'

The *miko* laughed Kodama's dreadful, melancholy laugh.

'There wasn't a soul on the riverbank that rainy night... Nor could I call out for help, because the man was so consumed by the desire to kill... Before I knew it, the boat was approaching the Eitai Bridge...'

By now they could see, standing on the deck of the steamboat, the bearded mien of Onimaru, as well as Ichinohata's wan, miserable-looking mug.

'Two sizeable lengths of rope were dangling from the southern railing of the bridge... Both of them had loops at the end... The boat drew nearer and nearer... The captain of the steamboat was indebted to the man, who had helped him get the position, so he had no choice but to obey his orders... Moreover, the captain had no idea what his plan was... I myself had no idea what was going to happen... Then, the moment the ship passed under the bridge...'

Suddenly, as the little steamboat really did vanish under the bridge, the *kagura* bells rang out.

'The man grabbed the rope and slipped the noose around my neck... Then he caught hold of the other end... In an instant, I was hoisted into the air, while the boat carried on... By the time the man let go of the rope, I was of course a dead man...'

When the boat emerged from under the bridge, only Onimaru remained on deck.

Later it transpired that Ichinohata had likewise been hanged under the bridge—only, of course, not by his neck. Instead, the noose had been slipped under his arms...

'*The man did all this with only his left hand... Instead of his right hand, he borrowed strength from the momentum of the boat... Two or three hoops of bamboo that had been cut in half were fixed to the midpoint of the rope so that it would stop when they got caught in the railing. He had prepared this the previous day when he came to Tokyo... The first two pieces of bamboo broke, but the third one held firmly in place, and so the trick worked...*'

The steamboat—the *Ginkō*-maru, which was the forerunner of what would later be known as the 'penny steamer'—was already vanishing through the wide, misty estuary and into the night.

'*Thus could a man who had been at the Eitai Bridge at around six o'clock be in Yokohama by eight...*'

The dull thud of the *kaen-daiko* rang out, and the *miko*'s voice grew quieter.

'*And so I, Kokuten Kodama, who dreamt of raising Japan out of clanship and factionalism, saw my great aim buried by a most foolish man... One thing I will say, though... Even here in the hereafter, I am impressed by the ingeniousness of the murder...*'

The voice faded into silence, and the *miko*'s head slumped forward.

'Get to your feet!' Kazuki ordered Teranishi.

Still dazed by what he had just heard, Kawaji watched as Esmeralda approached O-Nui and greeted her with a smile.

EYES AND LEGS

The following relates the particulars of an exceptionally difficult case, in which the witness reported having seen through a telescope a woman's leg being cut off. Although the leg was recovered, no victim could be found...

> — From a report made by Chief
> Inspector Toshiyoshi Kawaji of
> the Imperial Prosecuting Office

1

It was a certain day in the eighth lunar month of the third year of Meiji, and an intriguing item had arrived from France for Esmeralda. It was a brand-new kind of double-telescope. She said that she wanted to go to the Tsukiji Hotel again to take a look at Tokyo from the bell tower, so Kazuki had asked Kawaji whether he would care to join them and try out the instrument.

It turned out to be a pair of Boulanger binoculars. Kawaji had seen the singular kind of telescope before, but never anything as elaborate as this, so he agreed without any hesitation, thinking it a marvellous idea to survey the city.

They bundled Esmeralda into a palanquin and, with autumn already in the air, the three of them set off for the Tsukiji Foreign Settlement.

In the guardhouse at the Shinpuku-ji Bridge leading into the settlement, Sergeant Saruki was sitting alone in his chair, staring vacantly at a stack of coins on his desk—as ever, they had probably been swindled out of members of the public. When he saw the three figures pass by in front of the guardhouse, he quickly thrust the coins into his pocket and, hiding his astonishment, grinned at them broadly, like a monkey, before going after them, his enormous shoes clattering against the ground.

When Kazuki told him the purpose of their visit, he immediately asked whether he might have the honour of accompanying them.

Eventually, when the four reached the top of the nearly one-hundred-foot tower, they took out the binoculars. The view of Tokyo through them was truly exceptional; it felt as though they were looking at a city in an entirely different world. Even the ordinarily reticent Kawaji cried out in wonder several times.

'How does this compare with Paris, Miss Esmeralda?' he asked earnestly. 'Surely, Paris can't hold a candle to this?'

Esmeralda merely laughed and said nothing.

One by one, they each took a turn with the binoculars, and, when the commotion had died down, another voice asked:

'Excuse me, but… may I take a look?'

It was a boy of around ten, who had come up with a porter while they had all been admiring the view. With his forelock and pristine *hakama*, he looked every bit the child of a samurai. He even carried a short sword.

Kazuki had noticed the young lad's fascination with the binoculars and that he had been hesitant to ask up to that point, so he had in fact already been intending to show them to the boy, but since the very moment Saruki had set the binoculars before his eyes, he had been loath to let them go.

'For goodness' sake, Sergeant, will you let the child have a turn?!' Kazuki exclaimed. 'And show him how to use them.'

After a few moments, while observing the boy as his cheeks flushed and he aimed the binoculars in every which direction, Kazuki asked the porter:

'Is he the son of one of your guests?'

'No, sir,' the porter replied. 'He just came in and asked if he could visit the tower.'

As a rule, of course, only guests were permitted to go up there.

'I believe, sir, that he came to take a look at the church here in the foreign settlement, and that he availed himself of

256

the opportunity to stop by en route. The young chap asked so politely that I felt quite compelled to show him up.'

'The church, you say?'

Come to think of it, the child had an unusual, almost European look about him. He was not a child of mixed parentage, but a Japanese boy, to be sure. However, his features were deeply chiselled for his years, and he had none of the youthful beauty one would ordinarily associate with a boy of his age. For all that, his face was uncommonly intelligent, and he looked as though he had a will of iron.

It was unusual, at any rate, that he had come all by himself to the foreign settlement to see the church and the hotel tower.

Hearing this, Kazuki walked over to the boy and asked him what he would like to look at, helping him to adjust the binoculars.

'Are you from Tokyo?' Kazuki asked.

'No, I'm from Takasaki, in Jōshū.'

'From Takasaki? Is that where your father is?'

'No, he's in Iwanomaki, in Ōshū. He's a judge. My family lives in Takasaki,' the boy answered crisply, as he continued to look through the binoculars.

'So, have you come to Tokyo all by yourself?'

'Yes, at my father's behest, to learn English. I'm enrolled in a school run by an English lady.'

'Well, that's excellent, isn't it! I hear that you're on your way to see the church. Did your teacher tell you to go there?'

'No, a friend told me to go because he thought it was funny.'

'Funny?'

'Yes, he said there's a Western lady who taps a big box and music comes out, and then they sing songs in English. But these binoculars are much more fun!'

Belated though the sensation might have been, Kazuki felt a keen awareness that they were now living in a new era.

'You speak very properly for a young lad who's only recently arrived in the capital. There isn't a trace of any provincial accent.'

'That's because I was born in Tokyo and lived in Koishikawa until I was seven,' the boy replied. 'And my father used to be a samurai in the Takasaki Domain's Edo residence. He still lives in His Lordship's mansion even now.'

'Just how old are you, young man?'

'Ten.'

'And your name is…?'

'Kanzō Uchimura.'

Just then, the boy suddenly cried out in surprise.

'What is it?' Kazuki asked.

'Over there! There's a man and a woman doing something strange!'

'What? Let me see.'

Flustered, Kazuki snatched the binoculars.

'Where?'

'Beside the church… Third building to the left. First floor.'

'Hang on a minute…'

Kazuki scoured the city below with the binoculars.

'It's a Western building. Second window from the right.'

A few moments later, the binoculars found their objective, and Kazuki himself cried out in surprise.

'What can you see?' asked Kawaji, as he, Saruki and even Esmeralda gathered around with inquisitive eyes.

Through the large glass window, Kazuki could see a woman lying on a bed and a man standing beside her. The room was clearly decorated in the Western style, but the man and woman were not Westerners: they looked Japanese. A little off to the side was another man.

The strange act to which the boy had just alluded was apparently that one of the men had picked the woman up and laid her on the bed. Of course, even without the presence of the other man, this was not the sort of scene that one witnessed every day.

What had surprised Kazuki, however, was the realization that the woman was in fact not a woman at all.

In those days, the so-called 'Tanosuke cut'—a sort of chignon—was popular among young women, and Kazuki had realized that the 'woman' in question was none other than the originator of this style.

'It's Tanosuke Sawamura!' he exclaimed.

The binoculars were snatched away from Kazuki in turn, and Kawaji spent several minutes looking through them intently.

'I know that man. I'm sure that's Tateki Maki, from the Ministry of Popular Affairs,' he said. 'But who could the other one be? Judging by that expressionless face and those garish clothes, I'd say he must be another actor.'

It was now Esmeralda's turn to take the binoculars. Kazuki explained to her that, though the figure might have looked like a woman, he was really what was called an *onnagata*, a male kabuki actor who specialized in playing female roles. Yet no matter how he tried to convince her, Esmeralda refused to believe him.

As the *rasotsu* waited impatiently for Esmeralda to give him a turn with the binoculars, Kawaji called out sternly, 'Saruki! Over here!' and walked briskly over to the top of the spiral staircase.

'Yes, sir?'

'There's something fishy about a government official and an *onnagata* of dubious repute being found together in a Western house in the foreign settlement. We're going to check it out.'

After watching the two of them go, Kazuki took the binoculars and peered through them once more. The three figures in the glass window had vanished.

2

It was a journey of around fifteen minutes by foot. When Kawaji and Saruki finally located the house, they were told that the three men had left by rickshaw five minutes ago. The house was deserted, with only an old man there acting as caretaker.

All this was relayed back to Kazuki and the others at the Tsukiji Hotel when they returned there.

'What were they doing in an uninhabited house?' asked Kazuki.

'Well, I said it was deserted, and there indeed are a lot of houses in that area without tenants, but this one does apparently have one. And who do you think it is?'

'I've no idea.'

'Ginkō Kishida!'

'What?'

'Well, the caretaker didn't know much, but he did say that Kishida's been renting it for more than a year. Or did he say he owned it?' Kawaji recalled that Kishida had once said something to him about having a house in the foreign settlement.

'He said that Kishida rarely visited, but that today he'd promised to meet the three gentlemen there. Apparently, he sent word that he'd been called away on urgent business and

260

'couldn't make it, so the gentlemen ended up leaving shortly after they arrived.'

'Hmm... I suppose that isn't so odd, then.'

'Really? The combination of a student of Doctor Hepburn's, an official from the Ministry of Popular Affairs and an *onnagata* from the kabuki theatre doesn't strike you as odd?'

'Well, Kawaji, when you put it like that...'

'Anyway, what kind of an actor is this Sawamura? I've never seen him on the stage, but I've heard all kinds of rumours about him. Are you sure it's really a man?'

Like Esmeralda, Kawaji too seemed bewildered by the beauty of the *onnagata* he had seen through the binoculars.

'I've only been to the theatre a couple of times myself,' Kazuki added.

From the latter years of the shogunate to the early years of Meiji, Tanosuke Sawamura was celebrated as one of the most beautiful *onnagata* on the stage. So legendary was his beauty that his very name later became a byword for it. Born in 1845, the second year of Kōka, the son of Sōjūrō Sawamura V, he had played his first leading role at the age of fifteen, and his first leading female role at sixteen. Even for the scion of a distinguished family of actors, this was an exceptional feat.

That year he had turned twenty-six and had reached the very peak of his celebrity. Such was the actor's renown that Mine Imaizumi, the daughter of the renowned physician Hōshū Katsuragawa, wrote in her memoir, *Lingering Dreams*: 'He enjoyed such tremendous popularity, and people now often ask me why this was. He was truly a great actor. And he was beautiful. I do not believe I have ever seen such beauty before or since. His was not your common kind of beauty, but rather a divine kind of beauty.' Years later, Shōyō Tsubouchi,

261

in his novel *Portraits of Modern Students*, would even describe a certain beautiful geisha thus: 'She was tall with slender features, and her face was purest white. Her profile was arresting, with a high nose, and though her eyes seemed a little too bold, they were full of charm when she laughed. In her crimson lips and slender brow she bore a striking resemblance to the stage face of the late kabuki actor Tanosuke.'

These days, throughout the city, all manner of 'Tanosuke' products were sold, from rouge and face powder to collars for kimono—and the Tanosuke hairstyle, as well as Tanosuke *geta*, were much in vogue.

While Imaizumi might have described Sawamura's beauty as 'divine', and though it was said that he was easily embarrassed, blushing like a prim young maiden who had been cloistered away from the coarseness of the world, there were also rumours that said he would whisper cutting remarks about other actors even while on stage, provoking their profound resentment of him, and that, heedless of what others might think, he led a life of excess and debauchery, enjoying the pleasures of both male and female lovers. Among a multitude of eccentric characters, he was said to be an *onnagata* with a unique, almost other-worldly allure.

Being no habitué of the theatre, Kazuki knew none of this. Yet the few times he had gone there, he had been captivated by the bewitching spectacle of Sawamura, and so he shared his few recollections with Kawaji. For his part, Kawaji had never been to the theatre, but he had heard, in his capacity as an officer of the law, the salacious rumours circulating about the actor.

'I've heard it said that he's haunted by the vengeful ghosts of several dozen men and women. I doubt he rests easily,' he muttered. 'On another note, I wonder who the third man was.'

Judging by the look on his face, Kawaji was in no mind to let the matter rest.

For the next ten days or so, Kazuki and Kawaji were too busy to meet, but on the afternoon of the eighteenth, they bumped into each other at the jail in Kodenma-chō.

The exact date is relevant because it was the day on which Tatsuo Kumoi was sent to prison. Having plotted to overthrow the Satsuma–Chōshū government, this major political actor had been arrested some four months previously and imprisoned at Yonezawa, in his former domain, and now he had been sent to Tokyo to be placed in Kodenma-chō—and so, of course, the two chief inspectors had come to get a good look at the twenty-six-year-old criminal.

He was smaller than they had imagined and had the delicate features of a woman, and yet his bold, rebellious spirit was so much in evidence that anybody who saw him could only nod in agreement with the proceedings.

Afterwards, without any particular purpose in mind, the two of them sauntered leisurely towards the Asakusa Bridge, discussing Kumoi.

'You don't have any sympathy for Kumoi's motives by any chance, do you, Kazuki?'

'What makes you say that?' Kazuki laughed. 'I always thought that he was a fool.'

'How so?'

'People can mobilize and plot rebellion all they like, as if the government these days can be toppled from outside. No, if they're going to topple it, it'll be an inside job.'

'An inside job? Why?'

'It's just a feeling. I'm no strategist.'

They walked on in silence.

'Oh, about Sawamura,' said Kawaji all of a sudden. 'I paid Kishida a visit in Yokohama to ask him about that. Apparently, he's been a big fan of Sawamura's for some time, and it seems he hit it off well with Maki, who's also a fan. He said they'd agreed to meet at his house in the foreign concession and go sea-fishing—all four of them: Kishida, Maki, Sawamura and that other guy, who, it turns out, was another actor by the name Rikaku Arashi.'

'Hmm…'

'As for the house itself, he said he bought it with the intention of setting up a Western-style pharmacy in Tokyo. Anyhow, that morning, Kishida was seemingly called away on some urgent business and so he sent a messenger to inform them, but as there were three of them, there was some kind of mix-up and all of them showed up, only to have to go home again, disappointed.'

'Hmm…'

'At first, I thought it was a rather odd combination, but I suppose actors must have all sorts of fans. I laughed it off and almost bought it, but then I thought: what kind of government official patronizes *onnagata* actors? So, just to be sure, I looked into Maki.'

When it came to professional matters, the indefatigable Kawaji was exceptionally dogged.

'Tateki Maki, thirty-eight years old, born in Chōshū, deputy undersecretary at the Ministry of Popular Affairs. Lives in the Tawaramachi neighbourhood of Asakusa with his mother and niece. Unmarried. His character is every bit as jolly as his rotund frame would suggest, and his employer reports he is both meticulous and industrious.'

'Hmm…'

'Everybody says the only odd thing about him is that he's still single. I had Saruki do some digging, though, and it turns out that he owes vast amounts of money to loan sharks. He's very good at that sort of thing, is Saruki. Seemingly, Maki doesn't drink, gamble, womanize, or do anything else of the kind. Instead, he just lavishes money on Sawamura. It's as though he's indebted to the man. Naturally, he hides all this, and none of his colleagues knows about it.'

Kazuki burst out laughing. 'He's a bit of a queer fish, don't you think?'

'Compared to your average person, maybe. But not for a government official. On a practical note, if his superiors find out about it, he's sure to be dismissed.'

As they neared the Asakusa Bridge, Kawaji let out a curious exclamation.

'What is it?' Kazuki asked.

'Keep your head down. One of those loan sharks I was just mentioning is heading this way.'

And sure enough, walking towards them was a big, burly man, accompanied by a woman. The man must have been on the wrong side of sixty: his greasy body sagged everywhere, and not only was he repulsive to behold, but his ugly, rapacious nature seemed to have moulded his very features. As for the woman, her extraordinary beauty drew Kazuki's eye, and, after she passed the two men, staring in wonderment at Kazuki's *suikan*, she hastened to avert her gaze.

'They've ducked into the back alleys. Of course! He lives in Yagenbori,' said Kawaji. 'Maki borrows from other money-lenders, too, but that guy is the main one. He owes him more than three hundred *ryō*. His name's Kinpei Kobayashi, and, although he moonlights as a loan shark, he runs a legitimate pawnshop in Yagenbori. Saruki pointed him out to me the other day when we were walking together. The man was oblivious, needless to say.'

'What about the woman?'

'His mistress, O-Kinu.'

'His mistress? What a waste!'

'They say she was once one of the most sought-after geisha in Saruwaka-chō, but clearly that life was no match for the lure of lucre.'

'A geisha? It's little wonder.'

'Before that, she was the daughter of a footman to one of the shogun's bannermen.'

'And she lives in the pawnbroker's house?'

'The wife and mistress both live with him, although his wife is, by all accounts, bedridden.'

Kazuki looked at Kawaji in astonishment.

'You've certainly done your research. All this prying from a pair of binoculars! The subject of the investigation, of course, is up to his neck in all this. He won't stand a chance with you setting your sights on him.'

'Actually, it's all Saruki's work! As chance would have it, he'd gone to Kobayashi's pawnshop to leave some things in pledge. That's when he spotted Maki on his way out, which led to the discovery of all his debts.'

'Hmm, did he indeed?'

'On another note, those binoculars… They're intriguing. Would you mind lending them to me again sometime?'

'I'm afraid I don't have them any more,' said Kazuki.

Kawaji's eyes widened.

'Don't have them any more?!'

'They were gone before I knew it. One of the *rasotsu* usually stands guard at the house whenever I'm out, but somehow they've been pinched. Then again, they were the talk of the Saga mansion…'

3

One drizzly evening just over a week later, at the beginning of the ninth lunar month, Chief Inspector Kawaji, dressed in hat and cape, was doing his rounds in Yanagibashi, when suddenly he noticed a man and a woman running up behind him.

'Is that you, Saruki?' he asked, straining to see.

'It's me, sir!'

It was the figure of the woman, however, that caught Kawaji's eye. Could it be the mistress of Kinpei Kobayashi, the pawnbroker-cum-moneylender from Yagenbori? It certainly looked like her.

'What is it?' asked Kawaji.

'There's been a kidnapping!'

'What?!'

'There isn't time to explain. You've got to help us, sir! Don't worry, we'll catch them,' said Saruki, turning to the woman. 'They ran that way, didn't they? Towards the Ryōgoku Bridge? I'll explain it on the run, sir.'

With that, Saruki started running again, his enormous shoes clattering on the ground. Kawaji set off after him, leaving behind the woman, her fists clenched so hard that they had turned white.

'What's all this about, Saruki?'

'I was just at the Kobayashi pawnshop, sir. I'm ashamed to say it, but I'd gone there to leave something in pledge. Just as I got there, though, the young miss... Well, you already know her name, sir, it's O-Kinu... Anyway, she comes running out, saying that her friend has just been kidnapped.'

Saruki was already panting as he told the tale.

'The friend in question is a geisha from Saruwaka-chō by the name of Kikuchiyo. She'd had some business to attend to, and, once it was done, she climbed back into the rickshaw that had brought her there, ready to go home. Just as she was setting off, a man appeared, brandishing a sword. Apparently, he threatened the rickshaw-puller and abducted poor Kikuchiyo. As soon as I realized what had happened, I rushed after him and ran as far as the main street, and that's when I saw you.'

'Do you know why the geisha was kidnapped?'

'There was no time to ask for details, sir, but... Argh! My shoe!'

One of his enormous shoes had fallen off.

'Just carry it!'

Scalded by Kawaji, he set off again, running with one bare foot.

'Apparently, he means to use her to avenge his father.'

'What, you mean by...?'

'No, it looks as though his father was killed by Kikuchiyo's older brother. He found out about this only recently, and ever since he's been sniffing around her. It was getting out of hand, so apparently she'd come to have words with him. Ah, over there!'

Saruki was pointing ahead of them.

'That's it! She said it was a rickshaw with a collapsible hood!'

And sure enough, a rickshaw had just crossed the Ryōgoku Bridge and was disappearing into Honjo. There were few covered rickshaws in those days, and it was travelling unusually fast—doubtless because there was a sword-wielding man running alongside it.

The two of them ran after it through the rain. Several times they almost lost sight of it, but they closed in on it at the Rakan-ji temple in Itsutsume. The rickshaw had been set down outside the crumbling temple gate, but when they finally caught up with it, they found it empty.

'This way!' shouted Saruki, running through the temple gate. 'They must have gone in here!'

For a few moments, as he watched him, Kawaji just stood there.

He looked at the Buddhist temple, dedicated to the Five Hundred Arhats, and then to the north of it he spotted another building, the Sazae-dō, where one hundred statues of the Bodhisattva were enshrined. Kawaji knew none of this, but still, he could see the tall and narrow three-storey structure with its unusual spiral staircase wrapping around the outside of the building. The main temple had seen better days, but this bizarrely shaped three-storey pagoda was in such a terrific state of disrepair that it looked ready to collapse at any moment.

There, on the staircase leading up to the third storey, the kidnapper was standing with the woman, holding her arms behind her back. The rickshaw-puller had probably run off and disappeared into the temple grounds.

The man was in his mid-twenties and wore a black-crested kimono tucked up into his waistband. His features were pale and maniacal-looking. He opened his mouth like a wild beast and roared out:

'They didn't send the big guns, then? But this isn't just any kidnapping! My father met his end being tortured because of this one's brother!'

'Don't be a fool!' shouted Kawaji, even though his grasp of the situation was still rather shaky. 'She wasn't the one who killed him! Let her go!'

'If only you knew how he was killed! They cut off both my father's arms while he was still alive, and then they cut off his head!'

It was at this point that Kawaji realized the man was not only hysterical, but also drunk. He groped in his pocket for his pistol.

'Behold!' the man cried out. 'Now I'm going to cut this girl's arms off one by one. Then I'll let her go, all right.'

The girl screamed and tried to escape. The rain was getting heavier, blocking Kawaji's view, and, although he had managed to extract his pistol, he was worried.

Through the rain, he saw the flash of a naked sword being raised high.

The very next instant, however, the blade itself went flying into the air, falling at the foot of the pagoda, while somebody behind the man grabbed his arm and forced him down.

Kawaji then saw a familiar figure holding a rope in his mouth.

'I've got him!' the man in the *suikan* called out. 'Come and give me a hand, will you?'

Saruki had returned and he and Kawaji ran up and were dumbstruck when they discovered Kazuki standing beside a young man wearing the robes of an artisan. They seemed to have appeared out of nowhere.

'A fortunate coincidence. I'm glad nobody was hurt.'

'Kazuki, what on earth are you doing here?!'

'This gentleman will explain that later,' he replied, indicating the man beside him.

Presently, they tied the kidnapper up and took him downstairs for questioning.

There, in the dilapidated hall, with the rain blowing in through the wooden panels, row upon row of peeling statues of the Bodhisattva stood watching the proceedings.

The culprit identified himself as Hikomaro Kagawa, and it was surprising to learn, in light of his earlier insult to Kawaji's rank, that he himself worked as a minor functionary in the Grand Council of State. He was so drunk that, for the first few minutes, he could barely speak, but eventually his astonishing confession came out.

He was the son of Hajime Kagawa, a retainer for the Chigusa clan who was assassinated towards the end of the Edo period. Some seven years ago, Kagawa senior was set upon by several *rōnin* at his house in Kyoto after it was rumoured that he had conspired with Lord Aribumi Chigusa, his master, and Lord Iwakura to have a monk from Eizan lay a curse upon Emperor Kōmei.

During the attack, Kagawa senior hid himself in the gap in a double wall that he had had installed behind an alcove. The *rōnin* threatened his maid with their swords, but she was a courageous woman, and even when the blood began to flow, she insisted that she knew nothing; then, the rōnin seized Kagawa's eleven-year-old son, Bennojō, and threatened to take his life as an abettor to his father. It was at this point that, unable to hold back any longer, Kagawa revealed himself, only to be slaughtered. First, the *rōnin* cut off his arms one by one, and then they beheaded him. A few days later, the head was hanged from the drum tower of the Higashi Hongan-ji temple, while his right arm was unceremoniously delivered, along with a threatening letter, to the mansion of Lord Chigusa and the left was sent similarly to Lord Iwakura.

Among the many examples of terrorism that took place back then, Kawaji recalled this as one of the most dreadful and egregious.

'And where were you at the time?'

'On the night in question, I was...' Kagawa said, shaking. 'I happened to be staying with a relative that night, and so I was spared the ordeal.'

Then, after a few moments' silence, he added quickly:

'Several years later, I learnt that the men were led by Gen'ichirō Itami, who at the time was a retainer of the daimyo of Himeji. In the end, though, I never was able to find out where they had gone or what had become of them. But ten days ago, I received a letter informing me that in Saruwaka-chō there was a geisha by the name of Kikuchiyo, and that she was Itami's sister.'

He seemed to have sobered up considerably. A meekness and nervousness now appeared in his face, which had turned pale, as though he had caught a cold.

'I'm well aware that to take revenge on the assassin's sister is misguided, but when I think of the way in which my father was killed, I can't help feeling bitter. What makes matters worse is that the letter said that Itami died peacefully several years ago, in the comfort of his own bed. Then earlier today, I was off duty and having a drink at an *izakaya* near my house in Yanagihara. When I looked up, there was a piece of paper with a note scribbled on it, telling me that Kikuchiyo was going to an old friend's house in Yagenbori this evening and that it was the perfect opportunity to take my revenge.'

'What?! Show me the note,' demanded Kawaji.

'Ah, well, you see… To give myself some Dutch courage, I must have knocked back at least a pint and a half of sake. When I remembered the note later, it was gone.'

Kawaji looked at Kazuki.

'How, then, can we be sure that you're telling the truth?' asked Kawaji.

'It would be pointless for me to lie.'

'So, you meant to kidnap the girl and kill her?'

'No, I didn't want it to go that far.'

'But you meant to cut off one of her arms, didn't you?' said Kazuki.

'No! I… I didn't even know what I was going to do with her.'

Kagawa's face looked genuinely confused.

'At any rate, the fact alone that the lady has come to no harm doesn't absolve you of your crime. The very idea that an official of the Grand Council of State would take a sword and kidnap a lady!' said Kazuki.

'I know, I know… You'll have my full cooperation.'

No sooner had he said this, however, than he suddenly let out a desperate, high-pitched cry, bewailing his lamentable fate.

'Excuse me, but won't you please let him go?'

This unexpected phrase was uttered by none other than Kikuchiyo. The lady, who had until this point been sitting there as though in a trance, seemed to have come to her senses.

'It's my brother who committed the crime,' she said. 'My brother did many terrible things. Please, let this poor man go.'

There were tears in her eyes as she spoke. She was large, with vulgar features, but she had a kind nature.

'I just couldn't bear it if he were punished for this. Oh, please, won't you just let him go home?'

'What do you say, Kawaji? Shall we leave it here for now? After all, no real harm was done.'

Kawaji said nothing. He watched in silence as Kazuki untied the rope and Kagawa bowed two or three times, placing his head to the dust-laden floor, before staggering out of the pagoda, a wave of drink seeming to hit him once again.

'I wonder who it could have been, the person who incited him to take revenge—if such a person really exists, that is,' Kawaji muttered to himself.

Kazuki just looked at him quizzically. Then Kawaji turned to him:

'So why *were* you here?'

Up to that point, the young artisan—he could have been only eighteen or nineteen—had been standing there in a daze, as though spellbound by it all. He bowed and for the first time began to speak.

Because of the anti-Buddhist movement, he explained, the Rakan-ji temple had lost most of its worshippers since the Restoration, and their funds had reached such a nadir that they were having to sell off the Sazae-dō. The pagoda had been bought by a demolition business that wanted the place solely for timber. Only, the Sazae-dō had three entire floors dedicated to the goddess of mercy, and those hundred statues, which had been donated to the temple to repose the spirits of the dead in the hereafter, had been carved by master craftsmen in ancient times—and so there was much there that he wanted to preserve, if only for the artistry. Of all the statues of the deity, however, those decorated with gold leaf had been bought up by a goldsmith. Apparently, he wanted to burn them, collect the ashes and extract the leftover gold. When he heard about this, the sculptor—his name was Kōzō Takamura—had pleaded with the goldsmith to spare at least five of them from the ashes, but his plea had fallen on deaf ears.

'I was at a loss,' he said, 'but then I remembered a certain acquaintance of mine. I asked Kazuki here if he would mind having a word on my behalf, and so I brought him here first to show him the statues.'

'The divine grace of the Bodhisattva is miraculous, don't you think?' said Kazuki, smiling at the geisha.

4

Was Kazuki's decision to release Hikomaro Kagawa, the man who had kidnapped the geisha, Kikuchiyo, the right thing to do in the end?

The incident weighed on Kawaji's mind so much that he refused to let the man out of his sight.

When he looked into it, he found that the man's work record was not very impressive. On the occasions when he did turn up at the office, he would attend to his duties obediently enough, but there were also times when he failed to show up entirely. The reason for these frequent absences was apparently that he drank too much. Whenever he did, he would become violent and drink himself into oblivion, and then, the very next day, he would find himself in such a sorry state that he couldn't move. There was certainly a touch of the alcoholic about him.

One evening a few days later, Kawaji spotted him ducking into an *izakaya* on his way home from work and, so that the chief inspector wouldn't be noticed, took a corner seat and availed himself of the opportunity to observe his descent into inebriation.

When Kagawa was in a blind stupor, Kawaji heard him quietly lament:

'Oh, what a coward I am, a real coward. I hid between the walls while my own father was being murdered. When they were torturing my father, I heard my eleven-year-old brother, Bennojō, throw himself before them, screaming and wailing that if they were going to kill Father, then they would have to kill him as well. In the end, I was just too afraid to show myself. I may have survived, but really, I died back then. Now I'm just an empty shell of a human being.'

First, Kawaji had been convinced that it was Kagawa's state of mind that had led to the kidnapping, and now he thought that it was because of his weak nature that he had let his own father die. He would have only been eighteen or so at the time, but he was still the son of a retainer. For a young man from Satsuma, it was unconscionable. An experience like that, moreover, would ruin his life for ever.

Apropos of Kagawa senior's murder, there were some things that had been preying on Kazuki's mind after the incident at the Sazae-dō.

'What I don't understand,' he said to Kawaji, 'is why would Lord Iwakura want to have a curse laid on his late majesty?'

'I'm sure that was just a rumour.'

'But what were the grounds for it, then?'

'I've no idea. I gather that the late emperor wasn't really in favour of overthrowing the shogunate. There was talk of uniting the shogunate with the imperial court, of having them coexist, each with its own separate responsibilities.

That's why Lord Iwakura, who wanted to see imperial rule restored absolutely, was unhappy. Maybe his dissatisfaction was misinterpreted.'

'So, effectively, in order to re-establish the emperor system, they had no choice but to overthrow an emperor who wasn't so keen on it?' mused Kazuki.

'I'm not sure I'd put it in quite those terms.'

'You once told me that Lord Iwakura was one of the most terrifying men you knew.'

'Now, hold on a minute,' Kawaji hastily replied. 'I may have said that, but I never said anything about him laying a curse on the late emperor!'

But Kazuki, as was his wont, fixed him with a look of comprehension.

'Well, Lord Iwakura isn't the only man who'd stop at nothing to achieve his goal,' Kawaji said. 'People are strange, are they not?'

Kazuki laughed feebly.

Later on, Kawaji, too, would come to the disconcerting realization that Lord Iwakura was capable of anything…

To review the facts, Kawaji, one day, quite by chance, had witnessed Deputy Undersecretary Maki of the Ministry of Popular Affairs in the company of two kabuki actors at Ginkō Kishida's house in the Tsukiji Foreign Settlement. Suspicious of the group, he had Maki investigated and found that he owed large sums of money to several moneylenders. He had subsequently discovered that the moneylender Kinpei Kobayashi was keeping a former geisha as his mistress. Finally, he had learnt that Kobayashi's mistress, O-Kinu, was an old friend of the geisha Kikuchiyo, who was the sister of an assassin and, because of this, had been the target of an aborted kidnapping by the son of her brother's victim.

It was all very tenuous. What was more, the only reason that Kawaji knew any of this was that he had learnt if from Sergeant Saruki, or else had just so happened to be in the right place at the right time. And besides, as an officer of the law, who knew better than the average man how full of sorrows the world is, not one of these circumstances seemed especially out of the ordinary. In fact, you could even say that they were commonplace.

And yet, these circumstances were not unrelated. They were strands of a single affair—one that was steadily marching towards catastrophe.

It was only ten days after the incident at the Sazae-dō that Kawaji received word informing him that the geisha Kikuchiyo had gone missing.

On the previous day, at around five o'clock, she and three fellow geisha were summoned by the *okiya* in Saruwaka-chō to a certain restaurant in Matsuyama-chō. They travelled there by rickshaw and cut through the precinct of the Sensō-ji temple in Asakusa along the way. As they were passing through, Kikuchiyo, whose rickshaw was last in their procession, suddenly asked the driver to stop for a moment, telling him that she wanted to pay her respects. The driver watched her trot off towards the main temple, but she never returned—not that evening, nor even the following day.

On the evening that Kawaji received this report from Sergeant Saruki, he was understandably shocked. Saruki had come running after visiting Kobayashi's pawnshop again and hearing the story from O-Kinu.

The two then set out immediately for Saruwaka-chō. They questioned the other geisha as well as the rickshaw-puller, but the only answers they got were that nothing had been out of the ordinary that day, and that when Kikuchiyo had disappeared at the temple, she hadn't seemed to be carrying any money or belongings. The two men could only assume that Kikuchiyo had been kidnapped again. Their thoughts turned naturally to Kagawa, and so they ran straight to Yanagihara.

As expected, they found him drinking in a local *izakaya*. It was no after-work drink, either: he had skipped work that day and gone drinking instead. When Kawaji enquired, he replied that he had been drinking there all the previous evening as well. 'Why do you ask?' he said. He was pretty drunk by then, but now he seemed to sober up a little, and his expression grew anxious. It was impossible to tell, however, whether this was genuine or he was playing dumb. When they asked the proprietors of the *izakaya*, they replied that Kagawa had indeed been sitting there from four o'clock till eleven the day before. This seemed plausible enough, so Kagawa had an alibi.

Faced thus with a dead end, Kawaji and Saruki could not help looking disappointed.

Three days later, however, a horrifying incident occurred.

In Shiba Hamamatsu-chō, there was a house that belonged to Shūzō Toba, a junior secretary in the Ministry of Popular Affairs. It was early morning on the twentieth day of the ninth lunar month, and in front of the house stood a rickshaw with a long white object propped up inside it. It had been found by one of the servants, who discovered it to be a human leg that had been severed just above the knee at one end and just above the ankle at the other.

Needless to say, the discovery caused quite a stir. When they received the report, both Kawaji and Kazuki rushed to the scene.

Since the limb was missing a foot, it was not immediately clear whether it was the right or left leg, but the distribution of the flesh on the calf suggested that it was the left. It was still fresh, probably having been severed only the night before, and you could tell at a single glance that it had been cut off with a sharp blade. The blood had been washed off, and this pillar of white flesh was so plump and hairless that everybody agreed it could only have belonged to a woman.

The Toba family was at a loss to explain any of it. It transpired that the rickshaw had been stolen from a company in neighbouring Tsukiji. Kawaji's suspicions fell on two familiar figures, however: he believed that the leg was Kikuchiyo's, while the perpetrator must have been Kagawa.

Once again, he rushed to Yanagihara.

And yet…

It emerged that the previous day Kagawa had in fact gone to work at the Grand Council of State and that, after leaving, he had headed straight to his usual drinking den, where, as was his wont, he became blind drunk—so drunk, in fact, that he lay down in a corner of the *izakaya* and didn't stagger home until eight o'clock the next morning.

No matter who Kawaji asked—be it Kagawa, the couple who ran the *izakaya* or even the regulars who were there on the night in question—there could be no doubt about it. Kawaji was astounded.

And yet, once again…

The very next day, Kawaji received an urgent report from Sergeant Saruki. After questioning, Kagawa, whose alibi was supposedly watertight, had apparently absconded.

The barefaced liar!

Kawaji was upset at having let opportunity slip through his fingers once again, but after consulting with Kazuki, he summoned the usual five *rasotsu* and ordered a Tokyo-wide search for Kagawa. He then added:

'Oh, yes, that's right. There's also the matter of Kikuchiyo. Where is the woman?! After having her leg cut off like that, I doubt she's still alive, so keep an eye out for the body of a woman missing one leg!'

As Kazuki silently watched the *rasotsu* clatter out like a pack of bloodhounds—albeit not especially brave ones—he did not look reassured.

'But doesn't Kagawa have an alibi?' he asked.

'In a manner of speaking. But something here isn't quite right. And when I get my hands on him, I intend to find out what that is,' Kawaji grumbled. 'Maybe he didn't do it himself. He could have got somebody else to do it for him. After all, who, but for Kagawa, would want to do such a thing? And besides, isn't his sudden disappearance the best proof of it?'

'I know his father had his arms cut off, but then why would the victim have her leg cut off? To make it easier for her to haunt people when she's a ghost?'

'Don't be silly! Besides, her arms might have been cut off as well. We can't be sure until we see the body,' said Kawaji.

'Not only was the leg cut off above the knee, but the ankle was cut off as well. What do you make of that?'

'Heinous though it was, this guy's father had both his arms and his head cut off—so never mind limbs, it stands to reason that he might want to chop his victim, bit by bit, into little pieces. It isn't something any sane person would do!'

In his mind, Kawaji just couldn't get rid of the image of Kagawa's face, with its manic quality that appeared especially when he had been drinking.

Three, then four days went by, but still Kagawa was nowhere to be found. Kikuchiyo's body had not been discovered, either. But then, on the fifth day, Kagawa showed up—as a corpse, drowned in the river.

Just upstream of the Ryōgoku Bridge, on the bank of the Honjo's Yokoami-chō, there was a spot called Hyappongui, where hundreds of stakes had been driven into the riverbed to protect the bank at a bend in the river. It was a good place to catch carp and other fish, and so, early that morning, a fisherman had gone there, only to find a body floating in the water, caught among the stakes, and carried there by the cold autumn winds.

There were no injuries to the body, nor were there any signs of strangulation. Over the course of five days, however, Kagawa had grown so emaciated, with a scraggy beard now covering his hollow cheeks, that he almost looked like a different man.

'With nowhere else to turn, he must have taken his own life,' said Kawaji, staring down at the corpse blankly. 'But, Kazuki, now we'll never know what happened to the murdered woman.'

5

These events were shocking: a single leg found in a rickshaw, and now the man thought to have done it found drowned. Yet, in a sense, it was what occurred two days later that dealt an even greater blow to Kawaji.

Or, to be more precise, what came afterwards…

At around ten o'clock on the morning of the twenty-seventh day of the ninth lunar month, Kawaji was at the Imperial Prosecuting Office, listening to a report from Sergeant Saruki on the failed search for the woman's body. Just then, however, another report arrived from the Ministry of Popular Affairs in Marunouchi, informing him that, a short while ago, Junior Secretary Shūzō Toba had committed *seppuku* in his office.

'Shūzō Toba? I'm sure I've heard that name somewhere before.'

Kazuki, who also happened to be there, cast a quizzical look at him.

'Of course!' Kawaji cried out. 'He's the owner of the house where the leg in the rickshaw was found!'

Kazuki, too, recalled the long, dark, but rather wilful-looking face of Shūzō Toba, who at the time of the incident had said that he had no idea what it was all about and that it must have been a coincidence.

Dropping everything, the three of them rushed over to the Ministry of Popular Affairs.

When they arrived at the office, they found a dozen people standing around in a circle, frozen like statues. There, in the middle of the room, lying on the floor and surrounded by a sea of blood, was Shūzō Toba.

'What happened?' Kawaji asked.

'He killed himself because of the murder he committed,' a rather corpulent man replied.

Not only did this answer come as a surprise, but when Kazuki and Kawaji turned to look at the man who gave it, they were startled. Though they had never met in person until now, they recognized him as Tateki Maki, the man they had spotted through the binoculars. Maki was an undersecretary at the ministry, which meant that he had been Toba's superior.

'But... but whom did he kill?'

'Why, Hikomaro Kagawa, of course,' replied Maki.

'And what makes you say that?' asked Kawaji in astonishment.

According to the testimony of Undersecretary Maki and the other officials who were present, the events of that morning were as follows.

Shūzō Toba was a capable employee of the ministry who outshone many of his colleagues and was, moreover, a very upstanding man. A year ago, however, he had apparently fallen in love with a geisha: a certain Kikuchiyo from Saruwaka-chō. It had all started when Maki invited Toba, who was not only from the same province, but from the same village in Chōshū, to a restaurant and called for Kikuchiyo as well. The very upstanding Toba fell hopelessly for her and, after that night, began following her around. The man had an obsessive and brooding nature.

Eventually, Toba became visibly worried when he learnt that Kikuchiyo had a brother in the old capital, a *shishi* who had killed a man, and because of that she had been targeted and very nearly kidnapped by the son of her brother's victim, a minor official by the name of Hikomaro Kagawa.

About a week ago, Kikuchiyo vanished, and Toba felt certain that she had been kidnapped. Then, after the discovery of the severed limb outside his house and Kagawa's disappearance, Toba's frenzy peaked. He believed that Kagawa had somehow discovered his infatuation with Kikuchiyo and had done this to spite him.

Toba searched for Kagawa like a man possessed, and then, three days ago, he found him at night on the bank of the

Sumida River. He interrogated him, a fight ensued, and in the end Toba pushed Kagawa into the river. At the time, Kagawa was so drunk that he could hardly walk, so it was only natural that he drowned.

When Maki heard about Kagawa's death, he had a hunch that it was all down to Toba, but of course he had no evidence of this.

'This morning, I called Toba into my office and asked him outright whether he was responsible for Kagawa's death,' Maki explained. 'He blanched at the very mention of it, but then he played dumb and claimed not to know anything about it.'

Anticipating Toba's denial, however, Maki had already made certain preparations—one being that he had already summoned several officials connected with Toba.

'You say you know nothing about it, but there's no real proof of that,' Maki had said. 'So, permit me to show you something, and we'll see whether that changes your answer. Gentlemen, please keep a close eye on Toba's reaction!'

Then, right on cue, the door at the back of the room had opened to reveal a figure.

Upon seeing this, Toba had cried out, his eyes wide and his mouth agape.

'You… you're alive!' was all he could say.

He had frozen stiff, like a dead man. Standing before him was none other than the geisha, Kikuchiyo.

'And she isn't just alive! Look, she has both legs!' said Maki. 'Kikuchiyo, if you would do the honours?'

There, in front of the assembled men, Kikuchiyo blushed but seemed quite prepared to carry out Maki's order. Timidly, she raised the hem of her kimono, revealing two perfectly white, perfectly attached legs.

'But… this can't be! This cannot be!' Toba had cried. 'What, then, was that in the rickshaw?'

'It must have been somebody else's leg,' said Maki.

He now turned to the representatives of the Imperial Prosecuting Office.

'I was surprised myself, to be honest. I'd heard about the leg that was found outside Toba's house and was convinced that it had to be Kikuchiyo's. Imagine my surprise, then, when she turned up at my house last night, full of life and with both legs intact. When I asked her what had happened, she told me that she'd run off to a friend's house in Shimōsa. Ah, what a mess Toba had made of things! Though he wasn't the one who called for Kikuchiyo and the other geisha on the night of her disappearance, he had, a few days previously, insisted that she go to a hideout that he'd prepared for her. After her experience of being kidnapped, the very notion troubled her, but Toba was so worried for her safety that, being the kind-hearted person he was, he couldn't stand by and do nothing. For her part, however, Kikuchiyo disliked the importunate Toba even more than she did the man who had tried to kidnap her. How fickle the heart can be! So, with all these thoughts racing about her head, Kikuchiyo finally had had enough, and, on a whim that day, decided to run away from Asakusa to Shimōsa. Then, just last night, completely unaware of all the mayhem that had ensued, she decided, once again on a whim, to go and see an old friend of hers who is now the mistress of a pawnbroker in Yagenbori. There, Kikuchiyo heard at last about everything that happened since her disappearance, including Kagawa's body being found in the river. She was so shocked by this that she and her friend came to ask me what they ought to do. You can imagine my surprise when I saw her.'

Kawaji was stunned and for a few moments didn't know what to say.

'Why did the pawnbroker's mistress accompany her?' asked Kazuki.

'We know each other a little,' said Maki. Thinking that this wasn't a good enough explanation, however, he added: 'I was one of her patrons when she used to be a geisha.'

He was determined to keep a poker face and not let on that he had borrowed money at a very high rate of interest from the pawnbroker.

'It's obvious that Toba made a mistake. But mistake or not, this didn't change my opinion that he had surely killed Kagawa. And if this came to light, it would cause a scandal. As an official of the Ministry of Popular Affairs, and as Toba's superior, I couldn't possibly turn a blind eye to this. So, I decided to make Toba confess by having the living Kikuchiyo paraded before his very eyes, so that everybody could watch his reaction.'

Faced with Kikuchiyo alive and in one piece, Toba had looked as though he were in the middle of a nightmare.

'But... but I saw her leg being cut off!' he had cried out.

It was a curious remark, to be sure.

'What nonsense is this?! When?'

'The day before her leg turned up outside my house!'

'Where did you see it?'

'From the tower of the Tsukiji Hotel.'

Maki had looked aghast as Toba stood there, gasping for air.

'Maki-san, I saw it through the binoculars you gave me. You told me to go to the Tsukiji Hotel and take a look at Tokyo. You gave them to me yourself, didn't you? I really did see it!'

6

Kawaji gulped as he listened to the tale.

'He was right enough about that,' Maki continued. 'Just the other day, the pawnbroker's mistress—O-Kinu's her name—was telling me about an interesting item that had come into the shop. It was a pair of binoculars, which she lent me.'

'Hang on a minute,' said Kazuki. 'Did she say anything about the person who'd pawned these binoculars?'

'Indeed, she did. "Even in this age of opening up to the world," I said to her, "who on earth pawns something as rare as these?" And she said…' (at this point, Maki shifted his gaze) '… that it was a *rasotsu*.'

Saruki's eyes darted about. He looked at Kazuki and then at Kawaji, then started cradling his head in his hands. As a regular at the same pawnshop, Saruki was no stranger to Maki. Indeed, that was how Saruki had come to hear of Maki's debts in the first place.

Taken aback, Kawaji glared at Saruki, who appeared to be attempting to bury his head in the sand. So, in the end, it was Saruki who had stolen the binoculars while he stood guard at Kazuki's house. Was nothing beneath this man?

'Very well. We'll return to this subject later,' said Kazuki brusquely. 'Now, tell me, what happened after that?'

'Well,' said Maki, 'O-Kinu suggested that I take a look at Tokyo from the bell tower of the Tsukiji Hotel, so I took the binoculars and headed there. I was so impressed that, before returning them, I lent them to Toba with the same recommendation. He must have gone the day before the murder. According to him, while he was looking out of the tower, he witnessed a woman's leg cut being off through the window of a Western-style building. Apparently, she was lying on top of what looked like a bed.

288

There was blood everywhere. They were cutting her flesh with a dagger and sawing right through the bone.'

'Who was?' asked Kawaji.

'There was a curtain in the window half-blocking the view, so all he could see was the woman's legs, and the hands pinning her down and holding the dagger and the saw.'

'So, there was more than one other person?'

'It would certainly seem that way.'

'And the woman's face? Was it really Kikuchiyo's?'

'As I say, he could only see her legs.'

'But then, how did he know it was a woman?'

'Oh, there was no doubt about it. Or at least that's what Toba seemed to think. Ah, yes, there was a young boy there in the tower as well. He could have been only ten or so and asked Toba to let him see for himself. Seemingly, Toba obliged. Or no, that's it! He said it was the boy who saw it first.'

Kawaji and Kazuki exchanged a look.

'So, leaving the boy behind, Toba ran out of the hotel and tried to find the building he'd just seen through the binoculars. Only, when he found it, all the windows were covered in cobwebs and there was only an old caretaker there who told him it was unoccupied and sent him away with a flea in his ear, saying not to be so ridiculous. Toba said he returned home then in a daze, wondering whether it hadn't all been a dream. At that point, it hadn't even occurred to him that the girl might have been Kikuchiyo, but the very next day, when the leg turned up right outside his house, it was as though the scales had fallen from his eyes: he immediately thought it must have been hers. But he was wrong. "If you don't believe me, then ask the boy," he said. "Go to the hotel and you'll be able to find out who he is."'

'There's no need. We already have that information,' Kazuki interrupted.

Maki gave him a strange look.

'But what about Toba's suicide?' asked Kawaji.

'Even if Toba was mistaken about Kikuchiyo, there can be no uncertainty that he was the one who killed Kagawa. He said that he looked into Kagawa's movements on the day, and, since he had not showed up for work, Toba inferred that it was proof of Kagawa's scheme and decided that he had no choice but to kill him discreetly. It looks as though Toba'd been planning to feign ignorance over Kagawa's murder, but the shock of seeing Kikuchiyo alive betrayed his resolve. Toba could sense this from the way everybody was looking at him. All of a sudden, while we were still asking questions, he committed *seppuku*.'

The other officials nodded.

'Even a person of high rank cannot get away with murder. Toba was from the same village as I, and he came from a prominent family. Rather than face the shame of imprisonment, he died by his own hand, and I believe this was for the best. My colleagues and I humbly beg that you keep this affair as quiet as possible.'

'Saruki!' said Kawaji.

'Yes, sir?'

'Go and fetch the boy. You know the one I mean.'

'He said he lived in Koishikawa, in the Takasaki Domain's residence,' Kazuki added. 'I think his name was Kanzō Uchimura. Take a rickshaw and bring him here.'

Having escaped questioning over the binoculars for the time being, Saruki rushed out, looking rather pleased with himself.

Kazuki bid the whole group be seated, before seeming to lose himself in silent contemplation.

The renowned chief inspector looked so solemn as he stood there that none of the officials dared to sit, and instead they just stood around, trying not to look at the bloody corpse of their colleague lying on the floor.

It was about an hour later that Saruki returned with the boy. When the young lad saw Kazuki, he flashed a smile of recognition, but his expression turned serious as soon as the questions began.

'I did see it,' the boy declared. 'I really did see the lady's leg being cut off!'

'Be that as it may, what were you doing up in the tower again?' asked Kawaji.

'That morning, on my way to my English lesson, a lady stopped me and told me that if I went to the hotel at three o'clock, she'd let me look through the binoculars again. I really wanted to have another go with them, so after the lesson was finished, I rushed straight there.'

'A lady? What lady?'

'She was wearing an *okoso-zukin* headscarf, so I didn't really get a proper look.'

The two chief inspectors looked at each other.

'I feel as though I've got various links in a chain, but I still can't piece them together,' muttered Kazuki. 'Who could this woman in the headscarf be? She offered to let the boy use them *again*, so she must have known not only that Toba was going to be there that day, but also that we'd been there before. But who could have known that? Esmeralda would never have done a thing like that. And besides, if it was her, the boy would have noticed her blue eyes.'

'More to the point,' said Kawaji, 'if there really was a woman who had her leg cut off, then who is she? There's something distinctly odd about that house in the foreign settlement. I'll have to talk to Kishida again. Then again, there's something that seems distinctly queer about him too...

Two days later, Kawaji arrived with an update for Kazuki.

'There's not much to report, although I did find Kishida at Doctor Hepburn's house. He says he's no idea what's been going on at his house in the foreign settlement, because he hasn't been there lately. So, the day when Toba said he saw a woman's leg being cut off through the window was the nineteenth, right? Well, that day—or, more properly, from the fifteenth until around the twenty-fifth—Doctor Hepburn was suffering from a bout of rheumatism. Evidently even famous doctors can get it! Anyway, it was getting worse, so Kishida was run ragged, having to look after him and send away all the patients that had come to see him. Now that the doctor can just about stand the pain, he's back at work, but they're having to work through all the patients that have accumulated, and they're exhausted. Kishida just said, "Spare me the unnecessary questions," and slammed the door in my face.'

Kawaji was indignant.

'And there I was, thinking I'd hit it off with the man! As for whose leg it might be, or why this series of incidents has occurred, your guess is as good as mine...'

7

On the last night of the ninth lunar month, the inhabitants of the foreign settlement were startled when they looked up and saw the windows of the Tsukiji Hotel bell tower stained a bright crimson. They realized at once that it was not a fire, but still, they could not quite dispel the strange, rather eerie feeling that had come over them.

Two braziers were burning in the tower, but of course, they were being watched over, lest the fire spread. On a plain wooden dais were displayed various props used for ancient rituals, and, sitting in a long row, were the usual grandees of the Imperial Prosecuting Office, old Manabe and his daughter, Kazuki, Kawaji, and the five *rasotsu*. Also present in this spacious room was the pawnbroker's mistress, O-Kinu, the geisha Kikuchiyo, as well as a delegation of a dozen or so officials from the Ministry of Popular Affairs, including Tateki Maki.

The *kagura* bells suddenly rang out, and the *miko* Esmeralda's voice began to chant.

> *Awariya, asobihasutomo, mōsanu, asakurani,*
> *Shūzō Toba no mitama, mairitamae…*

This, of course, was the second time that this other-worldly ceremony had been held in the Tsukiji Hotel, though the first time it had been in the great hall below.

'*Ima… mairu!… I am… the spirit… of Shūzō Toba…*'

Kikuchiyo let out a faint, muffled cry.

'*For the first time since arriving in the land of the dead… I can see the land of the living without hindrance…*

'*I truly believed that Hikomaro Kagawa had murdered Kikuchiyo… And little wonder… Kagawa had borne a grudge against Kikuchiyo for some time and had even attempted to kidnap her… Then, after she disappeared, I witnessed the leg being cut off, and that leg was delivered to my house…*'

The enormous windows on all four sides of the room had been flung open to the vast autumn night sky with its countless twinkling stars. None of the assembled guests was looking at them, however. It was as though everybody were floating in another dimension altogether.

'*Some of this was true to begin with, but some had been contrived afterwards... Kikuchiyo disappeared because somebody encouraged her to do so... I was deceived!... Like a fool, I was ignorant of the degree of loathing that Kikuchiyo felt for me...*'

Kikuchiyo put her hands over her ears in horror.

'*The scene in the house in the foreign settlement... was Doctor Hepburn amputating the leg of the* onnagata *Tanosuke Sawamura...*'

Kawaji winced, as though he had felt the lash of a whip.

'*Sawamura is suffering from a disease called gangrene, which causes the leg to rot from the foot... The only way to cure it was to have the leg cut off... Only Doctor Hepburn could perform the operation, so Sawamura requested it through Ginkō Kishida...*'

The other-worldly strains of the *kagura* music continued to ring out.

'*Moreover, Sawamura did not want this to become public knowledge... and feared that he would become a spectacle if he went to the Hepburn residence in Yokohama... So he asked for the operation to be performed in secret at Kishida's house in the Tsukiji Foreign Settlement... Although Doctor Hepburn ordinarily never sees patients outside of his house, he agreed to this request... The disease was not visible to the naked eye, but it had spread... so they had no choice but to amputate the leg above the knee... What I saw was this operation being carried out with the help of an assistant...*

'*The reason Kishida did not mention it to the chief inspector afterwards was out of sympathy for the beautiful actor's vanity... and because Sawamura himself had asked him to tell no one... But* how could I, after having seen such a thing, have ever imagined that?...

'In fact, my witnessing of it was an artful affair... It was of course the boy who saw the incident and showed me... But he had noticed it only because he was fascinated by the building in the first place...

'What the child had originally witnessed was the preparations being made for Sawamura's operation... When the binoculars came into the hands of another person, Sergeant Saruki told them what the boy had seen... The real culprit took advantage of this and used the child to make sure that I saw what was going on in the same building a few days later...'

'Did I really say that?' muttered Saruki nervously, momentarily putting down his flute. Nobody other than Kawaji and Kazuki heard him, however.

'Indeed, the woman in the headscarf who enticed the child to go to the Tsukiji Hotel again that day was none other than the pawn-broker's mistress, O-Kinu... But she herself had been threatened by the real culprit and forced to play a part...'

O-Kinu shuddered. Her head slumped forward, as though her neck were about to break.

'It was also the real culprit who had given Kagawa the scrap of paper in the izakaya, inciting him to abduct her... The trap had been carefully laid...

'While the operation was taking place, the culprit was hiding in the next room... And when the opportunity presented itself, the amputated leg was stolen...

'With such meticulous planning, it was no wonder that when the leg turned up in the rickshaw I believed it belonged to Kikuchiyo... The reason the foot had been cut off was to hide the evidence of gangrene... Then, Sawamura's beautiful feminine leg was shaved so that it would look like the genuine article...

'I, however, believed it was all Kagawa's doing and flew into a rage, finally killing him... Seeing it all clearly now, it was always the culprit's aim to take advantage of my obsessive nature...

'Perhaps it was to be expected that the criminal would hatch a plan like this... We came from the same village, and, although my family enjoyed higher status, he had worked his way up, and feared that I would drag him down again one day... Then my chance came... I got wind that he was mad for the theatre and onnagata, and that he was up to his neck in debt from moneylenders... For a government official, that was scandalous enough... but if it were ever to become public knowledge, he could say goodbye to it all... And he knew that I knew this...

'So, he turned me into a murderer and pushed me to kill an innocent man... Kagawa was innocent... When he learnt of Kikuchiyo's disappearance, he knew the Imperial Prosecuting Office would suspect him... So he made the rash decision to run away, believing he had no other option...'

The kagura bells suddenly rang out.

'I fell right into the criminal's trap... Worse yet, I was placed in the unavoidable position of having to cut my own stomach before the Imperial Prosecuting Office could question me...'

The golden-haired miko's voice had already begun to fade away when the dull thud of the kaen-daiko resounded.

'Needless to say, the culprit is...'

The voice trailed off and Esmeralda's head slumped forward.

THE CORPSE
THAT CRADLED
ITS OWN HEAD

The following relates the particulars of an exceptionally difficult case, in which a rasotsu, *who happened to be conducting surveillance, discovered outside the walls of a certain villa in Imado a large, naked man whose body had been defiled and whose head had been cut off. Both the identity of the man and the significance of the circumstances in which he had been found were a mystery…*

> — From a report made by Chief Inspector Toshiyoshi Kawaji of the Imperial Prosecuting Office

1

It was the twenty-eighth day of the twelfth lunar month, and the sun was setting on the third year of Emperor Meiji's reign. In the jail at Kodenma-chō, the rebel Tatsuo Kumoi had been put to death by Gosaburō Yoshifusa, who was third son of the Tokugawa executioner, Asaemon Yamada VII.

'I was only seventeen at the time,' the boy would recall in later years, by then having taken on the family name and profession:

It was the month of Shiwasu in the zodiac year of the Metal Horse, and all throughout Edo rice cakes were being pounded for the season's festivities. Although the new year's fair at Yagenbori was taking place, I had been called upon that day to behead Tatsuo Kumoi, and so I made my way to the jail at Kodenma-chō. The former retainer of the Yonezawa Domain had a formidable reputation, and the prospect of beheading him was an onerous one, unlike that of executing any common criminal.

He had been subjected to a brutal interrogation, during which they tried to make him divulge the names of his comrades, but no matter how they tortured him, he would not give in. In those days, the torments inflicted on him would have been merciless beyond belief but, having burnt the round-robin, he sacrificed himself for his country with complete equanimity. He was of such a small physical stature that I do not know where he found such boldness and courage. It amazed me to think that here was Kumoi, who had made so impressive a name for himself throughout the country, and yet in an instant he was to disappear with the morning dew. He met his end with such unswerving composure that even now I feel only the deepest respect for him.

Even though the round-robin containing the names of his comrades had been burnt, as many as fifty-nine men were arrested for conspiring to overthrow the government. And so, on that fateful day, it was not just Kumoi who was to be executed, but also thirteen other ringleaders.

The setting was the by-now-familiar execution ground, and both Kazuki and Kawaji were in attendance.

The role of the Imperial Prosecuting Office was not only to monitor government officials, but also to root out sedition, and so it cannot be said that these two had nothing to do with the Kumoi case whatsoever. But since neither of them had played a leading role in the investigation, and since both of them happened to be otherwise unengaged, they were ordered to observe this rare spate of executions.

A short while before his execution, Kumoi asked to recite a poem of his own composition, permission for which was granted by Kawaji.

> At death, I fear no dying,
> As in living, I steal no life.
> The brilliance of the sun
> Is rivalled by the virtue of men...
> How insignificant my poor self,
> Against the great wall of ten thousand leagues!

After he spoke these lines, his voice reverberated throughout the execution ground and went on long after his death. After the fourteen corpses had been removed, the blood had been washed away, and the executioner and the other officials had gone, the place seemed even more like the underworld, frozen amid the cold twilight.

'The headsman today was absurdly young, don't you think?' said Kazuki, when he and Kawaji were the only ones left.

'He's Yamada's third son, apparently. The old man's getting old. His eldest, Genzō, was supposed to take over, but that one's seemingly a bit of a drinker and a womanizer, so he can't be relied on. The word is that this one actually likes the job—and is a master of his craft, too.'

'He bungled a few cuts towards the end, though!'

'Well, he did have fourteen to get through…'

'If they'd used my machine, there wouldn't have been any mistakes,' said Kazuki, glancing towards the little shed in the corner of the execution ground where the guillotine was stored.

'What can I say? The powers that be decided that the *shishi* deserved the honour of being beheaded the old-fashioned way.'

'You know, in France even the king was put to the guillotine.'

'If I were you, I'd content myself with seeing it used for those officials who are a disgrace to their office.'

Of the six assassins who had killed Shōnan Yokoi, the four *shishi* who had been arrested shortly after the incident, including Tsuge Shirōzaemon, had received a stay of execution after the directorate of the Imperial Prosecuting Office intervened. This had not been indefinite, however, and when the executions finally came to pass in the tenth lunar month, they were again carried out by the headsman. Indeed, until now the guillotine that Kazuki had taken such pains to procure had been used only for the worst criminals, although some exceptions had been made for corrupt officials—the reason being that the Imperial Prosecuting Office had accepted Kazuki's argument that, under the new government's policies, corruption was to be treated on a par with the worst kinds of petty crime. Hence, all of the perpetrators hitherto mentioned in this tale had already lost their heads under the iron blade of the guillotine.

'Anyway, you'll have another customer for it before long,' said Kawaji.

'You mean Yamashiroya?'

The two men looked at each other and laughed feebly.

Just then, they heard a strange commotion coming from inside the prison. They rushed from the execution block through the side door and into the jailhouse. There, by one of the interrogation rooms, they encountered a group of jailers and *rasotsu* who had come running from the main entrance. All were crowding around one of the prison servants who had his head slumped on his chest. He could only have been around twenty years old.

'What's going on here?' Kazuki asked.

'Take a look at this, sir,' a jailer replied, holding something up in one of his hands.

Kazuki and Kawaji gazed at the object in astonishment.

'Why, that's Kumoi's head, isn't it?!'

Sure enough, it was the head of Tatsuo Kumoi, which had been parted from his body only a short while ago.

'The guard at the gate stopped him when he saw him trying to leave with something big wrapped in a *furoshiki* under his arm. Turns out he was trying to take this away, sir.'

'Oh? What for?'

'That's just what we're about to find out.'

In view of his suspicious behaviour, the servant was taken immediately to an interrogation room, where he was subjected to a barrage of questions. At first, pale and trembling, he told them that his name was Zenkichi and that he had been taken on as a servant in the prison only three months previously, but later he confessed that his name was in fact Zennosuke Amanomiya and that he had once been a lowly vassal of the shogun. As he spoke, little by little his face took on a proud aspect of defiance that belied his former rank.

'I'd sooner feed Kumoi-sensei's remains to the stray dogs at Kozukappara than see them taken to the Imperial University to be dissected,' he said. 'So I tried to take his head at least, hoping to give him the proper burial he deserves.'

'What?' said Kazuki. 'He's to be taken to the East College to be dissected?'

True though this was, it was news to both Kazuki and Kawaji.

In those days, the East College—long before it became the Faculty of Medicine at the University of Tokyo—was the domain of Tadanori Ishiguro, the future surgeon general of the Imperial Japanese Army. 'For teaching purposes,' he later recorded, 'I had repeatedly asked the government to release the bodies of executed criminals. Finally, they acquiesced, and the first such body delivered to me was that of Kumoi. I remember it especially well because it was just a headless torso.'

It would surely have surprised Kumoi to learn that he was to be the first person to be dissected in Meiji Japan. His head had actually been destined for public display, but that Amanomiya had worked his way into the prison with the express intent of stealing Kumoi's remains was now beyond any doubt.

It was only natural that questions were asked about Amanomiya and whether he had been a co-conspirator of

Kumoi's, but it so happened that the lax security around the execution was also raised.

'Who was in charge?' Kawaji asked, marching out of the interrogation room, leaving Kazuki to run after him.

In one corner of the execution ground, there was a little hut known as 'the last office', where the dead bodies were kept. The headless corpses would be stored there temporarily, and then, later that day or the next, they would be taken to Kozukappara and buried—though dumped might be a better word—and, needless to say, no last offices were given.

'You!' cried Kawaji, as he entered the little hut and saw Sergeant Ichinohata standing there, disconsolate. The man, who always looked so pitiful, seemed to be on the verge of tears.

'I haven't seen anything like this in a long time,' he said, turning to Kawaji. 'I can't bear to look at it.'

That of course was no excuse, but when Kawaji and Kazuki saw the mass of coffins lined up there, even they felt a little unnerved.

These were not new coffins, although strictly speaking they were not old, either. They had been cobbled together from old reclaimed boards, which were already discoloured by all the blood oozing through the cracks. There were fourteen of them in total. A truly gruesome spectacle. And not one of them had its lid on.

'I'd set aside Kumoi-san's head, since it's to be put on public display,' Ichinohata began explaining.

However, the two chief inspectors just stood there in silence, paying no attention to what he was saying. The bodies had all been crammed into the coffins, their gaping necks in full view and their heads resting in their hands. Naturally, this was not the first time that the two had seen such a sight, and yet, far more disturbing than the grisliness of the beheading was the surreal, other-worldly vision of these convicts, in a practice carried over from the Tokugawa era, cradling their own severed heads.

2

Shortly after the fourth year of the emperor Meiji's reign began, there was another incident that shook the nation. In the early hours of the ninth day of the first month, Vice Minister Saneomi Hirosawa was murdered.

This was the third assassination of a high-profile government official in a year, after those of Shōnan Yokoi and Masujirō Ōmura. What made matters worse was that while first two had been carried out in Kyoto, this killing had taken place right in the imperial capital. No matter how many criminals they caught and executed, it seemed there was no end to these disturbing events, and as the new government entered its fourth year, violence yet stalked the country.

Needless to say, the Imperial Prosecuting Office, which was still in charge of public order, was alarmed by this assassination and desperately tried to seek out the perpetrators.

In the end, however, they were never caught, and the case remains one of the great unsolved mysteries of the Restoration. On the night in question, Hirosawa had been with his mistress at his residence in the Fujimi-chō neighbourhood of Kōjimachi, when the assailants broke in and killed him with as many as fifteen blows of their swords. The mistress testified that there had been only two or three culprits, but she too had been struck on her right temple and lost consciousness, so the they were never identified. Was this an act of sedition, as was the case with Yokoi and Ōmura? Or had Hirosawa, who once ranked alongside Kido as one of the leading figures in Chōshū, been a victim of the then-intensifying power struggle between Chōshū and Satsuma? Or could it have been the result of internal fighting within the Chōshū faction itself, or even a settling of old scores? Suspects were systematically rounded up based on all these hypotheses, but there were just too many of them, and the authorities were unable to narrow the search.

Naturally, Kawaji and Kazuki made a show of embarrassment over the situation. In reality, however, they felt rather indifferent—although only they knew this. Neither of them had been much impressed by the fact that Hirosawa had been in bed with his mistress. Their interrogation had revealed, moreover, that, while the mistress was possessed of a rare beauty even by Tokyo's standards, her mind appeared to be stuffed with cotton wool, and she had such loose morals that it was rumoured she gave herself to almost any man who asked.

And yet…

'Maybe this is somehow connected with the Yamashiroya case,' said Kazuki.

'I haven't seen anything to suggest that so far,' replied Kawaji, 'but it's certainly possible.'

The Yamashiroya case was one that they had been investigating secretly since the autumn of the previous year. The man at the centre of it all, Wasuke Yamashiroya, ran a trading company in Yokohama, with fifteen offices, a warehouse and 480 employees, which was an unusually large outfit for the time. As a purveyor to the Imperial Japanese Army, he single-handedly managed the purchase of munitions from abroad. In those days, the top brass of the army consisted almost exclusively of men from Chōshū, and it seemed that Yamashiroya had received this special warrant because he had at one time been a commander of the volunteer militia there.

That autumn it had come to the attention of the Imperial Prosecuting Office that Yamashiroya had lost a vast amount of money—some 150,000 dollars—in the raw-silk market. An investigation was launched after Sergeant Imokawa reported these particulars, having heard them from Ginkō Kishida.

The raw-silk market had plummeted because of the Franco-Prussian War that broke out in the summer of the previous year, and, even for a businessman like Yamashiroya, 150,000 dollars was an extraordinary sum of money.

And where had the capital come from? An internal investigation revealed that it had apparently come from the army. As its reserves for purchasing ordnance had been falling year on year, Yamashiroya had proposed to invest what capital there was, thereby not only preventing it from dwindling, but actually increasing its value, and so the Ministry of War, placing its faith in his business acumen, had seemingly given him the money as an unsecured loan. Yamashiroya had then put it into the raw-silk market and made an almighty mess of things. To make matters worse, 150,000 dollars was the equivalent of around 800,000 yen, or two per cent of the national budget.

'Hmm…' was all Kazuki had to say.

They had no solid evidence—and besides, the case involved the army. The natural place to start would have been Yamashiroya, but through their carelessness he had managed to slip the net. Wherever they looked, they were left with only hypotheses.

Then, towards the end of the previous year, Yasutari Yuasa, the first assistant finance director at the Ministry of War, left his post. Yuasa was another one who had served in the Chōshū militia. He had even lost an arm in combat during his period of service. Yet this one-armed soldier had proved to be a very capable accountant, and so he had risen up in the Ministry of War. The *rasotsu* were ordered to follow him, and thus they found that he dined out frequently with Yamashiroya's chief clerk, a certain Ihei Arisaka. Excited by this link, they began to delve deeper, but then Yuasa moved with his family back to Chōshū.

'He knows we're watching him,' Kazuki had said.

The investigation had stalled, and the only thing left was to find a chink in Yamashiroya's armour. As far as the Imperial Prosecuting Office was concerned, that was where it had all begun.

Could Vice Minister Hirosawa's murder have anything to do with this scandal brewing in the Ministry of War? Kawaji and Kazuki exchanged a knowing look, but there was nothing they could do unless they could form a picture of the culprits.

The month wore on, and the criminals remained at large. Then one day, quite by chance, Kazuki and Kawaji happened to receive two startling reports.

The first came when Sergeant Saruki nervously poked his head around the door of their office.

'Sirs, it looks like Kinpei Kobayashi's dead!'

'What?!' cried Kawaji. 'When did this happen?'

'I haven't been there lately, so I've only just heard about it. He apparently died on the seventh.'

'What did he die of?'

'They think it was a stroke, sir.'

Kawaji stood there, taking in the information.

'Who exactly is this Kinpei Kobayashi?' asked Kazuki with a quizzical look. 'I've heard that name somewhere before.'

'You remember the Sawamura case? He ran the shop where Saruki here pawned your binoculars.'

'Ah, yes, I remember now.' Kazuki scratched his head. 'The fat old man with the beetroot face? It's little wonder he had a stroke…'

'Apparently they didn't tell the neighbours about the funeral. The rumour is that the old boy died on top of O-Kinu.'

They didn't quite know what to say to this, and, just as they were looking at each other in embarrassment, the second report arrived.

In came Sergeant Imokawa, trying to catch his breath.

'Sirs… Yamashiroya's legged it!'

'What, Wasuke? Where?'

'To France!'

The two chief inspectors were flabbergasted.

'How could you have let this happen again?!' Kawaji shouted.

Imokawa was supposed to have been conducting surveillance down in Yokohama. He had been ordered to keep an eye on Yamashiroya's movements and to follow him whenever the situation called for it.

Imokawa told them that around ten o'clock that morning Yamashiroya and his chief clerk Arisaka had left the office and set off on foot towards the wharf. The *rasotsu* thought it was odd that Yamashiroya was wearing Western clothes and that Arisaka was carrying a large bag but had assumed that they intended to visit some of the large trading firms on the seafront. As he followed them, however, Yamashiroya boarded one of the barges and vanished onto one of the enormous steamers anchored in the bay.

Imokawa had been so horrified by this turn of events that he grabbed Arisaka while he was still standing there, seeing Yamashiroya off. The clerk told him that he was heading off to conduct some business in France at the request of the Ministry of War, and that his passage had been booked on the French ship *Marseille*, which was to depart shortly. Imokawa panicked and, without a moment's delay, ran all the way back to Tokyo.

'He's fled, hasn't he?' Kawaji groaned.

'Or he's been made to flee,' said Kazuki.

First, Yuasa's return to Chōshū, and now, Yamashiroya's flight abroad. It was clear that both of them had got wind that the Imperial Prosecuting Office was looking into the case, and now they were trying to draw a veil of darkness over everything. But to flee to France. This had caught them unawares.

'Enough!' barked Kawaji, getting to his feet. 'Here's what we're going to do: we're going to bring Yamashiroya's chief clerk in and have a little word with him. We're going to Yokohama! Imokawa, you're with me!'

And with that, he left, leaving Kazuki and Saruki behind.

When Kawaji reached Yamashiroya's office in Yokohama, however, he found that the chief clerk, Ihei Arisaka, had failed to return after seeing his employer off. It looked as though he, too, had gone to ground.

3

It was in the middle of the second lunar month when Kawaji arrested O-Kinu, the former mistress of the moneylender Kinpei Kobayashi.

According to Saruki, he had died while having relations with her, but even so, his business ventures had been extensive, and so it was somewhat odd that the funeral should have been held in such secrecy and with such haste, and without involving any of the neighbours.

In the case of the severed leg, O-Kinu, of course, had been prevailed upon by Tateki Maki to play a part in the crime. Kazuki's understanding of it was that the official had threatened her somehow, and so she had not been charged and got off with only a caution. Now, however, she had been arrested on a separate charge and taken to the police station in Yagenbori for questioning, where eventually she confessed to poisoning her lover.

Although the death had struck Kawaji as suspicious, it was the woman's confession that surprised him. O-Kinu had apparently dissolved some Iwami Ginzan rat poison in hot water and given it to Kobayashi as a cold remedy, but that was not the surprising part. The fact of the matter was that O-Kinu had been carrying on a secret affair with another man. O-Kinu had been Kobayashi's mistress, but in the last year the novelty had begun to wear off for her, and now he just forced his grotesque caresses on her. Then O-Kinu fell pregnant, which did not go unnoticed by Kobayashi. Still, difficult though this predicament was, Kawaji would never have expected it to drive her to murder.

Kawaji was then shocked to learn that the adulteress's new lover was none other than the actor Rikaku Arashi, and that the reason she had been unable to refuse Maki's request was that he had found out about the affair through Sawamura and was using it to blackmail her.

At last, thought Kawaji, the details of that case all made sense now.

When Kazuki learnt of this, he looked at Kawaji in disbelief.

'The only thing I don't understand,' said Kawaji, 'is why Maki didn't tell us that. Not that telling us would have saved his head, mind you.'

'I told him that there were two ways to go: one, the old Japanese way of beheading; the other, a new Western method using the guillotine. I said that if he conducted himself with the dignity befitting a government official, there would be a degree of compassion shown in the manner in which he died. Maybe he wanted to be beheaded the old way,' Kazuki laughed. 'Rice and bread nourish the body just as well as each other, but a Japanese will always choose rice. I think the guillotine is a more fitting way to go for corrupt officials, and I told him as much.'

Kazuki ought to have been as curious as Kawaji about the truth behind the case of the moneylender's mistress, yet he seemed to have little interest in such petty crime. Kawaji, on the other hand, could not help feeling that this was a real discovery.

The true purpose of the Imperial Prosecuting Office was to root out corrupt officials, however, and their current focus was the Yamashiroya case. Towards the end of the second month, the blanket of smoke that had been hanging over it suddenly lifted to reveal a body.

That day, after completing his morning rounds, Kawaji arrived at the Imperial Prosecuting Office to find a note from Kazuki, informing him that he had gone to the jail to supervise the guillotine, and that Kawaji should come there immediately, as there was an important matter to discuss.

Kawaji rushed through the rain, which was falling like threads of silk.

Since he was coming from the Sakurada Gate, he would enter through the back of the jail, but just as he was passing it, the rear gate creaked open.

This gate was only opened when executed criminals had to be taken to Kozukappara.

As he looked on, wondering whether the execution had already taken place and the bodies were now being transported, a horse appeared, pulling a cart. A peasant-looking man with a filthy beard and wearing a rain hat and straw *mino* raincoat was trudging ahead of it, holding the reins. The cart behind him was laden with crates. They were too small to be coffins, though, and, seeing them, Kawaji laughed. The gong farmer had come to take away the many pails of prison excrement.

Kawaji carried on around the side of the jail and entered through the front gate, only to find that the execution had indeed already taken place.

Having been informed that Kazuki had just stepped out with Sergeant Onimaru, Kawaji was asked if he would mind waiting. He smiled to himself, wondering what this 'important matter' could be, and took a stroll around the prison while he waited.

Naturally, he took a peek in the mortuary.

There, he saw five slightly stained coffins lying in a row and, beside them, sitting vacantly in the corner, Sergeant Ichinohata puffing away on a pipe. Surprised to see the chief inspector, he jumped to his feet.

'Don't worry, I haven't come for you,' said Kawaji. 'Kazuki asked me to come. Do you know where he's gone?'

'I've no idea,' the *rasotsu* replied, looking confused. 'He was here giving instructions for the guillotine just a minute ago. Has he gone out?'

'Could it be something to do with the execution?'

'I don't think so. It must be something else.'

Kawaji looked at the coffins. They all had their lids on, but, as ever, the blood was still seeping out, and the overpowering smell was nauseating.

'Who were they?'

'Rapists and murderers, the lot of them. Would you like to take a look, sir?'

'No, thank you.'

Kawaji shook his head. A corpse holding its own head was never a pleasant sight to behold.

'When are they being taken to Kozukappara?'

'It's scheduled for this evening, sir.'

'Make sure nobody steals any of the heads this time.'

'Kumoi-san was one thing, sir, but I doubt anybody would want these heads. That really was a disgrace the other day, but ever since then, somebody's been on guard until they're taken to Kozukappara. They've tightened up security at the gate, as well.'

Kawaji laughed and left him to it.

4

An hour passed, then an hour and a half, and still Kazuki hadn't returned. Then, a little after two o'clock, Sergeant Yokomakura came running into the jail, shouting, 'Is the chief inspector here?'

Ichinohata took him to find Kawaji.

'What's happened?' he asked. 'What's the matter?'

'Oh, Chief Inspector. You must come immediately. Chief Inspector Kazuki needs you.'

'Where?'

'Imado, sir.'

Imado lay just to the north of Asakusa, overlooking the Sumida River.

'That army accountant Yuasa's there.'

'What?! All right, tell me everything on the way!'

The two of them went running out of the jail, and along the way Yokomakura gave Kawaji the full story.

Two days earlier, Onimaru had been on patrol in Asakusa, when suddenly he had spotted Yatarō Aoki, a notorious scoundrel. He had once been in the shogun's service, but during the chaos that preceded the Restoration, he had gathered together a band of thieves and gone all across Edo, robbing people under the guise of expropriation, before finally being arrested. However, despite being subjected to torture more than a dozen times, he had persisted in protesting his innocence, and when the collapse of the shogunate finally came, he was granted a special pardon by Kaishū Katsu and released without charge. Since then, however, he had not mended his ways; only now his quarry were no longer petty merchants, but rather disreputable officials and government suppliers, because he knew that it was more efficient to extort large sums of money from them. In most cases, he could achieve his end by sending one of his henchmen, but, depending on the circumstances, there were also occasions when he would have to go in person and say menacingly, 'Yes, it is I, "the hardened criminal", Aoki. And you'd do well not to forget it when you open your mouth to me.' Those few words alone had been enough to convey the inhuman degree of his villainy and make his adversaries tremble. Of course, if they refused to listen even then, they would be set on fire and have their unidentifiable bodies dumped somewhere—such were the rumours of his violence.

And so it was this Aoki whom Sergeant Onimaru had followed, and whom he had spotted entering a certain villa in Imado.

In those days, just as the stretch between Yoshiwara and Asakusa was nothing but rice paddies, so too was Imado an area full of paddies and fields. Dotted around here and there, though, were a few forests, and the closer you got to the Sumida River, the more elegant the place became, with secluded villas scattered among the trees.

After about twenty minutes, Aoki emerged, wearing a sour look, and walked past Onimaru, who was squatting in the bushes. After half a dozen steps, he turned around.

'Hello, Sergeant,' he said, practically spitting out the words. 'You probably don't know this, but this here villa belongs to the famous Yamashiroya of Yokohama. There's a big army accountant hiding out there. Sure would be funny if the Imperial Prosecuting Office were to look into how that all came to be. He's a big fish, so it would be a crying shame to blow his cover. Might be an idea to stick around for now and see who's coming and going.'

Then, with his hands in his pockets, he sauntered off towards Yoshiwara.

Onimaru duly reported all this to Kazuki.

'An army accountant?' he said. 'Why, that could be Yasutari Yuasa! And you're saying that Aoki told you to keep an eye on the people visiting him? Hmm… Could this be retaliation if Yuasa rebuffed his attempt at blackmail? It would certainly stand to reason if he's a military man. Either way, he's right. Take a look and see who you find.'

From that day on, Onimaru and Yokomakura had been surveilling the villa, sometimes together, sometimes taking turns.

Kawaji realized that this must be the important matter that Kazuki had mentioned. It would certainly be a turn-up for the books if Yuasa, who they had thought was back in Chōshū, was really hiding out in Imado.

As they ran there, Yokomakura continued his tale.

Earlier that day, just before noon, somebody had pulled up at the villa by rickshaw. Since the vehicle had both a canopy and a curtain, they hadn't been able to identify the visitor. Whoever it was, however, they had come with two soldiers in tow. The two *rasotsu* were startled to see that the visitor was probably a military man of some rank, but, having realized this, they knew they had to find out who it was.

Yet no sooner had the rickshaw arrived at the villa than it left again. Had they just exchanged a few words standing at the door? What in the world could have made them come all this way to Imado in the rain? Unable to resist, Onimaru blocked the rickshaw's path.

'What's the meaning of this?' asked a soldier, glaring at him.

'By the authority of the Imperial Prosecuting Office,' Onimaru replied, 'I have orders to stop and identify anybody entering or leaving that house. Your name, please.'

From under the canopy, an ill-tempered voice replied:

'Yamagata.'

'Sir?'

'Aritomo Yamagata.'

Onimaru nearly jumped out of his skin. It was the deputy assistant to the Minister of War.

'Sir!' he said, growing more frantic. 'Forgive me, but I have orders to verify everyone.'

After a few moments of silence, the voice gave the order for the canopy to be removed. There, inside, Onimaru saw the long, sullen, stony countenance of His Excellency Aritomo Yamagata, whom he had seen somewhere before.

Onimaru stood to attention and saluted.

'Will that be all, Sergeant?'

The rickshaw then carried on past the *rasotsu*, vanishing as it raced off towards Asakusa.

This was why Onimaru had run all the way back to the prison, and why Chief Inspector Kazuki had gone running off the minute he heard the report.

Since Yamagata had already left, there was nothing that Kazuki could do, but he felt compelled to go there, nonetheless. When he arrived, however, he was confronted by something quite unexpected.

It happened as he was listening to the report from the two *rasotsu* in the woods near the villa.

All of a sudden, a girl of around sixteen came running out of the villa's main gate. The *rasotsu* knew from their surveillance the day before that the girl was employed at the villa. There was a field nearby where a peasant hut stood, and it appeared to be her home. The girl looked distressed, so Kazuki called over to her.

'We've found a body!' she cried in a high-pitched voice. 'The master's told me to report it to the police station in Asakusa.'

'Whose body?'

'I don't know who he is. But his head's been cut off.'

'What, inside the villa?'

'No, in the field behind it! He's naked, and he's covered in manure.'

Their surveillance of the villa was supposed to be a secret, but, hearing this, they had no choice but to investigate. The three of them rushed to the scene, guided by the girl.

What they found there was a horrific spectacle. And standing beside it was none other than Yasutari Yuasa. While he was asking what had gone on here, Kazuki suddenly recalled that he had requested Kawaji to meet him at the prison, and so Yokomakura was dispatched to go and fetch him.

5

The main gate was a modest affair, and the black wooden perimeter fence, which was hidden by a variety of trees and shrubs, was falling down in places. The building inside was not very large, but still, the grounds must have been around a thousand *tsubo*. It transpired that Yamashiroya had acquired the place, following the trend of wealthy men buying up villas in the area, but that his work had kept him so busy in Yokohama that he had scarcely had any time to make use of it.

The neighbouring plot was farmland, and it was the old farmer and his wife who usually looked after the villa. If ever somebody came to stay there, their daughter would cook meals and run errands for them. Her older brother, on the other hand, had been given a job in Yamashiroya's main office in Yokohama.

The rear gate—or, rather, the side entrance—opened onto the farmer's fields. On the far side flowed the swollen Sumida River, with Mukōjima perched on the opposite bank. When Kawaji arrived, he found Kazuki and the others in the field right outside the side gate, all of them congregating around the corpse.

Besides Kazuki, there was Onimaru, the old farmer and his daughter, and one other man, whom Kawaji recognized from a previous investigation. He must have been around forty and looked very respectable; both his head and his beard were shaved, with only a little stubble remaining, which was a rare sight in those days. It was Major Yuasa, the former first assistant finance director in the Ministry of War.

Only Kazuki and Yuasa had umbrellas, which they had taken from the villa. The girl was holding the umbrella for the latter, however, leaving him free to stand with his hand in his pocket.

Kawaji was already aware that one of Yuasa's arms was missing from the elbow.

So, this is where he's been hiding! Kawaji marvelled.

Rather than linger on Yuasa's face, however, he soon found that his eyes were drawn to the scene of devastation before him. What struck him most, though, was not the sight itself, so much as the foul stench that assailed his nose as he approached.

While it was only the end of the second lunar month, the end of March by the Western calendar, the fields and forests lining the banks of the Sumida River were already a great blur of verdure. Even in the cold mizzle, the air was filled with the fresh scent of spring, so what on earth was this terrible smell?

Leaning against the wall with only a *fundoshi* to cover his modesty, the large corpse had been positioned on his knees, facing forward, cradling a gruesome-looking head with dishevelled hair and no beard. The whole body was dripping with excrement.

Beside him were scattered almost a dozen pails, their offensive contents seeping out into the soil of the field.

'Onimaru put him here so that we could get a better look at the head,' Kazuki explained after a few brief introductions.

Then he began to relate the preceding events. Earlier that day, Yuasa had gone out to feed the koi in the garden pond, which was near the side entrance. When he got there, he could smell the stench emanating from the other side of the wall, so he pushed the side gate open. Then, although the door had barely touched them, the pails that had been stacked there went toppling over. That was when he found the decapitated body beneath them, covered in their contents.

He rushed to call the young servant girl and told her to run to the police station.

'Only, Yuasa-san says he doesn't recognize the body,' Kazuki added.

'I see,' said Kawaji, turning once again to look at the corpse's face.

The moment Yokomakura told him about the body, Kawaji had imagined it must be Ihei Arisaka, Yamashiroya's chief clerk who had disappeared the previous month. It was just a hunch, for other than the fact that the body had been found at Yamashiroya's villa, he had no evidence.

But it was not Arisaka, though the body somewhat resembled his. Arisaka had served under Yamashiroya in the volunteer militia, and he was also a large man; however, the corpse's face wasn't his. Since launching the surveillance operation, Kawaji had become familiar not only with the faces of all Yamashiroya's close associates, but also with those of certain army types—and not one of them had such a ferocious-looking, vile physiognomy. Each of them had at least had the appearance of a higher class of criminal.

The body was recently deceased. The rain had not let up, so they could not be certain how much blood there had been, but, in any case, the body could not have been more than a day old.

'How long has the body been here?' Kawaji asked.

'Well, that's just it. The old man said that he left the pails here yesterday, intending to move them to a nearby slurry pit today, but because of the rain he just left them where they were. So not before yesterday, in any case,' Kazuki explained.

The old man looked so pale that he might collapse any minute.

'So, we're left with the hours between yesterday evening and today,' said Kawaji, turning to the two *rasotsu*. 'Didn't you see anything when you were on duty?'

'Not a thing, sir!' said Onimaru, scratching his head. 'You see, there's quite a bit of distance between the front gate and the road, and there are trees blocking the view.'

'Still, it's odd that you couldn't hear any voices or sounds,' said Kazuki. 'He must have been killed elsewhere and brought here.'

'Are there any footprints?'

'It's too hard to tell after all this rain.'

'Why would they bring a body all the way out here into the middle of the fields? It's too far if they just wanted to dump it. Especially somebody as big as him. You'd need more than one man for that job.'

'This looks more like an act of intimidation or retaliation to me. Probably directed at the people in this villa.'

'I agree,' said Yuasa. 'If you ask me, this is Yatarō Aoki's doing. As you're investigators for the Imperial Prosecuting Office, you'll know just what a scoundrel he is. He came here the day before last, threatening me with false accusations, so I promptly showed him the door. He flew off in a rage. I wonder whether this isn't his way of getting back at me. He could have had some help from his henchmen.'

'But if this were retaliation, wouldn't it be odd to kill somebody you've no connection to and then dump his body here?' said Kawaji.

'So it's intimidation, then?'

'Maybe.'

A few moments later, looking as though he had just remembered something, Yuasa said:

'Yes, I thought it was odd myself. But if it wasn't Aoki—and I've given this a lot of consideration—I really don't know who it could be. Then again, I was responsible for the execution of more than a dozen rebels after the Boshin War, although it was really my men who saw to most of that. I did lose my right arm for it, though. Look... They ambushed me in the street one night in the autumn of the first year of Meiji. There were several of them. To this day, I don't know who they were, but they could still be after me. And not only me, but my men as well. Maybe this poor fellow was one of my men.'

'But, sir, wouldn't you remember if he were one?' asked Kawaji.

'I doubt it. Why, it was chaos back then. There were times when I even had men from Satsuma and Tosa under my command. The more I think about it, though, the more likely it seems. But, in truth, I cannot remember the man.'

'Why do you suppose he's wearing only a *fundoshi*?'

'Why, to get rid of the evidence from his clothing, surely!'

'But if it's so that the man cannot be identified, how will we ever know what it's all about?' asked Kawaji.

'Damned if I know. The corpse is every bit as much a mystery to me as it is to you. Surely you don't suspect *me*?' said Yuasa, fixing Kawaji with his gaze. Then, with open hostility, he added: 'You're from Satsuma, aren't you? Are you suspicious of every man from Chōshū?' He laughed. 'Even if you are, you can see perfectly well that I have no right arm, and I cannot wield a sword in my left with such brilliance. I do not know what he was like before he died, but even now I can tell he was the sort of man to put up a fight.'

Kawaji crouched down and lifted up the corpse's head to take a look at it. Brilliant was the word: horrifying in its skill, it was a near-perfect cut. There did not appear to be any other wounds. This was indeed a strange corpse.

'If you believe you're under suspicion, there are a couple of questions I could ask that would clear your name.' Kawaji replaced the head and stood up again. 'I believe that the deputy assistant to the Minister of War paid you a visit today, but I hear that he left almost as soon as he arrived. What, may I ask, was his visit in aid of?'

Though he didn't know what questions Kazuki had already asked, he wanted to hear this answer with his own ears.

Yuasa glanced at the girl.

'That is of no concern to the Imperial Prosecuting Office,' he replied with open hostility.

'Isn't it, sir?'

'It certainly is not! His Excellency heard a rumour that I was here and came to verify it for himself. He thought I'd returned to Chōshū. When he saw me, he was glad to see that I was in good health. And that was about it. He's a very busy man, you know. He made his excuses and left, just like that.'

Kawaji looked at Yuasa searchingly.

'You left your position at the Ministry of War. What was the reason for that, sir? And why did you come here, when you had your family return to Chōshū?'

'You're very well informed, Chief Inspector,' said Yuasa with a smile. 'I resigned from the ministry because I was worn out

324

by all the work that's come my way ever since the Restoration. However, I know that there have been some strange rumours going about, and that the Imperial Prosecuting Office has been poking its nose in lately. Given the Imperial Prosecuting Office regards my resignation as suspicious, that casts doubt on both my own honour and that of the military. I suspected there might come a time when I'd have to vindicate myself, so I decided to stay here awhile, renting this villa from Yamashiroya, while I recuperate.'

Suddenly he flew into a rage. 'But this is not my vindication! I don't have to explain myself to the likes of you!' He seemed to be angry not only at Kawaji, but also at himself. 'In any case, what does all that have to do with this body? Now clear off, the lot of you! And if you want to talk to me again, you'll have to come back with some evidence that this corpse has the first thing to do with me!'

Having said his piece, he turned and went back in via the side gate.

The rest of them just stood there silently in the rain, which by now had grown heavier. Suddenly the head that the corpse had been cradling tumbled down from its grasp, and the girl let out a dreadful scream.

6

Kazuki and Kawaji walked back in silence through the blustering early spring rain, while the two *rasotsu* were left behind to take the body to the local police station. Kazuki had his umbrella, but Kawaji was soaked to the bone. The inclement weather was the last thing on their minds, however.

When the shadow of the Sensō-ji temple's five-storey pagoda drew into view beneath the twilit sky, Kawaji finally broke their silence.

'Do you understand any of it, Kazuki?'

'No,' he said, shaking his head. 'One thing we can be sure of, though, is that that body has to be connected to Yuasa somehow. That, and the fact that Yamagata and Yuasa are connected as well. But as for what links that body to Yamagata, I've no idea.'

'More than that, I just can't see what this case is all about,' said Kawaji. 'Why was the body naked? Is there any significance in the fact that it had been beheaded and was cradling its own head? And what about all those pails?'

'Come off it, Kawaji. I don't know what the nakedness or the beheading mean any more than you do. But the business with those pails was just an accident, surely, and the fact that it was holding its own head was because I'd ordered Onimaru to sit it upright.'

'Yes, I know all that, but I can't help thinking it all has some meaning. How could something like this have happened in the first place? I just don't understand it.' As he walked, he stroked his beard. 'You know, I've had this strange, nagging feeling all this time, and I just can't seem to put my finger on it. Something's bothering me.'

'Well, I can't very well help you with that. Anyway, let's start with the fact that we still don't know whose body it is. Or should we cut to the chase and just bring Yuasa in?'

'No, let's wait,' Kawaji said, shaking his head. He had already overstepped the mark, accusing Yamashiroya's chief clerk of culpability. 'We don't have enough evidence for that yet. If we mess this up, we'll have the army to answer to, given Yamagata's involvement. Let's bide our time.'

As they were entering Asakusa, Kawaji suddenly gasped.

'What is it?'

'I've just put my finger on it!' cried Kawaji. 'That man... mightn't he be one of the condemned criminals from the prison?'

Kazuki stopped dead in his tracks.

'The corpse holding its head... It was positioned the same way! Couldn't the body be one of the ones you beheaded with the guillotine this morning?'

'Have you lost your mind?!' said Kazuki in a hushed voice. 'Didn't I just tell you that it was Onimaru who put him in that position? You think it was one of the men we executed this morning? Did you see the heads of those men?'

'No, I don't know.'

'Then what makes you say such an extraordinary thing? Ever since the incident with Tatsuo Kumoi's head, security at the jail has been tightened up. How could anybody get a body out of there?'

'Not a body. Just the head.'

'Just the head?!' Kazuki's eyes were wide with astonishment. 'Even if somebody could get a head out, who would do such a thing?'

'Him...'

'Him? Who?'

'It was Yuasa's face. It wasn't the first time I saw him, but when he was standing there by the pails. I'm only just remembering it now. He reminded me of somebody else. It was him.'

'Who? Whose face?'

'This afternoon, when I arrived at the prison, I saw the man who comes to collect the pails. He was coming out the gate at the back. He was wearing a rain hat and a straw coat. He looked like a peasant and had a beard, but if you were to shave him... he'd look rather like Yuasa.'

For a brief second, Kazuki was lost for words.

'But what you're suggesting is absurd! A former high official responsible for the army's accounts turned into a gong farmer?! For a start, Yuasa has only one arm. How could he do that job with only his left arm? That would be some pretty hard labour.'

'He wouldn't have to do much of it. He'd just have to pretend that he was doing it for long enough to make it out of there with the head. Of course, he wouldn't even have to collect the pails himself. He could have had somebody else do it. The farmer next door, for instance. But then, it's such a risky business. In practical terms, he'd have no choice but to do it himself. He really is the spitting image, you know—only without the beard. He must have done it himself. There were about a dozen pails loaded onto the cart. I bet one of those pails contained one of the criminals' heads. The sentry would never think to check.'

'You mean...' Kazuki stared intently at Kawaji's profile. 'You know, I must have underestimated you, Kawaji. I always knew you were a man of talent, but I never imagined your mind could work like that.'

'Is that a compliment or an insult?'

'It's a compliment! Although I'm still not convinced. Even if he could get the head, where would he get the body?'

'The body is probably Ihei Arisaka's. He was the same build.'

'What?!' cried Kazuki. For a good few seconds, he couldn't find the words, but then finally, in a hoarse voice, he said:

'You mean he's put Arisaka's body together with one of the prisoners' heads?!'

'Yes, I believe so.'

'But why? Why would Yuasa do such a thing?'

'To cover up the murder of Arisaka.'

'But why would Yuasa have murdered Arisaka?'

'We'll only find out if we ask Yuasa himself. There are still a lot of things I don't understand. How Yuasa came to know about today's beheadings, for instance. And even if it was him collecting the pails, he couldn't just turn up unannounced, so how was he able to do it? Then, as he himself pointed out, he's only got one arm, so how did he manage to behead Arisaka? And what's become of Arisaka's head? Still, there are a lot more things that make sense if you think about it like that. Could Yamagata have turned back from the villa immediately because he found that Yuasa wasn't really there? Because at that time, wouldn't Yuasa have been hurrying the horse and cart on, all the way from Kodenma-chō to Imado? The body had been stripped, of course, to remove any evidence that it was Arisaka, but it was no coincidence that it was covered in excrement. This was because even though he'd shaved the beard on the head, just as he had his own, no matter what he did, he couldn't get rid of the foul stench from its time in the pail, and so he had to cover up the discrepancy between the head and the pristine body.'

The lights of Asakusa, which by now had been lit, drifted past them. Seeming not even to notice them, Kazuki asked:

'But... but all this would mean that one of the coffins lying at the prison is missing a head, wouldn't it?'

'I would presume so, yes.'

'But the bodies are buried when they get to Kozukappara. A missing head would be noticed right away, surely?'

'Everything will become clear when we see those coffins!' Kawaji barked. 'And we'd better hurry up. It's almost time for the transport to Kozukappara!'

7

The two of them arrived back at the jail. Immediately, Kazuki asked the sentry whether anybody had left that day, carrying anything the size of a human head. The sentry shook his head adamantly.

Kawaji then ran over to the mortuary. He had made it just in time. The bodies were ready to be taken to Kozukappara, and Ichinohata was busying himself, securing the third of the five coffins with a straw rope.

'Sergeant!' Kawaji cried. 'Wait! Cut those ropes.'

Ichinohata looked puzzled.

'You've been here ever since they brought the bodies in after the executions, haven't you?'

'Of course, sir!'

'And you didn't leave for a single minute?'

'Well, sir, only to relieve myself.'

'Was that before noon?'

If a head was missing, it would have to have been taken before Kawaji arrived and Ichinohata asked him whether he wanted to look inside the coffins.

'I have some suspicions about the heads in those coffins!' Kawaji bawled at him. 'Remove the lids!'

Flustered, Ichinohata cut the ropes and lifted the lid of the first coffin.

There, illuminated by a dim shaft of light, lay the prisoner, cowering as he held his dishevelled, blood-spattered head in his lap.

'All right. Next…'

The second lid was opened to reveal another corpse cradling its own grim-looking head.

'Next!'

The third one was opened. It was the same story.

At this moment, there was a feverish sound just outside the mortuary, and it was getting closer. It was Kazuki's voice.

'Kawaji! Quick! Look at this!'

He went to the door. 'What is it?'

'One of the guards just showed me this. The emperor is displeased that Vice Minister Hirosawa's assassins still haven't been caught, so just this morning he issued an edict calling for the perpetrators to be apprehended. Take a look!' Kazuki was clutching what appeared to be a copy of the edict. 'This must be the first time that something like this has ever been distributed. Even for the Imperial Prosecuting Office, this seems like an impossible task!'

What Kazuki said was right enough, but Kawaji immediately turned back to the coffins. Ichinohata opened the fourth one. The head was there. Finally, he opened the fifth one…

Once again, the corpse was cradling its head. Each and every one of them had its own heinous, gruesome-looking head.

'Are any of them missing?' Kazuki came in and surveyed the group of coffins with their open lids. 'They've all got them, then. I thought as much. There's no way anybody could pull off anything as outrageous as stealing a head from here. That would be just too bizarre.' Then, clutching Ichinohata by the arm, he said: 'I hear you were the one who dealt with the man who came to collect the pails today?'

'It wasn't just today, sir,' said Ichinohata, scratching his head. 'It's my duty to look after the prison pails. The job does have its perks, though.'

By this, he probably meant that he received an extra payment of a daikon radish or some leafy vegetables.

'So, it was the usual man who came today?' asked Kawaji.

'No, sir, it was somebody else. The usual man was ill, so somebody else came in his place. There didn't seem to be anything suspicious, so I just let him get on with it. Did I do something wrong, sir?'

As he listened to the answer, Kawaji stood there dumbfounded. His hypothesis, which had come in a flash of otherworldly inspiration, was crumbling all about him.

The slovenly faces of a handful of prison servitors darted past.

'They'll be going to Kozukappara any minute now, sir,' said Ichinohata, turning around. 'May I tie them up again?'

Kawaji nodded, feeling like a fool. Assisted by the servitors, Ichinohata once again set about securing the five coffins with rope.

8

It was an evening at the very start of the third lunar month, but already there was a warm southerly wind blowing in across the water. Braziers were burning on the bank of the Sumida. With their backs to the river, the party looked out towards the woods and forests of Imado. There, to the unexpected strains of ancient music, the sound of a beautiful woman's voice with a strange accent began to float across the air.

Awariya, asobihasutomo, mōsanu, asakurani,
Ihei Arisaka no mitama, mairitamae...

Sitting in a row, as usual, were the grandees of the Imperial Prosecuting Office, old Manabe and his daughter, Chief Inspectors Kawaji and Kazuki, as well as the five *rasotsu*-cum-musicians.

'*Ima... mairu!... I am the spirit... of Ihei Arisaka... For the first time since arriving in the land of the dead... I can see the land of the living... without hindrance...*'

Sitting up on the embankment were Yasutari Yuasa, the old farmer and his daughter, and Yatarō Aoki.

Earlier that evening, Aoki had been detained and forcibly brought there. As they had dragged him off, he had kicked and screamed: 'Hey! Where are you taking me? I may have been "Aoki, the hardened criminal" a long time ago, but since the Restoration I haven't done anything to get arrested!' But now, even Aoki was placidly gazing upon the scene from his spot on the ground.

'*Yamashiroya has fled to France, whereas I was left behind... When I saw him off at the wharf, a* rasotsu *from the Imperial Prosecuting Office questioned me... If things continued like that, I, who was Yamashiroya's eyes and ears, would be arrested... And if I were arrested, I should not have the strength to feign ignorance about his dealings for long... So I fled...*'

The golden-haired *miko* spoke as though she were chanting.

'*Now that I had come to the attention of the Imperial Prosecuting Office, the army was the only place to which I could turn for help...*'

But the army had already sacked Yasutari Yuasa, who was hiding out at Yamashiroya's villa in Imado… I paid him a visit… As always, I entered via the back door…'

Yuasa looked on in disbelief, frozen, his eyes fixed on Esmeralda's beautiful, terrifying lips.

'But Yuasa said that when the time came… he and I should have to shoulder everything and die like men… I could not bring myself to do such a foolish thing, though… I have a mother, a wife and three children… I did not become Yamashiroya's chief clerk to suffer such torments… I begged Yuasa, but he refused out of hand…'

'It was *you* who threatened *me!*' Yuasa suddenly started shouting, losing control of himself.

'Then Yuasa carried out his plan to eliminate the dangerous witness that I was…'

'Of all the outrageous things!' Yuasa cried out. 'Silence that malign spirit!'

'The Imperial Prosecuting Office will hear its testimony!' Kazuki rebuked him.

'Meanwhile, Aoki had come to blackmail Yuasa… And the rasotsu *had started watching him… He had no choice but to act… But what could he do with the body after he'd killed me?… He felt uneasy about burying me in the garden of a villa that he would eventually have to leave… And he worried that I could be discovered if he dumped me in the river… So Yuasa decided that he could get away with it if he could make the body unidentifiable, or at least make it appear that he had nothing to do with it…'*

The strange, ethereal music of the spirit world continued to echo around.

'Yuasa happened to learn that the old farmer on the neighbouring estate was the pail collector for the jail in Kodenma-chō… and it was from him that he found out about the executions that were to

be carried out that day… So, disguised as the old farmer, he staked
everything on his plan to gain entry to the jail, steal the head, place
it beside my dead body and show it to the rasotsu…'

Kawaji's eyes opened wide. His guess had been spot on.

And yet…

'The previous night, as I always did, I entered the villa through
the back door, so that the rasotsu wouldn't see me… Yuasa killed
me by lacing my sake with rat poison… Then he cut off my head…
He placed my neck under a hay-cutter and single-handedly brought
the blade down… Then, he took my headless body and placed it
outside the rear gate, and threw the hay-cutter into a nearby field
latrine… The young maid knew nothing about this because it was
done at night…'

But if Yuasa's aim was to make Arisaka's body 'vanish', then
where did his head end up? Kawaji wanted to cry out. He
knew, however, that during these seances Esmeralda could
hear nothing from the real world.

'That day, Yuasa successfully managed to steal a head from the
jail… The main gate was under strict guard, but the sentry for the
mortuary was elsewhere, gossiping…'

With a mournful look on his face, Ichinohata was blowing
his flute as though in a trance.

'While Yuasa was gone, Yamagata arrived… The young maid
knew that he was out, but, as he left, he had given her a look that
told her to keep silent… The rest is as everybody knows… Yuasa
tried to explain it away by saying that it was probably harassment
from Aoki, or an old settling of scores, and, if that didn't wash, he
knew he could always just say that he didn't recognize the corpse…'

The *kagura* bells suddenly rang out.

The former assistant finance director just sat there, bolt
upright.

'*Together with Arisaka, Yuasa helped bury the army's secrets...*'

The voice was beginning to fade away—the usual sign that the spirit's possession of the medium was about to end.

'Wait!' Kawaji cried out.

Once again, his guess had been spot on.

And yet, and yet...

'Tell us one more thing, I beg of you!' he entreated the spirit. 'All the heads in the jail were there! But how can that be?'

'*The head...*'

Though the spirit could not hear anything spoken in this world, the foreign *miko* had just enough time to say these two words before falling silent, as though sinking into the ground.

Then there was nothing, and the *miko*'s golden head slumped forward.

CAN THERE BE A JUST GOVERNMENT?

1

It was a little after noon, one day at the beginning of the fourth lunar month, and Keishirō Kazuki was running late for work. He had been writing in his room at the Saga mansion, with the shadows of green leaves dancing on the white *shōji* screens, when two men arrived. One of these visitors was his colleague Toshiyoshi Kawaji, while the other was a military type with a magnificent beard, dressed in a smart black army uniform and exuding masculinity.

'This is Major General Toshiaki Kirino, a friend of mine from back home,' Kawaji explained. 'It's about the Yamashiroya case. I've brought him because my version of events was apparently unsatisfactory and he'd like to hear yours.'

'Trying to follow Kawaji's account was rather like trying to catch hold of a cloud,' said the major general.

Wasuke Yamashiroya, who had directed the import of foreign munitions to Japan, had borrowed such staggering amounts of money from the army that he had fled abroad, while the army's finance director, Yasutari Yuasa, had been dismissed from his post. Subsequently, Yamashiroya's chief clerk, Ihei Arisaka, had been murdered by none other than Yuasa, which had resulted in his arrest by the Imperial Prosecuting Office. When these facts reached the army, there was of course considerable uproar. It had been like setting a match to a tinderbox.

This, however, was a time before the advent of newspapers as such, so for the ordinary man it all felt as remote and intangible as flashes of lightning amid far-off storm clouds. And besides, the walls of clan allegiance were so thick and impermeable that the truth was not widely known even within the army itself.

'I had the army ledgers taken out and checked,' said Kirino. 'The entries clearly show that a lump sum was indeed deposited with Yamashiroya, but that it was safely returned before he sailed off. Still, there are many things about it that don't add up. What have you been able to ascertain?' His eyes glittered as he spoke. 'I asked Kawaji about it, but he tells me that you're better informed on this case.'

'Well, that's not quite true,' said Kawaji, shaking his head. 'After all, the Ministry of War does have a tendency to close ranks. You can see that well enough from Yuasa's actions after he was caught.'

'And Yuasa has been executed?' Kirino asked.

Although Yuasa had protested his innocence in the Yamashiroya case right to the very end, he had been put to the guillotine some ten days previously.

'That's correct, sir,' said Kazuki.

'But why did you execute him before you could get to the bottom of it?'

'He was exceedingly uncooperative. Kaieda got so angry that he ordered his execution at the earliest opportunity.'

'Old Shunsai did that, did he?' said Kirino with a chuckle. 'And what exactly was the crime for which he was executed?'

'The murder of Yamashiroya's chief clerk, of course.'

'And why did he kill him?'

'He claimed that the charges were trumped up and said that he'd been blackmailed. He even suggested calling on the *miko* again to summon Ihei Arisaka and hear more about it. He went to the guillotine with a sullen smirk on his face, telling us all to go to hell. He was a criminal, of course, but in another sense, he was quite a man.'

'It's because Chōshū men are stubborn like that,' said Kirino, tutting. 'So, has the Imperial Prosecuting Office given up on the case?'

'No, I believe we're still pursuing the Yamashiroya line of inquiry.'

'But if Yamashiroya's fled to France, and his chief clerk is dead…'

'That's why I'm thinking of going to France in the near future to catch him.'

'You are?!'

Kawaji let out a strange noise. He stared at Kazuki in disbelief.

'Are you serious, Kazuki?'

'I am. So long as the Imperial Prosecuting Office will permit it.'

'Excellent! Excellent!' said Kirino, clapping his hands, smiling for the first time. 'I'll have a word with the Imperial Prosecuting Office about it, too, then. But things can't go on like this. If that lot from Chōshū are allowed to carry on as they please, it'll be curtains for the army.' He suddenly looked around and lowered his voice. 'By the way, this French *miko* of yours… Is she here?'

'She is indeed.'

'I don't suppose I could take a look at her, could I? I came here today not just to discuss the Yamashiroya case, but also to catch a glimpse of this golden-haired *miko* you keep… err, I mean, live with.'

'I'm afraid she's working at the moment.'

'Working?' Kawaji interjected, sounding perplexed.

'Another French translation,' said Kazuki. 'This one's quite urgent. And it's hard going, even for her. She'll be upset if we disturb her while she's at work.'

'I see. Well, in that case, let's leave the audience with the *miko* for another time. At any rate, it's an excellent idea, your going to France to apprehend Yamashiroya. I'll put in a good word, by all means. So, my visit hasn't been in vain after all!'

After hastily getting to his feet, Kirino was shown to the main gate of the Saga mansion by the chief inspectors. After they sent him on his way, the two returned to Kazuki's house. Kirino and Kawaji were from the same place, but, despite Kawaji's advantage of two or three years, Kirino was the haughtier of the two, while Kawaji was more reserved. It was little wonder given their difference in rank.

'Well, that was interesting,' said Kazuki. 'That man's head is full of nothing but clan-based hatred. I'm well aware that only people from Chōshū are involved in the Yamashiroya case, but I'm not investigating it just to overthrow them.'

'I know, I'm sorry about that. He has a fierce reputation, and he has a bee in his bonnet about this case. He kept pestering me, and in the end I just couldn't take it any longer, so I brought him to you.'

'You're a good sort, Kawaji.'

'What makes you say that?'

'Though you're a Satsuma man just like him, you rise above all the clan rivalry with Chōshū.'

'Oh, I don't know about that,' said Kawaji with a wry smile.

Kazuki put his arm around Kawaji's shoulder.

'Well, it's a good thing that you and I at least know where our priorities lie: namely, cleaning up corruption in the government.' All of a sudden, Kazuki remembered something. 'Speaking of which, do you remember Fukuzawa?'

'You mean Yukichi Fukuzawa?'

'The very same. He's been lobbying the government for quite some time to sell him the Shimabara Domain's residence in Mita, and now it looks as though it's paid off. Just last month, he moved his school from Shiba Shinsenza over to Mita. What's more, he paid only five hundred and something yen to the Tokyo Municipal Office for a plot of more than fourteen hundred *tsubo*.'

'Oh?'

'The "magnanimous" Shimabara clan were furious that it had been sold without any consultation, so they went to confront Fukuzawa in person, but apparently he just stroked his chin and turned them out of doors, saying that he'd bought it fair and square and that they should address their complaints to the government. That was a little unsporting of him, don't you think?'

'Do you feel sorry for them?'

'The word is that the Shimabara Domain itself will cease to exist in the near future. Fukuzawa must have foreseen this. He's a privileged man and he's leading the government by the nose. I don't think we can turn a blind eye to this sort of thing, do you?'

'No, I don't.'

Kawaji had gone back with Kazuki so that the latter could change and they could go to the office together.

'By the way,' asked Kawaji, 'is this thing that Esmeralda's translating something to keep old Manabe quiet again?'

These translations had begun with the commission from Shinpei Etō—a treatise on French law—and ever since then Kazuki had kept bringing her more and more books to translate. It was obvious, though, that this had been just a pretext to stop old Manabe, who was urging that she be returned home.

'No, in fact this one came by order from Manabe himself,' laughed Kazuki.

Kawaji looked puzzled.

'You mean, Manabe wants a French book translated? Whatever for?'

'It's a very odd commission, I'll grant you that. It took me by surprise, as well. Around ten days ago, he just arrived with this book wrapped in a *furoshiki*, saying it had to be translated as a matter of extreme urgency. He asked me to keep it in the strictest confidence, though.'

'Hmm…'

'Manabe would never need anything like that, so I suspect it must have come originally from Etō or Ōkuma. But I just don't understand the need for all this secrecy around it. If I had to guess, I'd say it must have something to do with the contents of the book.'

'What kind of book is it?'

'It's called *Le Capital*, or something like that. Esmeralda's finding it rather difficult, and whatever she turns out, I'm having to rewrite into something that vaguely resembles Japanese…'

2

It was 1871 by the Western calendar, and towards the end of May, the Paris Commune was suppressed, while Paris itself burned. The world's first proletarian revolutionary government, brought into being by citizens who had had risen up after their defeat in the Franco-Prussian War the previous year, had fought the reactionary government forces for two months, which culminated in the so-called 'Bloody Week' that finally saw them annihilated. Meanwhile, half a world away, it was the tenth day of the fourth lunar month in the fourth year of Meiji…

In those days, the journey from Europe to Japan took around two months, and so news of this had yet to reach its shores. And even if it had reached them, the event would have been looked upon—even though the Japanese had their own 'revolution' but four years previously—as a tale from another world.

That day, the tenth, Kawaji was summoned to Takamori Saigō's mansion.

'There's something that Saigō-sensei would like you to do for him,' said Saigō's aide, Jūrōta Henmi, who had brought the message.

The summons shook Kawaji to his core. When he asked Henmi what it was all about, the messenger replied that he didn't know.

'I don't think it's anything untoward, though,' he added with a smile.

This was the first time that Saigō had asked for Kawaji by name. In fact, he had never met Saigō one-on-one before. Nor had he ever dared to approach the man himself. Kawaji hadn't the slightest idea what it could be about.

Henmi had come on horseback and had also arranged for a horse to be brought for Kawaji. The two of them rode to the former Owari Domain residence in Ichigaya, where Saigō lived. Having recently travelled home to Satsuma, Saigō had returned to the capital only at the start of the second lunar month, and, rather than make the mansion his own, he had turned it into a kind of barracks, keeping his own apartment deep inside it. When they entered through the main gate, there were soldiers milling about everywhere.

Henmi spoke to one of the guards, who led them away to a shaded, leafy inner garden where there were no soldiers.

There was a gazebo, and right in the middle was an enormous wooden table on low legs, around which sat two men wearing military uniforms. One was Saigō, but when Kawaji saw the face of the other one, it took his breath away. It was the deputy assistant to the Minister of War, Aritomo Yamagata.

Kawaji saluted.

'Ah, Kawaji! It's been a while, has it not? Please, take a seat,' said Saigō, smiling and indicating the seat opposite him. 'That will be all, Henmi. Wait over there.'

On the table were four or five dark-brown bottles filled with some kind of liquid, as well as three glasses. Beside them, piled high in a large bamboo basket, was a mountain of boiled broad beans.

'Kawaji, thank you for coming here today,' Saigō began. 'I believe you've been investigating the Yamashiroya case?'

Kawaji started in surprise.

'I'm not very good at this kind of talk, so I'll cut to the chase. I would like you to stop the investigation.'

'Sir?'

'The blunder was Yamagata's, you see. He was the one responsible for lending the army's money to Yamashiroya. He was taken in by Yamashiroya's reputation as a man skilled in commerce and put his faith in old ties of friendship from their days in the militia together. Yamagata tells me, however, that he himself never touched a penny of it—and I believe him.'

With his long, thin face, Yamagata just sat there, motionless, like a statue. Even his pallor was that of stone.

'Now, Yamagata isn't suggesting for a moment that you suppress all this—only that you wait a while before making the matter public. He's assured me that he will recall Yamashiroya from France soon and take responsibility.'

'With all due respect, sir,' Kawaji finally spoke. 'Even if His Excellency is innocent himself, he still bears grave responsibility for having lent the army's money to Yamashiroya.'

'Yamagata agrees, Chief Inspector. But he is indispensable to the army. I may be the commander-in-chief, but, as you will doubtless have heard, I'm a commander-in-chief who does nothing but nap in the afternoon. In effect, it's Yamagata who actually runs things. Without him, the newly formed national army would collapse. Worse still, who can say what would become of the new government that we've worked so hard to create? This is no small matter.' Saigō placed both his hands on the table. 'I ask you, Chief Inspector, leave this to me.'

As Saigō bowed his head, a shiver ran through Kawaji's body.

He had once taken Ōkubo's side in the face of Kazuki's deep admiration for Saigō. Yet that had been more to do with political ability. In terms of character, Kawaji's view of Saigō as a man of quality remained intact even now. More than that: he had begun to put Saigō on a pedestal.

'Sir, I'm only a minor official in the Imperial Prosecuting Office,' he finally managed to say. 'The case has already caused quite a stir—not least among people in the army like Kirino.'

'Leave Kirino to me,' said Saigō.

To put a stop to Kirino, who was from Satsuma, while helping Yamagata, who was from Chōshū? It was clear that Saigō's thinking went beyond clan loyalty.

'Yamagata has told me that it's the Imperial Prosecuting Office that worries him,' Saigō continued. 'Apparently, your investigation has been most thorough. That is why I've summoned you. Will you do this, for me?'

'Of course, sir!'

Many a man from Satsuma would not have agreed to this, but Kawaji was more pragmatic. He did not believe that the government could ever be just.

'Except...' Kawaji began to say. Suddenly the face of the very man who had cried out that the government ought to be the embodiment of justice flashed through his mind. 'There is one other person in the Imperial Prosecuting Office who is investigating the Yamashiroya case. He'll be a tough one to convince.'

'I've just been hearing about him. He's the one from Saga, correct?' said Saigō. 'That man seems to have it in for Yamagata. You can discuss that with the man himself presently. For the time being, however, my duty is done. Remember, Kawaji, I'm counting on you.'

Saigō drained his glass in a single draught.

'Ah, yes, I was given this by a foreigner. It's an alcoholic drink they call "beer". I'm told it's made from barley, but it's quite delicious all the same. Why not try it while you two talk things over?'

He poured some into another glass and pushed it in front of Kawaji.

'Oh, and one other thing. I didn't want to say this earlier, for fear that it might come as a shock to you, but I might as well tell you now. The Imperial Prosecuting Office is to be abolished in the very near future.'

'Sir?' Kawaji blinked in disbelief.

'The powers that be are starting to regret this monster they've created, which seems to be stuffed full of hardliners. These days, the very mention of the Imperial Prosecuting

Office is enough to send every official into a blind panic. The fact is, it's out of control!'

Saigō roared with laughter.

'No, I'm only joking, Chief Inspector! But there is a lot of crossover between the work of the Imperial Prosecuting Office and that of the Bureau of Penal Affairs, which I'm told is causing an almighty headache. So, they're being reformed into a single Ministry of Justice.'

Kawaji looked up at Saigō, dumbfounded.

In those days, there was in fact yet another branch of the judiciary, and Kawaji knew only too well the confusion that it all caused. To give a simple example, if ever a private citizen bribed an official, you could be sure that the Bureau of Penal Affairs would catch one of the men, while the Imperial Prosecuting Office would catch the other. Needless to say, it was impractical to have this kind of overlap.

'I believe Shinpei Etō is to become the first lord chief justice. The Hizen faction demanded that some positions at least should not go to Satsuma and Chōshū, which is reasonable enough.'

'Etō?' said Kawaji. 'But he's even more feared than the Imperial Prosecuting Office.'

'Indeed. And someday, you know, I'd like to see you in that position. But that would be a bit of a leap at the moment. In the meantime, I've asked them to increase the number of *rasotsu* to six thousand, and to put you in charge of them. I'm sure you're quite capable of taking the reins.'

Amid the leafy shade, Kawaji seemed to light up.

'This isn't a spur-of-the-moment decision, either. I've been thinking about this for quite some time. So, I hope you won't let me down.'

Had Shinpei Etō not mentioned something like this before? Yes, that's right. He'd said that if, someday in the future, the police force were to be properly reformed, he'd want a Satsuma man leading them, and that Saigō had said it ought to be Kawaji.

Though the memory came to Kawaji, he said nothing.

'Well, then,' said Saigō, ready to leave. 'If you'll forgive me, Yamagata.'

Suddenly, though, he bent down, and picked up a ball that was lying at his feet.

'I found this hiding under the table,' he said, handing it to Kawaji. 'It appears to have belonged to a child of one of the Owari clan's samurai. Can you read the name embroidered on it?'

It was a cotton ball with thread wrapped around it. Its hiding place under the table had protected it from the elements, but still, it looked old, and more than a little threadbare. Nevertheless, Kawaji was able to make out the characters.

'Tatsunosuke... Hasegawa...'

'Ah, so it belonged to a boy?' said Saigō, taking back the ball. 'In the Owari clan, even boys played with toys like this? And now we've turned their daimyo's elegant mansion into a barracks where bumpkins from Satsuma run riot. What times we live in!'

He laughed, tossed the ball into the air and then slunk off across the garden.

To show such childlike playfulness after so serious a discussion—perhaps this was yet another of Saigō's superhuman traits.

'Chief Inspector,' the statue spoke at last. 'I'm in your debt. The army's accounts have been replenished for the time being with accommodation bills—but that story won't hold up for much longer. This Keishirō Kazuki fellow… I know he's a friend of yours, but will he listen to you?'

'He's a friend, but he's also quite formidable. There are things about him that even I don't understand. I doubt he'd listen to me on this matter. After all, he's a man who's made it his life's work to put a stop to any kind of wrongdoing among politicians, government officials and the military.'

Yamagata grimaced.

'He has under his control this foreign *miko* with mysterious powers, while he himself likes to speak in words that sound like mystical incantations whenever he appears before the directors of the Imperial Prosecuting Office. One way or another, he enjoys a great deal of trust there. Or maybe it's precisely because of all this that he's won their trust. I believe it's all in aid of rooting out corrupt government officials, though. He's even said that he intends to go to France in the very near future in order to find Yamashiroya.'

'And if the Imperial Prosecuting Office is abolished?' said Yamagata.

'Well, Etō-san is supposed to be the new chief of the judiciary. He's not only from the same province as Kazuki, but Kazuki's younger brother is a favourite of his, which complicates things. On the face of it, of course, Kazuki's only investigating relatively minor officials, but I have a suspicion that he's using them as a means of looking higher up the ladder.'

'Etō should never have been appointed.'

Even now, his long, thin face was as expressionless as a Noh mask, but he was unable to conceal a flush of anguish.

'Something has to be done about that man before Etō becomes chief justice. And before he can go to France.'

As he spoke, a look of malice appeared in Yamagata's face.

'The thing is, my dear Kawaji, we've already looked into this Kazuki and certain measures have been taken. The plan is a little heavy-handed, and I myself am not entirely satisfied by it, but after hearing you speak just now, I've reached the conclusion that we no longer have any choice but to go ahead with it.'

'A plan, sir?'

'Since taking on Kazuki himself could backfire, we've decided to take a circuitous route and, to put it bluntly, set a trap for that foreign *miko*.'

'Namely?'

'She's to be arrested on charges of possessing and translating forbidden literature. If Kazuki wants her freedom, he'll have to keep quiet.'

Kawaji was speechless.

'But that must be... the book that Manabe-san asked her to translate?'

'You know about this?! Does anybody else know?'

'No, Kazuki told me about it in the strictest confidence, so I doubt anybody other than me has heard about it.'

'It's reached my attention that Manabe was keen to get that foreign *miko* away from Kazuki by any means possible—and not just to get her away from him, but to get her out of Japan entirely—so I summoned him and we discussed the matter. And he agreed.'

'You mean, the old man...'

'Even if it's revealed that the book came from Manabe, that will not absolve the girl of her crime. But if I may, I should like to request your help in ensuring that Manabe's part in this does not come out. Indeed, without your help, this plan may not work.'

'What exactly is the book?'

'The book I gave to Manabe is written in French, although the original was in German. From what I've read of the translation, it's a truly appalling work—far more harmful that anything those "Jesuits" write. It's a book that mustn't be allowed into Japan, not a single line on a single scrap of paper. The translator fully deserves the maximum punishment.'

The sky clouded over, and suddenly the silhouettes of the two men sitting in the gazebo turned black amid the verdure.

In the distance, there were bursts of laughter, and among them Saigō's voice echoed especially loudly. Perhaps he was tossing the ball about with the soldiers.

Yamagata and Kawaji lapsed into silence.

3

'We can go to France!' cried Kazuki, returning from work one day at the start of the fifth month. 'I've been granted permission to go!'

Yet his high-spirited announcement met with an unexpected reception.

'Keishirō,' said Esmeralda, a strange expression on her face. 'Monsieur Kawaji... he came for the book.'

'He did what?' said Kazuki, stunned by this news.

About three days previously, they had finally finished translating *Le Capital*, but although Kazuki had informed old Manabe of this, he still hadn't come to pick it up. Given the old man had insisted that it be done in record time, this was something of an anticlimax, but Kazuki had no choice but to wait.

Now, having been told that Kawaji had come to collect it, Kazuki was puzzled, but thought no more about it. He did not even want to chastise Esmeralda for having given it to him.

Over the next few days, Kazuki did not even see Kawaji at work, because the latter did not show his face at the office. Still, Kazuki did not suspect anything in particular; after all, the nature of their work was such that even he did not go to the office every day. Yet he did think it was odd that, despite having just received permission to go abroad, he should then receive orders from on high to put it off a little. Still, though, he didn't connect any of this with *Le Capital*.

It was on the tenth day of the fifth month that disaster finally struck.

That evening, Kazuki was alone in the office, getting ready to leave, when Kawaji appeared. They had not seen each other in almost ten days, and Kazuki was surprised to see him.

'Well, well! Where have you been lately?' he asked.

Kawaji's face was not pale or haggard, but for some reason Kazuki felt as though he had never before seen it look so solemn or pitiful.

'Kazuki, I have some bad news,' he said. 'Esmeralda has been arrested.'

'Esmeralda?!' said Kazuki, taken aback. 'What has she done?'

'It's in connection with that book, *Le Capital*.'

For several seconds, Kazuki was lost for words.

'When?'

'About an hour ago,' Kawaji replied. 'I was there at the arrest. They've already taken her to Kodenma-chō.'

'All because she translated that book?!'

'I'm sorry, Kazuki. It's all my fault,' he said, bowing his head in apology. 'I thought it was odd that old Manabe had asked her to translate the book in such a hurry, so when it was done, I borrowed it so that I could take a look. I didn't understand much, but it seemed interesting, so without thinking I showed it to Kaieda. He circulated it among the other directors—he even showed it to Ōkubo, Kido, Inoue and Itō—and they've kicked up a real fuss. They said that the book is dangerous and that if it were to be translated and disseminated throughout Japan, it could not only threaten Japan's future, but even bring about the total collapse of the government.'

For all the bombast of Kawaji's description, there could be no mistaking the book. It was of course Karl Marx's *Das Kapital*, which had been published as recently as 1867—that is, in the third year of Keiō.

Little by little, the blood drained from Kazuki's face. He, for one, did not consider Kawaji's description to be an over-statement, and he had suspected that old Manabe's reasons for asking him to keep the book a secret had to do with its contents. Like Kawaji, he, too, had found many of the words puzzling, but he also dimly sensed that it was one to be feared.

Kazuki, however, had believed that the book was just one of the many in the great deluge of foreign books that had entered Japan since the Restoration, and it had never crossed his mind that this book might be special in some way.

At last, he knew why his trip to France had been post-poned. The Imperial Prosecuting Office had launched an investigation.

'But...' he said, 'but why has Esmeralda been arrested and thrown in jail, when the commission for the translation came from Uncle Manabe?'

'Esmeralda hasn't told them that. I asked her about it when she was arrested, but all she said was that the book had been sent recently from France.'

'You asked her? But you already knew that.'

'But can we say that, Kazuki? Can we mention Manabe's name?'

Kazuki was utterly speechless.

'If Manabe's name comes out,' said Kawaji, 'all the higher-ups from Chōshū will be liable to stick the knife in. Saying that somebody from Saga asked her to do it won't make matters any easier.'

'That's it, I'm going to Kodenma-chō. I need to see Esmeralda.'

Having kept her promise not to divulge the name of the man who commissioned the translation, Esmeralda would of course be awaiting Kazuki's instructions.

Oblivious to Kawaji's attempts to dissuade him, Kazuki made to leave. When he got to the door, however, he suddenly stopped and turned around.

'Why haven't you arrested me, Kawaji?' he asked.

For a moment, Kawaji didn't seem to know what to say.

'You've thrown her in jail, but you haven't arrested me, who translated it with her? Isn't that a bit odd? Or did you come to arrest me?'

'I came to talk to you,' he whispered in a low voice.

'To talk about what?'

'The biggest hardliner in this investigation is Yamagata.' Kawaji cleared his throat. 'Couldn't you just drop the Yamashiroya investigation?'

Kazuki walked back and stood in front of Kawaji. He looked long and hard at his friend and rival.

'This is coming from Yamagata, isn't it?'

Kawaji looked up at the ceiling.

'Well, I knew you could be underhand, Kawaji, but this is really scraping the barrel.'

Kawaji looked back at Kazuki. His gaze was as lost as it was brazen.

'Your righteousness is dangerous. You're only a minor official, after all. Don't go after those higher up the ladder. If you do, never mind Yamagata, you could end up implicating Inoue, Itō, Kido, Ōkubo, Iwakura, even Saigō himself! What do you think the Imperial Prosecuting Office is for?! Isn't it an arm of the government?'

'The Imperial Prosecuting Office should be the agency of justice,' said Kazuki. 'The government itself should be a just government! Anybody who disagrees with that, even those in the highest places, should be removed from office!'

'That will have dangerous repercussions. Take my advice, Kazuki.'

'I'm not about to make any deals, Kawaji.'

'Not even for Esmeralda's sake?'

Kazuki fell silent once again. Tears welled in his eyes, as he glared at Kawaji.

Never before had Kawaji seen this man cry, though he knew the emotional side of Kazuki's character well enough. Still, the very sight of it took him by surprise.

'Kazuki,' he sighed. 'Can't you just overlook this?'

'Never!' thundered Kazuki, as if to strike Kawaji down.

Kawaji looked at the floor.

'You have a week,' he said.

Then he left the room.

4

Kazuki ran to the prison in Kodenma-chō, but when the guard saw his face he apologized, explaining that though the foreign woman was indeed being held there, she was forbidden from seeing anyone. And so Kazuki then went to see Manabe.

Old Manabe lived not in the Saga residence, but in the Aoi-chō neighbourhood of Akasaka. Night had fallen and it was raining, but when Kazuki arrived, Manabe himself answered the door with O-Nui standing behind him, holding a lantern.

'Forgive me, Uncle, but I must ask you about that book.'

'Wh-what do you mean?' the old man stammered. 'I don't know what you're talking about.'

Kazuki stood there in silence, his eyes boring into him.

The old man was stubborn by nature, but he had a kindly nature. He flinched under that gaze. He could see that Kazuki's heart was breaking and that he was desperately trying to hold it together.

The fact of the matter was that old Manabe would not name the man for whom he had served as the intermediary in the commissioning of the translation. Suffice it to say, however, the man in question was an influential figure within the Saga clan, and, since Manabe did not want to cause him any trouble, he had planned to order Kazuki to sever ties with the foreign woman. But as soon as he saw the desperation on Kazuki's face, he lost the will to take that line of action. He was not a bad man at heart, and his reaction was not as ruthless as it seemed. Kazuki had taken him off guard.

O-Nui's smile vanished, and she looked quizzically at the two men.

'Whatever's the matter?' she asked.

It was clear that she had no knowledge of any of this.

'Please, come in,' said the old man, his voice sounding hoarse. 'Keishirō, my boy, you need to give up that foreign woman.'

'I know,' he said. 'I'm sorry, but I can't stay.'

Kazuki smiled at O-Nui, bowed, and then turned to leave.

'Keishirō!' the old man shouted.

Without looking back, Kazuki hurried off, vanishing amid the darkness and pouring rain. Behind him, the stony visage of old Manabe and the shocked face of O-Nui stared out from the door.

What was most astonishing was that the very next day, Kazuki carried on working at the Imperial Prosecuting Office, writing reports and continuing to investigate cases of corruption. Most of his colleagues had no idea even that there was a case underway against him.

Instead, it was Kawaji who stopped showing his face at the office.

It was the seventeenth day of the fifth lunar month, and in Tokyo the rainy season was in full swing. It had been a whole week since Kawaji and Kazuki had their last encounter, and Kazuki had been summoned by the directorate of the Imperial Prosecuting Office. When he arrived, he saw Kawaji standing beside them.

'For the crime of spreading the most dangerous and most harmful literature that threatens to undermine the very foundations of our society, we sentence Esmeralda Sanson to death by beheading tomorrow at noon,' said Kaieda solemnly.

'However, you, who should be subject to the same punishment, are hereby exonerated with special dispensation.'

When no response was forthcoming, Shinagawa added, as though to rub salt in the wound:

'The execution received special authorization from Vice Ministers Ōkubo and Kido.'

Although a new legal code had been distributed at the end of the previous year, it was only in draft form, and this was, after all, an era of chaos in which nobody would challenge the arbitrary rulings handed down by judges—or rather, by government officials who were not judges by any means. And so, no matter whether Ōkubo and Kido had really intervened or not, what was clear was that Kazuki had made an enemy of the entire government apparatus.

Well aware that nobody could object, Kazuki did not look at all perturbed by these words, let alone make any protest.

'I believe that Kawaji has something he'd like to say to you as a colleague,' murmured Yukimasa Ozaki, while attempting to give Kazuki a comforting smile. 'Likewise, if you have anything to say, now is the time to say it.'

'I acknowledge your judgement,' said Kazuki quietly. 'I have nothing further to say.'

A look of astonishment appeared on Kawaji's face.

'Only, if I may be so bold as to ask…' Kazuki added, tripping over his tongue.

'Out with it, Keishirō!' one of the men thundered.

'If I may be so bold as to ask, I should like to request that the execution be carried out using the guillotine, as is the family tradition of the prisoner, and that you permit me, in my official capacity, to carry out the execution myself.'

As he uttered these words, all the members of the Imperial

Prosecuting Office, including Kawaji, could feel drops of perspiration running down their backs.

5

It was the eighteenth day of the fifth lunar month, which corresponded to the fifth of July by the Western calendar. The rainy season was not yet over, but that day the rain had let up, and leaden clouds were hanging low over the eaves of the prison in Kodenma-chō.

Four bonfires were burning in the execution ground, which was enclosed by a mud wall that was cracking and crumbling wherever the eye looked. On a fine day, fires at high noon would have looked odd, but in this dim, silver-grey air, the fires glowed red, as though burning in twilight.

The guillotine had been brought out and erected right in the middle of the execution ground, and at the very top of it, the triangular iron blade was glowing red as though it had already drawn blood. Sitting at the foot of it, as usual, were the grandees of the Imperial Prosecuting Office, the five *rasotsu*, old Manabe and his daughter.

Yet everything was not quite as usual. The guests were assembled here not to hear the golden-haired *miko*'s revelations, but to behead her. And now they were to witness, for the very first time, the guillotine in action.

Esmeralda was still in her cell.

The prison warden, Shigeya Ohara, who was normally present for executions, had also come, his keys jangling from his waist. The prison itself was still largely the same as it had been before the Restoration, only the keys and locks were now of

361

Western manufacture, and the warden always had at least three different types of key on his person.

The execution was scheduled for noon.

Kawaji's pocket watch showed that there were ten minutes to go.

'Well, it's almost time,' said Kazuki, sitting on the bench of the guillotine.

Everybody could feel their hair standing on end.

Just that morning, Kazuki had made a strange request. It was a pity, he had told Kawaji, that along with Esmeralda's demise, so too would vanish the one person who knew how to summon the spirits of the dead. He then revealed that he had recently tried his hand at Esmeralda's art, and with some success, and so he asked whether he might be permitted to conduct an experiment before the assembled guests prior to her execution. He said that he intended to summon the spirits of those who had already been put to the guillotine. Hence, he had asked Kawaji to ensure that the usual crowd was present at the prison.

Kawaji wondered whether his colleague had gone mad. He had expected that Kazuki would relent from his stubbornness and agree to stop pursuing the Yamashiroya investigation before anything could happen to Esmeralda. But after seven days, he still hadn't said a word, and Kawaji could only marvel at his colleague's resolve. Then came his request…

It was something of a surprise, but Kawaji granted it all the same, though he was still sure Kazuki was going to give in and take the deal.

And so, with the group gathered there, noon was fast approaching.

'What's going on, Father?' Kawaji heard O-Nui ask in a fearful voice. 'I… I have this feeling that something terrible is about to happen.'

But old Manabe could not answer his daughter's question. Evidently, O-Nui knew nothing of what was to take place, so her fear was only natural. Her father just sat there ashen-faced, as motionless as a stone statue.

With ten minutes to go, Shigeya Ohara, who similarly knew nothing of what was to happen, bowed to the dignitaries from the Imperial Prosecuting Office and turned to go and fetch the criminal. Just then, however, Kazuki said, 'It's time,' at which point the usual five *rasotsu* struck up their ancient instruments.

The *kagura* bells suddenly rang out.

Sitting on the scaffold where the guillotine stood, Kazuki, dressed in his *suikan*, was holding the bells aloft in one hand.

Was he really going to do it? Was Kazuki really going to transform himself into the bizarre spectacle of a male *miko* and summon the spirits of the dead?

Kawaji could scarcely believe his eyes and ears.

Intoned with great solemnity, the ancient words of the incantation flowed from Kazuki's lips.

'What's that?' he suddenly mumbled. 'Ah, you're already here?… You think it's fine for me to speak in the plain words of a chief inspector?'

Evidently, he was communing with one of the spirits.

Kazuki nodded and looked at everyone assembled below the scaffold.

'Well, then. Now I shall humbly tell the complaints of the departed in my own words.'

6

'First, there was the case of the murder at the Tsukiji Hotel in the autumn of the year before last, in which Kunai Nagasaka was responsible for the death of Tetsuma Sugi. Nagasaka was put to the guillotine, and what I have to say now comes from the confession of his spirit...

'When the murder took place, Nagasaka was at the top of the tower in the Tsukiji Hotel and he managed to kill Sugi by securing a sword through a pair of *geta* and sliding them down the spiral staircase as the latter was making his way upstairs. At the same time, he had the renowned swordsman Gensai Kawakami and his disciple, Ushinosuke Shimozu, lured to the scene of the crime in an attempt to pin the blame on them...

'However, no matter how ingenious Nagasaka's plan was, it would only work if Sugi arrived at the hotel at exactly the right moment, and if Kawakami and Shimozu appeared on the scene immediately after the murder had been committed. Without some guarantee, the plan could never have been put into action...

'It was Sergeant Yokomakura who fetched Sugi, and Sergeant Saruki who lured Kawakami and Shimozu to the scene of the crime. In other words, the murder was only possible with the cooperation of those two *rasotsu*...

'Nagasaka believed that the two men were helping him out of sympathy for his predicament, after Sugi had blackmailed him. In fact, the idea for the murder itself was given him by the two *rasotsu*...

'At the time, Chief Inspector Kawaji observed that there was something strange about the behaviour of the *rasotsu*.

But even he could never have suspected that they were the instigators of the affair...

'Sergeant Imokawa! Tie up Yokomakura and Saruki!...

'Next came the case in which the rickshaw crashed into the Kanda River in the second month of last year, and in which Magobei Akamatsu murdered Sagen Tagusari. Akamatsu was put to the guillotine, and what I have to say now comes from the confession of his spirit...

'Tagusari was blackmailing Akamatsu, having found out that he was harbouring Lord Ogasawara, and so Akamatsu plied him with drink, placed him inside two rickshaws that had been bound together and sent the four-wheeled contraption rolling down the hill and into the river, drowning Tagusari and making it look as though it had all been the work of Lord Ogasawara's *ikiryō*...

'So, in order to lend credence to the story, they bribed Sergeants Onimaru and Yokomakura, who were watching the house belonging to Lord Ogasawara's mistress, and had them concoct a story about seeing His Lordship's *ikiryō* in the graveyard at Yanaka. As you know, the details of this were exposed at the time, but not the reason for the cooperation of the *rasotsu*...

'In fact, the very genius of transporting the victim in this four-wheeled double rickshaw came from none other than Sergeant Imokawa. He was the one who approached Akamatsu after being bribed and gave him the idea. Were it not for that ingenuity, Akamatsu would never have been able to murder Tagusari...

'Sergeant Ichinohata! Tie up Onimaru, Yokomakura and Imokawa! Ah, Yokomakura has already been tied up? Well, see to Onimaru and Imokawa then...

'Next came the case of the hanged man at the Eitai Bridge in the spring of last year, in which Nijūrō Teranishi murdered Kokuten Kodama. Teranishi was put to the guillotine, and what I have to say now comes from the confession of his spirit...

'Teranishi forced Kodama to stand on the top deck of a steamboat and, as it passed under the bridge where the rope had already been prepared, he slipped the rope around his neck and hanged him, while he himself remained on the boat, escaping back to Yokohama. But didn't you notice, Kawaji? In order for it to work, they had to be in exactly the right spot, and so the captain had to manoeuvre the boat in such a way to make this possible...

'The captain of the *Ginkō*-maru isn't to blame, though. In fact, he sooner deserves your pity. For one, he was coerced into doing it. And he was also the father of the young girl who killed herself after being chosen for Lord Iwakura's collection of beautiful women. The captain's name is Naochika Asakura, and his daughter was the lover of the suspect Gitetsu Hikita...

'Incidentally, when we lost Hikita in the chase around Shinagawa, he had in fact boarded the *Ginkō*-maru, which was docked there. In other words, that day in Yokohama when Ginkō Kishida pointed out his steamboat to you, Kawaji, Hikita was already hiding on board...

'There is, moreover, something that I must reveal about the *Ginkō*-maru's owner. He was the one who lured Kodama out of the restaurant in Yanagibashi to the ship anchored at Hamachō, having told him to meet him there if he wanted to discuss the opium again. It was also Kishida who, in the Ogasawara case, made it look as though His Lordship had been sending money from America. And later on, too, in the subsequent case, it was he who arranged for Tanosuke Sawamura's surgery to be witnessed from the tower in the Tsukiji Hotel as though by chance...

'However, I would ask that you do not lay a finger on Kishida. He was only acting on instructions—and doing so out of his inimitable sense of loyalty. Yes, indeed, all of this was approved by none other than Doctor Hepburn. And if Kishida were arrested, the good doctor would have to be arrested too. And, if that were to happen, I need scarcely point out that the American government would have something to say on the matter...

'Despite all this, the reason that Teranishi was able to carry out his "grandiose" murder was that the idea had once again been given to him by somebody else. And this time the stroke of genius was provided by Sergeant Imokawa, who often went to Yokohama and had got to know Teranishi...

'Sergeant Ichinohata! Tie up Imokawa! Ah, I see there's no need...

'Next came the case with the leg amputation in the autumn of last year, and in which Tateki Maki manipulated Shūzō Toba into killing the innocent Hikomaro Kagawa, in consequence of which, tormented by his guilt, Toba committed suicide. Maki was put to the guillotine, and what I have to say now comes from the confession of his spirit...

'This two-part operation could only be pulled off if Toba believed that Kagawa might really harm the geisha, Kikuchiyo, in the first place. For this to be plausible, Kagawa would have to set his sights on her, but it would defeat the purpose if he actually succeeded in killing her...

'Hence the desperate scenes at the Sazae-dō. Kikuchiyo was threatened by Kagawa just after she got into a rickshaw, after which she was taken to the Sazae-dō, where a sculptor of Buddhist images and I happened to save the day. In fact, the rickshaw-puller was none other than Sergeant Onimaru in disguise. Onimaru knew that I was going to the Sazae-dō that day, and so, though he pretended to be afraid, he knew full well where to find me and took the rickshaw where he knew no harm would come to Kikuchiyo. When he heard about the abduction, however, Toba flew into a rage…

'It's clear from this that Maki had successfully manipulated Toba. Yet there was, in turn, somebody else who had manipulated Maki, and that person was none other than Sergeant Saruki, who met him at Kinpei Kobayashi's pawnshop…

'Ichinohata! If you would please do the honours…

'So, four of them have been tied up. That's quite enough for now. Throw them in a cell and we'll question them later! Ohara-san, it's time. Please, have the foreign *miko* brought here. Actually, no… Come to think of it, I still have more to say. Another twenty minutes or so should be enough.'

7

The prison warden, who had been in a daze as he listened to Kazuki speak, was suddenly jolted back to his senses. As he staggered off, he was followed out of the execution ground by Ichinohata, who was leading the four other *rasotsu* by the rope binding them.

By now it was clear that this was no confession from the spirits of the departed. This was Kazuki's own tale—which made its content all the more shocking and mysterious.

Kazuki continued in the same oracular tone:

'Then came the case with the five heads, in which Yasutari Yuasa killed Ihei Arisaka, swapping his head for that of somebody else in order to make it look as though he had no connection with the deceased whatsoever. What I have to say now...'

Here, for the first time, he laughed.

'Well now, we're in a bit of a bind with this case. Up to this point, the *miko* Esmeralda had recounted the confessions of the spirits to the satisfaction of all those gathered, but that wasn't the case with this one...

'Kawaji, even you suspected that the deceased's head belonged to one of the five men who had been beheaded earlier that day. And you were right. Little by little, you were revealing your true abilities as a chief inspector, and in fact the instigators of all this, who had been teasing you by having Arisaka's corpse cradle the head, were more than a little disappointed...

'Just as you thought, Yuasa, disguised as the gong farmer, was able to make off with one of the heads hidden in a pail. And he was given the idea by none other than Sergeants Onimaru and Yokomakura, who had been watching Yamashiroya's villa in Imado...

'You correctly guessed that one of the heads must be missing and went to investigate. Only, when you arrived, you were astonished to find that all five heads were there. And of course they were, because Yuasa had brought one with him that morning when he arrived...

'Did you really examine those five heads you saw? No, your so-called investigation surprised even Ichinohata—for of course it was he who had helped Yuasa to switch the heads...

'And that, my dear Kawaji, was not a very thorough examination. Just as you were on the point of discovery, I came in like a friend in need, and, while we were talking, Ichinohata swapped Arisaka's head, which was in the fourth coffin, with the one that was in the second. Of course, you'd only just seen the head in the second coffin, but you failed to recognize it, as it was no less heinous a sight than the others, with its dishevelled hair and blood-spattered face. That's why, when you asked about it afterwards, Esmeralda couldn't answer you. Do you see now?'

Kawaji just stood there, rooted to the spot. Had the mystery of the five heads really been down to that lazy, impudent *rasotsu*'s sleight of hand?

The case no longer confounded him. As he listened to Kazuki's explanation, he had blanched and blushed along with the other seated guests, but now, of them all, his sense of failure was by far the greatest.

'In other words, behind each of these elaborate murders, there was a gang of *rasotsu* trailing the suspects, watching them, investigating them—and all along they were the ones pulling the strings. Yes, despite the vacant expressions on each and every one of their faces, they're actually a pretty cunning bunch. They even manipulated some of the men so skilfully that they didn't know it!'

Kazuki beamed with satisfaction.

'Not one of those schemes actually originated with the perpetrators, though each had its origins in the bonds between the men involved in them. And for all that they were quick to take advantage of the opportunity given them, in the end they played only a supporting role—a fact that unavoidably came to light now and then, and which even raised your suspicions, Kawaji, on more than one occasion…

'And yet there's more. If you care to re-examine the facts, I dare say you'll hit on the answer to everything…

'You may well wonder why those men who went to the guillotine did not speak out about the *rasotsu*. As I've just said, this is because some of them were taken in but didn't realize it, while for others the shock of the crime and its punishment was so severe that they forgot all about the *rasotsu*, and still others found meaning in the belief that they had done it themselves. It's also true that most of them had killed people they wanted to kill, so they felt there was little point in speaking out now. Still, there were some who did mention the *rasotsu*, but they were silenced by me. Whenever one of them wanted to talk, I told them that if they kept quiet, they wouldn't be put to the guillotine.'

'Kazuki,' said his colleague, speaking for the first time, 'you silenced them?'

'I did.'

'Then the *rasotsu* weren't the only ones pulling the strings? There was somebody else pulling the strings behind them, using them—and that somebody was you!'

'Correct,' replied Kazuki coolly. 'As these were crimes of my own making, the above preliminaries were necessary.'

'But why?'

'To make a just government a reality!'

The *kagura* bells suddenly rang out.

'Every last one of those men who killed or were killed was an official or former official and woefully unfit for office. Our very own Kunai Nagasaka was so incompetent that he had the wrong man put to death, while Tetsuma Sugi was a maniac who took advantage of this to outstrip his rivals and demand his own boss's daughter. Magobei Akamatsu was pilfering from the

371

Treasury to support his former boss, and when Sagen Tagusari got wind of this over in the Ministry of Popular Affairs he tried to blackmail him. Nijūrō Teranishi, who had once been head of the Raw Silk Inspection Office, was a heartless man who abandoned a woman to advance his career, whereas Kokuten Kodama was nothing but a shameless pimp for a powerful man and pretended it was for the good of the nation. Hikomaro Kagawa, in the Grand Council of State, was a violent drunkard; Tateki Maki, who held high office at the Ministry of Popular Affairs, was borrowing vast sums from moneylenders just to lavish on female impersonators; and Shūzō Toba was a crook, who tried to leverage his boss's financial embarrassment in order to usurp him. The former army finance director, Yasutari Yuasa, was responsible for the loan of vast sums of public funds to a common merchant, while Ihei Arisaka was the merchant in question's chief clerk...

'What's more, if they had all simply been dismissed, they would have either gone unpunished or escaped. That's why I chose to punish them myself by making them turn on one another. And once they'd killed each other, all I had to do was execute the murderer.'

Even the grandees of the Imperial Prosecuting Office, who had been appointed as the very embodiment of just government, could not help shuddering at this moment.

Kawaji had turned pale. He had known very well that his colleague harboured a certain fanaticism, but he had never suspected anything of this degree of meticulousness. Suddenly he felt shaken by the prospect of any 'deal'.

As Kazuki had just pointed out, Kawaji had always had his doubts about the *rasotsu*. However, these had dissipated, in part because Kazuki had either defended them or avoided his questions every time, but more so because their aims had been too ambiguous for him to suspect them. Even before that, he had had his doubts about the messages from the hereafter relayed by Esmeralda. But then, even if Kazuki had been the one making her say all this, his ultimate goal, likewise, had been too unimaginable in the first place.

It was hard to believe that those five thugs had shared in Kazuki's vision.

But why was he even confessing all this now? Were all these men simply crazed lunatics?

'Kazuki, why are you telling us all this?'

'Ah-ha! There are three reasons for it.'

At that moment, a prison official appeared on the execution ground, looking confused.

'Is the warden here?' he asked.

'What?' asked Kawaji, turning around.

'... The first is that, when you think about it, my actions overstepped the authority of my office. They also overstepped its authority in that the punishment was meted out arbitrarily. When I looked back upon my actions, I concluded that I had a duty to judge myself...'

'What do you want with the warden?' Kawaji asked the official.

'Sir, Sergeant Ichinohata and four other *rasotsu* just left the prison with the foreign *miko*. They said they were taking her because they had orders that she was to be questioned again by the Imperial Prosecuting Office. They were all so calm and orderly that I allowed them to pass, but now it's weighing on my mind, so I came to check with the warden.'

'What?! When was this?'

'About fifteen or twenty minutes ago, sir.'

'… The second reason,' Kazuki continued, 'is of course that I did not intend to limit those punishments to minor officials. You see, Kawaji, I was planning to raise the matter at a higher level. I had even gathered a lot of material from the investigations! But at this rate, every cabinet minister and councillor would have to be punished! And so, coming to the realization that it would end in the complete destruction of the government, I fell into a state of utter despair…'

A second official came running into the execution ground.

'Quickly!' he shouted. 'It's the warden! He's passed out in the cell where that foreign *miko* was being held!'

Kawaji was about to run off, but his feet were pinned to the ground by Kazuki's voice.

'… And the third reason is that I am going to execute myself right here. That is why I have made my final confession…'

Kazuki threw the *kagura* bells down from the top of the scaffold, and they rang out one last time.

As Kawaji turned to look back, he saw Kazuki lying flat on the bench, his neck resting in the semicircular hole at the bottom of the end board. Whereas most of those condemned to die would ordinarily lie facing down, Kazuki was lying on his back. In his right hand, the rope was swaying.

'O-Nui!' cried Kazuki. As he twisted his neck around, he laughed. 'I loved you. But I couldn't marry you because I knew that this day would eventually come. Please, let your father choose a good man for you, and have a long and happy life.'

He pulled on the rope. The triangular blade came screeching down and sent an enormous spray of blood into the air. O-Nui fainted.

Thoroughly numbed by this spectacle, the onlookers were sure they had heard the last words uttered by the head just before it went tumbling down into the basket below.

'Banzai! Long live the Imperial Prosecuting Office!'

8

What an odd-looking chariot it was.

Two rickshaws had been trussed back-to-back, binding them together. Clutching one of the poles at the front was Heikurō Imokawa, while the other was pulled by Jirōmasa Saruki. Riding in the front rickshaw, covered by netting, was the golden-haired *miko*, Esmeralda. Pushing from behind was Heisuke Yokomakura, while Sohachi Ichinohata sat facing out of the rear rickshaw. With a baton tucked under his arm, Tamonta Onimaru came running behind this bizarre contraption.

'Come on!'

'Keep going!'

At the front, Saruki and Imokawa were running so fast that they looked as though they might take a tumble at any moment. But still, Yokomakura urged them on from the rear, pushing as fast as his legs would carry him. They were going at such a terrific speed that, had it not been for all their shouting, people milling about in the street could quite conceivably have been run over. As it was, however, their vociferous cries made people turn to look, before dashing out of their way and leaving the path clear for this strangest of rickshaws. They had already left Tokyo and were heading westwards.

After untying themselves, the *rasotsu* had subjected the prison warden to such agonizing torments that he fainted. Having then taken his keys, not only did they free Esmeralda, but Ichinohata came out of the prison storehouse that he knew so well, clutching three of the ten Snider rifles that had been recently acquired in case of prison escapes.

Shortly after leaving the prison, they had requisitioned these two rickshaws off the street, fashioned them into this 'chariot' and deposited Esmeralda inside, before setting off as fast as they could. By the time they reached Kawasaki, some ten miles from Tokyo, the wan grey clouds had turned a shade of dark ink, and the rain had begun to beat down on them.

It was around then that they first heard the cries of their pursuers.

Kawaji had been informed of their escape around twenty minutes after the fact, but he had no idea at all where they might be going. When it was finally established that they had headed west, along the Tōkaidō highway, he set out after them at great speed.

He realized now that the true purpose of Kazuki's long monologue had been to focus attention on himself and give Esmeralda sufficient time to escape.

'There!'

'Where are they going?'

'Stop!'

Hot on their heels, the prison officials were all shouting over one another. As the pursuers closed the gap on them, one, then another of the *rasotsu* went tumbling to the ground.

A series of gunshots then rang out.

The shots were being fired from inside the rear-facing rickshaw.

The pursuers scattered, until, urged on by Kawaji's cries and rebukes, several of them drew their swords and rushed forward desperately. But as they did, a giant with fury in his eyes emerged from behind the rickshaw and knocked every last one of them to the ground.

'Sergeant Onimaru!' shouted Kawaji, his eyes wide. 'Have you lost your mind? A *rasotsu* aiding and abetting a prison break?!'

'I'm sorry, Chief Inspector, but we won't surrender! Thanks to Chief Inspector Kazuki, we finally found a cause that made our lives worth living! And now the time's come for us to die like men!'

Several more men rushed at him, but after a couple of blows of Onimaru's baton, they all ended up in the mud.

The rain was getting heavier. More shots were fired. Two, then three of the pursuers fell to the ground. Under the rickshaw's canopy, Kawaji saw Ichinohata with a rifle slung over his shoulder. And to make matters worse, he appeared to have several of them.

It was seventeen miles from Tokyo to Yokohama, and both sides were half dead from running. Still, though, the fight continued on the move, and to see this rickshaw-cum-chariot moving backwards was truly a bizarre sight.

On the outskirts of Yokohama, Kawaji was saved when he came across a platoon of soldiers marching in the rain. Having explained to their stunned commander that the group running ahead was a gang of prison escapees, he asked for their help.

Onimaru and Ichinohata were shot dead at the entrance to Yokohama. Finally the giant lay sprawled out on his back, and Ichinohata, for all his puny stature, had managed to discharge

377

every last bullet from all three of his rifles before slumping out of the rickshaw, a bloodied mess.

Despite this, the rickshaw had continued to speed along as though pulled by phantoms, and, by the time that Kawaji and the others found themselves at the waterfront, the three remaining *rasotsu* had already bundled the golden-haired *miko* into a little boat that was waiting there and escaped out to sea.

Amid the rain and mist lingering off the coast loomed the silhouette of a foreign ship. The sound of its foghorn reached them. The ship was about to depart.

'They're getting away!' shouted Kawaji, jumping up and down. 'Fire!'

The guns of the soldiers lined up along the waterfront fired a single volley, and one of the *rasotsu* could be seen slumping over in the little boat and falling into the water. Kawaji could just make out that it was Imokawa.

Yet the little boat carried on through the rain and across the waves, getting further and further away.

Back on shore, Kawaji could only stand there, as white as a sheet.

The ship making ready to leave was the *Orléans*. Esmeralda learnt from the *rasotsu* that Kazuki had given them strict orders to make sure they arrived in time to meet the French ship.

The *Orléans* spotted the tender and lowered a rope ladder. Still dressed as a *miko* in her scarlet *hakama*, Esmeralda reached out her hand to it. Looking down at the little boat below, she saw Saruki and Yokomakura. So different now from the men they had once been, they had both rowed her with every last ounce of strength they had. But they were covered in blood, and now they were dead.

'*Merci, messieurs sergeants japonais,*' she whispered as tears welled in her eyes.

She looked up.

'*Sayonara, Keishirō!*' she cried out, gazing towards the distant shore of Japan.

Then, from the little boat floating there amid the pale-blue sea spray, she climbed the rope ladder, up towards the heavens, like a red-and-white butterfly.

In the seventh lunar month of the fourth year of Meiji, the Imperial Prosecuting Office was abolished. In the fifth lunar month of the following year, Toshiyoshi Kawaji was appointed chief of the *rasotsu*.

Seishi Yokomizo

PUSHKIN VERTIGO

THE HONJIN MURDERS

The award-winning
murder mystery classic

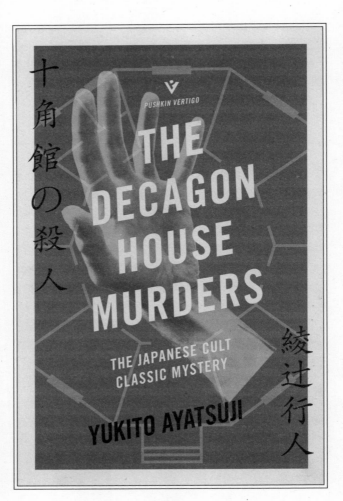

PUSHKIN VERTIGO

THE DECAGON HOUSE MURDERS

THE JAPANESE CULT CLASSIC MYSTERY

YUKITO AYATSUJI

十角館の殺人

綾辻行人